THE DEATH OF NORA RYAN

by James T. Farrell

YOUNG LONIGAN: A Boyhood in
  Chicago Streets
GAS HOUSE MCGINTY
THE YOUNG MANHOOD OF
  STUDS LONIGAN
CALICO SHOES
JUDGMENT DAYS
GUILLOTINE PARTY AND
  OTHER STORIES
A NOTE OF LITERARY
  CRITICISM
A WORLD I NEVER MADE
CAN ALL THIS GRANDEUR
  PERISH?
THE COLLECTED SHORT STORIES
  OF JAMES T. FARRELL
NO STAR IS LOST
TOMMY GALLAGHER'S
  CRUSADE
FATHER AND SON
ELLEN ROGERS
$1000 A WEEK AND OTHER
  STORIES
MY DAYS OF ANGER
TO WHOM IT MAY CONCERN
THE LEAGUE OF FRIGHTENED
  PHILISTINES
BERNARD CLARE
WHEN BOYHOOD DREAMS COME
  TRUE
LITERATURE AND MORALITY
THE LIFE ADVENTUROUS
THE ROAD BETWEEN
A MISUNDERSTANDING

AN AMERICAN DREAM GIRL
THIS MAN AND THIS WOMAN
YET OTHER WATERS
THE FACE OF TIME
REFLECTIONS AT FIFTY AND
  OTHER ESSAYS
FRENCH GIRLS ARE VICIOUS
AN OMNIBUS OF SHORT STORIES
A DANGEROUS WOMAN AND
  OTHER SHORT STORIES
MY BASEBALL DIARY
IT HAS COME TO PASS
THE COLLECTED POEMS OF
  JAMES T. FARRELL
BOARDING HOUSE BLUES
SIDE STREET AND OTHER
  STORIES
SOUND OF THE CITY AND
  OTHER STORIES
JAMES T. FARRELL SELECTED
  ESSAYS
THE SILENCE OF HISTORY
WHAT TIME COLLECTS
WHEN TIME WAS BORN
LONELY FOR THE FUTURE
A BRAND NEW LIFE
NEW YEAR'S EVE—1929
CHILDHOOD IS NOT FOREVER
INVISIBLE SWORDS
JUDITH AND OTHER STORIES
JAMES T. FARRELL LITERARY
  ESSAYS 1954–1974
THE DUNNE FAMILY
OLIVE AND MARY ANNE
THE DEATH OF NORA RYAN

The Death of
NORA RYAN

∾

James T. Farrell

Doubleday & Company, Inc.
Garden City, New York
1978

Library of Congress Cataloging in Publication Data

Farrell, James Thomas, 1904–
The death of Nora Ryan.

I. Title.
PZ3.F2465De   [PS3511.A738]   813'.5'2

ISBN: 0-385-13450-9
Library of Congress Catalog Card Number 77–83935

To Elizabeth & William V. Shannon

PART ONE

Chapter 1

I

Eddie Ryan looked at the calendar on his desk. January 1, 1946. What a way to start a new year. He had been trying to write a memorial article on Theodore Dreiser. Dreiser was no more. A great writer was dead. But *Sister Carrie, An American Tragedy,* and many other of his books would remain. This was the artist's aim, to preserve a moment, a memory, a person, for that uncertain future. Suddenly, Eddie crushed his cigarette in the ash tray and began to write.

II

It was late. He had been writing for three hours. The article was written. Theodore Dreiser would have liked it. He would mail it tonight.

Eddie closed the door gently. He didn't want to wake up Phyllis. She had been calm all day and had actually seemed to enjoy watching Tommy play with his Christmas toys. She had been charming and sweet with no tantrums. Poor Tommy. How could a six-year-old understand the violence of her explosions. Hell, he was over forty and after all these years he still couldn't. He wasn't going to think about this now. He would mail the article. There was a mailbox on the corner.

The few stores on the street were darkened. Even the East River Cafe was closed. God, he had made a fool of himself there. But he hadn't had anything to drink in over two years.

A couple, their heads bent against the wind, hurried past him.

Eddie forced the thick envelope through the opening in the mailbox, turned, and started back to the apartment.

4

III

Phyllis as still asleep. So was Tommy. He was sleepy too but he would read for a while. He went into the kitchen to make coffee.

"Oh, Eddie, it's late. Come to bed," Phyllis called.

"All right, dear."

As he got into bed, he thought, "Nineteen forty-six has begun."

Chapter 2

I

The telephone was ringing. He had heard it in his sleep and in his dreams.

"Eddie, the telephone is ringing," Phyllis called.

"I hear it; I'll get it."

He climbed out of bed.

"Oh, God, I hope it isn't bad news," Phyllis exclaimed.

Barefooted, Eddie walked into the next room and picked up the receiver.

"Hello, Eddie?"

It was his sister Frances, calling from California.

"Yes?"

"Oh, Eddie, I don't know what to do."

"What's the matter?"

"Haven't you heard?"

"Heard what? What is it?"

"About Mama."

—She's dead, he thought.

"What happened?"

"Clara hasn't called you yet?"

5

"No."

"Mama's had a stroke; she's dying. She might even be dead by now; it's been over two hours since Clara called me from Chicago."

"Well, she didn't call me. I'll wait a couple of hours, until morning, and call her."

Should he try to advise her? He had made up his own mind a long time ago that he wouldn't go back for funerals. He would go back to see his family and friends but not to bury them.

"It's terrible, Eddie. Clara says Mama's paralyzed on her whole right side. She can't talk and they don't know if she can hear."

"God!"

"Oh, Eddie."

"Do you want to go, Fran?"

"Yes."

He knew that she couldn't afford to go.

"I'll send you the money."

There was a pause.

"Send it to me in care of Clara in Chicago, Eddie. Are you coming too?"

"I don't think so."

"Thank you, Eddie. I'll never forget all you've done for me. I'll write as soon as I get there. Poor Clara must be beside herself."

"Do write and let me know how things are. Here's a kiss good-by for now."

Eddie sent a kiss through the phone.

"And here's one for you, Eddie."

II

"What was it?" Phyllis asked

"My mother's had a stroke."

"Oh, my God!" Phyllis exclaimed.

Eddie nodded.

"Frances called you from Los Angeles?"

"Yes."

"Why didn't they call you from Chicago?"

"I don't know."

"It seems to me that Clara would have telephoned you from Chicago."

"Maybe she can't."

"Poor thing. Maybe she can't."

His mother was dying. She might already be dead. Last summer, when the Commodore Vanderbilt had pulled out of the Englewood Station, he had seen the tears in her eyes as she stood on the platform waving good-by to them. It had made him sad.

III

It was late and he was tired.

"God, these early morning telephone calls," Phyllis grumbled.

"Yes."

He did not want to go back to Chicago. He didn't care what anyone said. He didn't want to go back for a funeral.

IV

Eddie was still drowsy. He had not been able to sleep after Fran's telephone call.

Should he go? It couldn't do any good. And judging from Fran, it could be too late to do anything.

It was seven-thirty. Eddie sat at his typewriter. He made a diary entry:

January 2, 1946
New York, New York

My mother had a stroke last night. My younger sister, Frances, phoned me from Los Angeles. It must have been about 4:00 A.M. She didn't know what to do. My other sister, Clara, had telephoned her. I have not yet heard from anyone in Chicago. I am waiting a little while before calling Clara. Mama might be dead by now. If she isn't, she will be, or so it appears. I am try-

*ing to decide if I should go back. This is an undecided question
for me.*

V

"Aren't you going to telephone Clara?" Phyllis asked.

"Yes, a little later. I don't want to do it too early."

"But your mother's had a stroke."

"She's probably unconscious and doesn't know what's happening
to her."

Even as he spoke, Eddie knew that he didn't believe this.

"You can't know that."

"I know."

"Oh God, it's awful."

She turned to the door.

"I have to get that kid ready for the school bus."

That was it. It had not occurred to him earlier. He was waiting for
Tommy to leave before he telephoned. The boy had already had his
breakfast and it was his slow eating that usually set Phyllis off. If
nothing happened now to provoke her, Tommy would be leaving
soon.

He thought of his mother. He remembered how she had started to
cry as their train pulled out of the station. That was the last time he
had seen her. It might be the last time that he would. Hurt was inevitable. The biological tragedy of life was death.

These thoughts and words had been with him many times before.
But now their meaning was concrete. His mother was dying. He felt
more pity than grief. His mother, Nora Ryan, was not a significant
part of his life now and much of his feeling was mixed with senti-
mentality. He felt some affection for her but at the moment he
thought of her as stricken and helpless, much as an animal. If she
were conscious, she would be terrified, more so than others who had
more intelligence.

Could he prove that?

The bell rang. It was the school bus.

VI

Eddie was on his way to the telephone when it rang.

"There's the telephone, dear," Phyllis called from the bathroom.

"I'll get it," he called back.

"Hello?"

"Hello, Eddie?"

It was his brother Steve, calling from Washington.

"Yes, Steve."

"You know about Mama?"

"Yes, Frances called me from California."

"She's had a serious stroke."

"Is she still alive, Steve?"

"She was an hour ago. I talked with Clara."

"What did Clara say?"

"Mama's had a complete right-side hemiplegia."

"That's bad," Eddie said.

"Yes, it is. Mama's in poor condition, Eddie."

"She's had the doctor?"

"Yes. Dr. Evans has seen her."

"What did he say?"

"Clara's waiting for him to make a call this morning."

"He saw her last night?"

"Yes, and he told Clara that Mama might die."

"What do you think, Steve?"

"Well, I only have what Clara told me to go on; but it looks awfully serious to me. I think she's dying."

"That's the impression Frances gave me," Eddie said.

"How is she? Is she still alive? Who is it? Clara?" Phyllis asked, coming out of the bathroom.

"She's still alive but it's bad."

"What did you say, Ed?"

"I was talking to Phyllis, Steve."

"Tell her hello for me."

"I will."

Eddie was waiting for Steve to say more.

"Well, Eddie, I can't say anything more than the way it seems to me. It's pretty bad. They can't move her. She can't talk. Judging from what Clara has told me, I would say that Mama's dying."

"I was afraid of that."

"Are you going out, Eddie?"

"No, I don't think so."

"I don't know yet whether or not I will," Steve said.

"Well, Eddie?" Steve began.

Eddie overlooked the question in Steve's voice.

"Well, Eddie," Steve repeated, "it seems that Mama is dying. She may already be dead for all we know."

"Clara would have called one of us."

"She's got her hands full but she did promise to get back to me. I'll telephone you if there's any change in Mama's condition."

"Do. And if I hear, I'll telephone you."

"It's a sad way to start a New Year," Steve said.

"Yes, it is."

"Good-by, Eddie."

"So long, Steve."

Eddie put down the receiver and turned to Phyllis.

"What's the news? What did Steve say?" her voice trembled.

"Nothing more than we knew."

"Did she die?" Phyllis asked.

Eddie shook his head but said nothing. He couldn't. His mother's stroke had affected Phyllis more than it had him. He ought to feel more. But you couldn't make yourself feel more than you did.

"Oh, the poor thing," Phyllis cried out, her eyes filling.

Eddie stared at her.

"Maybe you ought to phone Clara, darling," Phyllis suggested.

"Yes, I think so."

He had wanted to call Clara but now he hesitated. He didn't want to know the bad news.

"I'll have another cup of coffee first, and then I'll call her."

Phyllis frowned but she said nothing. She went into the kitchen and returned with his coffee. He drank it slowly. His mother was dying. He thought of the phrase "the pitifulness of humanity."

The telephone rang. Eddie rushed to answer it. It was a wrong number.

VII

Eddie Ryan picked up the receiver and asked the operator for long distance. He gave her Jack Boyle's name and address. He didn't know the telephone number. The operator called Chicago information for the number. Then she rang. Eddie could hear the telephone ringing at Jack and Clara's. It was a moment of suspense for him.

Instead of his brother-in-law Jack Boyle, it was his brother Jack who answered the telephone.

"New York City is calling for Mrs. Jack Boyle," the operator told him.

"Just a minute, Ed, I'll call Clara."

Then Eddie heard Clara's voice.

"Hello, Eddie."

"Hello, Clara."

She sounded tired.

"Gee, it's good of you to call, Eddie."

"How's Mama?"

"You're good to call, Eddie. I'm so glad to hear your voice. The whole family's called. Frances called from California and she's coming. Steve called from Washington. And Jack and Leo have both been here. And now you're calling."

Eddie waited.

"Mama's in very bad condition, Eddie."

"Yes?"

"She had a stroke last night at about ten."

Clara paused again.

"She can't talk. And she can't be moved. We're waiting now for Dr. Evans. He was here last night and he's coming back this morning.

"She keeps trying to tell me something but she can't talk. She tries to lift her arm and point. I think she's pointing to St. Julia's Church but I'm not sure."

"Yes, Clara."

"I have to go back to her. I haven't slept all night. I'll call you as soon as I have more news."

"No; I'll call you back, Clara. I don't know if I can come out."

"That's all right, Eddie. I understand. Frances told me that you're sending her a check so that she can come help out. That's awful good of you, Eddie."

"Do you need anything, Clara?"

"Not at the moment."

"If Mama can't be moved to a hospital, get a nurse to come to the house. I'll pay for it."

"That's awful good of you, Eddie, but I'll have to talk to Dr. Evans first and see what he says. We don't know how long she'll live and it may turn out to cost too much."

It was clear to Eddie from the way Clara spoke that it was not a question of whether or not Mama would die but a question of when.

"You can't spend another sleepless night, Clara. And if Mama's helpless, someone should be with her. Find out about a nurse and let me know what you'll need. I'll send it."

Phyllis stood near him, her face intense.

"How is she? What does Clara say?" she asked when he had re-placed the receiver.

"My mother is dying."

His voice was almost normal.

VIII

Eddie wrote out a check for two hundred and fifty dollars and put it in an envelope with a brief note. He dressed and went to the mail-box. Only last night he had dropped his article on Theodore Dreiser into this same mailbox. His thoughts had been on Theodore Dreiser, the artist, more than Theodore Dreiser, the man. And he had been aware of himself more as a writer than as the son of Nora Dunne Ryan.

—Poor Mama, he thought.

Should he go to Chicago?

Chapter 3

Another gray day, Eddie thought. But then many winter days were gray. His mother was not dead yet. Not to his knowledge. But she was as good as dead. She was dying. And the rest of them were waiting. Waiting for the dying to die. This was the death wish as Freud had written of death wishes. He was waiting and there was suspense in the waiting.

January 2, 1946
New York City

My mother is dying. She may be dead even as I write this. I do not know how I feel. But I am not called on to write how I feel now, at this moment, of this gray day. The postwar world is here. We are in it. Now when I write "The War," I must specify which war. The Revolution did not come.

Chapter 4

I

"Hello, Leo."

"Good morning, Ed. I'm a little late in returning your telephone call but I went to George, my barber, for a haircut. Did you have a good holiday?"

"Yes. I worked."

"You don't have to, you know. You're in a position to meet your needs for the rest of your life."

Eddie smiled to himself. Leo Berger was his publisher. The best kind of relationship between an author and his publisher was when the author's books were selling well and making money for the publisher. Eddie's books were selling and this made their friendship easier. He wished that this were not so but then he wished that many things were not so. And they were so. But Eddie felt sure that money could never weaken the bonds between Leo Berger and him. Their friendship meant something to both of them. He could talk to Leo about many things other than royalty statements. That was the reason he telephoned him so often. Leo Berger was one of the most intelligent men he knew.

"My mother, Leo," Eddie began.

"Yes?"

Was there a slight note of impatience in Leo Berger's voice?

"She's dying, Leo."

Some seconds passed before Leo spoke.

"God, I'm sorry to hear that, Ed."

"She had a massive cerebral hemorrhage."

"When did it happen?"

"Last night."

"God, I'm sorry to hear that, Ed."

Leo was sorry. Eddie could hear the sadness in his voice.

"When will you be going to Chicago?"

"I'm not sure I will be."

"Oh!"

A few moments elapsed.

"But won't you have to go out for the funeral, Ed?"

"Not unless I decide to."

"Oh, Ed, I'd go. You might regret it if you don't," Leo urged.

"I don't know yet, Leo."

"I'd do it, old man. And if you do, let me know when you go."

"Of course."

"Well?"

"I'll keep in touch with you, Leo."

"Thanks. And Ed . . ."

"Yes?"

"You know I'm sorry about this."

"Yes, I do, Leo."

"So long, Ed."

"So long, Leo."

II

It was a day of broken work periods for Eddie. He was not able to work in long stretches. But then many of his days were like this. As he tried to write, thoughts of his mother and of the past broke in. And of the day as it must be in Chicago. If a man went to work in an office or a factory while his mother was dying, most people would understand. But if he wrote while his mother was dying, the Philistines would not understand and probably criticize him.

What of it?

Thinking about what Philistines did or did not understand was a lifetime occupation.

But this did not settle the questions on his mind. Should he go to Chicago? This was the main question. He had decided not to go but the emotional tug in him was against this decision. So his decision was no resolution. He should go. But she might be dead already. Would it make any difference to her, or to him, if he were at the funeral?

The question would not rest.

As the day progressed, memories, memories of his mother and other members of his family kept coming back to him. His mother was part of his past. But he had lived with his grandmother. Grace Hogan Dunne had been "Mother" to him. There was so much of Nora Dunne Ryan that he did not know and could not recall. But he did not need to recall everything. He had a sense of her life.

Chapter 5

I

Nora Dunne Ryan had a stubbornness that was often manifested in exhibitionism. At times, her behavior was odd and bizarre. She was not as smart as her brothers and sisters. She knew this and they knew this. But she also knew that she was not stupid even though they thought she was. She was just different; she was like their mother.

It was out of vanity that Nora Dunne Ryan imitated Grace Hogan Dunne. Mother and daughter had seemed alike. And they were, in mannerisms. But Nora did not possess her mother's character. What was natural in her mother seemed to be eccentric in Nora.

Nora was the oldest of the daughters but younger than her brother Dick. She lacked the ambition of the others. It was not just that she was lazy. Nora did not know what she could do and she was afraid to take chances.

In school she had been poor in arithmetic. Simple addition and subtraction were difficult for her. Some of her most excruciating hours as a girl had been spent in arithmetic classes. There had been no one to help her. She was the second oldest. Her father and mother could neither read nor write, let alone do sums. Her older brother, Dick, could have helped her. He was good at sums. Nora had asked him a couple of times but he had become so impatient that he had cursed her and hit her. He had called her stupid. Maybe Dick was right. A girl should be able to learn what she was supposed to know. And if people her mother wouldn't speak to could do their sums, why couldn't she? But even if what Dick had said was true, he had no right to hit her the way he had. She had cried but he had gone right on punching her. That wasn't the only time, either. What a fool she had been to ask him for help. Eventually she had learned her lesson and she had stopped. But she had never learned how to do sums.

It wasn't fair. She wasn't a bad girl; she was a good girl. And she loved her mother and father; she loved them more than her brothers and sisters did. Dick and Jenny were always talking about "getting out of this." She knew that they were ashamed because Ma and Pa couldn't read or write. It didn't worry her; that was the way grown-ups were. Most of the parents of the other girls and boys she knew were Irish and poor. They didn't resent it and neither did she. But Dick and Jenny did. And so did Larry.

Well, she, Nora Dunne, didn't want to get out.

She knew how to read and write. And she could speak German too. The nuns at school were German-speaking and she learned it, by ear, not by book. She was asked to interpret, sometimes, for some German who couldn't speak English. And she was usually given a quarter for this. She talked better German than any boy or girl in her class except for the real Germans and they couldn't speak English the way she could.

Dick knew this but he never said a word about it. All he ever talked about was how stupid she was when she tried to do her sums. He never even praised her when she got her diploma from grammar school.

Nora had not wanted to go to high school. It was just as well; it would have meant ten carfares a week and other extra expenses. Any expense that wasn't strictly necessary was an extra expense and Joseph Dunne couldn't afford extra expenses, even with Richard working in a shoe store downtown and bringing home his earnings every week.

Richard hadn't been able to go to high school so Joseph Dunne didn't see why in the name of God a girl should be going. She could read and write, couldn't she?

Nora didn't want more schooling. She talked about entering a convent; she was sure she had a call. Her mother didn't think she did.

"Who are you to be thinking that God has given you the call to be a holy virgin?"

Nora did not go to work; she stayed home to help her mother. There was enough to do with two brothers and two younger sisters to cook and clean for. Nora Dunne liked it at home. She wished she could go on staying home. But she knew that her two younger sisters would soon be able to help and that she would be sent out to get a job so that she could bring home her pay.

The Dunnes were living on Twelfth Street. There was no bathroom, only an outhouse, and no hot water or electricity. In the kitchen there was a wood-burning stove. For lighting, there were kerosene lamps. There was always something to be done, to be picked up or swept, some household chore to be performed. The house was never in order. The Dunnes were used to this—except for Dick. There were times when he'd lose his temper the minute he stepped inside the door. And even though he blamed his explosion on the dirt and disorder, his anger was rooted in his shame.

Dick Dunne felt helpless. There were so many mouths to feed. And it was so hard to earn a decent salary with a grade school education. He hated the way they lived. He hated the neighborhood, the dirt—everything. He was ashamed of his parents, particularly his father. It was different with his mother. He loved her. He was her firstborn to survive and her favorite. She loved him. He wanted to give her a better life. He wanted more for her and for himself—for all of them. He wanted to amount to something.

His eighth-grade teacher, Sister Boniface, had told him that he had the makings of success. This had been encouraging. He didn't need it but it didn't hurt. He had asked Sister Boniface to pray for him and she had told him that she already had prayed for his rise in the world. This surprised him and gave him confidence.

Three days after his graduation Dick Dunne got a job at a shoe store on State Street in downtown Chicago. Felson Cohn hired him to wrap shoes and run errands for three dollars a week.

"See what education done for me son Richard. He has a job right away when he finishes school," his mother said.

"Good, he can help out at home," his father said.

"Of course I shall," Dick shouted.

"Sure and don't I damned well know you will," his father said.

"I knew you'd get a job," Nora interrupted. "I prayed for you at mass last Sunday."

"Thank you, Nora."

"Nora prays a lot," Jenny commented, smiling.

"Good, and it will keep her out of trouble," the father said.

"I wouldn't get in trouble, Pa."

"You do and I'll tan your behind till it blisters," Mrs. Dunne warned.

"But, Ma, you know I'm a good girl."

"And I'm telling you you'd better stay good," Mrs. Dunne said.

Then, turning to her husband:

"Pa, whist down to McCann's for a pail of beer."

Joseph Dunne was in his undershirt and pants. He started to put on his shirt. But what did he have this hungry band for?

"All right, Richard, here's a dime. Swish yourself to McCann's and get meself and your mother a can of beer."

"I'm working now, too. Let one of them go."

"Me razor strap is in need of more use," his father threatened.

He turned to his wife.

"Woman, where's me razor strap?"

"You'll not be using it on me son Richard."

"And who, woman, is the man in this home?"

"You'll not be using the razor strap on me son."

"You're telling him he's not to mind his father?"

"I'm not after telling him not to mind. I'm after telling you that you'll not be using the razor strap on me son."

"By Jesus, Mary, and St. Joseph," Mr. Dunne exclaimed.

"I'll go, Pa," Nora said.

"The divil you will, girl," Mr. Dunne said.

"What will the Sullivans next door be sayin' when they see a girl rushin' the can?" asked Mrs. Dunne.

"I'll go, Mother," Dick Dunne said.

"Yes, son, be mindin' your father and go. I need to be wettin' me own whistle, too."

"It's about time me own voice is heard in me own domicile," Mr. Dunne said.

Dick Dunne took the pail from his mother and a dime from his father. He went, but he hated it; he hated being seen rushing the can. Other boys rushed the can for their parents but he didn't like it. He wished his mother wouldn't drink beer.

"See that you're home quick, Richard, with the suds on top of the beer," his father said.

"Yes, Pa, I'll hasten."

He left with the can.

"Well, for the love of God!" the father exclaimed. "Did you be hearin' that? 'I'll hasten.'"

II

The prettiest thing about Nora Dunne was her black, silky hair. This and her clear blue eyes made her seem prettier than she was. Nora Dunne was plump and her face was plain. She was pious but her piety did not keep her from flirting. In time, she had dates. Nora enjoyed the attention but she wouldn't let fellows get far with her.

Occasionally she would go to a Saturday night dance. When she first started going, Dick had criticized her. She had bridled even though she was afraid that he would lose his temper and hit her. But he hadn't. He had clammed up and said nothing more about her going to dances. Nora was surprised. And glad. She was glad that she had gotten her way and Dick hadn't hit her. She had stood up to her brother Dick and he had backed down. It was like she had won.

Nora Dunne did not know that Richard Dunne had lost interest in her. He didn't care. He had decided that there was nothing much that could be done to improve Nora. The two youngest girls, Jenny and Rose, were far more promising in this matter of life and living. He couldn't waste his energies on Nora.

Nora, unaware of her brother's dismissal, continued to feel proud of her victory and to be afraid of him. But she wasn't the only one afraid of Dick's temper. Her sisters were too. When Dick lost his temper he lost control of himself. The only one who could stop him was Grace Hogan Dunne.

"Richard, that'll be enough," she would say.

And Richard would stop beating on one of them. Richard Dunne still toed the mark for Grace Hogan Dunne.

III

At times Nora Dunne wanted a beau. At other times she wanted to become a nun. This contradiction did not ruffle her. When one of her wants was strong in her head, she forgot the other.

Chapter 6

I

Eddie Ryan sat looking at the gray sky. His mother was still alive. He still had not made up his mind to go to Chicago. His mother wouldn't know if he were or weren't there.

Eddie got up from his desk and walked over to the big table on which Phyllis had placed the telephone. It was almost an hour since he had talked to Clara.

He reached for the phone but changed his mind. He wouldn't phone yet.

Should he call Steve? No, he didn't want to help Steve decide whether or not he should go to Chicago. He had offered to pay his way if he wanted to go. That was enough.

Eddie sat.

Phyllis was out shopping.

Was it the wake and the funeral that kept him from going to his mother's bedside? Or was it the people he might see? Was he afraid?

He was afraid that he was afraid.

There was Torch Feeney.

Torch Feeney had tried to shoot him in 1933.

Chapter 7

I

Eddie Ryan leaned forward to get a cigarette. He could remember it all. Whenever he thought of Chicago he remembered scenes from the past. But he had to focus on what was happening in Chicago right now, this very minute. His mother was lying in a bed, helpless. She couldn't speak. He knew that his sister Clara and her husband Jack would do everything they could. But how much could they do? How much could anyone do? His brothers, Leo and Jack, were there. And his sister Frances would be arriving from California with her son Michael. In fact, all the Ryans were there except for Steve and him.

He looked at his watch. It was past noon. He would phone again in a minute or two. He would tell Clara he wasn't coming. He didn't want to go.

He stood up. He had to make up his mind. He had proofs to correct. He hated correcting proofs but when it came to his work, he knew what to do. About this, there was never any indecision.

He should make up his mind about going to Chicago.

He picked up a book, and sat down and read for a few minutes. Then he went into the kitchen and heated some coffee. He gulped it down. He lit a cigarette, took several puffs, then squashed it in the saucer. He lit another one, walked into the front of the apartment, and stared out on the street. Automobiles were crowding by toward the ramp to the Queensboro Bridge. Fifty-eighth Street was dull—familiar and treeless.

He heard the key in the front door. He turned quickly from the window.

"Eddie?"

"I'm here," Eddie called, walking back from the parlor.

"Any news?" Phyllis asked.

"No, not yet."

"Did you call anyone?"

"No, I'll wait a little longer," he said.

Phyllis was carrying a bag of groceries. Eddie hurried to help her but she reached the kitchen before he could. He turned on the light.

"Thank you," she said.

He took a step toward the table.

"Oh, don't bother," Phyllis said, noticing that he was about to take what she had bought out of the bag. "I'll do it. You never put things in the right place."

He didn't care if she put the groceries away. It was her complaining that led him to try to help.

Eddie left the kitchen. He would not go to Chicago. It was definite.

Now that he had decided, he should go on with his routine. He had not been able to do much work today but he didn't think that he would be able to write now. He would be interrupted by telephone calls. And then dinner would be ready. He did not want to write now. That was the gist of the matter. But this was not precisely so. He always wanted to write. At least, he always had the wish to write.

II

"Isn't it odd that no one's telephoned you?" Phyllis asked.

"Oh, I don't know."

"You don't know?"

"No," Eddie answered.

"Well, I'd certainly know," Phyllis said.

She had walked into the living room.

"I would think one of them would have called you," Phyllis said.

"They must have no news," Eddie said.

"Oh, your poor mother!"

Eddie nodded. His mother was dying. And it was too late now. Too late for what? Too late for anything!

"Poor thing!" Phyllis said again.

"Yes," he mumbled.

This was all he could say. A wave of emotions had broken through. His mother was dying. The meaning had been penetrating all day but not until now had he fully felt it.

"I don't know . . ." Eddie began.

"What did you say, dearest?"

"I don't know."

"Why don't you telephone your sister Clara?"

"I will in a minute."

He would telephone but he wanted to delay it a little longer. He did not want to call but he knew that he should. It was a moral imperative. The fact that he didn't want to call did not mean that he wouldn't call. He would put through the call, later.

23

III

The front doorbell rang. It was a little early for Tommy to be coming home from school, Eddie thought.

"That's Tommy," Phyllis said, jumping up to go to the door. She hurried to open it.

"Why, Steve!" she exclaimed.

Eddie was pleased that Steve had come to New York.

"Hello, Phyllis, is Ed here?"

"How did you get here so fast?" Phyllis asked.

"I flew. I got in by priority because I'm a doctor."

"How is your mother, poor thing?"

"Well, the last time I talked with Clara there was no change in her condition."

In another moment Steve was walking up to Eddie and pulling his right glove off.

"Hello, Eddie."

"Why, hello, Steve, I'm surprised to see you."

"Well, I decided to come here. I got on a plane. It wasn't any trouble. I told them I was a doctor and that it was an emergency. I had my credentials."

"It is an emergency," Phyllis said.

Eddie wanted to ask Steve if he were going on to Chicago but he hesitated.

IV

Steve Ryan was taller than Eddie, about five feet eleven. His face was long and Eddie's round and yet it was easy to see that they were brothers. Steve was six years younger than Eddie but he had much more gray in his hair.

Eddie smiled warmly at his brother. He was proud of Steve who was a resident psychiatrist of a big government hospital in Washington.

"How are you going to Chicago, Steve, by train?" Phyllis asked.

"A plane is much faster," Steve said.

"But can you get on one?" she asked.

"Yes, I got one from Washington. I can get priority because I'm a doctor," Steve answered with a grin.

Suddenly Eddie wanted to go.

"Aren't you coming, Ed?" Steve asked.

"I'm thinking about it."

"I'll telephone now to see about getting an airplane ticket. Do you want me to try to get you one too, Ed?"

"I'm not sure."

"Eddie, I'd go, were I you. You might never forgive yourself," Phyllis told him. She turned toward Steve. "Don't you agree?"

"Well . . ." Steve began.

Phyllis looked at him impatiently.

"I think . . ." Steve went on.

Phyllis controlled her impatience.

"I think that it's terminal for my mother."

Phyllis said nothing.

"But of course, I haven't seen her," Steve said.

Phyllis maintained her control. Mrs. Ryan was dying. She was convinced of this. It was not the time to let Steve Ryan know that she thought him a fool.

Eddie watched her. He was afraid that she was going to hit the ceiling. Why did Steve always manage to sound so fatuous? But even if he did, that was no reason for Phyllis to blow up. But she had not blown up. She had contained herself. He had blamed her for doing what she had not done. Well, her eruptions were so frequent that he had come to overreact to the least sign that she might have a tantrum.

Phyllis could control her tongue but she could not hide the contempt in her eyes as she looked at Steve Ryan. Why was he standing there talking? Why didn't he telephone about an airplane reservation and try to get to Chicago where his poor mother was dying? Oh, the poor woman. Eddie ought to go too, but it would be better for her not to influence him.

"I'll telephone for a reservation. Do you want me to try for two, Ed?" Steve asked.

"I don't think you'll be able to get them."

"Oh, I don't know," Steve said.

"I'm glad you're going, lambkin. I think you should," Phyllis said to Eddie.

"Do you know the number for American Airlines?" Steve asked.

"No, look it up or ask information," Eddie answered.

He would go. After stewing all day long, he had decided in a single moment.

"I'll pack your suitcase, dear," Phyllis said.

"Thank you," Eddie mumbled.

Steve had the telephone directory out and was looking up the telephone number. When he found it he repeated it aloud to himself three times. Then, his lips still moving, he sat at the table on which the phone was placed and picked up the receiver.

"Damn it!" he exclaimed.

"What's the matter?" Ed asked.

"I forgot the number."

"That's what pencils are for," Phyllis said.

Steve put back the receiver.

"I'll have to look it up again."

"I'll look it up for you," Phyllis said impatiently.

"I can do it," Steve said, squatting to pull the thick directory from the ledge under the table.

"Let me, there's no time to lose."

Phyllis was annoyed. He was such an oaf.

"Let me see now," Steve said, thumbing through the pages. "Oh, here it is."

Phyllis watched him. He kept repeating the number to himself. Angrily, she walked over to give him a pencil and paper. He ignored her. Mumbling the number to himself, he reached for the phone again.

He dialed the number and was soon talking.

"Hello? I'm Dr. Ryan. I would like two tickets on the next flight to Chicago. Yes, it's an emergency. A medical emergency."

Eddie smiled. He was glad that his brother could manage this. It was usually he who managed such matters.

V

"Did you get the reservations, Steve?" Phyllis asked, entering the room.

"Yes, I told them that I was Dr. Ryan and that it was a medical emergency. But you heard me, didn't you?"

"To tell you the truth, I wasn't listening. I was packing Eddie's suitcase."

"Ed, your reservation is confirmed to Detroit. There is a good chance that you'll be able to go straight through with me but they couldn't confirm it from here."

"Well, if I do get bumped, I can get a train from Detroit to Chicago."

"Well . . ." Steve began.

"Why don't you take the reservation to Detroit? I'll do what I can to get you through from there but if I'm unable to you can get a train from Detroit to Chicago."

Eddie stared at him. That's what he had just said. He didn't get it.

"You'll both have to leave right away," Phyllis said.

"Yes, she's right, Ed, you'd better get ready."

"Or you'll miss the plane," Phyllis added.

"We won't miss the plane. I'll be ready soon. I'd better shave first."

VI

Eddie and Steve Ryan, were riding up front in the black airlines bus. They had just passed through the Midtown Tunnel from Manhattan and were going through streets in Queens. It was dark and neither Eddie nor Steve paid any attention to where they were. Traffic was heavy and the bus moved slowly. Both were thinking of what lay ahead. Steve knew that it would be both exciting and disturbing. And Eddie knew that it would be sad and pitiful.

Eddie looked out the window. There was still some snow in this area. Most of it had been cleared away in Manhattan.

His mother was dying. Life was far away from death. And death was far away from life. Death was the unspelled meaning of life. But this did not mean much. What could be said that would mean much about the meaning of life?

It was dramatic. Suddenly, in the gloom of a New Year's Day, his mother had been stricken. Death was not a separate agent, or an outside force. Death was a condition of the body.

"I hope Mama is alive when we get there," Steve said.

Eddie nodded.

"She had a massive cerebral hemorrhage," Steve said.

"That's what killed Papa, wasn't it?"

"Well, yes," Steve answered.

They did not talk for a moment.

A massive hemorrhage. Her poor brain must be flooded with blood. Unfed nerves and nerve centers were starving and would become still from a lack of nourishing blood.

"Eddie, don't be hurt if Mama is dead when we get there."

Steve's remark surprised him. It was an odd statement. But actually it wasn't, not from Steve. He was often reminded of Steve's humorless sincerity.

"I won't be hurt in the way I think you mean hurt, Steve."

"We're almost at La Guardia," Steve interrupted.

For a moment Eddie was taken aback.

"Yes, we're just about there," Steve said.

They rode along silently for a minute or two.

"Eddie?"

Eddie turned.

"If you can't get on the plane in Detroit, don't worry. You can get from there to Chicago by train."

Eddie was amused. He turned toward the window smiling. Steve was playing big brother to him. Poor Steve. He was deriving pleasure from reminding him that he, as a doctor, could get flight priority for a medical emergency. It was funny and a little pathetic.

The bus turned into the entrance of La Guardia.

"Well, here we are," Steve said.

The bus stopped. Steve and Eddie rose to their feet.

Chapter 8

I

The airplane was moving slowly down the runway. Eddie could see the snow crusted along the edges. On a parallel runway to his left, Eddie saw another plane taxiing out. The "No Smoking" and "Fasten Your Seat Belt" signs were on.

He felt a quiver of uncertainty. The greatest danger was supposed to be in the take-off and landing. But there was no sense in worrying about it. Chances were that nothing would happen. And if something did? It was too late now to alter his course.

The airplane stopped.

"I wonder what the matter is," Steve asked.

"I think we're just waiting our turn because of air traffic," Eddie told him.

"Oh, I never thought of that. Wouldn't you think that I would have?"

Eddie mumbled a yes.

The airplane stood, not moving, with the propellers still turning and motors humming smoothly. The delay was obviously for traffic clearance. But it was causing tension in the plane. Eddie felt it. The trip should have begun. It had, in fact, already begun even though the plane was not off the ground.

One by one, the passengers stopped talking. Those who continued to speak lowered their voices.

"I wish we'd get off the ground," Eddie said.

"Me too. But we have to wait our turn," Steve said.

Eddie sighed. An amused smile played upon his lips.

The airplane began to move. A few sighs escaped from passengers. Eddie's body sagged a little. Then the plane stopped again. The pilot raced one motor, then a second and a third, then all four. There was a bark and a roar, a mounting pounding, and the whole airplane vibrated. The propellers whirled so fast that they were visible as a dark whir. The motors roared. The entire plane seemed to strain.

Then it moved, roaring along the runway. It lifted and climbed up through the air. Tension in the plane eased. The passengers relaxed in their seats and started talking.

The "No Smoking" sign went off and several passengers lit cigarettes. Eddie Ryan did.

"I think I'd like a cigarette," Steve said.

Eddie handed him his opened pack.

Steve lit one and handed the pack back.

"Thanks, Ed."

In another moment the "Fasten Your Seat Belt" sign went off. The sense of danger was gone.

II

Dinner was being served by two uniformed hostesses moving along the aisles with trays.

"Say, Ed, this is good," Steve said.

"Yes it is."

"It really is," Steve exclaimed.

There was a steady echo of talk as the passengers ate.

"Some of the patients have a sense of humor," Steve was saying.

"I don't doubt it."

"One night a patient said to me, 'You know, Doc, I've been looking up at those stars for a long time. I've been watching and studying them for a long time. And you know, Doc, there's not a place like this on any one of them.'"

Steve and Eddie both laughed.

"And there's another patient who's been chased by the Red Army since 1923."

Eddie said nothing. He felt a hopeless sympathy for the man, not only because he thought that the Red Army was chasing him but also because a resident psychiatrist thought it was funny.

"The poor guy really thinks that the Red Army is after him," Steve said with a laugh.

It was funny, but not so funny. Lunacy was not funny. But that was not always true. Eddie remembered his visit to Steve at the hospital last June.

"Golly, I hope we get there in time," Steve suddenly said.

Eddie waited for Steve to say more. But Steve didn't speak for a couple of moments. Then, as a blonde stewardess passed in the aisle, Steve called to her: "Miss."

She stopped and turned. Not bad, Eddie thought.

"May I have another cup of coffee?" Steve asked.

She smiled.

"Would you like one, too, sir?"

"Yes, please," Eddie replied.

III

It had been a smooth trip so far. They were over Cleveland.

Eddie was reading. Steve had started to but had stopped and put down his book. He couldn't read, not at the moment. His mind trailed off. His thoughts strayed.

—Mama is dying.

He knew that his mother was dying, that she was on her deathbed, but he could not feel the truth of this fact.

—Mama is dying.

Steve Ryan was more than detached about this; he was aloof, psychologically removed from the personal meanings involved.

His mother's dying did not seem to mean much to him. What it meant was in his unconscious. It would be brought up in one of his visits with Dr. Eroica Gardner. He looked forward to his next meeting with Dr. Gardner when he got back to Washington. This experience—going to Chicago for his mother's death—would help him to advance in his analysis. It ought to be a big stride forward. It was a crucial time for Mama to die, a crucial time in his analysis. He would be able to go deeper into his own Oedipal situation. He did feel that he had been pushed off his mother's lap—first for his sister Frannie and then for his baby brother Vincent who had died. But that was sibling rivalry.

The plane was going smoothly through the night, thousands of feet above Lake Erie, a blackness down below with shiny spots of drifting bits of ice, turned by distance into pinpoints.

Eddie sat, idle. He had work to do but he didn't feel like doing much. Was it his mother? Or laziness? He was flying to Chicago because his mother was dying.

She might be dead already.

"Where are we?" Steve suddenly asked.

"I think we're over Lake Erie."

"Oh!"

Steve was more upset than he was about their mother. The truth was that he was not upset at all. He had pity for his mother. It was part of the sadness he felt for all of his family. There was a big gulf between his life and their lives. And this gap put him into the position of a spectator.

Was this true?

He wanted to think it true but he didn't know. He did know. It wasn't true. The difference was something else. It lay in values and purposes. It was in what he thought and what they thought. It was in what he did and what they did.

His mother was lying stricken and speechless. God, she must be afraid.

Death.

He was going to meet death. Eddie shook his head. He heard a low snore. He turned. Steve had fallen asleep and was crumpled up in his seat.

Steve slept for less than fifteen minutes. He woke up in surprise.

"Where are we?"

"Still over Lake Erie."

"I wasn't asleep for long then, was I?"

"No, only ten or fifteen minutes."

"I thought it was longer. We're nearing Detroit, aren't we?"

"Yes."

Would he be bumped in Detroit? He hoped not.

"I hope Mama is still alive when we get there," Steve said.

"I do too."

"She wouldn't want to die without seeing all of us," Steve added.

"I doubt she wants to die, seeing us or not seeing us."

"Of course. I didn't mean that. What I meant is that, if she is dying and can't be saved, then she would want us all there."

Eddie wondered. Steve was probably right. But seeing all of her children around could frighten her even more. She would know, then, that she wasn't expected to live.

"I wonder . . ." Steve began.

"Wonder what?"

"Wonder if Mama is dead yet."

"I have a hunch she isn't," Eddie said.

"But a hunch doesn't mean anything one way or the other."

"I know that."

What made Steve so fatuous?

"Still, there are things that we can't prove."

"Or disprove," Eddie reminded him.

"That's true."

"If my hunch were scientifically provable, that would mean that there is a scientific warranty for extrasensory perception, mental telepathy, and other such notions," Eddie said.

"Yes, it would. And I don't think that there is scientific basis for any kind of thought transference."

"Neither do I," Eddie said.

"It would throw a lot of confusion into our ideas should it turn out that there is a psychic capacity to perceive what's free of sensory perception," Steve said.

"And would create a whole series of problems."

"It sure would," Steve agreed.

"Science thrives on problems."

"Yes, it does," Steve said.

A moment or two passed. And he added:

"I had an anxiety for a minute or so. I was afraid that extrasensory perception might be true."

Eddie nodded. He understood how one could have such apprehension and fear.

Steve spoke again.

"I never thought that Mama would go because of a cerebral hemorrhage. She has an ulcer, a heart condition and I always imagined that one of these would eventually get her."

"I never thought of it much," Eddie said. "I knew that she didn't expect to live much longer because of her heart."

"Well, you never can tell," Steve said.

The airplane was riding smoothly. The engines were turning in a rhythmic humming tone. There were no signs of danger. But there could be a sudden, unexpected smashup. The probabilities were that there wouldn't be; but it could happen. He did not fly often because of Phyllis; she usually got terrified when he did.

He had not thought about Phyllis since they left the apartment. He felt a little guilty. She had gone out of his mind. But she was there, regardless of whether or not she was in his thoughts consciously. They had been together for over ten years.

He heard the motor droning.

Phyllis. What point had he been coming to?

He loved Phyllis but . . .

Should he say that there were grievances? If so, they weren't major ones.

"Phyllis is a good mother," Mama had said last June when he had Phyllis and Tommy in Chicago.

IV

Steve Ryan was troubled. He had seen death often enough. After all, he was a doctor and seeing people die had been part of his professional experience. But it was a relatively small part because he was a psychiatrist, not a medical practitioner. Even so, he saw death. But this was different. It was Mama. For a moment he felt sad. But then he told himself that he must accept the reality principle. You mature when you can accept your father and mother as separate human beings subject to all the weaknesses that flesh is heir to.

There was some comfort in these reflections. But there was still sorrow in him. Was it sorrow? Or guilt? Since he had gone into analysis he had not always been able to distinguish clearly between the two. It seemed to him that they went together. His not being able to distinguish between them didn't cause him any confusion. That was nothing to get heated up about.

He looked out of the window. It was dark and all he saw was a black blank.

Then, in the distance, he saw small lights. Suddenly the plane dropped. Steve looked down at the black water below. By the time he had clutched the arms of his seat the plane had righted itself and was flying smoothly again. Steve shook his head and let out a "Whew."

His fear was over. Let's see now, if the plane had crashed and he had been killed, the newspaper would print the story:

Dr. Steven Ryan Killed in Air Accident
While Rushing to Mother's Death Side

But even as he fantasized, he knew that this would not be the story that the paper would print. The newspaper would print a story on Famous Author Edward A. Ryan Killed. And it wouldn't be just the Chicago papers. Papers all over the world would print the story if something happened to Eddie. The story would tell how Edward A. Ryan and his brother, a psychiatrist, were rushing to their mother's death side. It might not even give his name.

A hostess passed along the aisle.

"Miss?" Eddie called.

"Yes, sir?"

She smiled at him.

"May I have another cup of coffee, please?"

"Yes, sir, but we are going into our descent pattern now. You will have time to drink your coffee before we land."

She picked up Eddie's white plastic cup and walked off.

"Oh, miss," Steve called. "Bring me some too."

Eddie wondered if Steve realized how loudly he had spoken. Well, he had more important things to worry about at the moment. He wondered if he would get bumped in Detroit. He hoped not; it would be damned inconvenient to get from the airport to the train station. And God knew what the train schedule was to Chicago.

The hostess returned with the coffee. Eddie thanked her.

As he drank his coffee and smoked a cigarette, Eddie wondered if there was a midnight train from Detroit to Chicago. If not, he might have to spend the night in Detroit.

"Well . . ." Steve began.

"Yes?"

"Well," Steve repeated, "it won't be too long a trip from Detroit to Chicago."

"No, it isn't a long train ride."

"I hope that Mama doesn't die before we all get there. It would be nice if all her children are present."

"Nice?"

"A nice kind of thing, I mean," Steve said.

There was suddenly a hard bump; the wheels had touched the

earth. The big plane roared forth at a high speed but it only went a short number of yards. Then it was taxiing toward the terminal.

Eddie was relieved. They had landed safely. Now, if he didn't get bumped, and could stay on the plane . . .

V

"The last lap," Steve said.

"Uh-huh," Eddie agreed.

The stop at Willow Run Airport in Detroit had been brief and Eddie had learned that he could keep his own seat to Chicago. But Steve had insisted upon checking with the stewardess. Eddie had been a little amused as Steve introduced himself to her as Dr. Steven Ryan who was flying to Chicago on a medical emergency.

"It won't be long now, Ed. If no one meets us, we'll have to take a cab."

"Oh, I'm sure someone will."

"Well, you never can tell," Steve said.

"You sure can't, Steve," Eddie teased.

There was a flash of resentment in Steve. Actually, there was no way of knowing whether or not someone would meet them. All he had done was state a simple truth. There was no need for Eddie's irony. But was he overreacting? He couldn't know. The answer would come out in one of his future psychoanalytical sessions. He would try to forget about it for now.

"Steve Ryan?"

Steve looked up. A full-shouldered blond young man was standing in the aisle.

"Why, hello, Al."

"It's a surprise to see you, Ryan."

"And it's a surprise to see you, Albert Sutter."

"That's me, plus an LL.D. after the name," the young man said.

"I heard that you became a lawyer," Steve told him.

"Aren't you a doctor now, Steve?"

"Yes, I'm resident physician at St. Margaret's in Washington."

"Glad to hear it. Going back to Chicago on a visit?"

"Yes—not to stay of course."

"I was in New York on a case."

"I'm not in New York; I'm in Washington," Steve said. "I'm an M.D.; but I'm a psychiatrist."

"Oh, I didn't know that."

Steve and Albert Sutter talked for a few more moments. Finally Steve walked to the front of the plane where Albert Sutter was sitting and stood in the aisle and talked for a few more minutes. Then he returned to his own seat.

"I went to St. Michael's with him," Steve told Eddie.

Eddie wondered why Steve hadn't introduced him to the young man. There was, he reflected, much that was odd in Steve.

"Gee, it will be an anticlimax if Mama is dead when we get there," Steve said.

Eddie nodded.

"I won't feel right if we get there too late," Steve went on.

The four motors hummed as the plane moved downward.

"We're descending; it won't be long now, Steve."

Chapter 9

I

Leo Ryan was waiting by the gate. Beside him, wearing a black fur coat, stood his wife, Florence. Leo was tall, about six feet, and well built. Florence was short and plump.

"Hello, Eddie; hello, Steve," Leo greeted them.

"Is Mama still alive?" Steve asked.

"Yes, but you have to be prepared for something," Leo replied.

Eddie walked through the gate; Steve followed.

"Hello, Florence," Eddie said, bending down to kiss her.

Steve then said hello to Florence and kissed her. They all walked toward the terminal building.

"How have you been, Eddie?" Florence asked.

"Pretty good," he answered.

Eddie glanced to his right. Steve was asking Leo questions.

"I don't know, Steve, you're the doctor."

Eddie heard the annoyance in Leo's voice.

Eddie turned to Florence and asked if it was bad. Florence said yes, poor Mama, it was bad. Florence then asked if they had had a smooth trip. Eddie said yes, they had. He moved closer to Leo and Steve. He wanted to hear what they were saying. By the time he had neared them, they were at the baggage claim area. Here, both Eddie and Steve were busy identifying their luggage.

"I'll go get my car," Leo said. "It's parked in the parking lot across the way."

"We'll all go with you," Steve told him.

"No, you wait here. There's no use in carting all that stuff for a block or two."

"Oh, we can do it," Steve insisted.

"It'd be much easier for Florence and me to get the car and pick you up here," Leo said.

"It will save time if we go with you," Steve persisted.

Eddie was irritated by Steve's persistence. After all, Leo knew where his car was; he was the one in the best position to decide what they should do.

"We'll go get the car and pick you up here," Leo snapped.

"All right," Steve grumbled.

Leo and Florence went for the car. Eddie and Steve waited for them on the sidewalk. Eddie watched the people. He reminded himself that many of them were returning to their homes after spending Christmas and New Year's holiday with friends and families. This would account for the number of people traveling so late at night. Cold air stung his face.

Mama is dying. This thought came to his mind. For her, the world was ending. She was ending. It was the end of Nora Ryan and the end of Nora Ryan was the end of the world for Nora Ryan.

Steve stamped his feet against the cold.

Just then, Leo drove up. He got out and helped them put their luggage in the trunk.

"Okay, let's go, folks," he said. "You both can get in back. Okay?"

"Suits me," Steve said.

Holding his stuffed briefcase carefully, Eddie got into the back seat of the car. Steve grinned. Eddie was used to being treated as first in the family. It never occurred to him that he was stepping ahead of his brother, Dr. Steven Ryan. Nor did Leo or Florence seem to notice.

Steve got in and sat beside Eddie.

Leo started up the car and it moved off.

"How is your mother, Florence?" Eddie asked.

"Oh, she's fine, thank you, Eddie."

"I'm glad to hear it."

"Now, Leo, tell me more about Mama," Steve asked.

Leo didn't want to talk about Mama. It wasn't just because he felt sad about her condition, although this was one of the reasons. It was because Steve was a doctor. He didn't know what to tell Steve; he didn't know the words to use.

He stopped at the gate to hand the gray-haired attendant his ticket and a dollar bill. The man gave him some change and Leo drove out through the gate to join the line of automobiles going north on Cicero.

II

Eddie looked out the window of the moving automobile. Although he slouched in the seat, he was tense. Steve was asking questions. Leo was controlling his patience but Eddie could hear the pain in his voice. They had turned off Cicero Avenue and were on South Ashland.

"You'll see, Steve, you're a doctor," Leo was saying.

"Yes, of course, but I'm trying to fill myself in," Steve said.

"Oh, it's just awful," Florence exclaimed, her voice trembling.

Eddie pressed his lips together. Steve reminded himself that he must take this with a doctor's calm.

❧ PART TWO ❧

Chapter 1

I

Nora Dunne Ryan lived with her daughter Clara and Clara's second husband, Jack Boyle. They rented the first floor of a two-story wooden house on Wells Street near Garfield Boulevard. Nora had her own room and was free to come and go. She went out every day no matter how cold it was. And she always managed to visit at least one church each day. At night, she would have supper with her brother and sister, Dick and Jenny Dunne.

She also visited her oldest son, Jack Ryan, and his wife Molly two or three times a week. This way, she could see their son, Andy. Occasionally she would baby-sit with him. But Nora never offered to baby-sit with Clara's son Eddie, even though she lived with the Boyles. Nor did she ever help Clara with housework. She excused her conduct by telling herself that it would be a bad habit to start; she didn't have the strength she once had, she had to favor herself a little. Thank God her children wanted her to take life easy. They all knew that she could not live too much longer.

II

Every time Clara thought about what had happened, it scared her. Mama had had a mild heart attack and didn't even know it. It wasn't until after she had suffered intestinal pains that Clara called Dr. Evans.

Clara liked to tell the story of how they found Dr. Evans. She and Jack, her husband, had gone to see a movie starring Humphrey Bogart. It was playing at the Halsted Theater at Sixty-third Street and Halsted. It had been a warm night and they had decided to walk home after the movie. They had turned onto West Garfield Boulevard. Suddenly Clara happened to notice a shingle in front of a two-story red brick house:

HAROLD EVANS, M.D.

The name had stuck with her because she had been thinking that she should find a doctor in the neighborhood in case of an emergency. She had been using Dr. Spender, a classmate of Steve's, but his office was downtown. And he lived way past Seventy-fifth and Jeffrey. He was awfully nice but she didn't like to have him go so far and then charge her so little because of her brother Steve.

It wasn't too long after that night that her mother had gotten sick.

For years Nora Ryan had known what it was to suffer. Before she had lost her teeth, she had had toothaches. She had had neuralgia, pains in her legs, in her stomach. And she had given birth fifteen times. By prayer, Nora had eased her pain. She was afraid of doctors. She had lived so long with the pain and the fear that they had become habit. But her ulcer had laid her low. The night pains were worse than any labor pains. There had been moments when she had thought that her time had come.

—Oh my God, I am heartily sorry for having offended Thee.

She groaned in the darkness. She couldn't remember the next words. A brutal penetrating stab shot through her. Oh, God, she was dying. Oh, God.

—Oh my God, I am heartily sorry for having offended Thee . . . and

She was sweating; her pillow was wet. Nora Ryan moaned again. She must be dying. She became solemn, solemn as a Mass for the Dead, solemn as the Stations of the Cross on Good Friday. She might be at death's door.

—In the name of the Father, and of the Son and of the Holy Ghost. Amen.

—Oh my God. Oh God, I am heartily sorry for all of my sins because I dread the loss of heaven and the pains of hell.

Now she remembered the rest of it.

—But most of all, because I have offended Thee Who art all good and deserving of all my love. Oh my God, God, forgive me my sins, and God, I firmly resolve with the help of Thy Grace to do penance, to amend my ways, and to sin no more. Amen.

The pain again. It was like a razor.

"Ooooooooooooohhhhh."

She didn't want to die. But if it was God's will. Another sobbing moan from her. She must pray.

—*Virgin Mary, Comfortess of the Afflicted.*

Finally her pains began to subside. The weakening effects of the pain had tired her. Her eyelids were heavy; her body weary. She slept.

Nora Ryan woke up the next morning later than usual and without pain. She did not tell her daughter of her pains. There was no need to worry Clara. She would say a novena. All she had had was a tummy-ache.

For the next two nights there had been no recurrence and Nora was able to convince herself that she had had nothing more than a stomach-ache.

However, on the third night the pain struck again and she could not hide it from her daughter.

Clara Boyle had looked up Dr. Evans' name in the telephone directory and had called him. She told him that she was worried about her mother. He had asked her a few questions.

"I'll be right over."

He arrived in less than twenty minutes. The minute Clara saw him she felt better.

Harold Evans was a tall man. In thirty years of neighborhood practice, there was very little that he had not seen in the way of illness and injury. He had delivered babies, performed emergency operations on kitchen tables, and had even amputated a leg.

III

Nora Ryan had always been afraid of doctors. She was afraid that there were things wrong with her and that a doctor would try to make her stay in bed. Being cooped up in a house would hurt more than any sickness ever could.

When Dr. Evans arrived, Nora was moaning between prayers. She prayed, not only for God, but for Clara and Jack, who were watching her. Dr. Evans looked at her. He knew that the pain was real; that the woman was suffering.

"You're not feeling well, are you, Mrs. Ryan?"

"Oh, Blessed Virgin Mary, no!"

"Well, let's see what we can do about it, Mrs. Ryan."

He opened his medical bag. Nora Ryan looked at him from her bed. What if she had appendicitis? She would have to be cut open.

Dr. Evans raised his shirt sleeve and looked at his watch. Then he took Nora Ryan's left hand, lifted it, and put his index finger on the artery in her wrist, counting as he kept his eye on his watch. Then he took her blood pressure. And listened to her heartbeat through a stethoscope.

He asked her questions about her eating habits, her bowel movements, and so on.

When he had finished his examination he asked Clara if he might use the bathroom. He went in and washed his hands. Clara waited, trying to control her fear. She remembered her father. He had died in 1923. There had been only two deaths in the immediate family since then; her grandmother in 1931; and Uncle Larry about three years ago.

"Your mother has an ulcer," Dr. Evans said, coming out of the bathroom.

Clara's face became grave.

"Ulcers can sometimes be cleared up by dieting," he continued.

Mama had a chance. That was all the reassurance Clara Boyle needed.

"Your mother must not overexert herself."

Clara became anxious. She foresaw a daily battle in the days ahead.

"Does she go out much?" Dr. Evans asked.

"Every single day. She goes to see this friend and then that friend. And she goes to church every day. And she goes to see her sister and brother every night."

"Do they live nearby?"

"At Sixty-fourth and Stony Island, Doctor."

"She shouldn't be doing that any more. Her heart won't stand it."

Clara Boyle had been expecting to hear this. It was sad in a way, Mama liked to go. But she couldn't take the time to be sad. She had to listen to what the doctor was saying. She had to find out how she could help and maybe prolong her mother's life.

"That will be hard on my mother. She loves to visit her friends and her brother and sister. And she just loves to visit different churches."

"I can understand that, Mrs. Boyle."

"She was tied down so long with all us children to look after that she enjoys gadding about now without any responsibilities."

"I understand. And I wish she could go on doing it but she can't. It would shorten her life."

"Then she will just have to stop it," Clara said.

"If she gets a lot of rest, is careful about her diet, she could possibly have another five or six years," Dr. Evans said.

Clara's eyes filled. It was funny, in a way. An hour ago she would have liked hearing a doctor say that her mother had another five or six years. Mama had been moaning and praying so hard that she had thought that she was dying then and there. But now that she was resting again, five or six years seemed mighty short.

"It will be hard to keep her in, Dr. Evans."

"Yes, but it's her best chance to live longer."

"Of course, Doctor, whatever you say."

"And whatever your mother decides."

Clara straightened up in her chair. Yes, it was what Mama decided. She was surprised at herself for not having thought of this.

"Yes, Doctor, that's what I mean. My mother will do what she decides. We're her children; we wouldn't think of telling her what to do."

"I understand that, Mrs. Boyle."

Dr. Evans took out a prescription pad.

"Now I'm going to give you a prescription that will quiet her down and make her less active. And it will help keep down her blood pressure. She's to take one of these three times a day, before each meal."

"I'll get it filled right away."

"It may make her drowsy but that's nothing to worry about. I'll come by tomorrow afternoon. But if you should need me before then, don't hesitate to call."

"Thank you, Dr. Evans."

Young Eddie Boyle had been playing with his building blocks and chattering to himself as he played.

"Mom?" he called.

"Just a minute, Eddie," she answered, her voice patient and tender.

"I must be going, Mrs. Boyle."

"Doctor, here, let me pay you now," Clara said.

"Mom!"

"I'll send you the bill, Mrs. Boyle."

"But, Doctor . . ."

"Mom!"

"It's easier to keep my records if I bill you. I'll stop by tomorrow."

"Mom!"

Dr. Evans went out through the front door.

"Yes, Eddie, I'm coming," Clara called to her son.

IV

The next day Dr. Evans found Nora Ryan in less distress but she was still a sick woman. The wear and tear of her life had exacted its toll. Her heart was damaged. And her blood pressure was up.

V

Clara had called the members of the family together for a meeting. She wanted them to know what Dr. Evans had told her about Mama's health. All of them had agreed that Nora Ryan should live as she wanted to; that she should be allowed to be happy during the time left her. If she were cooped up, kept in bed, she would be miserable. This was what Clara had thought and both her brothers, Jack and Leo, had agreed with her. Clara was glad that the meeting was going smoothly. She had wanted things to go this way because she was going to have to bring up the subject of money, too. Prescriptions had to be filled. There was no way that they could handle it on the money that they were getting from the rest of the family now.

Clara had no sooner explained the situation than Leo spoke out. He had never had a chance. Just like Pa, he had never had a chance. The rest of them had all gone off and gotten married and left him the burden of their mother to bear. He had been able to go to high school for only one year. Then he had gone to work for the Express Company as a helper on a wagon. Papa had never had a chance and neither had he.

Clara had tried to smooth things over. She didn't want the bitterness that had been gnawing at Leo to come out. She didn't want to see his suffering. But Leo was suffering. It wasn't just because of Mama; it was because of life. If he had had half a chance he could have become somebody. Eddie had become somebody. He was always hearing Eddie's name mentioned by people and he was getting fed up with it. Eddie wrote books. He was the first to admit that Eddie was smart. Eddie had always been smart, even as a little kid. But so was he. The nuns had told him he was smart. And there were others who seemed to respect him. But here he was a wagon dispatcher hauling things for the Express Company.

Leo spoke out for over ten minutes. And then he quit abruptly after claiming that he had been done out of twenty-five dollars of the burial expenses for Uncle Larry.

"Eddie's always been generous," Jack Ryan spoke up. "He wrote and asked us what was needed. He asked if there was anything that Mama needed."

"But he's got it," Leo snapped.

"He worked for it. He sent all he could to the Dunnes. And when I needed money, or when Steve did, he always came through."

"He's a Dutch uncle," Leo said, contradicting the resentment he had expressed only a few minutes earlier.

He didn't begrudge his mother anything. He would take care of her, by himself, if he had to. She was his mother. She had not been too good a mother but that didn't matter. She was the only mother he would ever have.

Jack spoke up again. He said that they all wanted to contribute what they could. Clara added that Frances out in California and Steve in Washington and Eddie in New York had all asked Mama to live with them. Leo said he understood all that; he got the picture; but the truth of the matter was, and they all knew it, that the three of them in Chicago would end up with the dirty end of the stick. Mama would not leave Chicago and Frances and Steve and Eddie knew that.

Clara interrupted. Mama would continue to live in her home. They had three bedrooms and Mama could occupy the room right off the kitchen. It was a fairly good-sized room and there were no stairs for her to worry about.

Leo said that they ought to be able to work out a plan so that it wouldn't cost any of them more than they could afford. They would all go equal shares, except maybe for Steve, who was just getting started as a doctor and had two baby girls to support.

It was worked out. Nora Ryan would be taken care of by her children. Leo and Clara figured that twenty dollars a month was enough from Eddie Ryan.

This, plus her old age relief check and money from the others, would cover her living and medical expenses. She would have to see Dr. Evans regularly. They couldn't take any chances on that.

They had also decided that Dr. Evans should be the one to tell her about her condition. She would be more apt to listen to him if he warned her. For the present, she was safe; she had a few years at least. And who could tell, it might be more.

Nora Ryan did go to see Dr. Evans a few times but she was closemouthed about these visits. Whatever he told her did not change the way she lived. She continued to go out every day.

Dr. Evans had tried to convince her. But Nora Ryan had protested.

"Oh, I feel good now, Dr. Evans. I don't have to rest so much."

"It's the best thing you could do to prolong your life."

"When He calls me, Doctor"—Nora lifted her eyes to the ceiling —"I'll go. It's all in His hands."

Dr. Evans looked at her. There was nothing he could do but keep her on the phenobarbital.

"Mrs. Ryan, you've got to promise me that you'll not go out of your way to waste your strength and energy."

"I'll do that, Doctor."

Dr. Evans knew that Nora Ryan would not change. And could he give a guarantee that she would live longer if she denied herself the pleasure of visiting her friends and churches?

"I'm going to keep you on the prescription I gave you, Mrs. Ryan."

"I take it, just like you told me to."

"Good. I want you to come in for a checkup about once a month so that I can see that you're all right."

"With the help of God, I'll be all right."

A bell rang. Another patient had entered the waiting room. Dr. Evans rose. Nora Ryan got to her feet too.

"God bless you, Dr. Evans; I'll pray for you."

"Thank you, Mrs. Ryan."

He walked ahead of her to the door that opened into the waiting room.

VI

Nora Ryan intended to be more careful but she went out every day. She showed no signs of having been sick and gave no indication of worry. But she did worry. When she did, she would tell herself:

—I'm too old to be taught new tricks.

Every night she had supper with Jenny and Dick. She was happiest when she was with them. To the three of them, the family dead were remembered presences. Both Nora and Dick hoped to meet their dead kin in heaven. Jenny sometimes feared the next world but at times she hoped to see her parents, all of the Dunnes, in heaven.

They lived in a present that was oppressive. The oppressiveness of the past was vague and less painful.

They were getting old and edging toward death. They lived for the small things of day-by-day life. They could not admit fully the sadness that was in them.

On some nights as she hurried over to be with her brother and sister Nora Ryan would think about how much better things were for them now than they had been a few years before. Things had been so bad then, so bad. Thanks to her children, she was better off than Dick and Jenny. Oh, but they had had a hard time of it.

And poor Larry, God have mercy on his soul. He had wasted away. Yes, her two brothers and Jenny had had it hard. They had gotten their comeuppance but it was not for her to rub it in. She was not one to lord it over them. But she would never forget how they had all treated her once upon a time. And the way they had talked about her Jack not providing her with anything but babies. Well, it was those babies who put the meat on their table. Not that she was one for reminding them, she wasn't. Any more than she would remind Dick of the way he had punched her when she was a little girl trying to do her sums. He had hurt her then, really hurt her. Why, she could remember having bruises from some of his punches. But that had been so long ago and she had forgiven him for hitting her.

None of them had liked it when she married Jack Ryan. On no, a teamster wasn't good enough for a Dunne. Even her mother, God have mercy on her soul, had called him a tinker, a long drink of water. But her mother had liked her Jack. Her mother had talked about him but that was just her way. She didn't look down on him the way her brothers Dick and Larry did. They had been shoe salesmen and were making good money in those days. Her Jack knew how her brothers had felt about him.

"After they sell a pair of shoes, what can they do? Tell me one thing that they can do with their own hands," he had asked her.

Her Jack had not liked Dick or Larry but he had some respect for Dick. Dick made good money and he had taken care of her mother and of her poor father. Her Jack always gave him credit for that. Why, when her father was sick and dying of cancer, Dick had gotten him a private room at Mercy Hospital. Her father had suffered so.

But all that was a long time ago.

Her father had loved her; she had been his favorite; she knew it. Pa and her Jack had gotten along.

"Nora, I have as little use for your relations as they have for me. The whole caboodle of them can go to the devil, all except the old gentleman," her Jack had said.

The two of them had liked to have their beer. And what harm did that do? Her Jack had respected her mother, too.

"The old lady is the best of the lot."

He had better respect her mother. She was her mother's daughter and her favorite. Her mother loved for her to go see her, especially after a funeral. And she had gone to many a wake and funeral.

"Tell me about it, Nora."

"Who was there?"

"How was she laid out, Nora?"

Her mother had asked her all kinds of questions. She was always wanting to hear more. But in those days Larry would sometimes come out to the kitchen and scream at her to go home. Even then, poor Larry didn't like to think about wakes and funerals.

"Can't you ever talk about anything but dying? Cripes, can't you do anything besides hang crepe?"

"I'm talking with my mother," she would tell him.

"Why don't you stay home and take care of your children?"

"That's my business; they're my children. I never had to borrow them from anybody else. I'm their mother, their real mother."

"Don't your kids need their mother?"

"Stop calling my children kids; my children are children, not goats."

Poor Larry, he didn't know what to say to her. They had had many an argument. But that was all a long time ago. Larry was dead. And she was an old woman. Dick was an old man. Even Jenny was getting old. But they were still brothers and sisters; they should be kind to one another.

VII

Dr. Evans had told Nora Ryan that she ought to lose at least twenty-five pounds. Jenny saw to it that what her sister ate at night was non-fattening. Nora began to feel better after she lost some weight. Jenny took credit for this and told people how much she was doing for her sister Nora.

This was all right with Nora. And with Dick too. Whatever Jenny did was all right with Dick. Nora had seen this happening ever since their mother died. Jenny had not touched booze for years now and Jenny was pretty smart when she wanted to be. And she made a home for Dick. Nora didn't mind that Jenny was boss of the home she had made for her brother. Neither one of them, Jenny or Dick, ever said a cross word to her. Why, the two of them couldn't be nice enough to her. Jenny bossing Dick around was no skin off her nose. And she didn't mind it a bit when Dick's talk went over her head, or when Jenny talked the same way. The three of them were getting along. They would talk about Mother a lot. And sometimes about Pa. But most often they talked about Mother. One night Jenny had come right out and said to Nora:

"Sometimes it's like you stepped in the place of dear dolly Mother. Isn't that so, Dick?"

"Yes, Jenny, it is."

Well, she was, in a way, taking the place of her mother with Dick and Jenny. The two of them depended on her. Her children were grown; they didn't need her any more. And she had had enough of diapers and feeding and cleaning house. When her Frances had married Harold Landry and her grandson Michael was a little baby, she had gone over and helped. But Frances had needed her mother around because Harold Landry's mother was around all the time. If his mother could be around, she could be around. Nora sometimes wondered how Harold's mother found the time to get so involved in the affairs of her married son. Of course, Mrs. Landry was alone; she had bossed that poor Mr. Landry, God have mercy on his soul, right into the grave. And she kept after Harold, too, but he hardly noticed. Harold always had a drink or two in him and he didn't notice too much happening around him.

"He's a boozer, Frances."

She had told her daughter Frances this.

Nora had enjoyed taking her first grandchild out in his buggy, and then in his stroller. When little Michael was able to walk, she had taken him out. She liked the feel of his little hand in hers. She had never been able to take her own children out like that except for John, her first-born. The others had come so fast, one after another, and there had been too much to do. It had not been easy for her in those days.

Little Michael was so good and so handsome. He minded well, too. He looked like her little Vincent who had died in her arms of diphtheria when he was only four years old. Oh, merciful Saviour, she had never gotten over losing her beautiful little Vincent. Yes, Frances' baby reminded her of her little Vincent. She would have gone to see him more often but it worried her to see the way Harold drank. She had told her daughter that he was a boozer and that was all that she was going to tell her. She wasn't going to be an interfering mother-in-law; she wasn't going to interfere in the marriage of any of her children. They were grown men and women.

They were good to her, but they did not pay much attention to her. Sometimes this hurt her feelings. Her children loved her and they took care of her but when they were all together they talked to each other. Most of the time she just sat and listened but a good part of what they talked about went right over her head.

Nora Ryan thought that she listened far more than she did. Most of what she heard, she let go in one ear and out the other. Nora believed that she was listening when she daydreamed. And she daydreamed a lot. Daydreaming allowed her to see what she wanted to see and to think what she wanted to think.

Chapter 2

I

When the bell rang and the horns were blown, and the shouting and kissing and wishing one and all "Happy New Year" was going on, Nora Ryan was asleep. She had done much gallivanting on the last day of 1945.

Nora had gone to see her oldest son's wife first. She had helped Molly with the housework and Molly had given her three dollars. She had left Molly's before noon to pay a visit to the Church of the Holy Family. She had prayed and lit three candles before the Blessed Virgin's altar.

To get to Molly and Jack's house from Clara's, she had had to get on a Wentworth streetcar at Garfield Boulevard, ride on that for twenty blocks until the West Seventy-fifth Street stop. There, she had gotten a transfer for the westbound Seventy-fifth Street car. She had had to wait for it for almost ten minutes. She had ridden that one to Halsted and then walked the four blocks to the building where Jack and Molly lived.

After she had left their apartment she took streetcars to Sixty-third and Woodlawn. Then had walked a block to the Hedgecomb Hotel. She entered the lobby.

The desk clerk nodded to her.

"Happy New Year, Mrs. Ryan."

"Happy New Year to you."

She went to the house telephone. When Nora heard the operator's

"Hello?" she asked for Mrs. Carney. In a moment a woman's voice spoke on the other end of the connection.

"Mother? It's me, Nora."

Nora Ryan listened. Then:

"I will, Mother."

She took the elevator to the eighth floor, got out, walked down the hall, and stopped before a door. She knocked.

"Come in, Nora," a husky voice called.

Nora entered the room.

"Hello, Mama."

"Hello, Nora."

Mrs. Carney sat in a wheel chair, withered and white-haired.

"How are you feeling, Mama?"

"Oh, I feel as good as I can, I suppose."

"Can I get you anything?"

"No, not yet. We'll have a cup of tea in a while. Oh, it's not a day for the last day of the year, is it, Nora?"

"No, it isn't. It's getting cold."

"It certainly feels like it."

Nora sat in a chair near Mrs. Carney and looked at the old woman devotedly.

"It's another year, Nora child."

"Yes, it is, Mama."

"Many's the year I've seen come to its end, Nora."

"I know."

"Hard ones and ones not so hard. Good ones and ones not so good," Mrs. Carney said, talking as much to herself as to Nora.

"Yes, Mama."

"Let's have our cup of tea now, Nora."

"I'll make it, Mama."

"No, I'll make it."

She rose from the wheel chair and walked slowly to the other room of her suite. Nora got up and pushed the wheel chair into a corner. Mrs. Carney used it to save her strength. Nora followed Mrs. Carney into the other room. There was a small electric stove on a shelf in a corner with more shelves along the wall. A small refrigerator was nearby. And a small table. On the other side of the room was Mrs. Carney's big-four-poster bed.

Mrs. Carney fixed the tea and toasted some bread. Nora set the table. Soon they were seated opposite each other eating. Nora's face was flushed.

"Do you feel all right, Nora child?"

"Yes, Mama, I don't feel so bad."

"Feeling not so bad isn't feeling all right, Nora."

"Oh, Mama, I've had aches and pains all my life."

"Maybe you should lie down here and rest, Nora."

"I have to go to church, Mama."

"Didn't you tell me that you went to church?"

"Yes, Mama, but I have two more to go to on the last day of the year. Then I'll go to my brother and sister's place."

"Will you be able to rest there?"

"Yes, Mama."

"And will you go home early and get a good night's rest?"

"Yes, I will, Mama."

"You promise?"

"Yes, Mama."

She did have a headache. It wasn't bad but her head did hurt. She looked out the window. The sky was gray.

—God will call me one day, Nora thought.

She didn't want to die, not yet. She had lived what was considered a long life. It had been a long life. When she thought this, something bothered her. She didn't try to think of what it was; all she knew was that something did bother her. Well, she wouldn't let it, not now. She was happy sitting here with Mrs. Carney having tea. They had tea together almost every day. She liked telling Mrs. Carney about her children and grandchildren, and about Dick and Jenny. And Mrs. Carney told her about her own life, of her past, and about the people who lived in the hotel. She usually stayed for about an hour.

After her second cup of tea, Nora started thinking that she should leave. Mrs. Carney looked sleepy.

"I must be on my way soon, Mama."

"It was good of you to come over, Nora."

"I love to visit you, Mama."

"I know you do, Nora child."

Nora kissed her good-by.

"Just a minute, Nora."

Mrs. Carney went to a small desk by the window, opened a drawer, and took out a white envelope.

"This is a remembrance of the New Year."

"Oh, Mama, you shouldn't do that."

"Now you take it, Nora. No words about it."

"Thank you, Mama."

She kissed Mrs. Carney again, wished her a Happy New Year, and left.

II

Nora Ryan visited two churches before she went to the Dunnes'. The natural shrine of the Mystic Rose of Jesus Christ in St. Charles's Church was directly across the street from the Hedgecomb Hotel. She had gone there first and had prayed to the saint who was called the Mystic Rose of Jesus Christ. To Nora, virtue and virginity were fixed on the face of the statue. The Mystic Rose of Jesus wore a lit-up golden halo. In front of the altar, by the rail, many candles burned, their flames wavering slightly.

She knelt close to the altar and prayed to the Blessed Virgin Mary first, then to the Mystic Rose. She prayed for her children and her grandchildren, for her living brother and sister, and for her dead parents and dead husband, her dead brothers and her dead sister, her dead children, for her son-in-law and her daughters-in-law, for the companies for which her children worked, for Mrs. Carney, for Chicago, and for America.

Nora was happy praying. She had the feeling that she was in direct communication with Mary the Mother of God and with the Mystic Rose of Jesus Christ.

She felt happy in God's house, praying and talking to Him, and she hoped that she would, one day, see Him in heaven. She was happy because she was storing up goods, the goods of God, for herself and for hers, living and dead.

Nora Ryan prayed with expressions and gestures. She knelt with her hands palmed together, resting on the altar rail. She was not praying to show off, she was setting an example. That was why she sometimes had to put on a little bit; she wanted to set a good example.

Nora prayed for a long time on that early afternoon of the last day of the year 1945. She wanted people to see her pray. She did not care if she was criticized. God would not criticize her!

III

Nora finally stood up. Her knees felt stiffer than usual. She walked over to the candles and lit some. She lost count but she must have lit at least eight or nine. With a final prayer, a final genuflection and blessing of herself, Nora left the church.

She walked slowly. She still had a headache. She didn't feel at all good today. She walked toward St. Basil's at Sixty-fourth Street.

Well, it was the last day of the year. She kind of felt like the last day of the year. She wished her headache would go away. As soon as she reached Jenny's she would have another cup of tea. That would ease it.

The walk from the Church of the Mystic Rose of Jesus Christ to St. Basil's was short. She had covered this distance she didn't know how many times. But today it tired her.

IV

Nora Ryan came out of St. Basil's Church still tired. She liked going to St. Basil's. Her son Edward had gone to high school here. And her Leo and Steve had gone here for a while too. She prayed especially for them when she went to St. Basil's.

She was tired but her headache was gone.

V

Her head was aching again by the time she had walked a short distance from Sixty-fourth and Dante. This time the pain was so severe that she stopped on the sidewalk and nearly cried out.

She felt dizzy, the sidewalk looked like it was waving. She was afraid that she would faint. Maybe she was going to die. Her eyes watered. The buildings, automobiles, people—all looked hazy. She was sick. She knew it. She would pray. But the pain was too much, she couldn't concentrate.

—Mother of God! she silently exclaimed.

She stood on the corner for a minute but it seemed that she had been there a long time. The blur in her vision was disappearing and pain in her head easing. She could walk now.

—*Oh, Mary, Mother of God, give me strength.*

—*Oh, Mary, Tower of Ivory, keep me in health.*

By the time she had reached the middle of the block Nora Ryan was smiling. With the help of God and His Blessed Mother she was over whatever it was that had been wrong with her. Her headache was almost gone. All she needed was a cup of tea. And she would be at Jenny's in two shakes of a lamb's tail. Her mother, God have mercy on her soul, used to say that a lot, "two shakes of a lamb's tail."

Nora reached the corner.

VI

After ringing the bell, Nora walked to the inner door. In a moment the buzzer sounded and Nora pushed the door open. She entered the hallway and slowly started up the stairs.

"Is that you, Nora?" Jenny called down.

"Yes," Nora answered, her voice tired.

"Happy New Year, my darling sister."

"Happy New Year, Jenny."

As Nora turned at the small landing, she saw Jenny standing outside the front door of the apartment.

Nora's breathing was labored.

"Jen . . ."

"Yes, Nora?"

"Oh, Jen, make me a cup of tea, please. I have a headache."

"Yes, dolly sister. I'll make you the best cup of tea you've ever had, and then it will be rats to your headache."

Nora tried to smile.

"I know it, Jen," she said, following her sister into the apartment.

VII

The furniture in the dining room looked as though it might have been salvaged from a junk heap. The two straight-back chairs had come from a nearby alley. They were badly scratched. The round dining-room table was also scratched and had watermarks from glasses. In a corner by the windows there was an old rocking chair. This had belonged to their mother. Nora often sat in this chair and rocked back and forth.

The peeling walls, the shabby furniture and the frayed curtains gave the apartment a wasteland atmosphere. Jenny had added to this by piling up cardboard boxes, wooden barrels and boxes in which she kept chinaware, wrapped in newspapers.

Jenny traded old clothes or anything else she could for china in thrift shops. Occasionally she would pay ten or twenty cents for a piece. This was her protection against disaster. It was all she had for a rainy day.

Jenny would say that she was going to put her treasures away where they could not be broken and then fix up the apartment so that it would look more like a home and less like a warehouse. But she never got around to it. From time to time the thought would occur to her but then she would look at how many there were and decide to do it at another time. She was content to leave them as they were. Some rich dealer or collector might hear about her collection and come ask to see it. She would, of course, show it to him and his eyes would all but fall out of his head.

Jenny Dunne had many such fantasies centered on her treasures. She did not think that her imaginings were merely dreams. They weren't; they were hopes.

And when this happened, she would take care of the whole gang of them the way she always had.

Jenny had been daydreaming about this when Nora rang the door-bell.

VIII

"Yes, Nora, I'll make you the best cup of tea you ever tasted," Jenny called from the kitchen.

Nora didn't answer. She scarcely heard her sister. Her head hurt so. What was Jenny saying? Oh, she could hardly wait for the tea. She would be all right; there was nothing to worry about. Wasn't it worry that killed the cat? Jenny was so good; she really was.

Jenny appeared with the tea.

"Here, Nora darling."

Nora lifted her head. She had almost drowsed.

"Oh, you're so good, Jen."

"Here's your tea, dolly, drink it. Here, sit at the table. I'll get some tea too, so that I can have a cup with you."

Nora did not move immediately. She looked at her worn pocketbook. Jenny was moving back toward the kitchen. Nora opened her pocketbook and dug into it. Jenny came back carrying her cup. Nora closed her purse. Jenny put her tea on the table. Nora opened a white envelope and pulled out a brand-new ten-dollar bill. Jenny pretended that she didn't see it.

"Come drink your tea while it's hot, Nora."

"I will, Jen, but take this."

"Nora darling, drink your tea."

"I will," Nora said, getting up and walking the few steps to the table.

Instead of sitting, Nora stood behind a chair, placing her hand on the back of it for support.

"Jenny."

"Yes, Nora?"

"Jen . . ." Nora started again.

"Nora darling, sit down and drink your tea. Drink it while it's hot."

"I'm going to, Jenny, but it's the end of the year. It's almost a New Year."

As she spoke, Nora extended her hand toward her sister.

"Take this as good luck for the New Year."

"You need it yourself, Nora dear."

"No, take it for you and Dick."

"Poor Dick. He does need so many things and he's a saint. He never complains. But I do keep him spotless, don't I, Nora?"

"Yes, you do."

"Oh, Nora, sit down and drink your tea. Please."

"I will."

Jenny took the ten-dollar bill and put it in her apron pocket.

IX

Nora smiled. Some of her weariness was gone.

"Do you feel better, Nora?"

"Oh yes, I do, Jen."

"I said I'd make you a cup of tea good for what ails you."

Nora sighed. She felt better.

"Have another cup, Nora," Jenny suggested.

"I think I would like another one."

"I'll get it for you," Jenny said, going around the table to get her cup.

She went into the kitchen. In a few moments she returned, carrying a steaming cup.

"Thank you, Jen."

Jenny looked at her sister. There was something about Nora's voice. She should lie down and rest. It would do her a world of good. But another cup of tea first would pick her up.

Nora drank the tea slowly. She had very little to say.

Nora was not acting like herself, Jenny thought.

"Why don't you have another cup too, Jen?"

"I think I will," Jenny said, rising from the chair.

X

Nora Ryan did not want to lie down. She would rather gossip with Jenny but she was tired.

"I think I will take a little nap, Jen."

"Take it in my bed."

"We're old now, Jen," Nora remarked, her voice sad.

Jenny had a lightning streak of fright. She had headaches, worse than any Nora had ever had. And she had pains in her heart, too. But she wouldn't give in to them the way that Dick and Nora gave in to their pains. They depended on her; both of them did.

Nora stood up.

"A little nap will make me feel better. And maybe when I wake up Dick will be home and we'll all be together to wish each other a Happy New Year."

"Do, Nora, take a nap and I'll tidy up things around here. Dick will be getting home any minute now."

"I'll just lie down a little while, Jen."

"Here, let me fix the bed."

"Oh, don't bother," Nora said, and started to walk out of the dining room.

Jenny moved ahead of her sister and went into her bedroom. She turned on the light. The bed had not been made. Two barrels stood between the bed and the door. The closet door was open and old shoes and dirty stockings were on the floor. The dust and confusion did not bother Nora Ryan. She was used to it. Besides, she was too tired to care. She was going to lie down on top of the bed with her clothes on.

"Here, Nora dear, let me help you get your shoes off and your dress off. I'll cover you up. You'll have a better nap if you get comfortable."

Chapter 3

I

Nora was lying in Jenny's bed. The shades were drawn and the bedroom door was closed. She was alone. God was up there. She was never alone, because He was up there. He was always there; God the Father. She was perspiring a little and her breathing was heavy. Her head still hurt but it was bearable. She was not really suffering. It only hurt a little, just enough to keep her from going to sleep.

Nora Ryan was drowsy. She had fallen asleep for a few minutes but she woke up. Her headache awakened her. She was afraid. She had awakened, not knowing where she was.

Nora Ryan said some prayers. She said an Act of Contrition, and then she said Our Fathers and Hail Marys, not counting how many she said. After a few minutes she said a second Act of Contrition. She was not dying but she had been afraid. She would die someday. This thought brought back her fear. She would be on a bed, just like this one, but it would be her deathbed. Fear paralyzed her. She could hardly breathe. She was afraid of the actual dying that would take place. This was what scared her. Nora never thought of her soul or her fate in the afterlife. The only times she thought of these was when she was saying her prayers and preparing for her afterlife. It didn't frighten her then because she didn't think of the actual dying that would have to take place before she reached her afterlife.

Nora felt helpless. Her lips quivered; her body was rigid. Death was sneaking upon her like a snake in the grass. She was stiff with fear. She could hear sounds. Automobiles on the street. A radio was playing somewhere, maybe in the flat upstairs. And footsteps; it must be Jenny.

Jenny was good.

Was Dick home yet?

Dick was good too.

She should get up now. The terror that she had felt was gone. She was vaguely sad. It was the end of another year. She was sad; another year made her older. Another year made Jen and Dick older. It took her further away from the time when her children were young and when Jack was alive and when her mother was alive, and her father. God have mercy on their souls. God have mercy on all their souls. They had gone. They had borne the sufferings of the flesh. God have mercy on their souls. When she did go, she would see them. She would see them in heaven with God. And her little Vincent, her little boy, who had died of diphtheria.

Nora Ryan was in tears.

II

"Well, well, the Dowager Queen," Dick Dunne said.

Nora Ryan, with cheeks slightly flushed, had walked into the dining room.

"Hello, Dick, Happy New Year."

"And Happy New Year to you, Nora."

He embraced her and kissed her on the cheek.

"Oh, my darling dolly sister," Jenny said as she came in from the kitchen.

"And the Princess of Graustark," Dick Dunne said.

"Happy New Year, dolly Nora," Jenny said.

"Happy New Year to you, Jenny. You're good," Nora said.

"And Happy New Year to you, Dick," Jenny said.

"Oh, Dick, Jenny is so good," Nora said.

"Oh, wait until you taste the supper I'm going to cook. I've just started it."

Jenny Dunne would not let either Nora or Dick help her. They sat in the dining room, Nora in the rocking chair.

Dick was quiet. She could tell that he was remembering too. This had been Mother's chair. She used to rock on it and say her rosary. And now Mother was in heaven, with God and the angels. And Mother was with Pa. She would be up there with them one day. Wouldn't that be a happy day? They all knew how much she had prayed for them, how many offerings she had given, how many holy candles she had burned for the salvation of their souls. She would go to heaven like a queen. A queen. Her mother was fit to be a queen but she herself wasn't. Wasn't that the word Dick had used tonight? Sometimes she didn't know what he was talking about. What was the word he had used? Dowager Queen? What did it mean? Dick was that way. He used big words like someone who had gone to college. What would her mother say to her in the next world? Everybody would know all about her, all of her thoughts, everything she had ever done. Nora shuddered. When she died, she would have to face her mother, her in-laws, some of her children, her relatives, a lot of them; and she would have to face God.

III

Dick Dunne was meditative and nostalgic. So much of life was in the olden days. His heart always softened when he thought of the olden golden days.

His ship had not come into the harbor safe and snug, laden with wealth of the Indies, good luck and fortune. If only his ship had come in. If only it had.

Dick Dunne looked around the room. This was what he had come to on December 31, 1945. A wave of emotion almost choked him. It was too late for his life to be different but he could still hope; he was still in the pink. The Lord would decide when he would go. Everybody's turn came. But, with God's will, he still had some years left.

"What's that you were sayin', Jen?" he asked.

Jenny had called from the kitchen.

"Oh, I was only saying that you just wait till you taste the supper I'm cooking. You just wait."

Nora's head nodded in sleep.

"I know you can cook, Jen," Dick said.

He did know. Jen was a superlative cook. He did not have much of an appetite tonight, though.

"Just you be patient, wait just a few more minutes," Jenny called.

"Take your time, Jen," her brother said.

Nora Ryan was nodding in sleep.

IV

Dick and his two sisters were seated at the round dining-room table. Small jets of stream were rising from the food that Jenny had set on the table.

"First, we must say grace," Dick said.

They bowed their heads. Nora put her hands palm to palm in a gesture of prayer. Jenny made a face but her head was lowered and neither Dick nor Nora noticed it.

"We give Thee thanks, O God, for these Thy bounties which we are about to receive."

"The boiled chicken will melt in your mouth, Nora," Jenny said.

Dick served slices of the white chicken. He handed the plates to Jenny, who put mashed potatoes and creamed spinach on them. There were only three of them and the serving was done quickly. There used to be six or seven at the table for a Sunday dinner. Seven . . . no, six. Larry, Mother, Jen, Clara, Eddie, and himself. Six. Nora had not been with them then. She had had her own family. But her family was raised. His generation was old. Most of the parents of his generation were dead now. Lord have mercy on their souls.

And on this the last day of the year, he thanked the Lord for all good things.

They ate.

"Next year's gonna be a better one," Jenny said, "I feel it in me, up here." She pointed toward her head. "And I feel it in my bones."

"With the grace of God, I think so too," Nora said.

"That's the ticket," Dick said. "That's the spirit."

"You deserve it, Dick, you're so good," Jen said.

Dick Dunne's enthusiasm was partly real and partly a habit of optimism. He drew comfort from what his sisters were saying. He needed this encouragement. His experience of a long lifetime had not provided him with much solid reason for hoping. Nevertheless, he had moments when he hoped. And the last day of a year was a day to hope.

"Yes, next year will be better than this one. I certainly hope so."

"It will be," Jenny said.

"Yes," Nora agreed tiredly.

Dick wondered if Nora felt all right.

Jenny could see that her sister did not feel well.

Nora felt tired. She felt no pain; she was just tired.

V

"No, Dick, I can do it myself easier," Jenny said.

Dick had offered to help clear the table and wash and dry the dishes.

"If the royal Princess wants help . . ." he said.

"No, Dick."

—Jesus Christ, doesn't he know he'd just get in the way? she thought.

Jenny masked her sudden anger with an insincere smile. She would not lose her temper on New Year's Eve.

It had gotten dark outside. And it had become colder, too.

Witches could howl and spirits could ride the cold winds of darkness tonight but he and his were safe. They were safely ensconced in their home, thought Dick Dunne.

Best it was to thank God for the gifts and not complain or bemoan other gifts. Dick looked at the shabby furniture and the boxes and barrels lining the walls.

It was comfortable enough for Jen and him. Cheerfulness was in the heart, not in things you owned. It did no harm to remember this. He had resolved to stay cheerful time and time again. Things would be worse if he wasn't. He had seen much that was not cheerful during his lifetime. He had never expected his later years to be the way they were. He certainly didn't expect that he would be living in an apartment like this. He had planned and saved so that he could be financially secure and respected. But there were reasons for the way his life had turned out. He had been the fall guy. But what good did it do to chew over bitter memories?

"I think I'll smoke a cigar," Dick said, making a motion as if he were going to rise from his chair to get one.

"Don't move, Dick, I'll get it for you," Jenny said.

She had just returned to the dining room from the kitchen.

"Thank you, Jen."

"Where did you leave them?"

"In the breast pocket of my suit coat hanging in my bedroom closet."

Jenny knew where Dick's cigars were. This scene was repeated almost every night after supper. Dick liked to be waited on. He sat while his sister went to get him a cigar.

He turned toward Nora.

Nora smiled at him; but it was a wan smile.

VI

Puffing on his cigar, Dick commented:

"It was a fine dinner, Jen, a superfine dinner."

"It was good, wasn't it? Maybe I could be a cook in a short-order restaurant."

"You could do better than that, you're a good cook."

"Yes, you are, Jen," Nora said.

"Oh, I always was," Jen said.

Dick nodded. Nora said nothing. Dick and Jenny were old now. She was too. And when you're old, you know that you will soon be going before God. You didn't complain about little things that you might have complained about when you were young. Jenny was good now. But it had been different when Jenny was young. But that was for God to judge. Dick was different, too. He had tried to run Jenny's life and now Jenny ran him.

They were the last three now. God had spared them for the New Year, and for years to come, Nora thought. Her head was aching again. Maybe another cup of tea would help her. She got up from her chair.

"Do you want something, Nora?" Jenny asked.

"I thought I'd make myself a cup of tea."

"I'll make it for you, Nora dolly. You sit down."

"I can make it, Jen."

"I'll make it. You sit down."

Nora sat. Jenny went into the kitchen. Dick sat, silent, puffing on his cigar. Nora was quiet too. Now and then she rocked.

Dick rose from his chair and turned on the radio. For a while they both listened to "The Hearth Family." It was on five nights a week and Jenny and Dick both liked listening to it. Nora did too, most of the time, but tonight she was silently saying prayers. She ought to be going home soon.

Jenny came back into the room with the tea. She sat down and listened to the radio. Nora smiled whenever Jenny or Dick laughed at something one of the Hearths said. She didn't want them to worry and she was afraid that they would. She would sit here a little longer. It was New Year's Eve and she liked being here with her only living brother and sister.

"The Hearth Family" ended with Happy New Year wishes. It was broadcasted good cheer, good cheer of paid announcers and paid performers cheering in the name of Pompadour Shampoo, the sensational shampoo sweeping the peacetime nation. Pompadour Shampoo was a product of the Grounds Corporation of Valley City.

"Sure and I let it go in one ear and out the other."

That's what her mother, God have mercy on her soul, used to say, Nora thought. And that's what she was doing now. Oh, she was tired, and . . . Nora caught her thought in time. No, she did not think that she was sick.

"Can I turn the radio off now, Dick?" Jenny asked.

"Of course, Jen."

Jenny turned to Nora. Nora didn't look well.

"Nora dolly," Jenny began.

"Yes, Jen?"

"Why don't you stay here tonight with Dick and I?"

Dick caught himself just as he was about to correct his sister's grammar.

The suggestion frightened Nora. She was used to her own room.

"Oh, I can't, Jen. Clara and Jack would miss me."

"I could telephone them, Nora dolly," Jenny urged.

Nora was disturbed. She couldn't stay here, not all night. She would have to leave, and soon.

"Do you feel all right, dolly?" Jenny asked.

"Oh yes, I won't have any trouble getting home."

"Dick can take you, can't you, Dick?"

"Of course, yes. Let me put on my shoes and a tie."

"Oh no, I wouldn't want Dick to go all that way and then have to turn around and come all the way back on a cold streetcar," Nora protested.

"It's nothing at all, Nora," Dick said.

"Well, at least take her to the streetcar and help her on," Jenny said.

"If I go now, I'll miss all the people out celebrating," Nora said.

Dick went into his bedroom.

"You're all right, Nora?" Jenny asked.

"Oh yes, I am, Jenny."

"If anything happened to you, Nora, I don't know what I'd do."

"It's the will of God, not us poor creatures, who decide."

Jenny's remark had upset her. She wanted to go home now, she wanted to get back to her own room. Dick reappeared, ready to put her on the streetcar.

"I'll get ready now," Nora Ryan said. She got to her feet.

VII

Dick watched as Nora paid the fare and walked to a seat. The streetcar moved on, going west.

He could not see Nora. She sat by a window. The streetcar had started up again before she had reached the seat and she had almost lost her footing. Thank God she had been able to grab the back edge of a seat and hold onto it. Then when she had regained her balance she had moved forward and sat down.

She looked out and saw the familiar store fronts. Most of them were darkened. There were people on the sidewalk and automobiles moved alongside the streetcar.

The streetcar stopped and started, stopped and started, stopped and started. Her headache had come back. She clutched her transfer. She would be getting off soon. The streetcar seemed to be shaking more than it usually did. She had been riding streetcars all her life. She was used to the rocking. It wasn't the rocking that bothered her; it was her head. It was aching. But she would soon be getting off at Wentworth. From there, it would be a short ride to Garfield and then she would be home.

She could feel her heart beating. She didn't feel right. She closed her eyes and began to pray to the Blessed Virgin Mary.

The streetcar stopped. Her lips moved in a silent Hail Mary. The streetcar started again. She could feel its vibrations. Oh, she'd be glad to get home. She closed her eyes.

VIII

Nora opened her eyes. Where was she?

"Halsted Street," the conductor called out.

She hurriedly rose from her seat and made her way to the platform. She shivered; it was getting colder. She crossed the street and waited for the light to change so that she could cross Halsted. She would have to catch a streetcar back to Wentworth. If she hadn't fallen asleep she would have been home by now. She waited for the cars. People were going out to celebrate New Year's Eve. It wasn't midnight yet. Her feet were cold, and her head still ached. The Sixty-third Street streetcar was coming.

Nora dragged herself toward the platform. A man helped her up on it. Nora handed the conductor her transfer.

"Lady, this transfer's no good on this car," the conductor said.

"I rode past my stop. The conductor didn't call me like I had asked him to."

"Listen, lady . . ." the conductor began.

"I was supposed to get off at Wentworth Avenue."

"This transfer will be good on Wentworth Avenue," the conductor said.

"Well, give it to me, then," Nora Ryan said.

"Let the lady through, she wasn't told right when to get off," a passenger called out.

"All right, lady," the conductor said, handing the transfer back to Nora Ryan.

"Happy New Year," Nora said, taking it and passing on toward the inside of the streetcar. She found a seat. It was only a short ride between Halsted and Wentworth, she would be there in fifteen minutes or so.

Nora half dozed. She still felt chilled. She wished she were home, in bed.

The streetcar rocked. There were a lot of people on this one but it wasn't crowded. It was New Year's Eve; people were going out to celebrate. She felt drowsy. She was shaken and bumped as she drowsed off. She had a feeling of peace and softness.

"Nora Ryan."

She was on a streetcar going home to her husband, to her Jack.

There was a voice calling something.

Nora heard a man's voice calling on the streetcar.

"Wentworth Avenue. Change here for the Wentworth Avenue streetcar."

Nora blinked. Something had happened.

"Wentworth Avenue," the conductor was calling.

For a few seconds she didn't know where she was. She had been hurrying home to her husband Jack Ryan.

"Wentworth Avenue," the conductor called out once more.

The streetcar stopped. Nora stood up and, clutching her transfer and her big black pocketbook, got off. Then she made her way across Wentworth Avenue to the opposite corner. She waited on the sidewalk, one of a small crowd. It was getting cold. There were patches of frozen snow on the sidewalk. Some of the people waiting for the streetcar were already having a good time. People going by in automobiles were blowing horns.

—Ring out the old, ring in the new, she thought.

"That's all right, lady, a Happy New Year to you."

The Wentworth streetcar arrived.

Nora handed her transfer to the conductor and went inside. She would be home soon.

Nora Ryan got off at the far side of Garfield Boulevard. She was almost home now. She had dreamed that she was going home. When she was on the streetcar on Sixty-third Street, she had dreamed that she was going home to her husband Jack. It had been a message from her husband, a message from Jack Ryan, her husband in heaven. She was going home soon.

—Oh Hail, Mary, full of grace! the Lord is with thee.

She stepped up on the other side.

— . . . of thy womb, Jesus.

Nora Ryan turned in at the little walk that led to the front door where she lived with Jack and Clara.

The door opened.

"Oh, Mama, I saw you coming," Clara called.

"It's getting cold out," Nora Ryan said.

—Hail, Mary, full of grace.

Nora went slowly to her bedroom. Her head was aching; she wanted to get into bed and sleep.

—The Lord is with thee.

Chapter 4

I

On New Year's Day, 1946, Nora Ryan went to twelve o'clock mass at St. Basil's at Sixty-fourth Street and Dante Avenue. It was a high mass and the little chapel was crowded. She was lucky to get a seat in one of the pews on the side of St. Joseph's altar. Some of the faithful had to stand in the rear of the church. A few others stood and knelt along the side altars. The mass lasted an hour and the air of the little church got stale with so many people in it. She had attended many high masses but none of them had ever seemed too

long. Before this was ended, she was breathing with difficulty. Her
cheeks felt hot and flushed. For a few moments she felt dizzy. She
was afraid that she would faint. But she didn't. When mass was over
she left the chapel and walked over to the Dunne apartment.

Dinner was almost ready when she arrived. Jenny said that everything would be on the table in a jiffy and they could all sit down to
the finest meal that they had ever tasted. Happy New Year, kiddos.

II

Nora Ryan did not eat much. The roast beef was tender. Jenny kept
urging her and she did eat more than she cared to because she didn't
want to hurt Jenny's feelings. Dick urged her to eat a little more too.
Nora still did not look well to him even though she did look better
than she had last night. He tried to signal Jen to lay off attempting to
persuade Nora to eat a larger portion. People could dig their own
graves with a knife and fork. He could remember years ago reading
in Donald Somers' column, "NOW" in the Chicago *Scope,* an idea
that was very similar to the one that just now occupied his cranium.
Donald Somers had been a brainy man and had a way of explaining
himself that caught the eyes of the mind. He was dead now, God
have mercy on his soul. But Donald Somers had had a good philoso-
phy of life. Dick thought that he would like to discuss Donald
Somers with his nephew, Eddie Ryan.

"That was good, wasn't it, Dick?"

"Oh yes, Jen, it was a swelliferous repast."

"It was good, wasn't it, Nora?"

"Oh yes, it was, Jenny."

"It's a shame you didn't eat more, Nora."

"Oh, I had a fine dinner."

"You didn't eat more than a bird, Nora."

"Oh, I had my fill."

Dick was getting nervous. He didn't want Jen to fly off the handle.
She picked up Nora's plate and, looking somewhat hurt, carried it to
the kitchen sink.

III

Jenny cleared the table, insisting that Nora and Dick just sit. Dick had said that it would be no trouble at all and Nora had said that Jenny shouldn't work so hard and that she, Nora, could do the dishes.

"No, I don't mind at all. You just sit where you are and take it easy, Nora dolly."

—It's all I'm good for anyway, Jen thought.

‹ She didn't want to think that way. But it was true. It made her sad, thinking this way, but didn't the truth often hurt? Well, she would wash the dishes. She was the youngest and the strongest of the three of them.

Jenny finished washing the dishes. It was almost two-thirty. She fixed herself a cup of tea, carried it into the dining room, and sat down facing Dick. Nora sat between them. She had been on the verge of dozing off when Jenny walked in with a cup of tea.

"Would you like a cup?" Jenny asked her.

"Oh no, thank you, Jen."

"It's no trouble," Jenny insisted.

"Oh, Jenny, I've had my fill, thank you, it was so good."

Jenny took another sip of her tea.

"This is delicious."

Nora told her that she would, later, have a cup of tea. She had had her fill for now. Jenny said that she would be glad to fix it for her whenever she was ready for it. She sipped her tea and smoked. Dick was smoking a cigar, blowing smoke rings and watching them rise to the ceiling in a blue-gray haze. He was thinking that if you had to smoke stogies and could not afford Corona Coronas, why, what the old Sam, a stogie could, under such circumstances, taste as fine as a Corona Corona. Take the stogie that he was smoking. Well, it tasted for all the world as mild and as satisfying as the Corona Coronas that he smoked. It did in so far as he was concerned.

"Let's have some radio," he suggested.

"All right," Jenny agreed.

He turned the dial.

IV

It was a long afternoon. Nora was drowsing. The radio was on. A jazz band was on the air. Dick didn't want to hear it, not now, he didn't, no, thank you. He had a book on semantics that he had gotten out of the public library. He would read that, but first he ought to get some fresh air in his lungs. He would go outside and take a short walk.

"Are you asleep, Jenny?" he asked.

Jenny didn't answer. He concluded that she was. He sat for a few seconds waiting to be sure. Suddenly she opened her eyes, looked directly across the table at him.

"What did you say, Dick? Gee, I was almost asleep."

"Oh, I'm sorry."

"Oh, don't be sorry, Dick. You didn't wake me up; I was only starting to fall asleep."

"I'm glad of that Jenny."

"But Nora is, poor darling," Jenny said, turning her eyes on her sister.

Dick didn't want to say anything, Nora might hear him, but he was thinking that Nora did not look well. Self-correction, Nora did not look well enough. She was showing signs of being tired.

"You had better go out now, Dick, while it's still light. It gets dark so early and it will be much colder."

"I think that you have judged correctly," he answered.

He stood up, fastening his shirt cuffs. "I won't be long, Jen."

"Oh, Dick, have a good walk, take your time."

"Yes . . ." he began, "yes, I'll be back shortly."

"All right, Dick."

He left the apartment.

V

Nora was still sleeping. Jenny sat at the dining-room table smoking a cigarette. The radio was still on.

VI

Nora's napping was fitful. She had not slept well the night before. She had strained and moved her heavy body in bed. Every few minutes she had awakened, sweating and terrified. She could hear her heart as it raced and thumped. It seemed to be pumping out loud. She had wondered if she should wake up Clara. But she lay still.

VII

It was a good beginning of the New Year. She had napped a little at the table after their meal and felt fine now. She and Jenny and Dick were having tea. It was raw and cold outside. It was better to be sitting inside having tea.

Today was the beginning of a New Year. There were so many things to remember. Jenny and Dick were remembering too. Jenny had just said something about Mother, God have mercy on her soul.

Jenny and Dick were sad about remembering and yet they were enjoying it, too. The years that they were remembering had been the best of their years. They were not remembering everything just the way it had been; they were remembering it the way they wished it had been.

VIII

"Mother was so proud," Nora Ryan said.

The three of them were still sitting at the dining-room table.

"Yes, she was," Jenny agreed.

The radio was still on. They half listened.

As he sat with his two sisters, Dick's mind wandered back to those olden, golden days when he was younger.

"Larry was a dresser," he said aloud.

"Yes, he was," Nora said to be agreeable.

"He could harmonize colors like a master," Dick said.

"Poor Larry," Jenny said.

"He would get a perfect harmony in his tie and socks."

—My Jack used to call him the dude, Nora thought.

"Yes, he could when he had the money, he was a swell dresser," Jenny said.

Dick Dunne was pleased that she had said this; Jenny had known he would be.

IX

Nora left the Dunne apartment at about eight o'clock. Her headache had come back. When she got off at Wentworth Avenue, the ache had become almost blinding. Her eyes were watering. In pain and fright, she appealed to the Blessed Virgin Mary to get her home. She could not walk fast; the short walk to Wells Street seemed long. She staggered several times. As she approached the wooden house the pain in her head subsided. She did not seem to have any headache as she began to climb the steps. The key was in her pocketbook. Instead of fishing for it, she rang the doorbell. Jack Boyle opened the front door.

"Hello, Mrs. Ryan, did you have a good day?"

Nora Ryan entered the house without answering.

"Yes," she finally said as she moved past him.

"Oh, hello, Mama," Clara Boyle called out.

"Hello." Nora's voice sounded weak.

"Don't you feel well, Mama?"

"Oh, I just have a headache," she answered, walking toward the back of the house. Her room was to the left of the kitchen. She reached the door of her room, turned the knob, and opened it. She went in and turned on the light and shut the door behind her. She started to take off her clothes; her head was pounding again. She would go to bed. Her head, the pain was unbearable.

Chapter 5

I

"Well, maybe this year we'll find a house," Clara Boyle said.

"I hope so," Jack Boyle answered.

"Gosh, it would be . . ."

She stiffened up. She and her husband stared at each other with a questioning, uncertain look.

The sound came again.

It was a moan, a moan from the back of the house.

—Mama, Clara thought in terror.

Jack Boyle was on his feet and hurrying out to Nora Ryan's room. His wife followed him.

"I hope . . ." She couldn't finish.

Jack Boyle opened the door of Nora's room.

"Mrs. Ryan . . ."

"Oh, Mama," Clara exclaimed, in shock and sudden agony.

Jack Boyle had stepped forward, pulled on the chain to turn on the overhead light, and stepped to the bed. Clara ran to the foot of the bed. Nora Ryan lay comatose, breathing with a wheeze.

"Thank God she isn't dead," Clara cried.

~ **PART THREE** ~

Chapter 1

I

Leo Ryan parked his car at the curb behind that of his older brother, Jack. They all got out.

Leo went to the back and opened the trunk. Steve rushed beside him in an effort to grab the luggage first.

"Just a minute, Steve."

There was an edge in Leo's voice.

Eddie stood by the curb, Florence beside him.

"I can get it, Leo," Steve said.

But Leo was already pulling suitcases out. Steve scarcely gave him time to set them on the sidewalk before he was pulling out one.

"What the hell!" Leo exclaimed.

"I'm sorry, Leo, I didn't mean to bump you."

Poor Steve, Eddie thought. His naïveté was irritating at times.

Suddenly Leo laughed.

"You never change," he said to Steve.

"Oh, I guess I am kind of impatient," Steve said.

Eddie walked over to pick up his briefcase and portable typewriter.

Leo pulled out another suitcase and set it down on the curb. He turned back to the car and slammed the lid of the trunk down.

The front door of the house opened. Jack Boyle stood in the doorway.

"Leave the luggage there, I'll be down to get it," he called, coming down the steps quickly.

"Here, let me take them," he said.

"That's all right, Jack," Steve said.

"Hello, Steve, how are you?" Jack Boyle asked.

"Oh, all right, Jack, all right."

"Hello, Eddie," Jack Boyle said.

"Hello, Jack."

"Here, Steve, let me take it," Jack Boyle said, reaching for the suitcase in his hand.

Steve Ryan let the big suitcase down on the sidewalk and walked toward the front door of the wooden house.

He wanted to get inside ahead of Eddie.

Leo was dragging Eddie's big suitcase and following Steve.

"Go on in, Eddie, and I'll follow you," Jack Boyle said.

"All right, thanks, Jack."

II

The light overhead was dim. The odor of urine was repulsive but his pity was stronger than his repulsion. His mother was lying on the bed. When she saw him she lifted her left arm and moved it in an irregular arc. She seemed to be trying to say something. The right side of her face was twisted and pulled out of shape.

Clara was standing by the bedside. She looked tired.

Steve had entered the room first.

"Oh, I'm so glad you both came," Clara said.

She looked more exhausted than sad.

"I haven't had a wink of sleep."

Steve went to the bedside and took his mother's wrist. He pulled out a watch.

Eddie waited. But Steve Ryan did not speak for some seconds. Then:

"Her pulse makes no sense."

Eddie left the room and walked toward the kitchen.

Jenny Dunne was there, pacing and wringing her hands. Wrinkles cracked her face.

"Oh, Brother, she was so good," Jenny said when she saw him.

He said nothing.

"Oh, Brother, it's so terrible."

"Yes, it is, Aunt Jenny."

"She was so good."

"Yes," Eddie Ryan said politely.

He could see that Jenny was going to try to corner him. He remembered how Jenny always behaved when there was a death in the family. She competed with the dying person for attention. He would have to be firm with her.

Eddie was about to say something to her when Steve came out of the bedroom.

"Oh, Stevie boy!" Jenny exclaimed.

This gave Eddie Ryan an escape. He went into the parlor. There, his oldest brother, Jack, was sitting, crushed into silence.

Molly, his wife, sat on a rocking chair. She was silent and dour. Leo and Florence were also there. No one spoke.

Jack Boyle came up from the cellar. He had gone down to tend the furnace.

He went to the closet, got his leather jacket and an old hat.

"You know we're on strike, Eddie," he said, buttoning the jacket.

"Yes, that's right."

"I got to go out on the picket line now."

There was honking from an automobile.

"That's for me," he said, hurrying out.

In a moment the motor could be heard, turning smoothly, as the car moved away.

Steve came into the parlor, Jenny following on his heels.

"Eddie, Mama is a terminal case," Steve said.

"Can we send her to a hospital?" Eddie asked.

"Oh, but your mother wouldn't want to be carted off to a hospital," Jenny intervened.

"Well, of course, Dr. Evans is the doctor in charge," Steve answered.

"What do you think?" Eddie asked.

"She could be taken; she would be more comfortable; physically, I mean."

He paused.

"I can take care of her better than any nurse," Jenny interrupted.

Eddie was irritated.

"I'm better than any nurse," Jenny repeated.

"Just a minute please, Aunt Jenny," Steve said.

"Psychologically, we can't know how conscious she is of her surroundings, and what effect moving her to a hospital would have, and how that would affect her condition. And then, too, moving her would tax her strength, and her heart, and it might be fatal. She's in poor condition, Eddie."

"I take it to mean that she shouldn't be moved," Eddie Ryan said.

"Well, I'd say so."

"Then we'll get nurses."

"We don't need nurses," Jenny said.

"You can't do it, Aunt Jenny."

Eddie's voice was firm.

"I can, too, and save the money."

"Aunt Jenny, I know that you are mother's sister," Steve explained. "But you are not a trained nurse."

"But I'm as good as a trained nurse," Jenny said. "Oh, I'll take such care of her."

"I know you would try to take good care of her, Aunt Jenny, but that is not a substitute for training as a nurse."

"Ask Brother here," Jenny said, turning to Eddie.

"Aunt Jenny, I'm a doctor," Steve began.

"But ask Eddie if his aunt won't be able to take care of your mother."

She looked at Eddie Ryan.

"No," Eddie said, anger in his voice.

Jenny was surprised. She could not speak for a moment. Her favorite nephew had betrayed her. He could just as well have slapped her face.

Jenny Dunne was already upset. She had been upset since last night when Clara telephoned and told them that Nora had had a stroke.

Now she was more upset. She never would have dreamed that Brother would talk to her, his Aunt Jenny, the way he had, just now, with her sister Nora, his mother, dying.

III

Dick Dunne was upstairs walking back and forth. Now and then his lips moved in a prayer. At any minute Nora might die. She gave every sign that she was dying. Her children were here because they all thought that she was. It was not unreasonable to deduce the general opinion. She was a mighty sick woman. But he was not going to admit it. He wanted his prayers to have the best possible chance of helping her or of soliciting the Lord's help, of asking God to spare Nora's life.

Eddie was here. Eddie would take care of matters now. Where he had left off, thanks to his fortune, Eddie had taken up.

Dick Dunne was thinking of the financial end of this tragedy.

Unless you were one of the rich, you had to think about sadness and sickness in dollars and cents.

Dick Dunne stopped pacing. He would like to smoke a cigar. But ought he to smoke a cigar in the same house where his sister Nora lay between life and death? Dick Dunne was so distraught that this question troubled him.

When Clara telephoned him last night, he asked if Nora had seen a priest. Clara told him that she had not been able to get the priest from St. Julia's, which was a block away.

Dick had said that he would get one. He had handed the telephone to Jenny and had dressed.

"Have you got your muffler on, Dick?" Jenny had called to him when he started out.

"Yes," he had thoughtlessly answered.

As soon as he did, he realized that he was not wearing it.

"No, I haven't."

"It's in the closet," Jenny had called.

Dick had hurried to the closet, gotten his muffler, and wrapped it around his neck, under his overcoat.

"I'll be back as quickly as possible, Jenny."

He closed the door.

He had walked the two blocks to St. Basil's on Dante Avenue. It was cold. He walked briskly. But even though he hurried, Dick Dunne was watching carefully for spots of ice or anything that might cause him to stumble and lose his balance. He had good footing; he wasn't worried about this; he was merely being careful.

The news of Nora had been a blow in the solar plexus. He was glad there was something he could do for his sister. And what he was doing was the most important thing that could be done for Nora.

He had almost reached Dante Avenue. Eddie had gone to high school at St. Basil's. He could not pass the school without thinking of his nephew.

Thinking of Eddie made him sad. This was not the time to dwell upon better days. There was a soul to save. He walked faster. When he reached Dante Avenue he crossed East Sixty-fourth Street.

He had had some mighty rocky moments in his life, he could say that. This was a rocky time for him, it was, for a certainty.

He walked by St. Basil High School. The priests lived on the first floor of the apartment building next to the school. He rang the bell. He wouldn't have to wait long. Someone would answer right away.

A few minutes passed. He still felt the cold. He said some prayers for his sister Nora as he waited.

He started to ring the bell again but hesitated. He didn't want the fathers to think he was impatient. But damn it, this was a matter of gravity. It was the matter of a soul. Just as he started to press the bell again he saw a shadow through the double glass doors, Someone was coming. He felt a sense of achievement, he had gotten a priest for his sister.

"Hello, who's there?"

It was the voice of a young priest.

"Father, God bless you," Dick Dunne said.

"God bless you," the voice came back.

"My sister has been stricken and we need a priest. I'm a parishioner here, Richard Dunne."

"Yes, come in."

Dick Dunne put his hand on the doorknob. There was a buzz and he pushed the door open. The young priest opened the inner door of the entrance hall with one hand and switched on a light with the other.

"My sister has had a stroke and needs a priest. Nora Ryan, née Dunne."

"Where does she live?"

"Garfield Boulevard and Wells, Father."

"That's not in our parish, Mr. Dunne."

"I know, Father, but she might be dying. I'll go to the police station and get a squad car to take you."

"Oh, I could get there but it's out of our parish. We can't go out of the parish for such a distance."

"She might be dying—there may not be time."

"I'm certain her parish priest will administer the rites of the Church. And I'll pray for her. I'll pray tonight, in fact."

"You can't come, Father, even under special conditions?"

"No, not there. Did someone try the parish house at St. Julia's. That must be her parish, isn't it?"

"Yes, Father."

"What was the trouble?"

"They couldn't get a priest."

"Why that's unheard of, Mr. Dunne."

"I don't know why, Father, I didn't take the time to get all the information. My sister is very ill. Her daughter tried at her parish."

"Well, Mr. Dunne, telephone your niece back and tell her to go back to St. Julia's. And I'll pray for your sister."

"Thank you, Father."

"God bless you, Mr. Dunne."

The young priest let Dick Dunne out. He stood for a moment, feeling the cold. He saw his own breath, like vapor, in the frosty night air. He was disappointed. But he had had many disappointments in his life. It had been a long life. He didn't have time to do any reminiscing now. His sister had to have a priest. Clara had not been able to locate one.

Dick Dunne decided what he would do. He walked to Sixty-fourth Street and Dante. He turned right and crossed the street. That young priest should have come with him. If Nora were dying, parish jurisdictions and street limits ought not to be of any consequence.

He was walking briskly along Sixty-fourth Street. The night seemed lonely and desolate.

It was one of the saddest moments of his life. His sister might be dying at this very moment, this was no time to falter. He had a job to do; he had to find a priest.

Dick Dunne walked north on Harper Avenue. Ahead of him, he saw a dim light coming out of a building in the middle of the block. He walked up to the building and entered. It was the Woodlawn Police Station.

IV

Dick Dunne was riding in a squad car with two policemen. Red Nolan was the officer driving the car and Ed Foster was the other officer's name. Lieutenant Morgan had ordered Nolan and Foster to help Mr. Dunne find a priest for his sister.

Dick Dunne had walked into the station and had asked to see the officer in charge.

"He ain't in," a rough-looking plainclothesman had told him.

"I want to speak with the officer in charge here," Dick Dunne had insisted. "I have to get a priest."

"A priest? This is the police station."

"Listen, I have no time for your irrelevant humor. Understand?"

"Say, who in the hell . . ."

Dick Dunne raised his hand.

"If you were a gentleman you wouldn't interrupt me," Dick Dunne said.

The detective was nonplused. Five or six police officers gathered around.

"Where's the lieutenant?" Dick asked.

"I'm Police Lieutenant Morgan," said a big, gray-haired man who had come through a side door.

"How do you do. Lieutenant Morgan. My name is Richard Dunne. I have to get a priest for my sister, Mrs. Nora Ryan. She has had an attack, a hemorrhage of the brain, and I must find a priest. I came to request the service of a squad car to help me."

"What's the matter with the priests over at the St. Basil's High School?" Lieutenant Morgan asked.

"My sister lives at Garfield Boulevard and Wells and it's not in their parish, I am told. God has no parishes."

Some of the policemen smiled.

"But there's no time to waste on arguments, Lieutenant Morgan. My niece could not get a priest at St. Julia's at Garfield Boulevard and Wentworth either."

"Is there a car here now?" Lieutenant Morgan asked.

"Nolan and Foster, sir."

"All right, take Mr. Dunne and try and find a priest for Mrs. Ryan."

"Thank you, Lieutenant Morgan. God bless you," Dick Dunne said.

"I'll say a prayer for your sister, Mr. Dunne," the big detective said, abashed.

"Thank you. Happy New Year, Officers," Dick Dunne said.

Chapter 2

I

"The wee small hours of the morning," Steve said.

"What?" asked Eddie Ryan.

"Nothing. I just said the wee small hours of the morning, that's all."

"It's about two-thirty."

"Yes, the wee small hours."

Eddie looked at him. Steve was grinning. Was he trying to be funny?

"Jack will be home soon," Clara said, coming out of her mother's bedroom.

"How is she?" Eddie asked.

"The same, I guess. As far as I can see, she looks the same."

Eddie was sitting at the kitchen table. Steve was standing near the door.

"Eddie? Steve?" Clara said.

They both looked at her.

"Don't you both think you ought to try to get some sleep?"

"I will in a few minutes," Eddie answered.

"I think you ought to try and get some sleep, Eddie," Steve said.

"I will."

Eddie tried to mask his irritation. He was fully awake now, he had no wish to go to bed.

"Well, I'm going to sleep unless you want me to sit up and watch Mama," Steve said to Clara.

"Oh no, I might as well stick it out until morning. I've gone this far," Clara said.

"I can stay with her," Steve insisted.

"No, I want to be up when Jack gets home."

She turned and went back to her mother's bedroom. Nora Ryan was trying to point again.

Suddenly an overpowering sadness gripped Eddie. He was here waiting for his mother to die. Again, he thought of her as she stood in the station waving good-by to him, Phyllis, and Tommy last June. He remembered thinking that it could be the last time that he would see his mother. It was not exactly a premonition. He had wanted his son Tommy to meet the Ryans and the Dunnes. He had hoped that Phyllis and he and Tommy could have a nice family visit. But Phyllis had, from the very first day, subjected the entire family to her tantrums and outbursts. That was why, when the train started out of the station, and the three of them were on the way back to New York, he had thought that he might not see his mother again. The sight of her waving good-by and crying touched him. His mother was old. Her health was not good. And Phyllis' behavior had embarrassed him. He would not be returning to Chicago soon. This was why he had wondered about seeing his mother again.

It had started on the very first day. He had been scheduled to lecture at Valley State University. He had planned to leave there on Saturday night and get into Chicago early Sunday. An hour later Phyllis was arriving from New York at the Englewood Station with Tommy. Clara and Jack Boyle were meeting his train and planning to drive to the station in plenty of time to meet Phyllis. But his train had been late. Clara had telephoned the Englewood Station and had asked the stationmaster to deliver a message to a young mother with a five-year-old curly-haired boy who would be getting off the Commodore Vanderbilt from New York City. Their names were Ryan, Clara had told him; and the message was that the Boyles were waiting for Mr. Ryan to come in from Valley City; that his train had been delayed but that just as soon as it arrived Mr. and Mrs. Boyle would rush Mr. Ryan over to meet her and the boy.

And that was what they had done. Phyllis had greeted them with an outburst. It was the first time that Jack Boyle had met her. Eddie had been embarrassed and had tried to explain. But Phyllis' fury had raged on.

"Why don't you try and travel in a small Pullman bedroom with your five-year-old monster!" she had screamed.

Phyllis had not let up during the drive to the Boyles'. When they reached the house she became worse. The delay in Tommy's breakfast schedule would undo all her efforts to teach "the monster" how to eat as other children. He must eat right away; everything else must wait.

"How do you want me to fix his eggs?" Clara had asked her.

"*I'll* fix his eggs," Phyllis had retorted.

Then Phyllis had complained about the difficulty in preparing a meal in a stranger's kitchen. Nothing was where it should be. Why did Clara keep this here and that there?

Clara and Jack had told their son Eddie that his cousin Tommy was coming to visit him. Eddie Boyle had looked forward to meeting his cousin.

"Maybe I'll fix Eddie a little something too, so that he and Tommy can eat together. He's been looking forward to Tommy's visit and I think they would . . ."

Before Clara could finish, Phyllis had turned.

"This kid's hard enough to feed with no one else in the room. I certainly don't intend to spend the whole morning standing over him like a policeman in order to get food down his throat."

Clara had been startled. What nerve, Clara thought. If it weren't for her brother, she would ask her to leave. But she was Eddie's wife.

Clara had let her have her way.

Eddie had hoped that Phyllis would behave better in front of his family. Once she got started in one of her outbursts, there was nothing he could do to stop her. He almost always ended up being screamed into a condition of almost agonizing impotence. Phyllis could only be stopped by physical force and Eddie could not force himself to kill her or to gag her. He couldn't lock her into a closet or knock her unconscious. All he could do was wish that she would die. Many people wouldn't approve of his wishing his own wife dead. He himself wished that he hadn't. It was a gloomy impasse in a marriage to wish a partner dead. And this was particularly true in his marriage because he loved Phyllis. And he was struggling to save his love. They had Tommy. At the University of Valley State he had, one afternoon, been taking a short walk on campus. He had looked at the girls and thought about them, about himself, his work, Tommy, the future.

—I'm trying to be a good and conscientious father and an unfaithful husband.

The thought had come unexpectedly.

—It will not work.

—Why won't it work?

But then:

—It could work.

Eddie had taken a cigarette out of the package in his pocket; lit it; and taken a puff. It might work but he would prefer to be a good father and a faithful husband.

He had decided that last week. And here he was now, ashamed and humiliated. He was being made to look like a goddamned, henpecked husband before his own family.

Eddie sat in the living room, too near despair to talk to Jack Boyle. Phyllis was still in the kitchen screaming about being kept waiting at the train station, feeding the monster, and how her role in life was reduced to acting as a policeman for the monster.

II

The first second that she saw her grandson Tommy, Nora Ryan had seen that Tommy was almost the image of her Vincent.

III

Phyllis Ryan scarcely relaxed during the ten-day visit in Chicago. Consequently, Eddie was continually on guard, waiting for Phyllis' next outburst and hoping that he could forestall it. On a few occasions he did succeed in averting a flare-up but he could do little to reduce the tension and strain that Phyllis created.

Nora Ryan spoke little in her presence. She would get up early in the morning and leave the house as quickly as she could. Her daughter-in-law was a very nervous woman, Nora thought, but she seemed to be a good mother. And she was being nice to her; she called her "Mama." Nora Ryan liked this. But she wasn't going to let them drag her into any fights. She was too old. Phyllis was a real nagger but every wife had to do some nagging. Oh, she didn't want to think about all this. She was old. She had raised her family. That was enough. She wasn't as strong as she used to be and she was tired. She wasn't used to someone like Phyllis who was always carrying on. She had gone through quarreling and name calling. Enough was enough. She was too tired to become involved in them now and she knew better than to get between a son and a daughter-in-law.

And besides, she hadn't raised Edward. She didn't really understand him. He wasn't like her Jack or her Leo. Even her Stephen. But Edward had always been a good boy. Her mother had brought him up well. How many times her heart had ached because she had let him go live at the Dunnes. Her husband Jack had never liked it, the years that Eddie was living with the Dunnes. He used to call them "your relations."

Eddie had been such a beautiful curly-haired baby. She had cried when she let him go. That was long ago. She didn't know where the years had gone. Edward was a man over forty now. And he wrote books. She had heard people talking about his books and she would see his name and picture in the newspaper.

She had read his books but she wasn't letting on that she had. She didn't want to get into any mix-ups over them and she didn't want anything she said about them to be held against her. Yes, she had read some of Eddie's books and she had cried.

"Nora, Eddie was such a darling boy. Why did he write the way he did about us? After all we did for him, why did he write those things?"

Jenny kept asking her these questions.

"I never read the books," Nora would answer.

She wasn't going to get into any fights about Eddie's books. She wasn't born yesterday.

"Me, I'm dumb like a fox."

That's what Mama used to say. And she was like Mother that way, dumb like a fox.

"Nora, I can't understand why Edward would write such things."

"I don't know either, Jen. When your children grow up, they grow away from you and you aren't even sure they want you around any more."

"Ain't that the truth!"

Chapter 3

I

Eddie Ryan slept on the big couch in the parlor. He woke up at about nine. At first he didn't believe that his mother was dying in another room of the house. It had been a dream. But he knew that it was real.

He lay there for a couple of minutes wishing that he did not have to get up. He would have to face the fact that his mother might be dead by tonight. What would happen when she died? There would be practical problems to be met. Decisions to make. The wake. All of this was depressing. But staying in bed another minute or five minutes would not solve anything.

There was a knock on the front door.

A few seconds later Clara walked through the parlor.

"It must be Dr. Evans," she said.

Eddie heard her open the door.

"Good morning, Dr. Evans."

"Good morning, Clara, how is your mother?"

"About the same, Doctor."

Eddie Ryan sat up and looked. He saw a big, gray-haired man.

"Dr. Evans, this my brother Eddie."

"How do you do, Doctor," Eddie said.

"Oh, you're the writer," Dr. Evans said.

He hurried through the room. Turning to Clara, Dr. Evans said: "I don't want to be written about by him."

Eddie was half amused by this remark. He would wait until the doctor left to get up. He might be in the way if he went into the kitchen now to get his breakfast and have a cup of coffee.

II

"Eddie," Steve said, "I spoke with Dr. Evans. He's going to call the nurses' register to get nurses. You wanted two, didn't you?"

"Yes, around the clock," Eddie answered.

"It'll cost you thirty dollars a day," Steve said.

Clara served Eddie bacon and eggs and toast.

"Don't you want a cup of coffee, Steve?" Eddie asked.

"Oh, all right," Steve answered.

He went toward the stove.

"I'll get it for you," Clara said.

Steve turned and sat down at the table again.

"What did Dr. Evans say, Steve?" Eddie asked.

"Well," Steve began.

Eddie sensed the change in Steve's voice. His brother was talking like a doctor, Eddie thought.

"Dr. Evans says . . ." Steve began again.

Eddie waited for him to go on.

"He says . . ." Steve said.

"Well, he says that Mama's condition is more than critical. But Dr. Evans won't give up. He's in there fighting."

"I can understand that," Eddie said.

"So can I," Steve said hastily.

Eddie was not eating as he and his younger brother talked.

"You see, Eddie, Mama's condition doesn't make sense. It doesn't make medical sense. Her pulse and heartbeat are so irregular . . ." Steve Ryan paused for a moment.

"Yes?"

Steve took a drink of his coffee. Then he looked up at the ceiling.

"Her pulse is so irregular and her heart is beating without any sense at all."

"She's dying," Eddie said as he resumed eating his breakfast.

"I know that." Steve spoke almost defensively.

III

Mrs. Landry, mother of Harold Landry, the divorced husband of Frances, who was en route to Chicago on the Chief, had come over to help Clara.

Hazel Landry was tall; her gray hair was turning white but she was a vigorous woman.

She arrived at the Boyles' home just as Eddie was finishing his last cup of coffee.

A nurse was expected at any minute and when the doorbell rang Clara had made a beeline to open it. Clara was as glad to see Mrs. Landry as she would have been to see the nurse.

"Clara dear, I was so hurt to hear about it. I came right over."

"I know, I know, Hazel."

Mrs. Landry stepped into the vestibule and she and Clara embraced. They both had tears in their eyes.

"I came to help, Clara," Mrs. Landry said, taking off her coat. "How is she?"

Clara shook her head.

"Oh, I'm so tired," she said, "so tired."

"You go take a nap, Clara. I'll manage for you."

"Oh, I'll be all right, let me give you a cup of tea, Hazel."

"I'll make it myself," Mrs. Landry said, going to the kitchen.

Eddie Ryan, wearing a bathrobe, was coming out of the kitchen as Mrs. Landry was entering.

"Oh, good morning, Mrs. Landry," he said.

"Hello, Eddie, how are you? A Happy New Year to you."

"A Happy New Year to you, Mrs. Landry."

IV

Clara was lying down and just getting to sleep.

Dick and Jenny arrived. Dick pressed the button to ring the doorbell. The ring was loud and sharp. This awakened Clara Boyle with a shock. Of course, she didn't blame them. Gosh, Uncle Dick and

Aunt Jenny must feel real bad. It was terrible, just terrible, Clara thought, getting up. Well, she would get some rest sometime; she couldn't now. She left the bedroom. Mrs. Landry was in with Mama. Jenny and Dick were taking off their coats. Clara wished that the nurse would come. A nurse would know what was best for Mama and how to make her comfortable. But Steve was here, he ought to know. He knew lots that the rest of them couldn't know. And Eddie had come home. He was so good and he was spending so much money. But then, he could afford it better than the rest of them could.

Clara's heart sank at the sight of Uncle Dick and Aunt Jenny. Well, not really at the sight of Uncle Dick. It was Aunt Jenny. She sure hoped that Aunt Jenny would not make trouble. Not now, not at a time like this.

"Oh, Clara, you're so good," Jenny Dunne said. "But you look tired. Did you get any sleep?"

"Yes, a little, Aunt Jenny," Clara lied. She didn't want her aunt on her neck insisting that she go in and take a nap. And that's what Aunt Jenny would do if she knew that Clara hadn't gotten any sleep.

Uncle Dick said good morning to Clara and asked her how she was. She told him that she was all right. Then she told them both to sit down, she would be right with them as soon as she went in to take a look at her mother. Clara went into her mother's bedroom. Clara had not seen her mother for about two hours, possibly a little less than two hours. Before Mrs. Landry came, she had been with Mama almost the whole time since she and Jack had found her in a coma. She thought that she was used to the way Mama looked. But when she looked at her on the bed now she was shocked.

The massive stroke that she had suffered had devastated her mother. She was helpless as a newborn baby, even more so. She could not talk. Her face was twisted, the right side pulled up so that her features were distorted. Her right eye was open and rigid, like a glass eye. The eyelid would not close over it. Her right arm and her right leg seemed to have shriveled and withered. They were useless. She could exercise no control over her bladder. It was the same with her bowels. She was helpless living flesh.

Her mother was dying, dying in an awful way.

It was horror. Clara stood horrified.

"Clara, you need more sleep," Mrs. Landry said.

Mrs. Landry's words broke in on her shocked state.

—Poor Mama! she thought.

A great grief came upon her; grief over her mother, for just about everybody. She could not have explained how she felt. For the first time in her life, she was seeing somebody die—her mother. Her shock was like a piece of ice held against her flesh.

Suddenly, she felt dull and empty.

She was so tired.

"Yes, I am tired," Clara Boyle told Mrs. Landry. "I'll go back and try to sleep a little more."

"You must, Clara, you look very tired. It must have been an exhausting time for you, Clara."

Mrs. Landry's voice sounded kind, sympathetic, and understanding.

"Yes, and thank you, thank you so much," Clara said.

Impulsively, Clara embraced Mrs. Landry and then she went into the kitchen from her mother's bedroom.

Chapter 4

"Oh, Eddie," Jenny Dunne exclaimed.

"Hello, Aunty Jenny."

He got up from the kitchen table and kissed her on the cheek. He sat down again.

"Oh, what are we going to do?"

Eddie did not answer. He knew what to expect. Aunt Jenny's scenes could not be allowed this time. They would have to be checked. It would be unpleasant, but unpleasant or not, she would have to be stopped if she started throwing scenes.

"Brother, Dick wants to have a little talk with you," Jenny said.

"What does he want?" Eddie asked.

Eddie had already guessed what Dick wanted.

"Brother, Dick worships you."

Eddie's patience was running thin.

"Here's Dick now, Brother."

"Hello, Eddie, how are you?" Dick asked.

"I'm all right."

"Have a nice talk now, Dick," Jenny said. "I'll fix some coffee."

She turned away from the table and moved over toward the stove.

"Well, Eddie, it's a sad occasion, a sad beginning of a new year," Dick started.

Eddie waited.

"Yes, Eddie, your mother's a very sick lady."

"I know," Eddie said.

"We'll have to mobilize everything to help save her," Dick said.

Eddie nodded.

"And you know, Eddie, there's nobody in the world like your Aunt Jenny when it comes to taking care of someone ill."

Eddie restrained himself from interrupting.

"Your mother knows her. Your Aunt Jenny will be a subtle morale builder, Eddie, like no one else."

"That won't do any good, Uncle Dick."

Dick looked pained.

"We thought, Eddie, that . . ."

Dick seemed meek. How different he had been when Eddie was a boy. In those days he had been a successful businessman and the head of the household he supported.

". . . I mean, Eddie, I thought that since your Aunt Jen is so much better than a nurse, we could save you a good slice of money. Jen is better than any nurse you can find."

He finished speaking, a hopeful and almost pleading expression on his face.

"My mother needs nurses, and I'm not trying to save money here," Eddie said.

Eddie was firm. He had to be. He felt resentment, but more against Aunt Jenny than against Uncle Dick.

She was going to make trouble. He knew how she could.

He was going to stop her, even if he had to have her taken out of here by the police.

"Shall I tell Jen, Eddie, that it's all settled?" Dick Dunne asked.

"No!" Eddie Ryan said.

Dick Dunne's head almost snapped at the firmness of Eddie Ryan's "No!"

"Eddie, I wish you'd consider it again. Jen was very good to you, you know."

Eddie Ryan felt a smothered embarrassment. Stronger than any feelings of embarrassment, there was sadness. It was a sadness about his family. This had been with him ever since he was a little boy.

And now he was back in the midst of it again. It was this, not any hangover of fear from the time when Torch Feeney had presumably wanted to kill him, that had conditioned his determination not to come back to Chicago.

He was back in the midst of it. And it was all still a mess.

Eddie wished that he hadn't had to be so curt with Uncle Dick. At the same time, he felt a sort of satisfaction. Eddie knew that this satisfaction was derived, in part anyway, from the cruelty bound up with his firmness. He could justify what cruelty he had felt.

But why bother? He didn't need to. He knew what he was doing and why.

To whom had he ever given guarantees that he would never be cruel?

He had to take over. He would not let his mother's death degenerate into a melodramatic farce.

Chapter 5

I

Clara Boyle was going back to get some more rest. It was hard to do with all that was going on and with her home crowded with the family, all of them upset, and feeling she didn't know how bad. But she could understand. She wasn't complaining. She loved Mama. They all loved Mama. She was just tired.

"You poor thing, you look so tired," Jenny said.

She had buttonholed Clara just outside the kitchen. Clara was too tired to talk and too tired to care whether or not Jenny Dunne's sympathy was genuine. She knew that Aunt Jenny didn't want them to hire nurses. Aunt Jenny insisted that she could nurse Nora and save the money for the kids, her nephews and nieces, and . . . Clara was too worn out to argue. Her brothers were here now. One of them was a doctor; he could handle it. She just wanted to go to bed.

"Yes, Aunt Jen, I am tired," Clara Boyle said. "I'm so tired I can't talk now."

"You look tired, Clara. Golly, you've been doing too much."

Clara didn't know how she could stand on her feet. She had never been so exhausted and Aunt Jenny wouldn't let her go.

"You go get yourself a rest, Clara dolly. Don't you worry, your Aunt Jenny, old reliable, is here to take care of anything that needs to be taken care of."

"I have to sleep," Clara said, unable to keep the petulance from her voice.

"You just let me take over," Aunt Jenny said.

She was planted squarely in front of Clara.

"You know your Aunt Jenny and you know that I am better for your mother than any two nurses would be."

"Steve is a doctor, Aunt Jen, and he and Dr. Evans talked . . . Oh, Aunt Jenny, please let me go to sleep or I'll pass out right here," Clara pleaded.

"That's just what I'm trying to explain to you, Clara dolly."

Clara looked helplessly at her aunt.

"Clara," Eddie Ryan said, stepping out of the kitchen.

"Brother, Clara and I are having a private talk," Jenny said.

Clara was afraid that Aunt Jenny would make trouble. She didn't know whether or not it would be best to give in to her about the nurses. She was so worn out, she didn't want to have to decide.

Eddie's butting in was such a relief but she didn't want any arguments.

"Can't I talk privately with my niece without interference?" Aunt Jenny demanded.

"Aunt Jenny, there's one thing I want you to know. It is definite and it won't be changed," Eddie told her, his voice so firm that it sounded angry.

Tears formed in his aunt's eyes.

"There are going to be nurses. That's all there is to this matter. You can't take care of Mother twenty-four hours straight and she needs someone in constant attendance."

Jenny was in tears but Eddie seemed to be unmoved.

"Clara," he said, turning, "you ought to go rest now."

"I want to; I just don't want any arguments," Clara said.

"Neither do I and there won't be any."

"I don't argue; I discuss," Aunt Jenny said.

Eddie remembered the days when they had lived at Fifty-eighth and South Park.

"I don't argue, I discuss."

He could almost hear his Uncle Larry pronouncing these words.

"The nurse will be here any minute now," Eddie Ryan said.

"Gosh, I'd better wait until she comes and tell her about things," Clara said.

Jenny Dunne turned away.

II

"Steve, Jenny has to be stopped before she goes too far," Eddie Ryan said. Steve listened with a thoughtful air. Eddie waited for a moment, hoping that his brother would agree. Steve maintained his thoughtful air. Eddie felt that he had to convince him. "I know, Steve; I know the symptoms."

"Yes," Steve said.

"Whenever there's a death, she competes for attention with the person dying," Eddie continued.

"Of course, but she must be distressed," Steve said.

"Then give her a Seconal or something to quiet her down."

"I don't know if she'd take it. Besides, I don't think we have to do that," Steve said.

"Well, if she starts cutting up, she'll have to be stopped and you know as well as I do that she won't stop by being asked."

"Well, I explained why she couldn't be the nurse," Steve said.

"And then she put poor Uncle Dick up to talking to me," Eddie reminded him.

"Yes," Steve said, nodding thoughtfully.

"And then she went at Clara again," Eddie added.

"Well, I will admit, she is persistent."

"I know she is."

Jenny walked in.

"I never merited such ingratitude, Brother," she said in a voice throbbing with self-pity.

Eddie was silent.

Jenny sighed as she left the kitchen, wringing her hands.

III

"After all that I did for you children," Jenny said.

She was standing by the kitchen window.

"But, Aunt Jenny, what have we done to you?" Clara asked.

She hadn't been able to sleep. She had lain down for a while but had finally got up and walked back into the kitchen. Although she had not actually slept, she no longer felt so tired.

"I told you that I would nurse my poor sister for nothing. I don't want a cent for it."

"But, Aunt Jenny," Steve interrupted, "you aren't a nurse."

"She's better than a nurse," Dick told him.

"That's not for you to decide, Uncle Dick," Steve said.

"Is it for you?" Dick asked.

"Yes, it is; he is a doctor," Clara spoke up.

"I apologize. I forgot that you are now Dr. Ryan, Steve." Dick spoke ingratiatingly.

"Oh, I'm so proud of my nephew Stephen, and he's here and I can do whatever he tells me to do to help my sister," Jenny said.

"Aunt Jenny, don't you understand that we need professional nurses?"

"But I'm better than any nurse."

Eddie took Clara aside and spoke quietly to her. Clara nodded. Jenny saw this and glared at him.

"Aunt Jenny," Clara Boyle began.

Jenny looked at her defiantly.

"If it's money you need, Eddie will give you money," Clara said.

"I said I'd do it without asking a cent," Jenny snapped.

"But you can't." Eddie's voice was curt.

"Oh, such ingratitude," Jenny sobbed.

Dick took a few swift steps over to his sobbing sister.

"Here she goes, Clara," Eddie said.

"There's no reason for this," Clara said.

"Jen, don't cry," Dick coaxed.

"All I wanted . . . all I asked . . ." Jenny let out a loud sob.

"Oh, God, all I did . . . I tried to . . ."

She sobbed again.

"And to be insulted this way. Oh, God!"

Everyone but Eddie was tense. He was angry.

"You," Aunt Jenny said, pointing at him.

Eddie slowly got to his feet and held her eyes in a hard stare.

"You, you ungrateful little . . ." Jenny Dunne was shouting.

"Shut up, Aunt Jenny," Eddie demanded.

"Don't you talk to me who raised you," Jenny Dunne spoke back.

"Aunt Jenny, I said, 'Shut up'!"

Jenny Dunne broke into wailing sobs.

"Get her out of here until she quiets down. Mama is dying and she is not going to do what she has always done," Eddie said.

"Eddie . . ." Dick appealed.

"I don't deserve this," Jenny wailed.

"Aunt Jenny, shut up," Eddie said. He turned to Steve.

"Either she shuts up or she gets the hell out of here," he said. He looked at Clara. "If she won't shut up and she won't leave, I'll call the police and have them remove her."

"Eddie . . ." Steve started to say something.

"She either behaves or she gets out. We can't have her making scenes and starting family fights." Eddie's voice was still controlled.

Jenny whimpered.

"Aunt Jenny, you heard me. Stop it or get out. If you don't, I'll have you taken out," Eddie said.

Clara looked at him uncertainly. She knew how Aunt Jenny was and she knew that something had to be done to check her. Aunt Jenny was starting to make trouble the way she always did. But still, the way Eddie was doing it seemed so hard. Clara had never seen Eddie acting this way before.

Jenny was quiet now except for a faint whimper.

Eddie felt sad, not because he had cracked down on his aunt but because she had made it necessary. Maybe the others, Steve and Clara, didn't like it but he didn't care. If Aunt Jenny were allowed to go on, she would have everyone fighting and confused, not knowing whether they were coming or going.

He lit a cigarette and sat down, grimly silent.

The front doorbell rang.

"That must be a nurse," Eddie said.

Clara went to the door. Jenny looked at Eddie accusingly. He ignored her gaze. They heard Clara speak and they heard a second feminine voice.

"I had better go talk to the nurse too," Steve said.

"Yes, I guess so," Eddie said.

Steve left the kitchen.

"You'll be sorry, Eddie," Jenny said.

He said nothing. He got up and walked toward the back.

—God! It's so depressing.

He looked in his mother's bedroom.

—Poor Mama!

He turned out of the bedroom.

Chapter 6

I

Cecilia Moran looked to be in her mid-thirties. She was tall and slender with an open wholesome face topped by dark brown hair.

"Hello, won't you come in," Clara asked warmly.

"Mrs. Ryan?" the nurse asked.

"I'm Mrs. Boyle, her daughter."

"I was sent here; I'm the nurse; my name is Cecilia Moran."

Clara closed the door and smiled at the nurse.

"I'm very glad to meet you."

"Thank you, Mrs. Boyle. The patient, Mrs. Ryan, is your mother?"

"Yes, she is. She's very sick; I think she's dying," Clara Boyle said.

"God forbid," Cecilia Moran exclaimed.

Steve joined them.

"This is my brother, Dr. Stephen Ryan. Steve, this is the day nurse, Miss Cecilia Moran," Clara Boyle said.

"I'm pleased to meet you, Doctor," Cecilia Moran said.

"Hello," Steve Ryan said stiffly.

Cecilia stood waiting in case young Dr. Ryan should have any special instructions for her.

"Cecilia, come, let me show you where you can put your things. And you can change into your nurse's uniform there," Clara said.

"Yes, Mrs. Boyle," but she did not follow Clara Boyle. She turned to Dr. Ryan.

Steve said nothing. He was trying to think of an order that would impress the nurse. The map of Ireland was all over her face.

"Nurse," Steve said.

He had called her "nurse" with deliberate intent. He wanted to establish a professional relationship here, right in the beginning.

"Yes, Doctor?"

"It's not good having too many people go in to see my mother. I don't think she knows any of us."

"I understand, Dr. Ryan."

She was used to doctors and she knew that she was a good nurse. She was used to sick people and dying people. She would do what she could to help this family in their troubled time. They were Irish —her own kind.

"I'll get into my uniform now," she added.

"All right, Miss Moran," Steve said, almost as though he were dismissing her from his presence in order that she could carry out his orders and instructions.

II

After this case, Cecilia Moran decided, she would take a vacation. She had planned to take one after her last case. She was in the bedroom, off the dining room, changing from her street dress into her nurse's uniform.

Cecilia Moran had taken this case because Mrs. Ryan was a patient of Dr. Evans. She just couldn't have said no to him. Why, Dr. Evans was too fine a man to say no to and she was first on his list whenever one of his patients needed a private nurse. In a few minutes she took a quick look at herself in the mirror, gave her hair a pat, and left the bedroom.

Cecilia Moran had begun work on another case.

III

When the nurse walked into Nora Ryan's bedroom she said a quick silent Hail Mary for strength and help on this case. She saw a poor helpless old woman who was soon to join her maker. Of that she was sure. And the poor woman needed to be bathed and to have clean sheets put on her bed. And her hair needed to be combed. If she was going to meet the Lord the very next minute, she would want to meet Him looking better cared for than she was. Cecilia did not think this in any critical way of Mrs. Boyle. One look at her and Cecilia had seen how tired she was and how hard a time she had had. This was one of the things that nurses were for.

Cecilia walked over to the bedside and looked down at Nora Ryan's face. She looked her directly in the eyes. The right eye was fixed and the right side of her face was paralyzed.

"Mrs. Ryan, I'm Cecilia Moran, your nurse," she said, speaking softly.

Cecilia Moran believed that she saw recognition in Nora Ryan's left eye.

"I'm going to make you more comfortable, Mrs. Ryan," Cecilia Moran said, again speaking very softly.

She passed Nora Ryan's bed and left the room to speak with Clara Boyle about what she would need to clean Nora up.

IV

Jenny Dunne stood in the kitchen, wringing her hands. There was a hard spite in her eyes as she watched Cecilia Moran go from Nora's bedroom into the bathroom.

Her nephew, Eddie Ryan. She was thinking of him. No, she did not want to be unkind or unfair. He was like everyone else, only worse. It just went to show how luck and success hit the wrong people. My God, after the way they had worshiped that boy, that he should bite them like a snake in the grass. Those lying books he wrote.

She had drunk, but did the world, or that snip of a nephew, know why?

Cecilia Moran went back into Nora Ryan's bedroom.

V

Dick Dunne sat on the sofa in the living room. He was in his shirt sleeves and looking down at the floor. He was bound up in thoughts of his own. His sister Nora could die. But no, he would not grant this. He could hold out and fight with her until the last minute. She did not have to die. The Lord granting it, Nora could live. He would concentrate on the thought of his sister Nora living.

Eddie walked into the living room. He noticed that his uncle looked grim and old. Eddie walked back out. Uncle Dick had not seemed to notice him.

VI

Molly Ryan had come, with her son, Andy.

"How is she?" she had asked Steve.

"Oh, Molly, she's the same," Steve answered, his tone almost formal.

"Oh, I feel so bad," Molly Ryan said.

"There's compensation in her knowing that her family is around her," Steve told her.

Steve did not know whether or not he believed what he had just said. But having said it, he decided that it was true.

"Where's Eddie Boyle?" Andy asked.

Andrew Ryan was almost six but big for his age.

Eddie Boyle, upon hearing his cousin, came into the front room.

Molly Ryan was taking her coat off when Jenny Dunne came to her.

"Hello, Molly."

"Why, hello, Jenny."

"Did you get any sleep, Molly?"

"Not so very much. I had to be up to make Jack's breakfast, before he went to work. Did you, Jenny?"

"No, but I'm as strong as a truck horse. I don't need much sleep."

"Everybody needs their sleep, Jenny."

"Oh, I'm strong," Jenny said. "I always was the strong one in the Dunne family."

Molly looked at her. What was Jenny getting at?

"But, Jen, no woman's too strong."

"You should see how strong I am, and what endurance I have," Jenny told her.

Molly Ryan wanted to go in to see her mother-in-law, but Jenny was blocking her passage. She didn't know what to do. She didn't want to say anything that would hurt Jenny's feelings. If there was any fighting while Jack's mother lay dying, she wanted no part of it. But Jenny seemed to be getting nasty toward her. She couldn't understand it; she hadn't done anything to Jenny Dunne.

"Yes, I could do for nothing what the two nurses will get paid for doing, were it not for my stinking nephew, Eddie."

"Listen, Jenny, I don't know anything about it."

She moved past Jenny and hurried toward the kitchen. In a moment Jenny followed, wringing her hands.

VII

Molly Ryan was surprised when she walked into the sickroom. A pretty nurse was sitting by the bed. And "Grandmother" was cleaned up, her face washed, her hair combed, her bed clean, the smell gone out of the room.

Now she could see why Jack's brothers, Steve and Eddie, had wanted nurses. Jenny, Clara, none of them could have done as much as this nurse had done to fix "Grandmother" up.

Cecilia Moran introduced herself to Molly, and Molly told her who she was.

"How is she?" Molly asked.

"She's more comfortable now." Cecilia Moran turned and bent a little toward Nora Ryan.

"Aren't you more comfortable, Mrs. Ryan?"

Nora Ryan could not answer but Molly thought that there was some flicker of recognition in her face.

"Does she hear?" Molly asked the nurse.

"We can't be sure that she doesn't," she answered.

They both believed that they had seen recognition in Nora Ryan's face.

VIII

Jenny was beside herself. Not one of them, not one of Nora's children, had bothered to pay any attention to their aunt, who had loved them so much, and who had done so much for them, and who had sacrificed so much in order to do all that she had done for them. No, not one of them had given the least sign of attention to their poor old aunt. She did not deserve such ingratitude.

Jenny Dunne was standing in the kitchen, partly obscured by the large wood-burning stove in the center of the room. She looked miserable. Her eyes, behind her thick lenses, seemed on the verge of overflowing. Her lips were pressed tightly together. Mrs. Landry and others of the family, and Cecilia Moran, moved in and out.

She had nothing to do, no one to talk to. With this thought, she welled up, closer to tears. She did sniffle a couple of times.

Cecilia Moran went back into poor, poor Nora's bedroom. Jenny stared after her. She didn't have a word to say against that nurse. The woman had only come here to do the work that she had been hired to do. It wasn't the nurse. It was her nephew Eddie.

She could have done everything Cecilia Moran did, and just as well, if not better, had she been given a chance.

"You couldn't have done it, Aunt Jenny," Eddie Ryan had said to her, a moment ago, when she went up and talked to him.

"Oh yes, I could. You forget how strong your old Aunt Jenny is," she had said to Eddie Ryan.

"Why didn't you think of it before and go and clean her up, then?"

To ask such a question! It was a dirty trick that she never would have thought that her nephew, Eddie Ryan, would be guilty of. To ask her that question when they would not let her help, and had told her not to help, and had stopped her from helping. It was a foul thing to do.

There he was, her nephew, whom she had loved so, Edward A. Ryan. He would not look in her direction. He couldn't look her in the eye, not after the ingratitude he had shown her. And his mother had wanted her, Jenny Dunne, to take care of her. He would flout his dying mother's wish. Jenny would never forget this.

IX

Steve Ryan had gone out to buy necessary medical supplies—rubber sheets, rectal thermometer, tubing for tube feeding, a syringe and alcohol. Eddie had given him twenty-five dollars when he left. When he returned later, he told Eddie that with cabs the cost had been thirty-eight dollars and forty-nine cents. Eddie told him that he'd give him a check for the difference. Steve said that would be all right, he'd take a check.

Steve enjoyed opening the packages, explaining the use of the items. Then he gave them to Cecilia Moran to take into his mother's room. She said that she would put rubber sheets on Mrs. Ryan's bed immediately. Steve said after she had done this they would tube-feed his mother.

Jenny hovered around, still looking hurt.

X

The day was passing and the sky was sunless. There was a chill in the air. Outside, on Wells Street, the passing of the day was marked by the usual small events of the life on the street.

Slowly, the gray day became darker.

Chapter 7

I

The darkness came early. It was already dark when Jack Boyle came home from work before five. Boy, was he tired. But he wasn't complaining about being tired. No sirree. He was lucky that he had something to fall back on. There was no telling how long the strike would last. He and Clara would be in some fix trying to live on the strike allowance from the union. And he didn't mind doing upholstering work. But it was hard. Working during the day and picketing at night. Besides, he hadn't had much sleep since last year.

—Ha-ha, it was since last year.

He had gotten a lift with one of the fellows, Marty Cilzik. It wasn't a long ride and the nearer he got to the house the more he remembered what was going on there. He didn't think of it much while he was working. He thought of it now and then but he would keep on working and the work took his mind away from his mother-in-law and her condition. He liked his mother-in-law. But anybody would feel sorry for someone in the condition that poor Mrs. Ryan was in.

"Here we are, Marty," Jack Boyle said, when they reached the house.

"Yeah, Jack."

"Thanks, Marty, see you tomorrow."

"Try to get some rest tonight, Jack."

"Yeah, if I can. I got to shovel out coal and I have to do picket duty tonight."

"Get what rest you can."

"Yeah, so long, Marty. Thanks again."

"Don't mention it, Jack, and so long."

Marty drove off. Jack walked up the steps to the front door.

II

"Oh, here's Jack," Steve said.

"Which Jack?" Clara asked.

"Your husband. Hello, Jack," Steve said.

"Hello, Steve. How is she?" Jack asked.

"Oh, about the same," Steve answered.

"She's more comfortable," Clara said, approaching her husband.

"Yes, that's true, she is more comfortable," Steve nodded.

"That's at least a little to the good," Jack commented.

"Oh, we got the nicest nurse, Jack," Clara told her husband.

"You did? Good."

"Cecilia Moran is her name."

"Fine, that's fine."

"Yes, she's so good," Clara said.

"I'm glad," Jack Boyle said. Then, "Clara, I'm going down and shovel some more of that coal in the basement."

"All right, Jack. Are you hungry?"

"I'll say I am."

"I'll get supper started."

"All right. Well, I'm going now and shovel some of that coal before I clean up."

III

The coal had been dumped in the passageway between the front and the back of the house. It had to be shoveled into the bins in the basement. These were under two basement windows along the passageway.

After a couple of shovelfuls he began to work up a sweat. He lost his tired feeling and fell in with the rhythm of the labor. He drove the shovel into the coal, and the contact caused loud, jarring sounds. This was followed by a cracking sound when the coal landed in the bin.

He could see his own breath in the darkness.

It was lonely, shoveling this coal. And it was cold. A fit of severe depression came upon him.

Of course, he was depressed because of the condition of his mother-in-law. Well, he and Clara had given her a home during her last years.

An engine whistle from the Rock Island tracks ruptured the silent darkness. A whistle in the darkness, especially when it was this cold, was a damned lonely sound, more than enough to put any fellow into the dumps. Besides that, his poor mother-in-law.

He shook his head.

He kept driving his shovel into the coal and tossing the shovelfuls down into the bin in the basement.

He was working up a sweat, all right. But hell, he didn't need any exercise. The last thing he needed was exercise. Clara's brothers wouldn't think of shoveling any of the coal for him.

Suddenly he stopped shoveling. He had done enough for tonight. And he just wanted to see if one of Clara's brothers would pitch in and shovel some of the coal.

IV

Jack Boyle was tired when he went up the back stairs and into his kitchen. The minute that he stepped inside he had a sinking feeling. The first thing he saw was Clara with her Aunt Jenny.

"It ain't right, Clara," Jenny was saying.

"Aunt Jenny, I don't want to talk about it," Clara said.

Jack Boyle got sore. Christ, he thought, he was really going to blow his top. Jenny was still yapping about the nurses as if he and Clara didn't have enough on their minds.

Jack Boyle's temper was short-lived. He got over it fast. But he was still sore. Jenny Dunne's gall was enough to make anybody sore. It wasn't her place to decide. It was Mrs. Ryan's children's right. He'd like to give her a piece of his mind. But he wouldn't. Jenny was Clara's aunt, not his.

He'd better stay out of it, especially at a time like this. It would be anything but smart to get mixed up in the Ryan fights. There was always at least one of them mad with another.

At a time like this, you'd think they'd all pull together. But it wasn't like that. He didn't get it. But he wasn't going to get involved. No, sir, he was going to have himself a can of beer and then take a nap and let Clara wake him up for supper.

V

"But it's my sister's dying wish," Jenny was saying to Clara.

"I don't know anything about that, Aunt Jenny."

"You don't think that with her on her deathbed, that I would lie about her dying wish?" Jenny challenged.

"Aunt Jenny, I said I didn't know anything about that," Clara repeated.

"Well, it was her last, dying wish."

"Aunt Jenny, I've got to cook dinner."

"I'll cook supper, and you, you poor thing, you need a rest, you go and rest, I'll cook supper," Jenny said.

Oh, how she wished that Aunt Jenny would just leave her alone.

"I know where everything is."

"Please, Aunt Jenny."

"Think nothing of it. Aunt Jenny will come to the rescue as she always did."

"Aunt Jenny, I have the supper planned. Please, you just sit and rest. It's just not practical."

"It's no trouble at all. You know what a wonderful cook I am. Why, your mother loved my cooking."

"Aunt Jenny, I haven't the time," Clara snapped.

"I'm only trying to help you."

"I don't need your help at this minute."

Clara immediately regretted her sharpness, but Aunt Jenny wouldn't stop.

Clara Boyle stepped away from Jenny Dunne and went to her pantry.

Jenny did not cry for ten seconds. Then the tears came. But she did not sob; she only sighed.

VI

Jenny Dunne was brokenhearted. She had told herself that she was brokenhearted many times since her poor dear sister Nora had been stricken on the night of New Year's Day.

—My poor broken heart.

—This is my reward for all I've done? A poor broken heart.

Jenny Dunne had convinced herself that she was brokenhearted and that her nephews and her niece Clara had broken her heart.

All she wanted to do was help. She wanted to carry out her dying sister's last wish. Jenny had convinced herself that her sister Nora's last wish was that she, Nora's sister Jenny, nurse her during her last, final hours.

—It's as true as the God's truth, Jenny Dunne thought.

—Nora asked me. And I said that I wouldn't fail her.

But her nephews and her niece Clara, and Clara's husband, Jack Boyle, wouldn't let her honor her poor sister's dying wish.

The worst of all of these was her nephew Eddie. And she had raised him. No, never, she never would have believed it, if anyone had ever told her that Eddie, the nephew she had raised and had always called favorite nephew, would turn on her like a dog biting the hand that fed it. No, never would she have believed that Eddie was capable of such ingratitude. All she had done was love him, and be kind and good to him, and sacrifice for him. And this was how he paid her back.

—Edward A. Ryan, big shot!

—Edward A. Ryan, pooh!

He was no big shot to her. Why, she had known men who could buy and sell Edward A. Ryan six times over.

But there he was, posing as a big shot, and did he act like one? She had known big shots. Big shots were generous. They were not tightwads.

But her nephew Eddie, Little Brother, sure was a tightwad. Why, if he wasn't a tightwad, couldn't he set her and Dick up in some little business, just a little store where she could buy and sell china? Sure, he'd say he didn't have the money. But word gets around and word

had gotten around that Edward A. Ryan was loaded with money from
the royalties his books had earned him.

Well, she wouldn't complain or whine.

But oh, God! Oh, God! Oh, God!

VII

It had been less than twenty-four hours since he and his brother
Steve had left New York. It seemed longer. Not only did it seem
longer, it also seemed as though it had been in some different di-
mension of time.

The idea of time was related to the impending death of his mother.
He was here for that death. He was here waiting for it to happen.
There were no developments that suggested a longer or a shorter
time before she would die. There was no measuring of gains or losses.
She was dying, and there was nothing else that gave light or hopes or
indicated change in the grim context of her impending death.

And there was the dual attitude of wanting and of not wanting this
all to end, which meant wishing and not wishing his mother's death.

Supper was being prepared. He felt much alone among the members of his family.

His Aunt Jenny Dunne was still trying to make trouble. Steve was
acting like a doctor instead of being himself. This had struck Eddie a
few minutes ago.

"Steve?" he had called.

Steve had been across the kitchen talking to Uncle Dick.

Steve had heard him but ignored him.

"Steve?" he had called a second time.

Steve had stopped talking to Uncle Dick. But then he had
started again. He had not turned in response to Eddie's call.

"Steve?" Eddie Ryan had called a third time.

Steve had given no sign that he had heard.

"Oh, Steve?" Eddie Ryan called a fourth time.

Eddie couldn't understand it. Steve had heard him.

—To hell with it! Eddie thought.

He turned and looked off through the back kitchen window.

In about a minute Steve spoke to him.

"What did you want, Eddie?"

Eddie looked toward him.

"Oh, it's not important."

"Well, if it's a question, and you want to know something, I'll answer it," Steve said.

"I forgot what the hell it was, Steve," Eddie Ryan said.

VIII

Clara had to put two extra leaves in the dining-room table for supper. There was herself and Jack and Eddie, their son, that was three people. And her brothers, Eddie and Steve, made it five. And Cecilia Moran made it six. Uncle Dick and Aunt Jenny raised it to eight. Her brother Jack and Molly and their son Andy made eleven for supper.

She had told Jack, her husband, that Eddie had given her money to help with the food. Jack had said it was all right. With him on strike, they couldn't afford to have a gang like this. She was glad that Eddie had said he would give her whatever more she needed to cover the cost of food with so many eating in her home. She had bought five pounds of hamburger. It was hardly enough. But gosh, so much had happened. She had enough on her mind to think about and there was nothing wrong with hamburger.

There was little conversation at the supper table. Cecilia Moran twice left the table to go into Nora Ryan's bedroom to see how she was. Each time Jenny's eyes followed her.

She could have done as much for her sister, she thought.

"Oh, isn't this murder awful?" Jenny exclaimed.

"It gives me the chills," Molly said.

"It must be some madman," Jack Boyle said.

"He's committable," Steve Ryan said.

"Ho!" Jack exclaimed. "You got to find him to commit him."

"Maybe it's not a he," Steve said.

"Then she," Jack Boyle said.

"It makes me sick to read about it," Clara said.

"How can there be such sick people in the world?" Cecilia Moran asked.

"That's what I'd like to know," Jack Boyle said. They all fell silent again. A mood of gloom hung over the supper table. "But there are."

Chapter 8

On January 2, 1946, a nineteen-year-old girl, Rosanna Herndon, was found murdered in her kitchenette apartment at the Lincoln Arms apartment hotel on North Winchester Avenue on the North Side of Chicago.

The girl had been stabbed and hacked with a butcher knife. Examination indicated that the victim had also been raped.

Chapter 9

I

The references to the murder had been depressing. There was cause enough for gloom in the Boyle home without adding the murder of a nineteen-year-old girl.

Nora Ryan's condition was virtually unchanged. Her pulse was fast and irregular. Her heartbeat was fast, and her blood pressure was high. She had a low-grade fever. There was some congestion in her lungs.

Nora Ryan was dying. But it seemed that either consciously or unconsciously she was struggling against death with all the will she possessed inside her maimed and helpless body.

Dr. Evans came back to look at her. He would not admit that Nora Ryan had to die. She could live. And he would do whatever he could to try to help her live. Death was his antagonist. It was death that he fought. It was death that he attempted to head off and postpone. It was death that he strove to thwart. And it was death that sooner or later defeated him.

But in every instance where Dr. Evans was defeated by death, and he lost a patient, he had fought that death to the last second. This was the only way he knew how to be a doctor. He had had patients, rarely, it is true, but nonetheless he had had patients who had been just about as close to death as Mrs. Ryan and they had survived.

After examining Mrs. Ryan he said to Steve that he would like to order oxygen tanks for her. He did not think that these could be delivered before morning, but he would advise ordering them, if the family could afford it.

Dr. Evans intended to pay for the oxygen tanks himself if the Ryans couldn't afford them. But Steve told Dr. Evans that they would order the oxygen tanks. After Dr. Evans had left, Steve went to Eddie, who was sitting at the kitchen table having a cup of coffee.

"Eddie, Dr. Evans said that Mama should have oxygen tanks. I told him that we would order them. I thought you wouldn't mind paying for them and I didn't want to ask you in front of Dr. Evans or stop what he was saying."

"Of course. Will you find out where to order them?"

"I know where to call."

"Will you do it?"

Steve suddenly took on an almost pompous tone. "Yes, I'll put the order in."

"All right," Eddie said, looking at his brother and shaking his head.

II

Time dragged. Nobody said much. Leo and Florence Ryan had driven over.

The first thing he did was go to his mother's bedroom to see how she was. He had stared at the almost depersonalized mass of flesh. In his mind and memory he held many living images of her. The contrast of his mental images of his mother and of his mother as she lay helpless hurt him. It was such an awful thing to happen. It was awful to see it, and to remember.

It?

He had meant "her," and "her" came out "it" in his mind.

Holy God! He could almost believe that he didn't know where he was or what he was. His thoughts had come together quickly and in a flash, while his thoughts had come as they had, Leo was taken aback by the presence of Cecilia Moran.

"Hello, I'm Cecilia Moran."

"I'm Leo Ryan, one of her sons, and this is my wife Florence."

"I'm pleased to meet you," Florence Ryan said.

"How do you do," Cecilia said.

Florence gave a little smile.

The sight of Leo's mother frightened her. She had seen death before, her father, and Chuck McPhelan, her first husband. Death was terribly sad, but you could bear it. You had to bear it. You had to. But she was afraid. She was afraid, about her own mother. Tears came into her eyes. She must not, no, she would not cry.

Her mother!

Poor Mrs. Ryan.

Her mother!

Chapter 10

I

Mrs. Ann Hasek, Florence's mother, lived with Florence and Leo. She was seventy-one years old. Born in a little town in Bohemia, she had arrives in Chicago in 1893 at the age of eighteen. In her years in the United States she had learned only a few English words. She was convinced that if she didn't speak the language she would stay out of trouble.

Ann Frankel's first months in America were marked by hard and bewildering times for her. She had heard so much about how rich America was, how money was to be made in ways undreamed of in the old country. She had come to America to gain a better life. Instead she saw suffering, the like of which she had never seen in the old country. Anna had a severe fright. This had much to do with her decision not to learn English.

She had been in America less than four months when she married Anton Hasek, a foreman in the Midwest Agricultural Implements factory. He managed to keep his job all through the bad times. Anna was protected in marriage by her husband. He was a big, strong man and also a kind one.

Anna Hasek was pregnant within a year after her marriage; the baby, a boy, was stillborn. She was shaken with sorrow and Anton felt a deep sadness. However, they were a solace to one another and time dissipated the worst of their sorrow.

A second child, a girl, whom they planned to name Helen, was very frail and she lived only four days. Grief as black as coal dust fell upon their happiness.

Again, the rawness of their disappointment and sadness went away in time.

And a third time Anna became pregnant; and this time Anton and Anna Hasek hoped desperately. She and Anton lived through agonies of dread. They refrained from naming their expected baby in advance.

The third child lived six hours.

Their cup overflowed. Anna Hasek was strong in her faith, and this had much to do with pulling them through their ordeal of sorrow and their struggle not to be bitter.

If God had meant for them to have healthy living children they would have such children. If it were God's will that the two of them, Anton and Anna, should suffer, then they would suffer. They were God's creation and God knew best.

Anna believed this. And she believed it with unquestioning simplicity. And her belief served her well. It sustained her in the face of what she had gone through. Her belief in God had given her the strength she needed to bear up under so heavy a cross.

Anton Hasek had been shaken. His pride, too, had received battering. Three times his wife had been pregnant. Three times and what was born each time was dead or dying.

It looked as though either Anton Hasek or his wife had something wrong with them, and that was why they could not make babies that would come out healthy and would live to grow up in strength and health. Sometimes at mass when Anton saw other people, he would feel ashamed. He was not as good as other men. Either that, or else he had a wife who was not as good as other women. In the most important of all things about a woman she was not as good. And if it was Anna, this still would be a reflection on Anton Hasek himself. It must be himself or Anna who had something to make what had gone wrong go wrong each of the three times that Anna had been with child.

Feelings of shame and guilt would gnaw in Anton Hasek. He did not know what to do. He was of the belief that he had to do something.

But what could he do?

There was nothing. He could leave Anna but that would be bad.

Anton Hasek was spiritually and psychically wounded. These wounds seeped into his pride and his self-confidence was infected.

Anna Hasek sensed the hurt in her husband and the effects of that hurt on his personality. She knew that she must be more steadfast. She had to be steadfast for Anton until time softened the harsh blows he had felt.

Anna Hasek was attentive and loving to her husband. If he was moody, she would sit with him and say nothing unless he spoke to her, waiting until his mood passed. She ministered to his wants. And often she anticipated them. She made herself helpful to him in every way that she could.

Anton Hasek was a good man. Because he was, the loss of three successive children had hurt him all the more. What had happened seemed so unjust. He had always done what he thought was right. And the three dead infants were like a punishment to be meted out to an evil man. Sometimes he feared that others thought that he and Anna were being punished and that, since it was so severe a punishment, there must be something very bad about the two of them.

And Anton Hasek was not sure that he was not being punished. How could he know that he was not being punished by God!

For a while life was torment for Anton Hasek. But during this time his wife Anna was most steadfast. He gradually became more aware of how strong she was, how she lived in a faith which gave her a grace of serenity. He even believed that what his Anna had was the grace of God.

And in time Anton Hasek's health asserted itself. The three losses receded. They were a distance away, a distance back in the past.

Love had not ceased to grow between Anton and Anna Hasek. Their sorrow was accepted, and to a degree this was assimilation of that sorrow.

They expected not to have more children and had come to accept this prospect even though there was a sadness in their acceptance.

And what they did not expect, happened. They did have children. Anna Hasek gave birth to two daughters. Vera was the first daughter. And a few years later, Florence.

II

That had been long ago. And now Anna Hasek's younger daughter, Florence, was almost forty. And Anna Hasek was over seventy. She could scarcely walk because of her arthritis; her strength was slowly but surely deserting her.

Neither of Mrs. Hasek's daughters had been married when Anton Hasek died on West Madison Street. He had crumpled and dropped to the sidewalk in severe pain, gasping helplessly for breath. His chest felt as if he was being crushed by two closing steel beams. After a long minute of pain and terror, he was no more.

Something of Anna Hasek had died when she was told of her husband's death. A policeman had come to the Hasek home. Vera Hasek was there but Florence had not yet come home from work. The policeman told Vera. Vera told her mother in Bohemian. Mrs. Hasek was speechless for a full minute. Then she waited like a hurt, stricken animal.

It was instinct with Anna Hasek to live. But ever since her husband's death she had also waited to rejoin him in heaven. Her faith that she would rejoin her dead husband in the next world was unshakable.

With the passing years, a passing that frequently seemed slow, but that sometimes, in reverse, seemed to be all too swift, she gradually came to think more and more of rejoining Anton in the next world. With Anton, she had not felt useless. Her daughters loved her. But nevertheless she had the fear that she was useless, in a way, a burden. Vera and Florence both tried to convince her that she was not useless, not in the way, and not a burden but they could only partially succeed. Their genuine love and affection for her did reach beyond their words and conveyed to her how much she was wanted, how much she was loved. But Mrs. Hasek was alone much of the time. She was home all day, and her daughters were at work. She could go out, and there were neighbor women whom she knew, who spoke Bohemian. Hers was a mitigated loneliness. She brooded and time seemed to go by slowly.

When Florence married Chuck McPhelan, Jack Ryan's best friend, Mrs. Hasek at first thought that she was in the way. But Chuck McPhelan was an easygoing and sweet-natured man, and he did not mind Florence's mother living with them. Mrs. Hasek came to realize this.

The death of Chuck McPhelan was a personal loss to Mrs. Hasek. She grieved. It was God's will that a man would not live long in her home, or in her daughter Florence's home. But since this seemed to be God's will, it might also be God's will that she should live and be a comfort to Florence. Her daughter Florence was good.

Anna Hasek began to age more noticeably. It became harder for her to walk.

Her older daughter, Vera, moved to Kansas City, Missouri, when her husband, Joe Janowski, was transferred. Mrs. Hasek became more dependent on Florence. She was almost useless. She had been able to keep the house clean and orderly, but now her legs were failing her. It was because of her, Mrs. Hasek was convinced, that her daughter Florence could not find another husband. But Florence did find a husband in Leo Ryan. Anna Hasek was happy. She liked Leo Ryan and Leo liked Mrs. Hasek. Anna Hasek tried to make herself useful again. Supper was ready for Leo and Florence every day when they came home from work. The apartment was clean.

5

126

Anna Hasek knew many happy moments after the marriage of Leo
and Florence, even though she felt her decline into old age. By 1946,
Florence Ryan could not fail to see that her mother was aging. She
prayed to God to keep her mother alive longer. Florence dreaded the
thought of her mother dying. She tried not to think of it.

Chapter 11

I

Florence Ryan could not shake her sadness. It was worse than
sadness. She felt helpless. Nothing could stop death. That was why
she felt so helpless.

Florence had come out of Mrs. Ryan's room and gone back to the
front of the house. Leo had been a step behind her. They both sat,
not speaking.

II

Leo Ryan was more depressed than he had ever been in his life. He
could not talk. He drew a package of cigarettes from his pocket, took
one, and lit it.

He had just thought how he couldn't talk. He was a little bit
puzzled by his own thought. What did he want to say? And who
would he say it to?

In another moment Leo Ryan was no longer puzzled. He did want
to talk. And he knew what he wanted to talk about. He almost knew.
The way Mama was out there dying. He could die that way too. But
he couldn't tell anyone this. He didn't have to, they knew it. He, or
anybody else, could die like Mama was dying.

He squashed his cigarette out in an ash tray.

He was up against a blank wall and he could do nothing. A dead
end.

—Death's end, he thought.

There was something to do, but there was nothing to be done. That was the way it was. There was nothing to do but to sit and wait for Mama to die.

He stood up. He couldn't stay sitting. But once on his feet, there wasn't much moving to do. The parlor was too small to do much moving in. He took a step forward, away from the chair in which he had been sitting, and then stopped.

"Do you want anything, Leo?" Florence asked.

She could see that he was agitated. She had asked him if he wanted anything because she wanted to help him, if she could.

Leo didn't answer. He turned around and sat down beside her again.

III

Eddie sat on the big couch set against the parlor wall. This was an ordeal. It would have been better not to come.

"All personality is gone, and it's no longer really Mama. It's a mass of flesh."

Steve had said this today.

"Suffering flesh," Eddie had said.

Remembering the conversation now, Eddie thought:

—And humiliated flesh.

Death was the humiliation of everyone's flesh, and spirit even more.

He lit another cigarette. Puffing, he thought how hard it was to free himself from the gloom that hovered over his thoughts.

Leo and Florence were silent.

Steve entered the room and dropped into a rocking chair opposite Eddie.

"Stephen Daedalus wouldn't pray when his mother was dying," Steve said to Eddie.

"I know."

Leo looked at Steve and then at Eddie, with an irritated expression. Florence simply glanced.

Neither Leo nor Florence knew who Steve was talking about. Eddie wished that Steve hadn't brought up Stephen Daedalus. But maybe Steve was trying to impress him.

"It's the same situation, isn't it?" Steve asked.

"In some ways."

"It's the same in the important essentials," Steve persisted.

Eddie raised his brows, behind his thick glasses.

"Obviously," he said.

Steve waited.

Eddie knew that Steve was waiting for him to say something. But he really didn't feel like talking.

"Well, are you going to do what Stephen Daedalus did, or what he didn't do, I mean?" Steve asked.

"It doesn't matter one way or the other."

"It mattered to Stephen Daedalus, didn't it?"

"Yes, because Joyce strongly motivated Stephen's reaction," Eddie answered.

"Well . . ." Steve began.

"I wouldn't be proving anything," Eddie said.

He was irritated that Steve had brought up the question.

"I don't know about proving, Eddie."

"I used 'proving' in the sense of convincing himself."

"Yes, I know. That's what I don't know about," Steve said.

Eddie puffed on his cigarette.

"When Stephen Daedalus refuses," Eddie said, "he is a young man, and he has to act ardently and resolutely. It's not going to affect anyone."

"I'm not going to pray," Steve declared.

"Neither am I," Eddie said, "but I don't make much of the fact, either way, if I did, or if I didn't."

"I'm not going to."

Eddie shrugged. Why should Steve sound so challenging?

Steve got up and went to the back of the house.

Leo and Florence were still silent.

IV

Clara Boyle answered the doorbell. It was the night nurse.

"Oh, please come in," Clara invited.

"I'm Miss Daugherty, Bridget Daugherty," the big woman said.

"Well, I'm Mrs. Boyle," Clara said.

"How do you do, Mrs. Boyle," Bridget Daugherty said.

She set down her small suitcase.

"And here are two of my brothers, Eddie and Leo, and Leo's wife, Florence."

They all acknowledged the introduction.

"My mother is very sick. She's in the back bedroom," Clara said.

"We must pray to God," Bridget Daugherty said.

Bridget Daugherty was a big woman, broad and hefty, in her middle fifties; her dark hair was beginning to turn gray.

Clara led her to her mother's room. They met Steve, who was returning to the parlor. Clara introduced him as Dr. Ryan. Steve talked for a moment with Bridget Daugherty. Then Cecilia Moran came out of Nora Ryan's room and met Bridget Daugherty.

They talked for a minute or so.

Bridget Daugherty went in to see Nora Ryan, her patient. She blessed herself and said a prayer.

Then she changed into her nurse's white uniform and, carrying two holy candles, went into Nora Ryan's bedroom.

While Bridget Daugherty had been changing into her nurse's uniform, Clara had slipped into her mother's bedroom and picked up copies of three of the novels that Eddie had written. She was afraid that Eddie's books would offend Bridget Daugherty.

Bridget Daugherty set the two holy candles on the dresser. She lit them and said a few prayers.

She was now on duty.

v

"Hush," Molly Ryan said to her son Andrew.

"I'm tired," he whined.

"Go to sleep here and we'll wake you when we go home," Molly told him.

"Let him lie on the bed in my bedroom," Clara said.

"I wanna go 'n' lie down," Andy said sleepily.

"Daddy will take you," Molly told him. She turned to her husband, Jack Ryan. "Daddy, take Andrew into the bedroom and let him lay down on the bed."

Jack Ryan made a face and stood up.

"Come on, Buster."

Rubbing his eyes, Andrew got to his feet. He stumbled.

"Don't let him fall," Molly said.

"Come on, Buster," Jack Ryan repeated.

He took his son's hand and led him into the bedroom.

Chapter 12

I

Jack Boyle was picked up by Stan Wilek. He was an inspector. Bart Knight and Jan Janewicz were both in the back seat. Bart was a trimmer and fitter, and Jan a welder.

It was a long ride to the plant. Nobody said much for a few minutes. Jack Boyle lit up a Camel.

"Goddamn it, when's this goddamned strike gonna end?" Bart Knight suddenly exploded.

"You tell me," Stan said.

"My old lady," Bart began.

"Don't tell me no more," Jan said.

They all laughed.

"Well, my old lady doesn't understand strikes," Bart said.

"Don't you mean she don't like strikes, Bart?" Jack asked him.

"My old lady, she ain't interested in understandin' strikes. She just don't like 'em," Jan Janewicz said.

"Who does?" Jack Boyle asked.

"But I wouldn't like workin' for May Motors," Jack Boyle added, "if we didn't have no union."

"Who would, but some clown?" Bart Knight laughed again.

"Oh, a lot of women, too," Jack Boyle said.

The car was traveling along. Stan Wilek took a right turn to go north on Cicero.

"Take my wife's aunt," Jack Boyle said.

"No, thanks, Jack, I got my old lady's aunts," Jan Janewicz said with a laugh.

"Well, you threw one past me that time," Jack Boyle laughed. "But what I was gonna say is, you fellas know how, when the war was still goin', there was those women, they couldn't do enough work, my God, you'd think that winnin' the war depended on them alone."

"I know 'em," Bart Knight said.

"Well, women like that don't care about a union," Jack Boyle said.

"You son of a bitch," Stan yelled out his window.

A driver had almost swiped Stan's car at an angle. The big automobile had cut in front of them, from nowhere.

They all cursed the crazy driver who had almost killed them and they thanked their lucky stars they hadn't been killed. It had been a close call.

"That crazy bastard will probably get killed before this night's done with," Bart Knight said.

"Let him," Jan Janewicz said.

"Sure," Bart Knight said, "but do innocent people who don't even know him have to be hurt and maybe get maimed or even killed because of that no-account prick?"

"I just want him killed, no one else," Jack Boyle said.

They all laughed.

Then, as Stan Wilek drove on, they fell to silence.

"You know, fellows," Jack Boyle said, "I beef about it a lot."

"What do you beef about a lot?" Bart Knight asked.

"The union."

"We all do," Bart Knight said.

"But I say that a bad union is better than no union," Jack Boyle said.

"I second that," Jan Janewicz said.

"Do you fellas think we got a bad union?" Stan Wilek asked.

"No, not at all, we got a good union," Jack Boyle said.

"Yes, I second that," Jan Janewicz said.

The car had passed West Madison Street and was now on North Cicero.

"Any of you fellows feel like some coffee?" Stan Wilek asked.

"I know I do," Jack Boyle said.

The other two said they did too.

"There's a place right along here," Stan Wilek said.

"Yes, I know the place," Bart Knight said.

"So do I. They have good coffee," Jack Boyle said.

"Oh yes, I know that restaurant too. They do make good coffee," Jan Janewicz said.

"Well, it's about two blocks ahead on the right," Stan Wilek said.

II

> *"Solidarity forever!*
> *Solidarity forever!*
> *Solidarity forever, for the union makes us cold!"*

A cheer went up from the moving line of pickets.

"Ho! Ho! for the union makes me cold," Jack Boyle said.

"Say it straight," the fellows behind Jack Boyle and Bart Knight called to them.

"Say it straight, some dumb cop will think we mean it."

"Fellows sing 'Solidarity' straight now," Jack Boyle said.

"Sing 'Solidarity Forever' straight or them cops will think we mean it," Bart Knight called ahead of him.

In a moment the marching line was singing again with some lusty enthusiasm.

> *"Solidarity forever!*
> *Solidarity forever!*
> *Solidarity forever, for the union makes us cold!"*

The singing injected energy into the men marching on picket duty. They moved back and forth before the main gate of the big May Motors plant at Grangeville, Illinois, a suburb of Chicago. Several bonfires were blazing in wire baskets near the curb. Inside the gate were uniformed company police and blue-uniformed local policemen, plus a borrowed contingent of Chicago policemen. Outside, there were local policemen, Chicago policemen, county policemen, and state troopers.

But the strike had been peaceful. No one expected it to become violent. The authorities of May Motors had made no effort to break the strike.

The factory loomed in the darkness, an impenetrable black block.

Moonlight gleamed on some unlighted windows, and the effect was somewhat strange.

Back and forth. Back and forth the pickets walked.

Suddenly, an hour had gone by, and they were being relieved.

"The comin', the gettin' home, and the goin' back home," Jack Boyle told Bart Knight, as they stood for a moment by a blazing fire, "that's worse than bein' here."

"You can say that again."

III

Jack Boyle found everyone sitting in his parlor except for the boy, Andy, who was sleeping in a bedroom. Jack had hoped that they would be gone or else asleep. It wasn't that he had anything against any of them; it was only that he was seeing and hearing too much of them in one dose.

"Hello, Jack," Eddie said. "How was it, picketing?"

"Oh, it was all right, a little cold, that's all."

He took off his coat and turned back to the entrance hall to hang it up. He also took off his boots. At least the picketing had gotten him away from this for a little while. He wasn't complaining about the situation. Hell, he wasn't saying anything. It wasn't good all around, or good for anybody.

Jack hung up his coat. He was wearing a blue sweater over his checked shirt. Steve started to say something to him but Jack said he had to go down into the basement to tend to the furnace.

In the cellar he shook out the ashes but he didn't bank the fire in the furnace. The nurse would be up all night, and Clara's mother and the night nurse would need heat. After he had tended the furnace he returned upstairs. He yawned. He ought to go to bed. Tomorrow was another day of work for him. Hell, he meant today. It was well after midnight. But he decided to stay up for a few minutes. They were all sitting around and moping. But after all, their mother was dying.

He yawned again as he sat down.

"Hello, Jack," Jack Ryan said.

"Hello, Jack," Jack Boyle said.

"Two Jacks," Jack Boyle laughed.

"Clara," Molly said, "your Jack and my Jack."

"Yes, our two Jacks," Clara smiled.

"How's Mrs. Ryan?" Jack Boyle asked. "Still the same?"

"Yes, she's still pretty much the same," Steve said.

Jack Boyle shook his head.

IV

The atmosphere in the Boyle home was tense. They all were trying to act normally in a situation that was abnormal. They were trying to go along as though nothing out of the ordinary had happened when something extraordinary had begun to happen, and was still in the process of happening.

They were trying to hold up, Jack Boyle thought. He would be doing the same thing if he was in their shoes. He was in the same situation with them. After all, Mrs. Ryan was his mother-in-law. Nobody liked it if a person spills their guts out; he knew he didn't.

Jack Boyle was sitting in a rocking chair. He rocked two or three times and then stopped. His hands lay folded over his stomach. There were lots of things that he could say, but he didn't know exactly how to say them.

He yawned again.

He ought to go to bed. He continued to sit.

Clara's mother was dying. She was dying and nothing could save her. And everybody was waiting around for the old lady to die. And he was doing no different himself.

But there was nothing else to do.

He felt as if he was being held here in his own parlor. He guessed that the others, the Ryans, must feel the same way.

V

Eddie Ryan was beginning to find the silence oppressive. It was not, of course, a total silence. Ever so often something would be said. But then there would be the silence again.

Eddie noticed the others.

Jack Boyle sat with his hands in front of his stomach, scarcely moving. His face was drawn. He seemed to be looking at everything and at nothing.

Behind Jack, sitting in the shadow in the next room which opened on to the parlor, Jenny sat. Her lips were tightly closed. Her eyes looked puffy and were almost lost behind her gold-rimmed glasses. She kept making small movements and gestures with her hands and then dropping them on her lap. His Aunt Jenny was jealous of his mother dying because his mother, by dying, was the person on whom attention was centered.

Eddie Ryan's attention was distracted from Aunt Jenny by Steve, who had come into the room. He had been with Nora Ryan.

Steve sat down opposite Eddie.

"Mama is about the same," he said.

"Yes," Eddie said rather absent-mindedly.

"You say that she is the same, Steve?" asked Jack Boyle.

"Yes."

"That wouldn't be a good sign, would it? That she was holding her own?"

"No, not in her condition, Jack."

Jack Boyle shook his head.

"It's amazing that she's hanging on," Steve said.

No one said anything.

They all sat.

VI

Steve suddenly became talkative. He was in analysis and he was full of psychoanalysis. He was talking about it.

"This is an almost classical case of the Oedipus complex," Steve said to Eddie.

"Yes, maybe," Eddie said.

"I wouldn't say that there is any maybe. It all stands out clearly. It sticks out like a sore thumb."

Eddie didn't want to discuss what was going on in the context of the Freudian conceptions of the Oedipus complex.

"What about that murder?" Jack Ryan asked.

"Oh, did I tell you?" Jack Boyle asked.

"No, Jack, not that I heard," Leo Ryan said.

"There's a second one killed," Jack said.

"By the same nut, you mean?" Jack Ryan asked Jack Boyle.

"That's what they think," Jack Boyle answered.

"Well, after all, everybody has an Oedipus," Steve said.

"Where does that take us?" Eddie asked.

"It does not take us any place, necessarily."

"People get over their Oedipus troubles," Eddie said.

"I'm sure, in a sense, yes, that is what analysis should accomplish," Steve agreed.

"Another girl, she was twenty. I think she was twenty," Jack Boyle was saying.

"Isn't that terrible!" Jack Ryan exclaimed.

"It is," Jack Boyle said.

"It's a maniac who kills like that," Leo exclaimed.

"Where did you say she was killed at, Jack?" Jack Ryan asked.

"I forget the street but it was about half a mile from where the other murder was committed on the North Side."

"I don't know what to think about the Oedipus situation. It's something we have to get out of," Eddie said.

"Well, now," Steve began, "since I've been in analysis, and I can say that I find it all fruitful . . ."

"I don't doubt it, Steve," Eddie interrupted. "I simply did not have any thoughts, I had no conclusions to draw from, say, a statement that the Oedipus situation is universal."

"Well, there are conclusions to draw," Steve said.

"Undoubtedly, there are," Eddie Ryan said. "In fact, I know it. But I just didn't have them at hand. I mean, I didn't see that we were heading to conclusions."

Eddie didn't think that he and Steve should sit here and talk about Oedipus. He was not interested in the subject, for the present. Another time, perhaps, he would be, but not now.

VII

Steve was feeling hostility. He had to figure out why. What was behind his rising hostility?

This was why he wanted to talk to Eddie, and why he had mentioned the Oedipus. But Eddie didn't seem to be in the mood to talk. He wondered why. Sometimes you couldn't get a word in edgewise with Eddie. Heck, it was a mess here. It was a psychic mess. Talk about your Oedipus. Steve started slowly filling his pipe.

Eddie and Jack Boyle were talking about the strike at May Motors. Jack Boyle was saying that it was anybody's guess when the strike would end.

Steve Ryan had his pipe full, the tobacco well packed in the bowl. He put the pipe between his lips, took a kitchen match out of a pocket, leaned forward down toward the rug, struck the match on the sole of his shoe, and brought it up to the pipe. He drew on the pipe with satisfaction. The hostility which had been rising in Steve Ryan dissipated with the puff he had taken. He had forgotten his hostility of a few seconds ago, and he wished that he hadn't. But gosh, this seemed foolish. Well, we have to face the fact that we are foolish, a little foolish anyway, and far too often. Analysis, of course, would cure a person of a lot of this. That wasn't the way to look at the matter, though. The meaning was what was important. And behind foolish meanings there sometimes were other and important meanings.

Steve Ryan puffed on his pipe. He looked about the parlor and casually noticed as he looked. He felt a need to talk. He could not be with people long and not want to talk, and to be himself. He wanted to talk. It was more than wanting to talk, he had something of a compulsion to talk.

He didn't know just what he wanted to say, he just wanted to talk.

"Many things that seem foolish ain't as foolish as you might think they are, once you begin to examine them."

"Yeah, Steve," Jack Boyle said.

Eddie raised his brows. What in hell was Steve trying to say?

"Now take . . ." Steve continued. He paused.

"Take what?" Eddie asked.

"Oh . . ." Steve had suddenly become lost for an example.

Eddie leaned forward on the couch, waiting for Steve to go on.

"Oh, what I was thinking of, what I had in mind," Steve said, "well, this is what I mean. Take anybody, he'll think a lot of things that are foolish. But now, if you ask, 'Are they all so foolish, or do they have a hidden meaning and significance, an unconscious meaning and significance?' "

"That's beyond me," Jack Boyle said.

"Me too, Steve," Leo said.

"Well now," Steve said, "let me put it this way. We can have many foolish thoughts that are infantilisms."

"We do." Eddie nodded.

"This is what I am saying," Steve said.

"But what's the point of saying it?" Eddie asked.

"Well, when we think something that seems just, oh, senseless, it isn't senseless in terms of our psychic economy."

Eddie shrugged.

"The problem of what is significant is at the heart of psycho-analysis," Steve declared.

"That's so." Eddie nodded again.

"Well, that's about what I meant," Steve said.

Eddie decided that Steve was trying to get at something and he should be more patient.

"You see, Steve, I'm not sure what you are getting at, that is, if you are getting at something more than a true generalization," Eddie Ryan said, but he said it patiently.

"Well, I am." Steve was defensive.

"I didn't say you weren't. Ah, hell, I was impatient, Steve," Eddie said.

"Oh, that's all right."

Eddie waited for Steve to go on. But Steve had lost the thread of his own thoughts. He busied himself in emptying and refilling his pipe. Then he used three matches in lighting his pipe. While Steve was busy doing this. Eddie returned to his own gloomy thoughts.

VIII

Eddie Ryan was unable to sleep. He was on the sofa in the parlor. The lights were out. There was a light back in the kitchen.

The others had gone. Everyone in the house was trying to sleep, except the nurse, Bridget Daugherty.

And his mother!

She was trying to live!

He wished that he could sleep. He had taken a seconal, but it was not having much effect.

He thought of his mother again.

What did she understand? What did she think of, if she were conscious?

She was conscious! She couldn't talk. She was conscious and utterly helpless.

His poor mother. She must be afraid. The thought of her helpless, in fear, not really knowing what had happened to her, but knowing, she must know it, that she was dying.

He was getting drowsy.

Suppose he should close his eyes and never wake up?

He wouldn't know anything about it.

And his mother.

Through his drowsiness, he again thought of her, helpless, but in spirit frightened and dying.

He drowsed away to sleep.

IX

Bridget Daugherty had holy candles burning on the dresser.

Bridget Daugherty had already said many prayers. She prayed more. It was almost dawn. They were all asleep in the house. Mrs. Ryan was resting comfortably. And Bridget Daugherty was reading. She had found, on a table in the corner, a book written by Edward A. Ryan. Clara had overlooked this one when taking Eddie's books out. He was one of Mrs. Ryan's sons; she had met him when she came in last night. Bridget Daugherty was reading *A Son and His Father* by Edward A. Ryan.

Chapter 13

I

Clara was bleary-eyed from lack of sleep. It was early. A few seconds after she opened her heavy eyes, Clara put on her winter robe and walked to her mother's room. Even though there was no hope, she still had hope.

She opened the door and walked in. Bridget Daugherty looked up at her and smiled. Clara glanced over to the bed where her mother lay. That was Mama. She was barely alive, her breathing was shallow and loud. She lay there, so many pounds of flesh, blood, arteries, veins, skin, nails, and hair.

Clara asked Bridget Daugherty how her mother was and the nurse answered that Mrs. Ryan had been made as comfortable as possible and that she was doing well, but of course that was considering, but still, Mrs. Ryan was doing well.

—She's like Mama, Clara thought.

Bridget Daugherty wouldn't admit the worst. She was a nurse so she had to believe in medicine and in doctors; but more than in medicine and in doctors, she believed in God. Bridget Daugherty had lit holy candles and she had prayed to God, asking Him to save Nora Ryan's life.

Clara was touched. Tears formed in her eyes, and she almost cried. But she was beyond tears.

Clara told Bridget Daugherty that she was going to fix breakfast. Bridget Daugherty said any time, not to hurry. Clara said that she was not hurrying. She had to fix breakfast for her husband, who went to work early. And her two brothers would probably be getting up soon.

"Will the doctor be getting up?" Bridget asked.

"He probably will. Did you want to tell him anything or ask him anything, Miss Daugherty?"

"Oh no, no, no, oh no," Bridget said.

Clara looked at her mother, a looming misshapen form under the covers, a face with one side twisted and distorted, an eye open, starkly open and motionless, a hand and arm outside of the covers, shriveled and lifeless.

—Oh, Mama, poor Mama!

Clara left the room.

Bridget Daugherty rose and walked to the dresser. She snuffed out the burning holy candles. She turned and went to Nora's side.

Nora Ryan's shallow breathing could be heard in the sickroom.

II

Jack Boyle was dressed and shaved. He was wearing an old blue shirt and a sweater. He came into the kitchen, unfolding a copy of the Chicago *Daily Representative* which he had picked up off the front porch. Clara was fixing his breakfast. Neither she nor Jack spoke.

"Holy!" Jack Boyle exclaimed as he opened the newspaper.

"What's happened, Jack?"

"Can you imagine that?" Jack Boyle exclaimed.

"What, Jack?"

"Another young girl was murdered on the North Side," Jack Boyle said.

"God, that's terrible," Clara Boyle said.

She served her husband a hot cup of coffee and put a plate of toast on the table.

Bridget Daugherty came and sat down at the breakfast table.

"I have your breakfast just about ready, Mrs. Daugherty," Clara said.

"Good morning," Jack Boyle said.

"Good morning, Mr. Boyle," Bridget Daugherty said. As she sat down she said to Clara, "It's Miss, not Mrs., Mrs. Boyle."

"Oh, I'm sorry. I'm so sorry." Clara was flustered.

"Oh, it's nothing, Mrs. Boyle."

Clara set fried eggs and bacon before her.

"Thank you, Mrs. Boyle," Bridget Daugherty said.

"It's nothing," Clara said, setting a cup of coffee down on the nurse's right side.

Jack Boyle put his newspaper aside and began to eat.

Clara sat down with a cup of coffee.

"Jack, what was it in the newspaper?" Clara asked.

"Did something happen in the newspapers?" Bridget Daugherty asked.

"Another young girl's been murdered," Jack Boyle said.

"Oh, gracious! Mother of God!"

"Yeah, on the North Side," Jack Boyle said.

There was shock on Bridget Daugherty's face. There was more pain than shock on Clara's face.

"It's the third one that's been killed," Jack Boyle said.

"Oh, that's terrible. I hope they catch him," Clara said.

"How was this one done?" the nurse asked.

"Oh, he stabbed her," Jack Boyle said.

Clara shuddered. It was an unwilled response. It was almost an anguished shivering. She thought of the poor girl, and another shiver shot through her. How awful, how unbearable it must be to be slashed and stabbed, cut to death with a knife.

"Oh, the poor girl, and her poor mother and father, I hope she wasn't Irish," Bridget Daugherty said.

"No, I don't think she was Irish," Jack Boyle said. "Her name was . . ."

Jack Boyle stopped and tried to remember the girl's name.

"Now, what was her name? I just read it, just this minute, but I can't seem to remember."

"Whatever the poor girl was, may God have mercy on her soul," Bridget Daugherty said.

"Yes," Clara said.

"Yeah," Jack Boyle muttered, affected by the murder and by the reactions of the two women.

Jack Boyle ate. So did Clara and Bridget. Jack Boyle reached to the vacant chair on his right, where he had put the newspaper, and picked it up. He unfolded it back to the first page, looked at the page, and said:

"Here it is, Louella Youngler."

"Louella Youngler," Clara said.

"How old was she?" Bridget Daugherty asked.

"Only seventeen, it says here," Jack Boyle said.

"What a sinful shame!"

"Yeah," Jack Boyle agreed.

It was getting lighter out.

"Bridget, would you like some more coffee?" Clara asked.

"I don't care if I do," Bridget answered.

Clara stood up, leaned forward, and got Bridget Daugherty's cup. She went to the stove and poured more coffee.

"Thank you," Bridget Daugherty said when Clara had placed her second cup on the table.

Clara started making her husband's lunch. She put the food into a lunch box.

Jack finished his breakfast, went down into the cellar, and tended the furnace, shaking out ashes and shoveling in new coal.

When Jack got upstairs his lunch was ready. Bridget Daugherty was reading the paper.

"Stan Wilek didn't honk yet?"

"No, not yet," Clara told him.

"He'll be here any minute. I guess I'll put my things on so I'll be ready."

He turned and went to the front of the house and put on his sheepskin coat and his hat. He came back out to the kitchen putting a woolen glove on his left hand. Clara handed him his lunch box.

A horn honked in front of the house.

"There he is," Jack said.

Clara and Jack said good-by to each other. Bridget Daugherty looked up and said good-by. Jack said good-by to her. Jack turned to leave for work. As he went out of the parlor, into the vestibule, and grabbed the handle of the front door, Eddie wished him good luck. Jack said thanks and so long to Eddie Ryan.

III

Eddie Ryan was just waking up as his brother-in-law, Jack Boyle, was leaving for work. He spoke to Jack, sat up, stuck his bare feet into his slippers, picked up his bathrobe and his glasses from the floor. He put them on, stuck his arms into the sleeves of his bathrobe and, tying the belt, walked out to the kitchen.

Bridget Daugherty was going back into his mother's room with the newspaper in her hand as Eddie came into the kitchen.

Eddie and Bridget said good morning. He asked how his mother was, and she told him that his mother had rested comfortably. Eddie said good morning to his sister. Clara set a cup of coffee on the kitchen table for him and asked if he had slept well. He said that he had. He had taken a pill to be sure that he would, he said. Clara said that she didn't believe in taking pills. Eddie said they didn't hurt you if you took them when you needed them. Clara said she didn't know about that. She was at the stove, fixing his breakfast.

Eddie poured cream into his .coffee and added some sugar and stirred. He took his cigarettes from a bathrobe pocket, lit one and, inhaling, lifted his cup of hot coffee.

Clara set bacon and eggs and toast before Eddie. He thanked her and asked her to have a cup with him. She wished she could but she had to get breakfast now for little Eddie. He would be waking up any second now.

Eddie Ryan smoked and ate his breakfast.

IV

Eddie Ryan had about finished his breakfast, but he was having another cup of coffee. Eddie Boyle was seated on a pillow at the table, eating. He took his food without any fussing.

This was so different from the way it was in Eddie's own home. He thought of Phyllis and Tommy at home and the fights over Tommy's eating. He could do nothing about this, not now, here in Chicago, while his mother was dying.

Eddie Boyle finished his breakfast.

V

It was only eight o'clock. The new day was gray and chilly.

There was not much to do in the Boyle home. The nurse was taking care of Nora Ryan. Steve Ryan was also keeping a check on his mother's condition and reporting to Dr. Evans if necessary.

Clara Boyle had finished her chores by eight. Eddie Boyle played by himself. Eddie sat waiting for the first mail delivery at nine. He looked forward to this more than the others because he was most likely to receive mail. There was the change of nurses at nine o'clock, or a few minutes after nine. That was one thing to be looked forward to. Another one, Eddie thought, was Cecilia Moran's arrival. She was rather attractive. He and Steve had both noticed this. And there was Dr. Evans' visit.

There was also Aunt Jenny's arrival. It was problematic whether or not Dick would come with her. If he did, he would miss a day's pay.

VI

Jenny Dunne was beside herself. But Jenny had been beside herself yesterday.

Her sister was still dying and her nephews and her niece Clara, and especially her nephew Eddie, were depriving her poor sister of the care that Jenny was prepared to give her.

But hurt and suffering as she was, she would bear this cross, and bear it bravely.

This she had decided at home as her poor brother Dick went off to work, trying to sell printing on a commission basis.

The westbound Sixty-third Street car rocked and shook. Jenny slid a little in her seat. This bumpy streetcar was giving her a bumpy headache.

Oh, everything happened to her.

Her heart was heavy as a stone. Her dear sister Nora, dying. And her dear sister's children were treating her like dirt.

The streetcar bumped and swayed again as it approached State Street.

Jenny wished that the ride was over.

"State Street," the conductor called as the car stopped.

A few passengers got off. A few passengers got on the streetcar. The streetcar started up again.

It would be soon now.

Oh, she must bear up.

But she was beside herself, beside herself, because of such black ingratitude.

The streetcar rocked and swayed.

Oh, poor dear Nora!

The conductor called from the back platform:

"Wentworth Avenue."

Jenny Dunne got off the streetcar. She felt the chill morning air. She crossed the street and waited for the Wentworth Street car. The wait was short. Jenny gave the conductor her transfer and went inside toward the rear platform. The moving streetcar jumped and Jenny was almost knocked off her feet. She was able to grab the back of a seat to keep from falling. She was close to tears. Almost falling had frightened her. Everything was going wrong, going against her, everything.

The streetcar reached Fifty-ninth Street. It stopped, then started again. Jenny sat down in a seat that had just been emptied. She would soon be at Clara's house. Her poor dear sister Nora!

Jenny was near tears again. She did not know what she would have to put up with at Clara's house, what insults, what humiliations.

Oh, everything was going against her, yes, everything.

The streetcar neared Garfield Boulevard. Jenny got up and carefully moved to the back platform.

"Garfield Boulevard," the conductor called out.

Jenny stepped down when the streetcar stopped.

VII

Jenny was still distressed when she reached Clara Boyle's house. Clara answered the doorbell.

"Good morning, Aunt Jenny."

Jenny stepped into the vestibule without answering. She took her coat off and hung it on a hanger without saying a word. Then she took her galoshes off. Clara watched her. At first she was perturbed, then she became angry. Jenny walked by her. She did not speak to Eddie Ryan or to Steve Ryan. She went straight into the kitchen. Then she turned around and walked to the parlor.

Silently and ominously, she paced back and forth. First to the kitchen, then to the parlor, parlor to kitchen, kitchen to parlor.

"She's looking for trouble," Eddie said to Steve.

"So you think we ought to do something?" Steve asked.

"No, not unless she starts disrupting," Eddie answered.

Jenny kept pacing back and forth, the full length of the house.

The front doorbell rang.

"That must be Dr. Evans," Steve said.

"I'll get it," Clara called.

Jenny stopped pacing and sat down. From the kitchen, she could hear Clara greeting Dr. Evans. She should be the one talking with him. Dr. Evans would see how intelligent she was and how much better she would be for her sister than two strangers. He'd understand right away.

—Miss Dunne, you're as good, if not better, than most nurses, he would tell her.

—Miss Dunne, I've never had such good assistance in the care of any patient.

He would say something like that. But Dr. Evans would never know how capable she could be in taking care of her sick sister. She was here in the kitchen, unnoticed, while her dear darling sister lay near death in the next room. She was no better than some poor relation. It was awful.

The front doorbell rang again. Eddie, who was in the living room, answered it.

A Western Union delivery boy stood there.

"Boyle?"

"Yes."

"I have a telegram for Mrs. Clara Boyle."

"I'm her brother; I'll sign for it."

The boy handed Eddie the telegram and a slip to sign. Eddie signed and returned it to him.

"Thank you," he said, reaching into his pocket for some coins.

"Thank you," the boy said, taking the quarter that Eddie gave him.

He bounded down the front stairs. Eddie closed the door behind him and turned into the hall. Clara met him.

"What is it?" she asked.

"A telegram for you."

"It must be from Frances," Clara said, opening it.

She read the telegram.

"Yes, it is; she and Michael are both coming. Let me go tell Mrs. Landry, she'll be so glad to see little Michael again."

"What's happened? What's the matter?" Jenny asked.

"Frances is coming," Clara answered. "I can't wait to tell Hazel Landry that she'll be seeing her grandson. She loves that boy almost as much as she does Harold. And she's been so good to all of us Ryans. The minute she heard Mama was sick, she came right over here. And she's been here every day since to help in the kitchen. She's so good and you know, Eddie, things got ugly between Frances and Harold by the time they were divorced but Mrs. Landry never took sides."

Chapter 14

I

Eddie Ryan had known Harold Landry since 1912 when the Dunnes lived at 5131 Prairie Avenue and the Landry family lived on the 5300 block of Prairie. Harry was a year younger than Eddie and a Protestant. He was one of the kids who played on Prairie Avenue. Eddie often played with the public school kids. This was how he met Harry.

Harold Landry was an only son. His mother, a tall, serene-looking woman, indulged him, practically from birth. His father, Tom Landry, a short stocky man, dealt in construction materials and had a profitable business going. He was satisfied with what he was and satisfied with what he earned in his business. But he was not satisfied with his life at home. There was no finer woman walking the face of the earth than his wife Hazel, and he wouldn't have any other wife than the one he had. But Hazel liked to have her own way. He didn't think that he was complaining when he said this but he did sometimes think that Hazel would have been smarter if she had treated their son the same way she treated him. There was no telling how much better off the boy would be. Not that she wasn't a good mother, Hazel was a wonderful woman.

Tom Landry thought this until the day he died in 1938.

II

After graduating from high school Harold Landry went to college. He flunked all the tests the first semester. He went to a second college. And a third. By the time he had failed in five schools, Harold decided that he did not want to try a sixth one. His mother agreed with him.

Harold had become a heavy drinker. But anything he did his mother usually excused. It wasn't because she liked some of the things he did, she didn't. It hurt her to see him drunk and slobbering. And his failures at college were a lasting disappointment to her. But she was incapable of speaking a harsh word to her son. There were times when she had been so mad with him that she wanted to give him a good sound shaking, even wring his neck, but she couldn't. She couldn't even reprimand him, much less punish him. She served him, waited on him, and stood behind him, no matter what he did.

Hazel Landry knew that she was not always good for her son Harold but she believed that she was more good than bad for him. Harold had never been arrested. He didn't steal. He wasn't a criminal. He drank, yes, but many men did. As for his not finishing college, well, if she had gone to college when she was young, she wasn't sure that she would have wanted to finish. All things considered, she was proud of her son.

After Harold Landry had made up his mind not to try a sixth college, he decided that he would get a job and have a good time on weekends. He knew that he had the brains to do better but he didn't have the ambition. He would always live the way he had. No matter what happened, his mother and father would guarantee this.

He got a job as a mechanic. Harold Landry was mechanically talented and inventive. Even as a high school student, he had made things. But he soon lost this job. He lost two more jobs.

At this point Harold decided to take a civil service exam. He passed it with a high mark and became a mailman.

III

One night, when he had nothing to do, Harold Landry went to see Fred Morris. He had gone to school with Fred. Fred asked him if he would like to go with him to see a couple of girls. What kind of girls? he asked.

"They're rich," Fred answered.

"That sounds pretty good. Tell me some more."

"You'll like them, Harry, I promise you."

Harold had gone with Fred to see Minnie Bloomer.

"Some joint, ain't it?" Fred asked as he led Harry to the front gate.

Minnie Bloomer met them at the door. She said hello to Fred, who then introduced her to Harry.

"Hello, Harry," she said cordially.

In the living room, Harry was introduced to Della Lyons, a plump girl with red hair. They talked a few minutes and then Minnie suggested that it would be cozier in the basement. All four went downstairs. As he got up to follow the other three, Harry had thought that this was an invitation to neck. What other reason would there be to go into a basement? But when Harry saw the basement he wasn't so sure. It had been fixed up into a very comfortable room. There was a big Victrola and radio on one side. By the opposite wall there was a billiard table. And there were two comfortable sofas and several chairs. There were bookshelves, many of them. The four of them had sat around and talked. Harry kept looking over at Della until finally he caught her looking at him. Their eyes met; they smiled.

Della and Minnie were the daughters of rich parents. Even as little girls they had been treated as special. They were important; they had always been important. They took this for granted. They regarded their self-importance as separate from the wealth of their families. And even though Harold Landry was not, nor ever had been, rich, his mother's devotion and attention had helped him grow up self-important. Both girls sensed this. They both knew that he was more like them than Fred was.

Harry knew that Fred was in love with Minnie and had been for three years. He had been in the Bloomer home for only a short while when he knew that Minnie was not in love with Fred. Harry was sorry. He wished she were. But she wasn't. Still, he couldn't make a play for her, not under the circumstances. So he was ready to go for Della. She appealed to him more, anyway. She was well rounded and sexy.

The four of them sat around talking randomly for about thirty minutes. The girls were getting restless. Harry could sense that Fred was getting tense.

"The light gets in my eyes," Della laughed.

"It's shining directly into mine," Harry said.

"God forbid," Minnie said, "that the Bloomer home doesn't have a place where a guest can sit without getting light in his eyes."

"Oh, Harry will see the light soon," Fred laughed.

"I do already," Harry quipped.

"There's too much light on the subject. It hurts my eyes," Della said.

"I'll brave the monsters of the dark, Della, if the light hurts your eyes that badly," Minnie said, continuing the joke.

"There are monsters of the dark," Harry said.

"What are they like?" Della asked him.

"I can't tell you."

"Why?"

There was a challenge in her voice.

"There are ladies present."

Minnie Bloomer stood up.

"Now you boys have to protect us," Minnie said as she walked past Harry, "because I simply cannot permit my best friend Della to get an eyestrain."

She reached the light switch on the wall. Harry crossed to Della on the sofa.

"Oh, a monster!" Della Lyons exclaimed.

She said no more. She moaned as she leaned toward Harry with her arms open. Her breathing was audible. The movement of their bodies could be heard in the darkened room. Both Fred and Minnie could hear Della when she gasped:

"Oh, give me that monster, hurry."

IV

Harry and Della were gone on one another. Harry Landry did not know if he loved Della but he knew that he went for her. She couldn't seem to get enough; it was like an orgy; she always wanted "the monster." Whenever he thought of this phrase and its private meaning for Della and him, he smiled.

There was something about Della that Harry did not perceive at first. It was several months before he did. Just as he was at the point of seeing, Della herself told him. She would have told him sooner, she said, but she thought he knew.

They were in Harry's car. She was in his arms. They had driven far out on Jeffrey Road and Harry had parked in a dark secluded spot on a side road for about two hours.

"Why, I'm a nymphomaniac, Harry. I thought you knew."

Della's admission surprised him. It did not provoke any jealousy. He believed that he was getting the best of Della Lyons; and he was. He loved her but he was not ready to marry her. After all, she was rich. Harry knew that marriage to her would be disastrous. He could not earn money as fast as she could spend it and she would not be capable of understanding why. Even though Harry did not feel that he was ready for marriage with Della Lyons, or with anyone for that matter, he did give thought to the idea of marrying her. Most of the time when he did this, he was drunk. There was a variety in his drunken fancies about marriage to Della. He would marry her and she would live with him on his earnings and what he got from his mother. He would go back to college, become an engineer, and then go out and make a fortune. He would become an inventor and become a millionaire through his inventions. Or he would have a stroke of good fortune through gambling. Or some millionaire uncle of whom no one in his family had ever heard would die and leave him millions.

Sobered up, Harry would laugh over his wild notions. There was nothing that he could get from Della married that he was not getting now. And most certainly Della could not improve on the home that his mother gave him. Della could not do all the things for him that his mother did. The thoughts of wedding bells had been the products of booze. An intoxicated mind was not the cleverest of all minds, etc., etc.

It was Della who brought Harry around to the Fifty-seventh Street Art Colony. He ran into Eddie Ryan. He was glad to see Eddie again. And Eddie's girl, Marion Healy, was a very sweet girl. She seemed to be.

Della could not stand Eddie Ryan.

"Why don't you like him?" Harry asked her, sitting in her parlor one evening.

Harry and Della had been over to Joan Jackson's studio to visit Joan and Eddie had been there.

"I can't stand him."

"What did he ever do to you?"

"Why, I wouldn't let him touch me," Della said, with disgust.

"Did he ever try to make you?"

"He was never given the chance."

"Did he insult you, darling?"

"Yes," Della answered. She all but spat out the word.

"What did he say?"

Momentarily, Harry was apprehensive. Della hated Eddie Ryan. She hated Eddie so poisonously that the situation might get out of hand. He might be put in a position where he would have to fight Eddie. God, he hoped not. Eddie Ryan was tough. Around Fifty-eighth and Prairie, everyone who knew him warned you not to be deceived by what Eddie seemed to be; he was tough. He wasn't afraid of Eddie Ryan but he didn't see the point of his fighting him. It would be damned foolish.

"Yes, he insulted me."

"How? What did he say?"

"He didn't say anything; his presence insults me, whenever I have to see him."

Harry Landry was relieved. He would not have to have a senseless fight.

He laughed.

"I can't help it, Harry."

"Eddie's a nice guy. I've known him since we were seven or eight years old."

"I met him in about the summer of 1925," Della said.

"Where?"

"At my home."

"How come?"

"Oh, Fred Morris and Peter Moore came to see Minnie and me; they brought him along."

"What did he do—get drunk and break the furniture?"

"I was a girl of seventeen then, Harry."

"But what did he do?"

"He didn't pay any attention to me, none at all," Della Lyons said.

"And you've held that against him ever since?"

"I can't help it, Harry."

"But it's senseless."

"I can't help it."

Harry didn't say anything but he decided that Della Lyons re Eddie Ryan was none of his affair, none of his business.

"Harry," Della exclaimed, a note of urgency in her voice.

"Yes?"

"The monster, please!"

V

There was a tapering off, a slowing down, in the sexual relationship between Harry and Della. But even so, they still practiced sex together regularly. They fed on each other's desire. Between them, inhibitions had broken down and they were able to share a relationship that many couples would have lacked the capacity to equal. There were days now when both Harry and Della felt satiation. There was still a strong and firm affection between them, but once the tapering off of sex had begun, there was more. By the fall of 1931, sex was rare for them but their affection continued. In December 1931, Della Lyons moved to Los Angeles, California.

Chapter 15

I

Harry Landry met Frances Ryan for the first time on January 1, 1932, at Alice Healy's New Year's Day party. The year before, her sister Marion had had a New Year's Day party. The two girls had convinced their mother to give her consent and pay for the party. There had been a big crowd at Marion's party and Mrs. Healy had been impressed by Eddie Ryan's friends. She liked the young man, he seemed decent enough, but she had always thought he was a little touched. He had to be; he was going to be a writer. Or so she was told. And anyone who wanted to be a writer had to be touched.

When the bills came in, Mrs. Healy had grumbled. She had said that she would never have another such party. But by then Eddie and Marion had already eloped and were living in Paris.

Alice did not want to lose the precedent that Marion had started. She kept at her mother until Tessie Healy finally consented to another party on New Year's Day, 1932. Eddie's youngest brother Steve was invited and he had brought his sister Frances. Frances Ryan had never been to such a big party. In one way she liked it. She liked meeting new people and there were lots of fellows here. Some good-looking ones, too. But how could she get to meet them? Where was her brother Steve? Frances looked around. The Healy parlor was crowded. Steve was gone; she had lost him. She kept looking around. Finally she saw him on the other side of the room talking to someone she didn't know. She started over; she was going to give him a piece of her mind. Just then she saw Peter Moore. He saw her at the same time. He smiled and moved through the crowd toward her. Two fellows were with him.

"Hello, Frances, remember me?"

"Of course."

"Peter. Peter Moore."

"Yes, Peter Moore," Frances said.

"Frances, these are two friends of your brother Eddie. May I present Fred Morris. Fred's known Eddie longer than I have. And Harold Landry. Harry's known Eddie longer than I have too."

"How do you do?" Frances said.

"I'm pleased to meet you," Harry said.

Frances smiled at him.

The four of them stood and talked for a few minutes and then they were separated. Frances thought that Harold Landry was good-looking. And Harry told Peter that Eddie's sister was cute.

II

Frances Ryan moved to an apartment at Fifty-seventh and Harper Avenue a few days after New Year's Day, 1932. The next week her roommate, Josie Corcoran, lost her job and had to move back with her parents. Steve heard someone around the Fifty-seventh Street Art Colony mention that a girl named Hannah Patterson, a social worker, was looking for a roommate. Steve had gotten her address and given it to Frances. Frances went to see her and they talked for about an hour. She and Hannah liked each other.

Hannah Patterson, a dark-haired Jewish girl, was twenty-six. She had gone to the university and had a master's degree in social work and worked for a private agency.

Frances told Hannah how she had, about a year or so ago, sneaked out of the house and run away. Her mother had forbidden her to live away from home. And her brother Leo had told her that she could not leave home. He wasn't going to let some bum ruin his baby sister. Frances laughed as she recounted all this to Hannah. Hannah asked her how she had gotten away. Frances said that her younger brother Steve—well, he wasn't younger than she, he was older than she, but he was younger than Leo—Steve had helped her get away. He had carried her suitcases.

"Good for Steve," Hannah Patterson laughed.

Frances smiled. She was proud of her brother Steve.

Hannah Patterson suddenly sat up straight and put a hand to her lips.

"That reminds me," she said.

Frances waited for her to go on.

"Ryan, you aren't related to Edward A. Ryan, are you?"

"He's my brother."

"You must be proud of him, Frances."

"I am."

They talked some more and Frances told Hannah that she would like to be her roommate and Hannah told her that she would like to have Frances as a roommate.

III

Frances Ryan moved in with Hannah Patterson three days after she had visited her. She was excited about the change. She'd have a better chance of meeting fellows, sharing an apartment with Hannah. She would be living near the university, and practically in the Fifty-seventh Street Art Colony.

Frances was not looking for someone to get married to. Not yet. She just wanted to be in love. She was looking for some fun. To have good times, you had to know interesting people. Having fun was pretty much up to yourself, but still, she would be meeting more interesting people, she thought. People who knew more than the people she had been meeting.

IV

Frances Ryan saw Harold Landry on the street two or three times. He would smile and say hello and Frances would smile back. They would go on walking in opposite directions. Then she did not see him again for months, not until December. She saw him downtown at Randolph and Michigan. Frances was surprised that he remembered her. He had seen her first and greeted her. He asked her how she was and how her brother Eddie was. She told him that her brother was fine. When they parted, Harry said that he hoped that he would be seeing her again soon.

But it was almost two years after they first met before Harry Landry and Frances Ryan started getting to know each other.

In December of 1933, Harry met Frances on a downtown I.C. train. They sat together and talked all the way from Fifty-seventh Street to Randolph. Frances enjoyed talking with him. She remembered that Harry was good-looking but she had not remembered how good-looking. Why, Harry Landry was handsome.

But she had a kind of feeling about Harry. There was something sad about him. She didn't know what it was but there was something sad. Still, he had brightened up when he saw her. She could tell that he was glad to see her. Well, he wasn't the only one who was glad. There were two of them who were glad. Because she was. They hadn't talked about much of anything but it was interesting. Frances wished the ride were longer. She enjoyed sitting next to Harry Landry and talking. But before they knew it they were getting off the train at the Randolph Street station.

Harry Landry asked her for her telephone number and asked if he might call her sometime for a date. She gave him the number and told him please, by all means, call her any time. She would be glad to see him.

Then they parted.

Frances walked away from him hoping that he would call her, call her soon.

V

Eddie Ryan's kid sister Frances was cute. And she was sweet. He liked her smile. And he liked her cute little figure. He would call her for a date. Soon.

It was almost a week before Harry Landry called.

VI

When Frances Ryan picked up the telephone receiver, she hoped that it would be Harry Landry.

"Hello."

"Hello, Frances?"

Recognizing his voice, she said:

"Yes, this is Frances Ryan."

"Frances, Harry Landry . . ."

"I know," Frances interrupted, "I recognized your voice."

"You did? That's nice to be told."

"We had such a nice talk on the I.C. train," Frances Ryan said; but she couldn't remember much of what they had talked about.

"Yes, we did, didn't we?" He could remember no more of the conversation than could Frances but the memory of their conversation was pleasant.

Harry asked Frances for a date the next night. She told him she'd be glad to go out with him.

VII

She had a date with a new fellow. She had a date with Harry Landry, and he was handsome. A new first date. It was exciting.

Frances Ryan warned herself that she must be careful and not let her excitement carry her away so that she didn't use her head to tell her what to do and what not to do.

Oh, she wasn't worried about that.

—I'm old enough to know better, she thought, smiling.

She was smiling because this was what she thought when she had lost her virginity.

—I'm old enough to know better than to stay a virgin.

That had been with Trotter Kelly. She had never gone out with him again. He had never called her after that night. She had been hurt. But she wasn't hurt now. In fact, she was glad that Trotter Kelly had not telephoned her again. But it wasn't a very nice thing for a fellow to do.

He had taken her to a dance at the Shafter Hotel. She had never been to a dance at a hotel like the Shafter. This was not why she had said yes to Trotter Kelly. It wasn't why, but it had had something to do with why she had. The Shafter Ballroom was beautiful. The music was wonderful. And the dance was good. Everything had fitted together into such a wonderful night, and she was so curious as to what it was like. Everything fitted in right. She had just decided it was the right way to end the evening. Maybe it wasn't, though. Well, it was spilled milk. And the new bottle of milk wasn't spilled.

She wondered how much she would get to like Harry Landry.

VIII

Harry Landry was about twenty minutes late.

Frances was miffed but she decided to overlook it. After all, this was only a first date.

Harry knew that he was late and he wondered how Frances Ryan would take it. He didn't think that she would take any offense. He was less than a half hour late. Harry had his own car—a 1929 model Hudson. He parked it at the curb.

HANNAH PATTERSON

F. RYAN

He rang the bell. When the buzzing started, Harry pushed open the inner door and started up the steps.

"Hello," called a girl's voice.

When Harry Landry got to the third-floor landing, Hannah Patterson was standing in the apartment entrance.

"Hello, Mr. Landry?"

"Yes."

"I'm Hannah Patterson, Frances Ryan's roommate."

Had he been stood up?

"Come in, please. Frances . . ."

Harry Landry stepped inside as Hannah Patterson was talking to him.

"Go in the parlor, Harry, please," Hannah Patterson said as she closed the front door.

"Harry," Frances called from the back of the apartment.

"Yes, Fran."

"I'll be with you in a minute."

"Take your time. I was late anyway."

"Sit down, please, Harry."

"Thank you, I will."

"I know Frances' brother Eddie," Harry said to Hannah, making conversation.

"I never met him but Frances talks a lot about him."

Frances Ryan appeared, smiling.

She looked damned cute, Harry thought.

And Frances Ryan was convinced that Harry Landry was handsome.

IX

Harry Landry took Frances to a movie and then he took her for a drive. He kissed her. She told him that they must wait to find out how much they cared for one another before going further than petting. They had waffles and coffee, and he took her back to the apartment. He said he would call her up again, soon.

He liked Frances Ryan. He could tell that she liked him. He would call her again. Maybe tomorrow. Or the day after. It might be best to wait a few days before telephoning. If he looked too anxious, he could lose out.

Harry Landry waited three days before he telephoned Frances Ryan. He had no strong reason for the delay. It was just the way he was. He did things when he got around to doing them.

X

Harry Landry was on time for his second date with Frances Ryan. He asked her if she would like to eat Chinese. Frances said she'd love it. He told her that there was a Chinese restaurant downtown where he wanted to take her. She said that it was a dandy idea. That's just what she would like, a Chinese meal downtown.

They went downstairs and got into his car. He turned east from Harper Avenue. He drove across Stony Island into Jackson Park. It was dark out. Lake Michigan was streaming out of the distant night. They looked at it as Harry drove downtown on the Outer Drive.

Harry drove fast.

"OOOOH!"

Harry's Hudson had hit a hole in the drive. Frances had cried out as she was bounced.

"Are you hurt, Fran?"

"No, but I almost was."

"Slump low in the seat," Harry said. "There may be another."

"Ouch!"

"Are you all right, Fran?"

"Yes, for the second time, I survived," Frances laughed.

"We're almost downtown," Harry said, still driving fast.

"There's Soldier's Field. And the Planetarium," Frances said, pointing.

"If they don't repair the Outer Drive," Harry said, "the city will have to build a hospital by the drive."

Frances laughed.

Harry slowed down to make a left turn.

"Are you hungry?" he asked.

"I'm starved."

"I'm hungry too but we'll be eating Chinese in not too long."

"The sooner the better," Frances said.

XI

Harry Landry and Frances Ryan were finishing up their tea.

"Gee, the food is good here," Frances said.

"Yes, it is."

"You know, Harry, it was a nice thought on your part, bringing me downtown to supper."

"It's my pleasure, Fran. There's no use in kidding around the bush, because I'm sure you know that I like you."

"Yes, I do, and I'm sure you know that . . ."

"Of course I do," Harry smiled at her.

For a few seconds she felt shy. Then she smiled.

"Now, before I was so romantically interrupted, I want to say that it was a nice thought. I hardly ever get downtown to supper, and it's all the more fun for me being downtown with you, Harry."

"Thank you, Frances."

"You thank me and I'll thank you."
"That's a bargain," Harry said.
Frances blew him a kiss.

XII

After they had eaten, Harry suggested a movie. Frances said good; she'd like to see a movie. He said that he had been hoping that she would like the idea. Did she have some particular movie that she wanted to see?

Frances Ryan couldn't think of any particular movies that she wanted to see, because she didn't know what movies were running. But they were all within walking distance; they could go and look and then take their pick.

Harry and Frances left the restaurant and turned north toward Randolph Street. Frances took his arm.

"I haven't seen too many movie pictures," Frances Ryan said.

"I don't go too often," Harry said. "Oh, do you like Mae West?" he asked.

"I never saw her."

"*She Done Him Wrong* is at the Randolph State Theater," he said.

"Oh, I'd like to see it."

"Let's," Harry Landry said.

They walked to State Street.

XIII

Once seated in the movie, Harry put his arm around Frances. When he did, Frances almost trembled from excitement. Harry felt this and left his arm on her shoulders. She wanted him to. It was cozy and assuring, as well as exciting.

As they watched the movie, Harry Landry was thinking of kissing Frances Ryan, and she was thinking of being kissed by Harry. They were both glad when the film ended. They wanted to pet, to touch one another. And Frances wanted to be kissed and petted and stroked; and she was thinking that maybe she wanted more than that.

She did want more. But should she let herself? It would be better to wait.

They walked to the garage where Harry had parked his car. Harry Landry hugged Frances to him the moment they were in the car. He drove out of the garage.

"Harry, you'd better watch your driving," Frances cautioned.

He was a few seconds slow in taking his right arm down.

"I can drive with one arm," he said defensively.

"Not with me in the car, you can't."

"Oh."

For a minute he was angry. Frances Ryan had repulsed him. She was right, he guessed.

"You're right, Frances."

"About what?"

"One-arm driving," Harry laughed.

"Well, I don't want to get myself killed or disfigured in an automobile accident that could be avoided."

"I see your point," Harry agreed.

"It's something I won't tolerate, Harry."

"What is?" he asked, teasing.

"You know," Frances laughed.

"You won't allow a fellow to put his arm around you? Is that what you won't tolerate?"

"A lot of fellows, no."

"All fellows?"

"You'll have to figure that out for yourself, Harry."

"Don't interrupt my thought processes and I will think about it."

Harry was driving into Jackson Park. He slowed down the car, took a right turn to the Fifty-seventh Street exit. He turned the car slightly to the right, slowed down more, and then stopped. He leaned toward her, put his arm around her and kissed her. Frances kissed him back. They were locked together in a long kiss when they heard a loud voice.

"Break it up!"

Harry released her, slid back a little, and started the car.

"I'm blushing," Frances said.

The car was out of Jackson Park now, across Stony Island Avenue and moving under the I.C. viaduct.

"Do you want to come up, Harry?"

"Yes, I'd like to, thank you."

"You're very welcome," Frances laughed as the car reached Fifty-seventh Street and Harper Avenue.

XIV

Harry wished that he had brought a bottle along. He needed a drink. He wanted one, anyway, whether he needed it or not. He was nervous. Frances Ryan was very pretty and seemed to be getting prettier by the minute. He smiled at her.

She had sat down on the couch beside him.

"I know what you want, Harry, you want to sit on the couch with me."

"You are intuitive."

He laughed but his laugh was strained.

He put his arms around her shoulders. Frances turned toward him and put her arms around him. Her dark eyes were bright, her face soft and lovely.

They kissed.

Frances was not sure how far she would go when she first put her lips to Harry Landry's mouth. But when his hand dropped to her thigh she mumbled:

"Please don't."

"Frances, you can't tease me this way; I don't want to be teased."

"Harry, I don't intend to tease you, but I just don't know . . ."

She put her arms back around him and kissed him again.

"I don't know when, darling, I mean I don't know, tonight . . . or later . . ."

Her voice was strained.

His breathing came faster. He kissed her again, passionately. She responded.

"Frances, do you know now?"

"Oh, God, yes," she answered.

When his hand touched her thigh again she murmured:

"Darling, let's lie down."

Harry began to take her dress off; she helped him.

Chapter 16

I

Frances Ryan was in love. She knew what love was now. She was in love with Harry Landry. She had never known what love was before. Now she did. Now she knew, she could tell anyone who asked that love was wonderful. Of course, she couldn't tell them what was the most wonderful; that would be too embarrassing. But she knew and she could think about it.

She did think about it.

She went to sleep after Harry had left, thinking about the wonderful feeling that she had had when he made love to her.

It really was the most wonderful thing that had ever happened to her. She felt sorry for all of the people in the world who were not in love. Everything that had ever happened to her before seemed to have happened a long time ago. But she didn't want to think of anything that had happened to her before last night. She didn't want to think of anything except Harry. Harry and her. She was in love with Harry. She could say this over and over again.

—I'm in love.

She had awakened with these words in her mind.

—I'm in love.

II

Harry Landry had awakened thinking:

—Damn it, I think I'm in love.

His memory of last night was sweet. But he didn't want to fall in love. He knew that Frances Ryan was in love with him. He was sure of it. And he wasn't sure he wanted her to be. She would want to tie him down. And he didn't want to be tied down. But he was afraid that he was tying himself down; he was afraid that he was in love.

He was in love with Frances Ryan.

He knew it. But maybe he wouldn't have to tie himself down right away. He made up his mind not to phone her for a day or two.

It was a cold day. The wind was strong and bit sharply into his face. He walked along Kenwood Avenue, south of Sixty-third Street. He was wearing his mailman uniform with the mailbag hung over his shoulder.

He went into a building, took out a pack of letters, and looked at the top one. He put it in the mailbox of the person to whom it was addressed. He took the other letters addressed to the same address. It was a three-story brick apartment building with six flats in it. Harry separated the letters in the pack and put them in the proper mailboxes. He rang each doorbell as he put letters in the box. Then he left the building, turned right, and walked to the next building where he did the same thing.

He kept remembering last night. Tonight, he could pick up where he'd left off. But what about his decision to let a little time pass before he called? What about it? He could change his mind if he wanted to.

It was a mean day, raw. What was he thinking? Oh yes, he did not have to decide about telephoning her, or not telephoning her, right this minute. He had to deliver the mail and allow neither the rain nor cold nor wind nor love to interfere with his putting the right letters in the right boxes. For now, he was only concerned with getting rid of his mail load. And getting out of this cold. He could be out of the cold for a little while before he set out with his second delivery. He didn't have to think about Frances Ryan and what he was going to do. But he had Frances Ryan on the brain. There was no guessing about it, he was in love with that cute, dark-eyed Irish girl.

Chapter 17

I

Harry Landry and Frances Ryan were much lonelier than either of them realized. Their readiness to fall in love was an escape from it.

Harry had always been lonely, an only child. A big gap had been forced into Frances Ryan's life by the death of her father, Jack Ryan, when she was thirteen. But neither she nor Harry had any clear idea of what they had missed, even though they both believed that they had missed something important.

When Harry and Frances fell in love, they rebounded out of their pessimism about the things they'd missed. They had gotten each other. And wasn't that wonderful compensation for all the things that they had not had.

Their future could be less lonely than their past. Still, they were hesitant about that future. Before they met they had both day-dreamed about getting married. But as they matured they discovered that they had no desire for marriage. Neither of them felt that they could find a compatible mate. What they actually believed was that they would not find anyone good enough.

Frances knew that she had been spoiled as the baby of her family. And Harry Landry knew that his mother had spoiled him. They had both liked being spoiled. And they were both convinced that they had deserved the special treatment they had received.

They were both taken with each other. They were both on guard against acting spoiled. Each made an effort to be considerate.

This was the way they behaved during the first few months. But then the months stretched into a year. They had come to know each other in that year and they didn't make as many concessions to each other, but generally they would decide together on what they would do, where they would go.

They continued to avoid the subject of marriage.

They still believed that they were in love but they did not possess the same ardor. They believed that their flame had burned down to a steady glow. They did not have as much to talk about and went to see movies often.

Harry Landry drank less during the first months that he and Frances Ryan were going together. He would only get drunk when they went to parties. Frances herself drank, and sometimes got a little high. Whenever they went to parties around the Fifty-seventh Street Art Colony they'd drink. After one party, they quarreled and broke up. They remained broken up for two weeks. But then Harry, looking woebegone, went to see Frances and apologized. But Frances wasn't the only reason he looked woebegone. In the two weeks since they had seen each other, Harry Landry had done some heavy drinking. Once he got going with the booze, he had felt very sorry for himself and had declared that the reason he drank was that the girl he loved had left him. It was easy to find drinking companions who sympathized with his suffering.

But after almost two weeks of sodden drinking and sodden self-pity, Harry felt an urgency to love, to be the lover, to act like the lover. It was a need to say something when there was nothing more to say. He needed to convince himself and Frances that the emptiness he felt was not emptiness.

And so they resumed. They both tried to act new to each other. And they tried to feel newness. They played at being "two turtle-doves." Their new excitement lasted for several months.

Frances Ryan did not think that it made any difference whether or not you were married. She did not accept many of the conventions of society. But Frances Ryan had grown up believing in these conventions. They had influenced the shaping of her character and her personality. Before she had ever flouted them, acceptance of them had become a habit. To deny them did not eradicate them. She believed in them without believing in them. They were inescapable, like part of her skin.

And there were stirrings of ambition in Frances Ryan. These were vague but there were stirrings. The only external support of her sense of importance was the fact that she was Edward A. Ryan's sister. He had two novels published. She had not thought so much of this before but gradually she began to realize that her brother was important. And she would mention that she was Edward Ryan's sister.

But she was only temporarily borrowing his importance. One day she would be as important. This influenced her attitude toward Harry Landry. She began to think of breaking up with him.

And Harry Landry had thoughts of breaking up with Frances Ryan.

But they did not break up.

II

Two years passed. Frances Ryan and Harry Landry still saw each other regularly. They had very little to say to each other. Often Frances would sit, an almost blank look on her face. They would find themselves trying to think of something to say. And when one or the other of them did say something, the response was almost casual, sometimes listless.

Harry Landry began to drink more.

And Frances Ryan had changed from a bright young girl to a dull and unhappy young woman.

III

One evening, when Harry Landry called for her, Frances Ryan told him that she thought she was pregnant. Harry was taken aback. He did not want to become a father, particularly of an illegitimate child. She didn't know what to do about it. She could ask her brother Steve; he would know something about abortions. Harry Landry could ask someone. He could find out.

Harry sat, not speaking. She waited for him to say something.

"Can't you have an abortion, Franny?"

"I wouldn't know how to go about having one."

"Are you sure you're pregnant?"

"No, I'm not. I don't know for sure."

"How late are you?"

"Eight days."

"That doesn't sound so good," Harry said.

"No, it doesn't."

"Well, we have a little time; it's supposed to be safe up until three months."

Harry Landry was worried. He didn't know how safe an abortion was. And if something went wrong and Fran died, it could land him in jail. He didn't speak for some moments. Fran sat with her shoulders slumped, hoping that she wasn't pregnant.

"Franny, do you want to see a movie tonight?"

"Yes. Yes, I would."

IV

The next night, Frances asked Harry if he had gotten any information.

"Gee, Franny, no; but I'll do it tomorrow."

"I didn't talk to Steve either but I'll call him tomorrow."

It was the same the next night.

"We've got plenty of time," Harry told her.

"Yes, I guess so. I'll get in touch with Steve tomorrow."

"That's a good idea, Fran."

"Um-humm."

Another silence.

"Franny, there's a movie playing that I'd like to see."

"All right, I guess."

V

Frances Ryan put off talking to Steve. She knew that she couldn't ignore the problem; she would have to face it; but she was hoping that it was a false alarm. Besides, she would be embarrassed to talk to Steve about it. She shouldn't be but she would be. Steve wouldn't criticize her. Leo might, but Steve wouldn't. Steve liked to manage things and he'd start rushing her into an abortion. He would start planning everything and she wasn't sure he would plan right, or if he would plan left-handed. Her grandmother used to say that when something was done wrong:

"It was done left-handed."

She remembered when she had left home. The minute she told Steve that she was thinking about it, he had told her that it was a good idea.

"When do you want to leave, Franny? I'll help you move."

She had thought it would be best to move without giving Mama and Leo any warning because, well, she knew how the two of them would carry on. But Steve had talked her into telling Mama. And once she had agreed to tell her, Steve had nagged at her to do it.

Jesus Christ!

The way her mother had carried on. It had made her ashamed.

"I'll call the police. I'll call a squad car. Leo, do you hear what I'm saying? I'll call the police."

And Leo got his big brother's worth into the ridiculous situation.

"Ma, you don't have to call the police. I'm here. I'm the head of this household and I say that she's not moving out."

"Who'll stop me?"

"I'll stop you, I, Leo Ryan, your big brother."

"But listen, Leo . . ." Steve interrupted.

"Steve, I don't want you to put your two cents' worth in this situation."

"I'm her brother, too."

"I'm her older brother, my word goes. And as for you, Steve, quit talking like your brother Eddie. One Edward Arthur Ryan in this family is too much."

"Leo, that's not rational. . . ."

"Steve, go tell it to your big brother Edward A. Ryan."

"That's no argument about the problem."

"Oh, Blessed Virgin Mother of God, my daughter is ruined."

"Oh, Mama, cut it out."

"Franny, you'll be respectful of your mother."

"In the name of the Father, and of the Son, and of the Holy Ghost, Amen. My daughter will become a hussy, and her dead father's name will be smirched."

Frances thought she was in a crazy house.

She had had to sneak out with Steve's help.

It was not until a long time after that Frances realized that Steve had encouraged her and had helped her to leave home.

But he had not left home himself.

No, she hoped she wouldn't need Steve's help. This problem was too serious to be handled in his left-handed way. She hoped that it wouldn't have to be handled at all.

VI

Two more days passed. Frances was certain that she was pregnant. And Harry was convinced that she was.

"Harry, I can't stand the suspense any more," she said one night as they sat in Henrici's restaurant after seeing a movie.

"What are you going to do?"

"I'm going to see a doctor, Harry."

"That's a good idea. Have you got a good one?"

"I know four or five I can go to."

"This is just for an examination?"

"Yes, of course. I don't even know if I'm pregnant yet, but I think I am."

"Have you got the money, Franny?"

"Yes, I have."

"You better let me give it to you, Franny."

"If you think you can afford it better than I."

"I think I can."

Frances smiled.

"All right, then," she said.

"When we get outside, I'll give you the money," Harry Landry said.

VII

Frances Ryan went to Dr. Joseph Kamin, who had an office over a drugstore at East Fifty-fifth and Kimbark Avenue.

Dr. Kamin told Frances Ryan that she was pregnant.

"Jesus Christ!" Frances had believed that she was pregnant but it was only after Dr. Kamin had told her, definitely, that Frances Ryan felt the full weight of her condition. It was as if her doom had just been pronounced. That was how she felt.

She was afraid that she was going to faint. She did not faint but she did feel embarrassed. She hastily paid Dr. Kamin and left his office. She walked slowly back to the apartment at Fifty-seventh and Harper.

VIII

"I never had an abortion, knock on wood," Hannah Patterson said, "but I've had friends who have." .

"I don't know anything much about them," Frances said.

They were sitting in the living room.

"It doesn't seem to be too bad," Hannah Patterson said.

"How?"

"Well, my friend Sunny Jacobson had one about two years ago," Hannah Patterson said, "and she was able to come home by herself and she went to work the next day."

"Then it couldn't have been too awful."

"Oh, it'll hurt," Hannah warned.

Frances smiled at her.

"I would have imagined that there would be some pain, naturally," Frances said.

"But it must be bearable, Fran. Girls and women have abortions every day, and nobody knows about it, and they come out all right."

"I only hope that the knife doesn't slip on me."

"You definitely want to have an abortion?" Hannah asked.

"I don't want to have a baby."

"Does Harry know?"

"Not yet, for certain. But he knows I'm late."

"Will he stand by you?"

"He goddamned well better stand by me."

"When are you going to tell him?"

"When he comes around tonight, if he's sober."

"He does drink a lot, doesn't he?"

"He drinks too much," Frances said, "or at least, I think he does."

"Yes, he does seem to drink a lot."

175

"Oh, I forgot to buy cigarettes," Frances said.

"Here, I have some."

Frances got up, walked over to Hannah, took a cigarette, and lit it.

"Thanks."

She took a glass ash tray off of a stand and carried it with her, back to the chair in which she had been sitting. She put the ash tray on a little table beside her.

"Well," she began.

Hannah waited for her to go on.

Frances forgot what she had been about to say.

"Oh, I was going to say something but it slipped my mind."

"It'll come back to you, Fran."

"It couldn't have been important or I wouldn't have forgotten it."

"No, I guess not."

Frances puffed on her cigarette.

"Oh!" she exclaimed.

Hannah looked at her.

"Darn it," Frances said. "I thought I remembered it, but I didn't."

"You are worried, aren't you?"

"I can't help but be a little worried," Frances told her.

"Try not to be, I'm sure that everything will come out all right."

"Well, let's hope so."

IX

"The doctor said you're definitely pregnant?"

"Yes, he did, Harry."

"Hum-hum," Harry muttered.

Frances waited for Harry to say something.

"Well, what do you want to do?" he finally asked.

"There's no choice," Fran began.

"Yes?"

"But for me to have an abortion," Frances finished.

Harry was silent again. Then he spoke.

"I believe you're right."

"Did you find someone to perform it, Harry?"

"No, I haven't. Not yet."

"But will you?"

"Now, yes."

"When, Harry?"

"I'll start trying tomorrow."

"Harry, can I rely on that?"

"Yes, Franny."

She still had a little time; she was only in her fourth to sixth week. That was a source of some consolation. She didn't have to act immediately like, say, tomorrow morning. What she wanted was a little time in which to think. She did not know what there was to think about, but nonetheless she felt a need for time so that she might think. She positively did not want to have a baby. She would not change her mind about this. The only choice for her was to have an abortion. She did not have to think about this. Her mind was made up about it. All she had to think about was how to get the abortionist, and how to get the money to pay for the abortion. And Harry Landry would have to attend to both of these matters.

She was afraid in a vague way, and she didn't know why. She didn't think that she would die as a result of the abortion. She was quite certain that she wouldn't. She guessed that she was just afraid.

It was not only that she was afraid; it was the indignity that she felt about the whole thing.

Once Frances Ryan was aware of what it was that bothered her, she knew it was something other than fear. It had been suppressed anger. But her anger was no longer suppressed. She was angry in a general way. She was angry at life. She was angry, not because she was a female, but because she felt that being a female exposed her to indignities such as the abortion that she would have to allow to be performed on her.

Her indignation grew.

It wasn't fair. The differences between the male and the female of the species wasn't fair. Why should she be the one to bear the burden? She and Harry had made love. They had both committed a sexual act but he was a man and she was a woman. As a woman, she had to pay the price. It made her mad.

But what good would it do to get mad? This was an unalterable and unchangeable fact of life. Instead of wasting time thinking of things that couldn't be changed, she should concentrate on things that could be changed. And one thing that could be changed was her pregnancy. Two weeks had passed since Harry had promised to make all the arrangements. He had promised to find a doctor, get the money to pay him, and set the date. She knew him well enough to know that he intended to do what he said he'd do. But intending to do and actually doing were two different things. And she had better start thinking about what she was doing to do about an abortion. There was still time but she would be a fool to depend upon Harry for something so serious. She should know by now that Harry was a procrastinator and that she would have to do everything herself.

Just as Frances had decided this and was getting ready to make some telephone calls, Harry told her that he had raised the money and would be making the arrangements soon.

Frances was surprised but grateful. And she was a little bit ashamed of herself for the kind of thoughts that she had been thinking. Harry had done what he was supposed to do. She felt guilty. She reached over, put her arms around him, and kissed him warmly. He kissed her back. It was a desperate kiss.

"Franny?"

"Yes, Harry, yes, yes, yes."

X

That night as she was getting ready to go to bed Frances decided that it was best not to think about the abortion. The less she thought about it the better. It wouldn't do any good to worry. And it was useless to wish that she weren't pregnant. What was done was done. It would have to be undone. The only thing to do was to go through with it. Harry was being good about it. He was standing by her. And she appreciated his attitude.

She needed a good night's sleep. She was really tired. And her back ached a little. She must be more tired than she thought. Her body felt almost strained. And she had a slight case of cramps, almost like the ones she got sometimes before her period. She used to complain about them. Now that she was pregnant, she would welcome them. But these were milder. They couldn't actually be called cramps. It was probably fatigue. She hadn't been sleeping well. She had been worried and she really had thought that Harry was going to leave everything up to her. The worrying and the lack of sleep were causing her to feel this way. At least she hoped that this was all that was causing these cramps. There was something funny about them. Maybe she ought to ask somebody.

Suddenly her pain disappeared. They were gone. Well, she was certainly relieved about that. She picked up a book and started reading. It had been nothing, nothing at all. She had been silly to worry. She read for a while. Steve had recommended the book to her. So far she liked it. She was reading *Of Human Bondage* by Somerset Maugham.

Frances gasped. The pains had returned. They were sharp. She clenched her fists.

—Oh, God, help me!

She knew that something was happening. She felt a gushing. She got up and staggered into the bathroom. As she walked, she left a trail of blood.

XI

Frances lay in bed, too tired to care about anything. She was weak but calm. It was a great relief but it was sad, too.

Hannah had come home early. She had found Frances Ryan weak after her miscarriage. Hannah had been frightened.

She telephoned Steve Ryan first. Then she telephoned Mrs. Ryan. And then a doctor. Hannah's telephoning had awakened Frances, who was drowsing.

"I had a miscarriage," she said, her voice weak.

"I've called a doctor."

"I think I should see one. Thank you, Hannah."

"He should be here any minute. And your mother is coming, too."

"My mother?"

"Yes; I didn't know what to do, so I called her."

"Oh, God," Frances sighed. "She'll throw a fit and then she'll pray."

Hannah said nothing.

"Where's Harry?" Fran asked.

Hannah explained that she had not been able to reach him on the telephone.

—He's probably out on a toot, Frances thought. Oh well. She was so tired. She didn't want to think about anything. All she wanted to do was to sleep.

The doorbell rang.

"Hello," Steve said as Hannah Patterson opened the front door.

"Hello, Steve, please come in."

"How's Frances?" he asked, entering the apartment.

"I think she's going to be all right. She's in the bedroom. You go in and see her."

Steve took off his hat as he walked toward the bedroom door. Hannah closed the front door and followed him. As she entered the bedroom, Steve bent over and kissed his sister.

"You look all right, Frances," he said.

"I think I am," she answered.

The front doorbell rang again. Hannah turned and went to answer it.

"I hope that's the doctor," Frances said.

"Who else could it be?" Steve asked.

"Hello, who's there?" Hannah called at the opened front door.

Then:

"Won't you come in, Mrs. Ryan?"

Steve and Frances looked at each other.

"Where's my daughter?"

"She's in bed."

"Oh, Blessed Mother of God, my daughter!"

Limping on a cane and looking disheveled, Nora Ryan walked into the bedroom.

"Hello, Mama," Steve greeted her cheerfully.

"Hello, Mama," Frances said.

"Oh, Blessed Mother of God, Jesus, Mary, and Joseph, protect my baby," Nora Ryan cried out.

Hannah stared at Mrs. Ryan.

"Mama, what's the matter with you?" Frances said.

Nora Ryan ignored her daughter. She dropped her cane and slowly got down on her knees near the bed. She blessed herself:

"In the name of the Father, and of the Son, and of the Holy Ghost . . ."

Nora Ryan pressed her hands together, palm to palm. Her lips moved as she silently mouthed words of prayer. Occasionally there

was a mumble but then it was silent again as Mrs. Ryan's lips continued to move.

"Mama, what is the matter with you?" Frances asked, annoyed.

Steve grinned.

The doorbell rang again. Hannah Patterson, who had been standing nearby, amazed by Nora Ryan's performance, turned to answer
the door once more. This time it was the doctor, Dr. Anthony J.
Forman.

Nora Ryan rose and picked up the cane. Steve went into the living
room to meet the doctor.

"Hello, Doctor, I'm the patient's brother, Steve Ryan."

"How do you do, Mr. Ryan, I'm Dr. Anthony J. Forman."

He turned toward Hannah Patterson, "And . . ." he hesitated.

"I'm Hannah Patterson, Miss Ryan's roommate."

"How do you do, Miss Patterson," Dr. Forman said.

Nora Ryan entered the living room.

"And this is the patient's mother, Mrs. Ryan, Dr. Forman. Mrs.
Ryan, this is Dr. Forman."

"How do you do, Mrs. Ryan?"

"How do you do, Doctor."

"Now, may I look at the patient?" Dr. Forman asked.

Hannah led him to the bedroom, went inside with him for a moment, and then walked back out, closing the door behind her.

XII

They all looked up when he came out of Frances' bedroom.

"She's all right. Miss Ryan had just had a little hemorrhage but the
flow is stopping now. However, she ought to rest for another day or
two."

"Oh, thank God," Nora Ryan said.

"Well, I thought it best to phone you, Doctor," Hannah said.

"You did the right thing, Miss Patterson," he said.

"There is no danger, you say, Doctor?" Steve asked.

"I'd say that she is in no danger. If anything develops—and I'm
reasonably sure that nothing will—but if anything should, call me up
immediately and I'll come back as promptly as I am able to."

"Thank you, Doctor," Hannah said.

"Well, I'll be going now," Dr. Forman said.

"About the bill . . ." Hannah began with an air of embarrassment.

"Oh, that was taken care of by Miss Ryan herself."

"Well, we thank you, Doctor," Steve said.

The doctor left the apartment.

"What's he talking about?" Nora Ryan asked. "My prayers did it. He didn't do anything for my daughter."

"What do you mean, Mama?" Steve asked.

"It was St. Anthony who saved Frances' life. I prayed to St. Anthony."

Hannah looked at her. The woman was right out of the Middle Ages. No wonder Frances had left home. And that cane. Frances had told her that her mother had fallen and broken her ankle over two years ago. From the way she limped, you'd think she had broken it last week.

Frances called from the bedroom. Hannah rushed in. Steve was right behind her. Nora Ryan limped in behind him. Frances had started to tell Hannah what the doctor had told her when she saw Steve coming in. She started to tell him to get out so that she could talk to Hannah, but before she could say anything she saw her mother coming in.

"Later," Frances told Hannah.

"Yes."

No one said anything. Frances frowned.

"Well . . ." Steve started.

"Well what?" Frances asked.

She was annoyed with Steve. He should have stayed out and he should have kept Mama out of the bedroom.

"I had a slight hemorrhage but it's all right now," Frances said.

"You're all right?" Steve asked.

"Just tired."

"You're all right now, Frances, aren't you? I'll be going back home if you are," Mrs. Ryan said.

Frances had her pocketbook on the bed. She opened it and took out three dollars.

"Steve, take this, get a taxi and take Mama home in a cab."

"No, I won't ride in a taxi."

"Oh, Mama, I'm too tired to argue with you. Just let Steve take you home in a cab."

"No, I won't."

Frances looked at her. Why didn't they go and let her sleep?

"Mama, why won't you be reasonable?" Steve asked.

"I refuse to ride in a cab," Nora Ryan said, folding her arms and holding her lips together in a grim line.

"But why?" Steve asked.

"I won't waste money that way."

Hannah was annoyed. Couldn't Mrs. Ryan see that she was upsetting Frances? Hannah wanted to say something to her but she decided not to; it was best to mind her own business.

"I won't do it, Steve," Nora Ryan repeated.

Frances was on the verge of tears. What was the matter with Mama? Hadn't she heard what Dr. Forman said? Dr. Forman said that she needed some rest.

"Steve?" Frances' voice shook.

"Mama, you aren't being reasonable," Steve said, ignoring Frances.

"For the last time, I'm saying it, I won't ride in a taxicab."

"But why, Mama?" Steve asked.

"I told you."

"Oh, please, please, let me go to sleep, for Jesus Christ's sake, stop it!" Frances cried.

She began to cry.

"Don't cry, Franny," Steve said.

"Just let me alone," Frances sobbed. "Just let me alone, all of you. I want to sleep."

Steve was confused.

"Gee," he exclaimed.

Frances continued to sob.

Nora Ryan stood up, picked up her cane, limped over to the bed, bent over and kissed Frances.

"Good night, my baby doll."

She turned from the bed.

"Steve, kiss your mother good night."

"But Mama . . ."

"Kiss your mother good night."

Steve kissed his mother on the cheek.

"Good night," Nora Ryan said, walking out of the bedroom. Hannah followed her.

They said good night at the door. Hannah walked back into the bedroom.

"Just let me sleep," Frances said.

Chapter 18

I

Harry Landry acted almost shy when he walked into the apartment that Frances and Hannah shared. Frances, looking pale, was sitting in the living room.

"Hello, Franny."

"Hello, Harry."

She stood up. Harry went to her, put his arms around her, and kissed her.

"Sit close by me," Frances said.

He sat down on the couch beside her. Frances took his hand and held it. He smiled at her but it was still restrained.

"Well, Harry, we didn't lose Frances," Hannah said.

"No, I see we didn't."

"But then I could have lost all my nuisance value to you, Harry," Frances said.

"And all other value, too," Harry said.

"See, Hannah, Harry didn't want me to lose all kinds of nuisance value to him."

"I never thought that he did," Hannah said, leaving the room.

Harry put his arms around Frances and kissed her.

II

One year later, Harry Landry and Nora Frances Ryan were married in High Point Valley State by a justice of the peace named

Carter Redmond. The marriage took ten minutes. While Justice of the Peace Redmond was going through the prescribed motions, Harry had a fierce headache.

Justice of the Peace Redmond pronounced them man and wife.

Five minutes later they were a married couple getting into Harry's automobile to drive back to Chicago.

Chapter 19

"I told Frances," Nora Ryan was saying, "not to live with his family. But she wouldn't listen to me. Well, she's sorry now, I can tell you that."

Nora was visiting the Dunnes.

"Oh, the poor little dolly," Jenny said.

"I told her, I said to her, 'Frances, let's you and me ask for wages here.'"

"How awful. Don't you want another cup of tea, Nora?" Jenny asked.

"Yes, thank you, Jen. I would like another cup."

"His mother has waited on that Harry Landry hand and foot from the time he was born," Nora said, resuming her conversation.

"But Harry's a nice boy," Jenny said.

"And what do you think Frances is?" Nora asked.

"A darling girl," Jenny answered.

Nora sipped her tea.

"Can't Harry get a better job than a mailman?" Dick asked her.

"That's just what I said to her. I told her, 'Frances, can't he get anything better than putting letters in mailboxes?'"

"He went to college, didn't he?" Jen asked.

"Yes, but he always got kicked out."

"I never knew that."

"Yes, for boozing. And it was more than one college, Jen, it was three or four. Maybe even five."

"Oh, Nora, not five colleges! Why? He's smart, isn't he?" Jenny asked.

"He's a boozer, Jen."

"Nora, can't you bring us news that will cheer us?" Dick asked, smiling.

It had been so long since Jenny had imbibed. Still, he saw little purpose in dwelling on the topic. Jenny was nervous and there was no way to know how she would react to such a conversation.

"Well, he is. He's a boozer," Nora said.

"Oh, that's too bad," Jenny said. "My only hope is that he doesn't mistreat my darling niece."

"What about the baby?" Dick asked.

"Michael is a good baby," Nora said.

"I'll bet your boots he is," Jenny said, "and he's a beautiful baby."

"Oh yes, he is," Nora said, "but do you know what?"

"What?"

"Frances is like Steve and Eddie; she's a pagan, a heathen atheist."

"She'll be all right," Dick said. "She'll come back. All three of them will come back."

"I pray to God they do," Nora said.

"They will," Jenny assured her.

"Say some prayers that they will, Nora. And I'll pray also," Dick said.

"I always do; I always pray that my three lost sheep will come back to the fold."

"But, Nora, weren't you going to tell us something?" Jenny asked.

"Yes, I was going to tell you this," she said, leaning forward and lowering her voice. "I baptized my grandson Michael."

"Good for you, Nora!" Dick said.

"Didn't Frances have Michael baptized in the church?" Jenny asked.

"No, Frances wouldn't allow it; she's become a heathen."

"But even so, what harm could she think it would do to the baby to have it baptized?"

"I don't know but she didn't so I baptized my grandson," Nora boasted.

Chapter 20

I

For a year or so after his marriage, Harry Landry drank much less than he did before. He got drunk only a few times. Sometimes Harry liked it, being married. But he didn't know whether or not he loved Frances. Whether he did or didn't, he was resigned to his marriage. He saw no alternatives. He was a father now. Michael was his responsibility. And then, too, his marriage hadn't made serious inroads on the way he lived. Maybe marriage wasn't so bad for him. Oh sure, he got pissed off once in a while. One of the things that really pissed him off was Frances rubbing it in that he was only a mailman while Eddie Ryan was a famous writer and Steve was studying to be a doctor. He didn't know why she kept bringing them up. She ought to see that it had no effect on him. He wished she'd stop. But she wouldn't and he knew it.

Franny wanted him to be a success. That was down low in his interests and up high among the things that he didn't care to become. Hell, he'd rather be happy than famous. It wasn't just his success that Franny wanted. She wanted to be important. Maybe she would come down to earth and get over this yen. He certainly hoped so. In the meantime, he hoped that they could have some peace. They would have to move soon. He really didn't want to leave his parents' house but he thought that he'd have to agree to it. Franny was his wife, the mother of his son. She had a right to her own home. She had already told him that she didn't mind living close to her in-laws but that she had to be in her own place.

Franny found a six-room apartment on Kimbark Avenue for seventy-five dollars a month. Harry signed the lease. They had saved some money. Hazel Landry helped out with the furniture as well as silver, dishes, linens, and other things.

Frances was very hopeful when she and Harry moved into their own apartment. But she could only hope, she thought. She was excited about the apartment. It was her first home, her first home of her own. She never realized how much she had wanted a home of her own. She loved it.

Frances and Harry were quickly settled in the new apartment. Frances had hoped that this happiness would continue but the days soon became dull. She had Michael to take care of but Michael had two grandmothers who liked to help take care of him. At first she had been determined not to ask for help from either of them unless it was absolutely necessary. But she soon learned that a mother could love her baby and still be bored with taking care of him. And as much as she hated to admit it, both of Michael's grandmothers were better with him than she was. They had had more experience than she had. Maybe it wouldn't be so bad if she didn't have to pick up after Harry all the time. Harry's mother had always waited on him hand and foot. He had never had to do anything for himself. It made her furious. He left his socks wherever he happened to take them off. He never hung up his coats. As for shoes, half the time when he wanted to put on a pair he couldn't find them—or he would find just one of them. It was funny watching him look for them. So funny that she couldn't stay mad. She would have to laugh. Sometimes Harry didn't like it when she laughed but she couldn't help it, she just had to. Once in a while he saw how funny it was and he would laugh with her.

They had been in their own apartment less than two weeks when Harry went on a binge. This one lasted longer than the others had. He didn't seem to be able to control himself. He had never drunk like this when he was younger, before he met Franny. He was drinking a lot more than he used to. It was her fault.

And the more Harry drank, the more it was Fran's fault. And the more it was her fault, the more belligerent Harry began to feel about her.

Frances thought of leaving him and taking Michael with her. She could threaten to leave. But what if her threat didn't work and she had to make it good? It could be a mistake. Sooner or later Harry would go on the wagon. When he went on the wagon he would feel sorry and he would promise to go on the wagon for good. And she would believe him. She always did. She believed him because she kept hoping he would. It was because of Michael. Michael loved his

father. He could be badly affected if she left Harry. She didn't want
to take a chance on this. She didn't want to do anything that would
hurt Michael or give him complexes. This was why she wouldn't do
something drastic like leave Harry. But she had to do something. She
couldn't let her life go on in the way it was with Harry's drinking.

II

"I think that I'll stay on the wagon this time, Franny."

They were having supper.

Frances smiled but her smile was sad.

"You just wait and see, Franny."

"Oh, I believe you, Harry."

"Yes, Franny, it will be different this time."

"Good."

Harry wished that Fran could be a little more enthusiastic and encouraging. Well, she would see for herself. He meant it this time.

"This is a good supper," Harry told her.

"You like it?"

"Yes, it's good."

III

Harry stayed sober for four months. This was a strain for him.
Frances ought to give him some credit for what he was doing. She
was so cold; he didn't like it. Well, he would show her. He would
stay on the wagon this time. It didn't matter to him whether or not
she cared; he cared. But why should he if it didn't matter to her?

Then Harry went on another big binge. He had put up with
Franny's indifference and her talk about her famous writer brother
and her soon-to-be-a-doctor brother for as long as he could. Sometimes you'd think that she wanted him to get drunk. She was always
rubbing it in about him being a mailman.

That Sunday night, while he was drunk, Harry Landry slapped
Frances in the face. It was a hard stinging crack and her cheek

turned red instantly. She started to cry from the pain and from humiliation.

Harry left, slamming the front door behind him. When Fran heard the door she broke into hysterical sobs. Her face no longer hurt and she no longer felt humiliated but she continued to sob. She could not have explained why even if she had been asked. She felt awful. Simply awful. Harry Landry was so mean and unfair. She was married to him. He was the father of her son Michael, who loved him.

And he had slapped her face.

She broke into a fresh fit of sobbing.

A half hour passed. Frances had stopped crying. She sat, her eyes red from crying, thinking about leaving Harry Landry.

But she did not leave him on that Sunday night. She undressed, went to bed, and fell asleep. She was asleep when he came home.

The next morning she was up early to fix his breakfast and feed Michael. She was silent. Harry was glum. He remembered slapping her in the face. He wished he hadn't done it. He felt anything but good about last night. He wished he hadn't gotten drunk. But he didn't have time to brood about it; he had to be off to work.

Wearing his uniform, Harry Landry was off.

Frances saw no sense in thinking about how he had slapped her. She wouldn't forget it but she wouldn't dwell on it either. It had happened. Harry had slapped her in the face, hard, but it wouldn't do any good to feel sorry for herself. There was no use in batting her brains out about it now. It had happened. It was done and past. She was going to stop thinking about it. It wasn't worth it.

Frances became less cool toward Harry. She acted as if nothing had happened between them, as if Harry had not slapped her on the face that Sunday night.

Two weeks later Harry came home drunk and beat her. The next morning Frances knew that absolutely she would have to do something. She was living the only time that she would ever live. She had a right not to want to spend her life as the wife of a mailman, a drunken mailman who beat her.

Look at her mother. She didn't want her life to be anything like that. Times had changed and her life couldn't be the exact repetition of her mother's. But there were some things that would be like her mother's life if she were to leave Harry. It had been hard on her mother after her father died. She had tried to raise her children and it had been hard because she didn't have any skills. Her mother had had some compensation. She believed in God and fully expected to go to heaven when she died to receive a reward for all that she had not gotten in this world.

Well, she didn't believe in any life after death. None of this heaven or hell made sense to her.

So if she were to amount to anything, if her life were to mean something, it would have to be in this world because there was no other. And she couldn't believe that her life would mean anything if she were married to a mailman. And Harry was more than satisfied to be a mailman.

IV

Frances went to work. She liked working and she liked getting a salary. And she didn't have to worry about Michael. Her mother came over to take care of him most days. When she didn't, Hazel Landry did. She should have looked for a job sooner. She had lost time, valuable time. She would have to have special training to get the kind of job that would give her the opportunity to make something of herself. She would have to go to school at night. She could have had enough money saved for school by now if she had gone back to work sooner. She had lost lots of time, all right. Well, she was on the right track. She would save her money and bide her time. And when she had enough money saved she would leave him.

V

She was ready. All she wanted was a good excuse. The next time he got drunk, that would be her excuse. And if he should hit her it would be even better. It would be all the reason she would need. The only thing was that Harry was so mean when he was drunk that he terrified her. He didn't always know what he was doing and she could be crippled for life.

Well, her mind was made up. She had made up her mind before and had changed it. No, she hadn't really changed it; all she had done was postpone it. But now she had to do it. She couldn't go on delaying.

VI

It was a cold Tuesday in February. Harry had been on the wagon for two weeks. He came home from work and parked in front of the building. He rang the doorbell. There was no answer. Frances must be busy with Michael. He let himself in with his own key.

"Hello, where is everybody?"

There was no answer.

He knew what had happened instantly. There ought to be a note, he thought. He looked for it. There wasn't one.

He was furious. The least she could have done was write him a note. She owed him that much. He picked up a lamp and threw it against the wall. It fell near the telephone. He walked over. Propped against the phone was a note.

Dear Harry,

There's no use in our staying together. You'll hear from me when I'm settled.

Frances

—Goddamn it!

VII

Harry Landry telephoned Fran's sister Clara Jack Boyle answered the telephone. Harry asked for Clara. In a few seconds he heard:

"Hello, Harry? How are you?"

"Oh, I'm well, Clara, and how are you?"

"Fine, Harry, fine and dandy."

"Is Franny there, Clara?"

"Why, no, Harry. Did she say she was coming here?"

"No, she's left me. When I got home I found a note saying that she was leaving me."

"Oh, Harry, that can't be so."

"It is so, Clara."

"I wonder where she went?" Clara asked, as though thinking aloud.

"I don't know but if she comes there will you let me know?"

"I sure will; but since she hasn't come here up to now, I don't think that she will."

"You never can tell," Harry said. "If you asked me out of a clear sky where Franny would go in circumstances like present ones, I'd have said right off, 'to her sister Clara's.' "

"Well, she didn't."

Clara's voice had turned cold. She could no longer hide her hostility. Harry became suspicious.

"You will let me know if she comes to your place?"

"Yes, I will, Harry."

They said good-by and hung up.

"I don't know, Franny," Clara said, turning away from the phone.

"Do you think he suspects I'm here."

"Definitely, or else he believes you'll come here."

Frances looked disturbed.

"It's only natural that he'd think that. Where else could you go?"

"Yes, I suppose so," Frances said.

"Franny?"

Frances looked at Clara.

"Let Jack take Michael over to his Grandma Landry's."

Frances said nothing for a minute or two.

"I really think that you ought to send Michael to his grandmother's now," Clara continued. "And you'd better do it before Harry has a chance to get here. If he rings the bell and asks to come in, or asks if you're here with Michael, we can't say that his son is not here if he is."

"I suppose not. Well, if Jack will take him to Hazel's."

"Oh, I'll take him, all right," Jack Boyle spoke up.

"You'd better do it now, don't you think, Jack?"

"Sure, but we better telephone the old lady first."

"You call her, Clara," Frances said.

"I will but I think it would be better to call her after you've left."

"All right, I'll get him ready."

"And I'll call for a cab," Clara said.

VIII

"No, Hazel, I don't know," Clara said into the telephone.

Her mother, Nora Ryan, was standing in front of Clara and shaking her head.

"Yes, she did come here. She was very upset," Clara was saying.

Nora Ryan kept signaling her.

"Yes, she told me that she had left Harry. She had Michael with her."

Clara listened while Hazel spoke.

"Well, yes, she was upset."

Frances started smiling.

"I'm sorry too," Clara said, her voice growing cold.

Nora Ryan shook her head, trying to signal her daughter.

"I don't know where she went, Hazel."

Clara listened again.

"Yes, and well, good-by, Hazel," Clara said, and she hung up the telephone receiver.

"You shouldn't tell her anything, Clara," Nora Ryan said.

"I didn't tell her anything, Mama."

"How did she sound, Clara?" Frances asked.

"Oh, she was friendly," Clara said.

"You can't trust her," Nora Ryan said. "Not when it's her son you're talking about."

"She wanted to know if you were here," Clara said, "and how did you feel when you had been here. You heard what I said, Franny?"

"Yes."

IX

"Oh, the old lady was pleasant enough," Jack Boyle said, coming in the house.

"She was to me on the telephone, too," Clara told him.

"How was Michael?" Frances asked.

"Oh, he was all right," Jack said. "I talked to him about bowling and baseball. He told me he liked swimming better than baseball or bowling, and so I said I like to go swimming myself.

"Yeah," Jack Boyle went on, "me and Michael got along all right, and so did me and the old lady."

"She didn't try to pump you?" Clara asked.

"Well, maybe a little," Jack Boyle laughed, "but I ain't getting in the middle, between cross fires."

They all laughed.

X

"Franny," Clara said, her manner serious, "I don't want you to think that I want to try to tell you what to do, but you've got to make up your mind."

"I know it."

"You can't let things go on like they are. This is no way to live."

"I know, Clara."

"Do you know what you want to do?" Clara asked.

Frances sat, silent. Clara and Jack Boyle sat, their faces grave. They said nothing.

"I want to do something, but what is there to do?" Frances asked.

"I know it's hard, Franny, but you're an intelligent person."

"Yes, I understand."

"I'm telling you for your own good."

"I know, Clara. And I don't resent what you're saying to me. I really don't."

"Well, I'm only talking to you for your own good."

"Yes, I know."

This was becoming painful. Didn't Clara understand? There was more to it than just making up her mind and doing it. She didn't have enough money, for one thing. And for another, she had to consider Michael.

Before any more was said, the front doorbell rang.

"I bet that's Harry," Frances said.

"Do you want to see him, Franny?" Clara asked.

"God, no."

"Then hurry, go upstairs. We'll get rid of him."

Frances was on her feet, so was Clara.

The front doorbell was still ringing.

Clara turned to Frances.

"Hurry, get upstairs."

Clara glanced about and picked up a sweater of Frances'.

"I'll answer the door," Jack Boyle told her.

He went to the front door. Clara put Frances' sweater in her mother's room, off the kitchen, then she fussed as though she were busy in the kitchen.

<h1 style="text-align:center">XI</h1>

"No, Harry, she came, dropped Michael off, then left. I don't know where she went. She didn't tell us where she was goin'."

"She didn't give you any indication?" Harry asked.

"No, none at all," Jack said.

Harry Landry shook his head.

"That's funny. It doesn't sound like Franny."

"Well, if it does or doesn't, Harry, we're telling you the truth."

"Oh, I know that. I don't doubt you."

"She left Michael here and I took him to your mom's in a Yellow Cab."

Harry nodded. He sat, not speaking. He didn't believe either of them, Jack or Clara. Franny was probably upstairs. But he couldn't just bolt up the stairs. This wasn't his home. And even if he should dash upstairs and find Franny up there, what could he do about it? He stood up.

"All right," he said. "Thanks, Clara, and thank you, Jack, for taking my son to my mother's."

"Oh, don't mention it, Harry," Jack said. "It's nothing at all."

Harry put on his coat, said good-by, and left.

Frances spent the night with Clara and Jack. Harry telephoned three times. Once in bed in the downstairs bedroom, Frances cried herself to sleep. Around eight the next morning Clara brought her a cup of coffee.

"How sweet of you to bring me coffee, Clara."

"It was no trouble, Franny."

"Still, it's sweet," Frances said, smiling at her sister.

"Did you sleep well?" Clara asked.

"Oh yes, I did."

"Good."

"I think I'll get up now," Frances said.

"You'd better or you'll be late for work."

"Oh, didn't I tell you, Clara?"

"Tell me what?"

"I took a week off," Frances said.

"Will you have your job when you go back?"

"Oh yes, I'll have it."

She finished her coffee.

"Here let me take the cup, Franny."

"I think I'll get up now," Frances said, handing her sister the empty cup.

Chapter 21

I

She had done the whole thing wrong. She had no place to go. No money. Her life was disrupted. Michael's life was. And Harry's life was. So were Harry's parents'. And so were her family's. She had made a mistake. She talked with Clara. Clara agreed with her. Frances hated to admit that she had been foolish but there wasn't much else to do unless she wanted to compound her mistakes.

Frances did the only thing she could do at the time.

She went back to Harry Landry.

II

At first Harry didn't seem to hold it against her. He said that he would try to let bygones be bygones. Harry meant this; he was going to try to let bygones be bygones. He wasn't going to throw anything up to Franny's face. But he expected her to do the same.

Frances returned thinking that, if Harry would let bygones be bygones, so would she.

In this spirit, Frances and Harry Landry tried to make a go of their marriage. Trusting one another, and letting bygones be bygones, that was how they were going to try to be. This marriage depended on whether or not they could forget.

Chapter 22

I

Clara had suggested to Frances that she talk to Peter Moore. Peter was a good friend of Eddie's and a lawyer. Frances said yes, she knew Peter Moore. Frances had telephoned him and asked if she could see him. Peter invited her to come to his apartment the next evening. She found both Peter and his wife Geraldine very friendly. Geraldine said that she too had known Eddie back in the days when she had been a student at the University of Chicago. Frances said that she was glad to know that.

Peter was an old friend of Harry's as well as Eddie's. They had gone to grammar school together.

There were a few minutes of friendly talk. Presently Geraldine excused herself. This was nice of her, Frances thought, she appreciated it. Some wives would have been jealous under the circumstances. They would have resented a woman coming to their home to talk to their husband alone. But Frances could see that Geraldine felt no resentment. She and Peter must be happy.

After Geraldine had left, Frances couldn't think of how to start. This was foolish. She had come here to talk. She would just have to force herself.

"I want a divorce. How do I go about getting one?" she blurted.

Peter Moore was surprised. Peter had always liked Harry but as Frances talked, he realized that the marriage was no good.

Frances was hoping that Peter would offer to talk to Harry but Peter made no such offer. Instead he suggested that the wisest step for her, in his opinion, would be to talk to Gus Inwood. Gus was a friend of Harry's but Gus and Harry had never been as close as he and Harry had been. And Harry respected Gus, Peter said, and he thought that Harry would trust Gus, too.

Frances' hopes rose. She would try to see Gus Inwood. Peter told her that he would phone him first thing in the morning. Frances thanked him.

Frances left Peter Moore's apartment with her hopes high.

II

When Frances telephoned Gus Inwood he told her that Peter Moore had telephoned him. She was relieved. Gus asked her to come to his office and talk things over.

Frances went to his office on North La Salle Street. She did not have to wait; Gus had her come right into his office. Frances knew immediately that she could trust him and his judgment. This put her at ease.

Frances told him that she was afraid of Harry because of the way he sometimes drank. He had gone on the wagon many times, of course, every time he had fallen off. Even if he were to go on now, she wouldn't be able to believe he would stay on. She couldn't help it; she had been disappointed too many times. And Harry's drinking wasn't all of it. She was worried about her future. What was she going to do with her life? She wanted to make something of herself. Harry was satisfied with where he was and what he was doing. And she didn't like spending her life as the wife of a mailman. Not that she looked down on mailmen, she didn't. She simply wanted more out of her life than she could get by being Mrs. Harry Landry.

Gus Inwood said that he understood.

Frances believed that he did.

At the end of their talk Gus said that he would think about what she had told him and if he thought that he could do anything helpful he certainly would try to do it. He would get in touch with her as soon as there was anything for him to communicate to her.

Frances left Gus Inwood's office feeling that at last things were on their way. She felt good.

III

Gus Inwood convinced Harry Landry that the best thing for Frances and for Harry himself, and for Michael, would be a divorce. Harry had seen the sense in what Gus said. And, to be absolutely honest, he was not happy in his marriage. He and Fran had tried to let bygones be bygones but neither of them had been able to.

Neither of them was getting much out of the marriage. Michael was one reward. They both loved the boy. He was bright and good-natured, a curly-haired beautiful boy. But Michael was more apt to be hurt than helped by their continuing such a marriage.

"Gus, I know you're right; it's the only sensible thing to do."

"Okay, Harry, then why don't you agree to do it?"

"I will."

"Do you mean that, Harry?"

"Yes," Harry laughed.

"Have I got your word on it?"

Harry hesitated for a few moments.

"Yes, Gus, you've got my word on it."

IV

Harry and Frances Landry were divorced. It was an amicable divorce. Harry agreed to give fifty dollars a month toward the support of Michael. He was given visiting rights; he would be able to take Michael on weekends and during school vacation periods.

A load was lifted off both their minds; but Michael became obstreperous. Frances hoped that he would come to accept it just as he would one day come to accept the deaths of either of his parents whether he wanted to or not. She was older than Michael; he had far more time in which to find happiness than she did.

Harry went back to live with his mother. Mrs. Landry was happy to have her son back and she showered him with little attentions.

Because of the war, there were jobs for women. Frances landed a new job in a chemical factory. She saw her chance for her future. She went to night school to study chemistry. At first she thought that she could never get through the courses. She did not have a disciplined mind and she had had only one year of high school. But she could not fail. She was on her own now; she had to make something of her life. This was her big chance. Frances persisted. On weekends, she would fall asleep over her textbook. She dragged herself through long days.

A few months passed.

Frances realized that she was learning. She knew that she could become a qualified chemist. She could make plans with this in mind.

V

Harry was still a mailman. He both envied and admired Frances for what she was doing. He knew that he could do as much, or even more, if he wanted to. Knowing this was enough; he felt no need to prove it.

With his mother's help, he bought a sailboat which he named the *Fancy Face*. He spent weekends sailing on Lake Michigan. Sometimes, when the lake was calm, he would take Michael sailing. The boy loved it. Harry taught his son to swim. Michael loved this even more than he loved sailing.

Harry knew that he would be drafted. The only way to escape it would be to go to work in a defense plant. But he had no yen to work in a factory. He talked this over with his mother. He told her that he wouldn't like working in a defense plant.

"This is our country, Mother, we've got to fight this war."

Hazel Landry thought for a couple of moments. She wished she could go into the army herself.

"If they want me, Mother."

"I understand, Harry."

Harry had known that she would understand.

"You're pretty wonderful, Mother."

"I only wish I were."

"Well, we'll see what disposition Uncle Sam makes of your one and only son," Harry said flippantly.

Chapter 23

I

"Harry is meeting Franny," Steve said.

"Maybe I ought to have gone to meet her," Eddie said, "but . . ."

"You don't have to be there, Eddie," Steve said reassuringly.

"I know that," Eddie said, a little put off by Steve's patronizing reassurance.

"I'll be glad to see Franny," Steve said.

"So shall I," Eddie said.

Steve didn't realize how patronizing he was, Eddie thought, so he would just overlook it. Steve had a number of traits that had to be overlooked. But Steve was worth it.

"Frances seems to have done a good job about herself," Steve said.

"I guess so," Eddie agreed.

"I wonder what's going to happen when she and Harry meet?" Steve said.

They were sitting in the parlor. The day outside was gray. Cecilia Moran was in the bedroom with Nora Ryan, whose condition was unchanged.

"I'll be glad to see Franny all right," Steve said.

"So will I."

"Judging from her letters, I think that Franny has grown a lot since she went to California."

Eddie nodded.

Steve stood up and looked out through the front window.

"Not much of a day," he said.

II

Harry Landry, his mother, Hazel, and Clara Boyle and her son
Eddie Boyle met Frances and Michael Landry at the Northwestern
Station. The train from Los Angeles came in a few minutes late.

—I can hardly wait, Clara thought.

"I hear it, don't you, Hazel?" she said to Mrs. Landry.

"I'm nervous as all get out," Hazel Landry said. "But the train is
almost here now."

"Yes, in a minute or two we'll see it," Harry said.

"I hope the train hurries up," Eddie Boyle said. "I hope the train
hurries up."

"Are you nervous, Harry?" Clara asked.

"What do you think?" Harry asked.

"Oh, there she comes," Eddie Boyle shouted.

They could see the engine coming closer, and growing bigger as it
did.

III

Michael stepped down from the Pullman car first. Frances was right
behind him. They looked ahead to their left.

"There's Frances, there they are."

Frances recognized her sister Clara's voice. She felt a surge of happiness. Then she saw her and she was even happier. Then she spotted Harry, and next, Hazel Landry. She was happy to see them.

They were calling.

"Frances!"

"Frances!"

"Franny!"

They were running toward her. She stood and waited, happy and
proud.

Frances' moment of being proud and happy on the station platform was blotted out by the thought of her mother, dying. But she shouldn't be guilty; she didn't have to be. In her gladness to see Clara, she had forgotten about Mama.

But she did feel guilty.

Frances could tell by the way Clara looked that Mama had not died.

IV

They were all riding in Harry's car.

"You look well, Frances," Hazel Landry told her.

"Thank you, Hazel."

"Yes, Franny, you're looking very good," Harry said.

"Thank you, Harry. All of you are looking good too."

"And we're all damned polite," Harry laughed.

Frances and the others laughed too. But then Frances, looking worried, turned to her sister.

"Clara, tell me more about Mama."

"You'll see in a little while," Clara said.

"Yes, I know. I was so afraid that I wouldn't get here in time."

"Is Grandma dead?" Michael asked.

"No, honey," Clara told him, "she's very sick but she isn't dead."

Frances was impressed by the gravity on Hazel Landry's face.

"Can Mama talk?" Frances asked.

"No, she can't," Clara answered.

"That's terrible."

Clara nodded.

"What's terrible, Mother?" Michael asked.

"Death is terrible," Harry said.

They did not talk for a while.

V

"Franny looks good, Eddie," Steve said.

"Yes, she does."

Eddie had been moved at the sight of his sister.

"Don't I look good?" she had asked.

"You look like a million dollars," Steve had told her.

"Yes, you do, Franny," Eddie had answered.

"Did you have a good trip on the train?" Steve asked.

"It was all right but it took too long."

"It must have been awfully tiring," Clara said.

"We'll talk later, I want to see Mama," Frances said.

"Just go in. There's a nurse in there, in Mama's bedroom," Clara said.

Cecilia Moran stood up when Frances walked in.

"I'm Frances Landry," Frances told her.

She was looking at her mother, helpless, on the bed.

"I'm the youngest of my mother's living children."

"Oh, how do you do, I'm Cecilia Moran."

"I'm glad to meet you," Frances said.

"And I'm pleased to meet you, Mrs. Landry."

Frances had approached the bed. The mass of living material on the bed couldn't be her mother. But it was. It was Mama. She reached the side of the bed. Outwardly, there was no sign that the sight of her mother had affected Frances.

Nora Ryan was staring upward. Frances did not know if her mother were staring at her or at the ceiling. Her mother's right eye was open but it didn't move; it was fixed. Her mother's mouth was pulled down, out of shape.

"Hello, Mama," Frances said, speaking in a low voice.

Frances thought that she saw some recognition from the left side of her mother's face but she couldn't be sure. She looked down at the disfigured face. She felt pain. This was her mother; it was her mother's face. But there was nothing left of her mother as she had known her, just a resemblance of features.

"Mama, this is Frances, your daughter. Mama, this is me, Frances."

Again, Frances thought she saw a flicker of recognition in her mother's left eye. She wanted Mama to know that she was here; she wanted Mama to know that she had come from California to see her. She wanted very much for Mama to know.

"Mama, it's me, Nora Frances," she said again, speaking in a low soft voice.

There was a flicker. Yes, her mother did recognize her. There had been a slight flicker. Had there been or had she imagined it? She couldn't be sure. She wanted to cry.

Cecilia Moran watched her. She wanted to suggest to Frances Landry that she had been in the room long enough but she didn't want to come right out and say so. Her patient might hear her.

But Frances had just decided that it was long enough for a first visit.

"I'll be here now, Mama," Frances said softly.

She bent down and kissed her mother on the forehead. Once again, she almost was in tears. Then she straightened up, turned from the bed, and stopped for a moment before Cecilia Moran at the foot of the bed.

"I don't think I'd better stay any longer now; it might not be good for her."

"I think it best not to prolong the visit," Cecilia whispered.

"So do I," Frances said.

She left the room.

VI

"Poor Mama!" Frances exclaimed when she walked into the kitchen.

"You know, of course, Mama's dying?" Steve said.

"Yes, I know. It's so terrible."

"What you see in there now is hardly Mama any more. Mama's personality has been destroyed by the stroke."

Frances nodded slowly, tears in her eyes.

"For all practical effects she was eradicated when she had her massive cerebral hermorrhage," Steve went on.

"I knew it, I knew it," Frances said; she was crying now.

"I know how you feel, Franny."

Frances wiped her eyes, blew her nose, and managed to stop. Eddie came into the kitchen.

"Hello, Franny," he said.

She smiled at him.

"I didn't thank you for sending me that check, Eddie."

"Was it enough?"

"Oh yes, it was enough for me to get here but I'll need carfare back."

"I'll give it to you."

"Thank you, Eddie."

VII

"I don't want to hear about your gripes and troubles here in Chicago," Frances said.

She was sitting at the kitchen table with Clara, Steve, Eddie, Harry Landry, and Hazel Landry. Eddie wondered why Frances had just made this announcement. He didn't understand it.

"I came here determined not to get involved in family quarrels and situations," Frances said firmly.

Nobody said anything.

"Do you want more coffee, Frances?" Clara asked.

"Why, yes, thank you."

Clara got up and got Frances a fresh cup. Frances put cream and sugar into it and stirred it. They were all looking at her; she was conscious of their attention. She stirred her coffee again and then lifted the cup to her lips.

"You make good coffee, Clara," she said.

"Thank you."

Frances hesitated a moment before speaking.

"I have developed since I went to California. I have new friends, new interests."

"Good," Steve said.

"I now have a life of my own to live and I am living it in California."

Eddie was puzzled. He looked at Hazel Landry. Frances was talking again.

"You see, I have left Chicago. I live in California now."

"Well, I'm mighty glad that you do," Clara said.

"Now Mama has her whole family around her," Steve said.

"But does Mama know that we're here; does she recognize us?" Frances asked.

"I think so," Steve answered. "At least, I hope so."

"So do I," Clara said.

"I'm glad," Frances said.

"I'm not," Eddie disagreed. "Think of the fear and agony she must feel."

"Do you think she knows she's dying?" Frances asked.

"Yes, I think she probably does," Steve answered.

"Why, that's terrible!" Clara exclaimed.

No one spoke.

"Oh, I hope she isn't suffering," Clara said.

"I really don't think that she is," Steve told her.

Clara turned to him. She wanted him to say more. Frances waited for him to speak again.

"I think that, with the stroke that Mama suffered, there must have been some dulling of her consciousness. We don't know, you see, how much of her brain has been damaged. For instance, for all that we know, there might be an aphasia, I mean an amnesic aphasia, which is an inability to remember words."

"What you say makes sense," Eddie told him.

"Oh, I hate to think of it," Clara said.

"Well, there's this way to look at it," Steve began. "Mama is seventy-two, isn't she?"

"No, she's sixty-nine," Clara corrected. "She's seventy-two for the old-age people."

"Oh, I didn't know that."

"Yes, we thought it would be better if we made Ma a little older," Clara said.

"Well, what do you know about that!"

"I never knew how old Mama was," Eddie said.

"Her real age is sixty-nine," Clara said.

"I never did know Mama's real age. And neither did I realize the real ages of Uncle Dick, Aunt Jenny, and Uncle Larry," Eddie said. He added, "When I put them in my novels, I might have screwed up their ages. But then, that's fiction."

"Well, as I was going to say," Steve started again, "Mama has lived sixty-nine years; and she's lived a full life."

"But it's been a hard life, Steve. After all, Mama had fifteen kids," Clara reminded him.

"Did she have that many?" Harry asked.

"Yes," Clara said.

Harry shook his head. "I never realized she had that many."

"It's a wonder she's lived this long when you think about it," Frances commented.

"Oh, Mama was strong," Clara said.

"She had to be to have fifteen kids," Frances said.

"But Mama's life was hard, I mean when we were kids," Clara said.

"But still, it was a full life, in a way," Steve protested.

Eddie looked at him in astonishment.

"She had children," Steve said. "She had fun a number of years; she was able to do what she wanted to do. I think she had a good time during these last years. And now she has her family gathered around her."

"I see what you mean, Steve," Clara said.

"Well now," Steve added, "if you look at it that way, you can see it differently and we can more readily console ourselves about what's happening to her now."

They all fell silent.

They had said and heard enough.

Chapter 24

I

"Oh, Frances, your old Aunt Jenny's so happy to see you," Jenny Dunne said, embracing her.

Jenny and Dick had just arrived. The moment they had seen Frances they began making a fuss. Frances wanted to escape all the hugging but Jenny held her tightly and rattled on.

"You're such a beautiful doll, Franny."

"She most certainly is," Dick Dunne repeated.

"You don't know how glad your Aunt Jenny is to see you, Franny."

"And I'm glad to see you, Aunt Jenny. You're looking well, and so is Uncle Dick."

She put on a big smile.

"Oh, Frances, I'm heartbroken," Jenny said, changing immediately.

"I know, Aunt Jenny."

"It breaks my heart, Franny."

"Yes, Aunt Jenny."

"I'd give anything," Dick Dunne said, "if this had not happened to your mother."

Frances shook her head sadly.

"I know, Uncle Dick."

She thought that she was going to cry.

II

Frances was unpacking. She had spread her belongings out on the bed and chairs, so that she could put them away in the two dresser drawers that Clara had cleared for her. The closet door was open and many of Frances' things were already hanging there. She didn't know how long she would be staying. Of course, it depended on how long Mama lived. Or how soon she died. Mama was dying. It was hard to believe. Frances hung a new blue dress in the closet. She turned and saw Aunt Jenny.

"Hello, dolly Frances."

"Hello, Aunt Jenny."

"Here, let your old reliable Aunt Jenny do that for you," Jenny said, coming forward as Frances picked up her black dress.

"Oh no, that's all right, Aunt Jenny, but thank you just the same."

"Oh, it's nothing for me to do," Jenny said, picking up some underthings off the bed.

"Please don't bother, Aunt Jenny."

"It's no bother, Frances dolly."

"But please, Aunt Jenny, I want to put my own things away."

"Don't think of it, when you have your Aunt Jenny to do it for you."

"Jenny, won't you please . . ."

Frances had spoken with exasperation in her voice.

"Oh, all right, but I was only trying to help."

Frances looked at her angrily, but then the anger vanished. Aunt Jenny looked crushed. Frances felt both pity and resentment.

Jenny began to cry.

Frances was nonplused. What was the matter with her? She must be upset because of Mama.

"All right, Aunt Jenny, you can help me."

"You go rest and I'll put your things away," Jenny said, "and then we'll have a nice talk."

Now she was in for it. Aunt Jenny had fooled her, had taken advantage of her pity.

"Oh, I would do just anything for my doll baby niece."

Jenny had stockings in her hand.

"Nora Frances, doll baby, where do these go?"

Frances didn't like being called Nora. That was why she had dropped the name. And she wasn't used to it any more. But still, there wasn't any use in saying anything about it now, since her mother's name was Nora. And Mama was dying.

"In the first drawer, there."

"Oh, I'll put them away so neat and orderly."

Irritated as she was, Frances wanted to laugh.

"There," Jenny said, folding the stockings in the top drawer.

Maybe her Aunt Jenny was working for a touch. How much ought she give her? Maybe five dollars? But she didn't have much money on hand. It might be better to see Eddie before she gave Aunt Jenny any money.

"There, it's all done, and put away as neat as a pin," Jenny announced.

"Aunt Jenny, I'll see you later, I don't have much change on me."

"Oh, don't worry, Frances, baby doll."

"I'm not worried, I'm just mentioning."

Aunt Jenny was always building things up into scenes.

"Oh, Frances," Jenny said, "your poor Aunt Jenny is so unhappy."

Frances looked at her.

"Oh, Frances, when I heard that you were coming, I was so glad. You can't know how glad I was. I said to Dick, 'Dick, Frances will understand.'"

Frances was beginning to be bored.

"How I wish you had been here when it happened," Jenny said.

"Well, I wasn't here."

"I know it, oh, how I know it, dolly."

But what was Aunt Jenny getting at?

Jenny began to cry.

"What's the matter, Aunt Jenny?"

"Oh, Frances, you don't know."

"What? What don't I know, Aunt Jenny?"

Jenny Dunne shook her head sadly.

"Oh, your poor, poor mother," Jenny said through her tears.

"Aunt Jenny . . ." Frances began.

"And they won't let me nurse her," Jenny interrupted.

—What is this? Frances wondered.

"I could have done it myself and saved them all of that money."

Dick Dunne hurried into the room.

"Jen," he said sympathetically.

"Oh, tell her, Dick, tell Frances what I've suffered."

"Why is Aunt Jenny crying?" Clara asked, sticking her head in the doorway.

"I don't know. She's unhappy," Frances said.

"What's the matter, Aunt Jenny?" Clara asked.

"I wanted to talk privately with my niece Nora Frances. Why is everybody in here interrupting my talk with my niece?"

"I'm sorry, Jen, I'm sorry," Dick Dunne said, flustered.

Clara looked at Frances with a question on her face.

"She came in and insisted on hanging up and putting my things away and then she started talking about getting sad, and then she started to cry," Frances told her sister.

"What is it?" Clara asked her Aunt Jenny, bending down.

"I want to talk privately with my niece Frances," Jenny snapped.

Dick Dunne, still flustered, said:

"She wants to converse with you, Frances."

Frances frowned.

"Why don't you all clear out and let Frances and me talk?" Jenny Dunne asked in rising anger.

"I have to talk with Clara," Frances said, as Jenny stood up and took Frances' arm.

"Let's get out and leave them alone," Dick said to Clara.

He stepped out of the bedroom, but Clara did not follow him.

"I haven't had a chance to talk with my sister or my brother yet, Aunt Jenny," Frances said. "Later, I'll talk to you."

"You won't give your poor old aunt five minutes?"

Dick tapped Clara on the back.

"Clara, they want to speak privately."

"Frances doesn't want to speak privately to Aunt Jenny," Clara said.

"What?" Dick asked.

"I'm getting out of this room," Frances said.

She walked out of the bedroom and into the dining room. Dick looked at her, disappointed.

Clara came out of the bedroom and Jenny Dunne followed, looking utterly miserable and wretched.

"What did I ever do to you, Frances?" Jenny asked.

Frances walked into the parlor and sat on the couch. Jenny Dunne stood over her.

Frances looked up at her. Aunt Jenny was making her nervous.

"I never did anything to you, Nora Frances," Jenny said.

"I didn't say you did."

"You won't even let me tell you."

"Tell me what?"

"What's the matter?" Eddie asked, walking in.

"Nothing's the matter, Eddie," Dick said, stepping in front of his nephew. "They are just having a little conversation, that's all."

Eddie didn't say anything.

"Say, Eddie?"

"Yes, Uncle Dick?"

"I have an idea for a story that will knock 'em sky high. It ought to be a best seller."

"I can't do anything about it, Uncle Dick," Eddie said impatiently. "I can't write that way."

"But this is a wow of a story, Eddie."

Jenny sat down on the couch.

"Frances, all I wanted to do was help out," she said.

"But, Aunt Jenny . . ."

"Please, Nora Frances, let me tell you."

Frances looked at her.

"I wanted to do it."

"You wanted to do what?"

"I wanted to nurse your mother and relieve Clara."

"What can I do about it?" Frances asked.

"I just wanted to tell you. I thought you'd want to know."

"Aunt Jenny," Clara's voice was firm.

"What have I said now? I was only telling . . ."

"Cut it out, Aunt Jenny," Eddie said.

"Eddie," Dick Dunne said, "the soft pedal, the soft pedal."

"You're trying to make trouble, Aunt Jenny," Eddie said.

"What's going on in here?" Steve asked.

"Aunt Jenny's telling Frances that we wouldn't let her be the full-time nurse," Eddie told Steve.

"Aunt Jenny," Steve said, "I explained to you."

"But I'm as good as your nurses, I'm better," Aunt Jenny said.

Eddie walked back toward the kitchen.

"Frances, she wanted to be the nurse, day and night."

"Doctors have told me, 'Miss Dunne, you're better than any trained nurse I've ever worked with,'" Aunt Jenny told Steve.

"Oh, Aunt Jenny," Steve said.

Frances stood up and walked quickly to the kitchen.

"Would you like some coffee, Eddie?"

"That would be nice, Fran."

Frances poured two cups.

"Thanks."

"Oh, it's nothing."

"Aunt Jenny was buttonholing you, Franny."

"I know she was. Why me?"

"Because she thought you would listen."

"What's she complaining about?"

"She's complaining because we haven't let her take the center of the stage away from Mama."

"Do you mean that, Eddie?"

"Yes, I do."

"It sounds too ridiculous for words."

Steve came into the kitchen.

"Well, you caught it," he told Frances.

"What did I catch?" Frances asked Steve, as he sat.

"Aunt Jenny's sob story."

"I don't understand it," Frances said.

"She wanted to take over as nurse," Eddie said.

Clara and Jenny entered the kitchen.

The three of them stopped talking. Jenny looked at them with suspicion.

214

"Well, Franny," Clara said, "you're here at last."

"Yes, I'm here," Frances said.

"I never would have treated any of you the way you have treated me."

"How did we treat you, Aunt Jen?" Steve asked.

"You know how you all have treated your poor old aunt," Jenny complained.

"No, I don't know."

"As God is my witness, that's all I wanted, was only to help." The tears came.

Dick Dunne came into the kitchen.

"Jen, what's the matter, Jen?" he asked solicitously.

"Oh, God, Dick, I can't stand it any more."

She broke into sobs and left the kitchen.

Dick followed her.

"Jen, Jen . . ."

III

"Did you go to a psychiatrist, Frances?" Steve asked.

"Yes, I went to one for help."

They were sitting in the dining room. It was about one-thirty in the afternoon.

"And what happened?" Steve asked.

"He told me I didn't need him."

"Well, good for you, Fran."

"But when I come back here, what do I find? Trouble. I don't mean Mama, either. Poor Mama. I mean the rest."

"Well, what do you expect, Franny? Especially at a time like this?" Steve asked.

"Maybe you're right, but that's why I left here and went to California."

"I know. But you should have seen it when Eddie and I got here. Was it a mess!"

"Well, I'm glad I didn't. I can imagine what it was like," Frances said.

"It was something."

"God!" Frances exclaimed.

Clara walked in and sat down.

"I don't know what's the matter with Aunt Jenny," she said.

"She's a troublemaker," Frances said.

"She always was," Clara agreed.

"I remember once when she got about three hundred dollars; she took me with her and she started drinking. She kept telling me how unhappy she was," Frances said.

"Oh, she did that to me three or four times," Clara said.

"She did?" Steve asked.

"Yes, she did," Clara said.

"And to me too," Frances said.

"She's sick, all right," Steve remarked.

"Well, I can't make her well," Frances snapped.

"She didn't want us to hire nurses," Steve said. "She wanted to do all the nursing herself. That's why she's cutting up now."

"Yes, that's what you told me," Frances said.

They could hear Jenny pacing back and forth.

"Isn't that something!" Clara exclaimed.

"What's that?" Steve asked.

"Uncle Dick. He went out to work from here."

Eddie and Steve went over to the front window. The air was full of flying snow; there were drifts of snow along the sidewalk.

"He shouldn't have gone out on a day like this," Steve said.

"Well, you know Uncle Dick; he never was lazy like Uncle Larry."

"But he doesn't have to work on a day like this," Eddie said, "I'll give him what he'd make."

"Not Uncle Dick. He's not too proud to earn whatever he can at any kind of job he can get," Clara said.

"But he could catch pneumonia," Steve said.

"And you know, I think he's at least seventy-three. I'm not sure but I think he's around that age."

"He doesn't look it," Steve said.

"He still goes swimming," Clara told him.

"He looks healthy, all right," Steve said.

"Well, he's always taken good care of himself," Clara said.

"He's in good shape, all right," Steve said. "But I still say that he shouldn't have gone out on a day like this. I hope he doesn't catch pneumonia."

"I don't think he will, Steve."

"Neither do I; all I said was that I hope he didn't get it."

"Yes, we know what you said, Steve, we heard you," Eddie said.

"Hey, Franny," Steve called.

"Yes?"

"Did you know that Uncle Dick is seventy-three years old?"

"No, I didn't but I can't say that I'm surprised."

"I think he's doing very well, considering his age."

"Where's Aunt Jenny?" Steve asked, turning to Clara.

"She fell asleep."

IV

It was cold and snowy outside. Eddie was correcting proofs of his novel. The galleys were piled on the floor. He turned to look out the window. The houses on Wells Street looked drab and old. The wind was whipping down the street.

Eddie turned from the window.

"You don't get weather like this in California, do you, Franny?" Clara asked as she and Frances came into the parlor.

"No, that's one of the reasons I like it out there."

"It isn't a bad reason for liking it."

"I wish you could all come out there."

"Don't I wish it!" Clara said.

"Well, maybe you can someday."

"Gee, I hope so."

Eddie picked up a galley.

"What's that?" Franny asked him.

"Another novel."

"It is?"

V

How soon would she die?

The question hung over the house. Outside, it was getting dark. The snow had stopped.

"I didn't see Aunt Jenny leave," Eddie said.

"She went home to cook Dick's supper. I'll give her credit for that. She takes wonderful care of Uncle Dick."

Frances was sitting on the couch. She seemed restless. So did Michael.

"I was correcting proofs. I guess that's why I didn't notice her leaving."

"She didn't say good-by to any of us," Clara told him.

"She certainly is mad," Frances smiled.

"Let her be," Steve said.

"Jack will be getting home soon," Clara said.

"You're pretty hard on Aunt Jenny, Steve," Frances said.

"You have to be with her or she'd have this whole house in turmoil."

"Oh, I guess so."

—How long will it be? she thought.

"Steve?"

"Yes, Franny?"

"How is Mama?"

"She's just about the same."

"Is there any chance that she'll live?"

She suddenly felt a wild kind of hope.

"No. And if she does, she'll be helpless. She won't be the same person any more; she won't be our mother."

"Oh, she'll always be my mother," Clara said.

"Yes, of course. What I meant is that her personality, the Mama we know, was destroyed by this stroke."

A look of pain crossed Frances' face.

Jack Boyle let himself in the front door. He kicked off his rubbers and put his gloves and stocking cap on the shelf in the closet. He took off his jacket and hung it up. He also hung up his old suit jacket. He walked into the parlor without speaking. Young Eddie Boyle ran to him. Jack Boyle bent down and held his son, asking him how his day was.

"Hello, Jack," Steve called.

"Oh, hello, Steve," Jack answered without looking up.

"Eddie," Clara called. "Eddie Boyle, come eat your supper with your cousin Michael."

She walked into the parlor.

"Hello, Jack."

"Hello, Clara, how's your mother?"

"She's the same."

"Did Frances get here?" Jack asked.

Eddie walked in.

"Hello, Jack.

"Oh, hello, Eddie."

Frances came into the room.

"Come on and eat, Eddie," Clara called to her son.

"I'm hungry, Ma."

"Well, it's ready; come on out to the kitchen and get it."

"Hello, Jack," Frances said, smiling broadly.

"Why, hello, Frances."

They shook hands.

"She looks good, doesn't she, Jack?" Steve asked.

"Yes, she looks real good."

"Thank you, Jack. I feel wonderful."

"I can see that California agrees with you," Jack said.

"I like it," Frances said, sitting down.

Jack turned around to Steve.

"How's your mother, Steve?"

"She's the same."

"How did work go today, Jack?" Eddie asked his brother-in-law.

"Oh, it was all right," Jack answered, sitting down and taking some cigarettes out of his pocket.

"Did you have a good trip out?" Jack asked Frances.

"Yes, we did. Of course, it was a long trip."

"Where's Michael?"

"Here he is," Frances said as Michael Landry walked in from the kitchen.

Chapter 25

"That poor girl who was murdered. Her name was Endicott, Mildred Endicott," Clara said.

They were all sitting in the dining room eating supper.

"It's terrible when you think about it. Gosh, it could happen to anybody," Clara said.

Steve turned to his brother Eddie at the other end of the table.

"It was a terrible murder, wasn't it, Eddie?"

"I don't suppose it's the best subject for the supper table," Clara said. "We should talk about something else. But I don't think any of us has much to talk about that's pleasant or happy right now."

"A person has to take what comes along," Jack said.

"You sure do," Clara agreed.

"And a lot of the things that come along are things that you wish you could sidestep," Jack said.

"I sure agree with that," Clara said.

"That fellow who did that murder was a fiend; that's all he is, a fiend," Leo said.

"He sure is," his wife Florence agreed.

"I don't care what they do to him when they catch that one," Leo declared.

"Well, I do," Jack Boyle interrupted. "I don't want him goin' free."

"Oh, they won't let him go free, Jack, you can be sure of that," Leo told him.

"No, I don't think there's any danger of his going free," Cecilia Moran said.

"Well, I don't know about that, sometimes they let them kind of guys go by sayin' that they ain't all there in the head. Then a few years go by and the next thing you know the guy is let out and killing another innocent person."

"Oh no, Jack, not when they do things like this fiend did," Clara protested.

The table was piled with food. Eddie had given Clara more money to help feed the family. There were a lot of Ryans to feed while Nora Ryan was dying. The house was crowded.

"But I say . . ." Steve said in a rising voice.

What Steve said was not heard because Leo Ryan and Jack Boyle were saying something at the same time.

Eddie had started to speak a couple of times but there was too much commotion. No one seemed to be interested in what he was trying to say. He knew that it was no time for him to talk. He was willing to be silent and to sit and eat and listen.

Nora Ryan lay on her deathbed in a room off the kitchen, her condition unchanged.

Chapter 26

I

"Are you going to pray at Mama's bedside?" Steve asked.

Eddie and Steve were sitting on the couch.

"No, why?"

"They think a priest should come and pray over Mama," Steve said, "and I was wondering if you were going to kneel and pray with the others."

"It would be an insult to them if I did."

"Why would it be an insult?"

"They know what I think," Eddie said.

"Oh, I see what you mean, but I still don't see how it is an insult."

"Well, it would be," Eddie said. "And anyway, the point here is, I've answered your question."

"You know, it's really something, the way the priests acted when Mama was stricken."

Eddie nodded.

Frances joined them.

"Franny, did you hear about the trouble there was getting a priest the night Mama had her stroke?" Steve asked.

"I heard something but I can't get it straight. Just what did happen?"

"Well," Steve began.

"What happened?" Frances asked.

"That's what I'm going to tell you," Steve said. "Clara called up the priest at St. Julia's. No one answered the telephone."

"Yes, Clara told me that."

"Did she tell you that when she and Jack went over to the parish house, the priests didn't answer the doorbell?"

"Yes, she did."

"And how Uncle Dick got the police and went in a squad car, looking for a priest?"

221

"Yes, so I guess I did get the whole story."
"It seems that way," Steve said.
"It was like a farce," Eddie commented.
"I never heard of anything like it before," Frances said.
"Maybe the priests at St. Julia's were sleeping off a New Year's Eve drunk," Eddie suggested.
"Well, I hand it to Uncle Dick," Steve laughed. "Getting a squad car and touring around to find a priest. It's just like him, all right."
"Those priests are hypocrites," Frances said.
"Here was Mama, one of the most religious women in this whole city, and she could have died without a priest." Steve paused.
Eddie and Frances didn't speak, waiting for him to go on.
"Of course," he said, "Mama didn't know it. At least I don't think she did."
"I'm glad of that," Frances said.
"Yes, it's better that she not know about it," Steve agreed.
"Do you think she did, Steve?"
"No, I don't but I can't say for sure because I don't know for sure."
"But it's very likely that she doesn't know?" Eddie said, putting this as a question.
"Yes, that's probably true," Steve said.
"What was that?" Frances asked.
"Oh, it's most likely and probable," Steve explained, "that Mama didn't know anything about that business about the priests not coming, and about how hard it was to get a priest for her."
"Well, then it doesn't matter so much, maybe, that they didn't want to come."
"I think it does," Steve argued.
Frances gave him a questioning look.
"Well, what about the hypocrisy of priests?" he asked.
"What about it?" Eddie asked.
"Yes, what about it?" Steve repeated.
"All you can say is that that's the kind of hypocrites they are," Frances said.
"I don't know," Steve said.
"I could do something about it," Eddie said. "I could write about it."
"That's what I was thinking about," Steve said.

"But I won't write about it," Eddie said.

Steve looked disappointed.

The front doorbell rang.

"That's the priest from St. Julia's, I guess," Steve said.

Clara Boyle hurried from the kitchen to the front door.

II

Eddie, Steve, and Frances remained in the living room. The two brothers sat on the big couch, Frances sat on a rocker nearby.

The priest had been led to the rear of the apartment and was talking with Clara.

"What did he say his name was? I didn't get it when he told Clara."

"Father Fulton," Eddie told her.

"Yes, that's it, Father Fulton," Steve nodded.

They listened as Father Fulton talked to Clara.

"I want to know what excuse he gives," Steve said, "if he bothers to give one."

"Well, Father," Clara was saying, "my mother was so devout, and when we had so much trouble getting a priest, I didn't know what to think."

"I'm very sorry, Mrs. Boyle. It will never happen again."

"I should think it wouldn't happen again," Steve muttered to Eddie.

"We didn't hear the bell ring," Father Fulton said.

"Well, Father, Mr. Boyle rang the bell a number of times."

"Oh, yes, Father Fulton," Jack Boyle said, "we rang your bell real loud."

"Oh, I don't doubt it, Mr. Boyle."

"He didn't say why he didn't hear the bell when it was rung loud," Steve said to Eddie.

"Hell, Steve, he was probably boozing all New Year's Eve and he and the other priests were out cold. That's my guess, anyway."

"You see, Mrs. Boyle," Father Fulton explained, "we were robbed. The burglars drugged us so that we didn't hear the telephone or the doorbell ring. The burglars must have used a spray gun to spray some drug in the parish house that put us to sleep."

Eddie looked at Steve with amazement. He began to laugh.

"They sprayed the air with some drug that put us to sleep," Father Fulton was saying.

Frances started laughing.

"Gee, Father, I'm sorry that all this misfortune happened to you," Clara was saying.

"Oh, it wasn't so much, Mrs. Boyle," Father Fulton said.

"Steve," Eddie said, "Father Fulton's a faker."

Frances smiled.

"Well, Father, I'm not the kind of a person who broods over bygones."

"That's a very sensible attitude, Mrs. Boyle."

"I think so, Father."

"Yes, it is sensible, Mrs. Boyle."

"Thank you, Father."

"And now, Mrs. Boyle, where is your mother?" Father Fulton asked.

"Right in there, that's her bedroom door, right there."

Eddie, Steve, and Frances stayed in the parlor. The others were in Nora Ryan's bedroom with the priest. All but Jack Boyle, who stood with bowed head, had knelt. They followed Father Fulton in prayer for the speedy recovery or the grace of a happy death for Nora Ryan, and for the repose of her soul if she were about to be called to God.

The mumurs of prayers being said in the bedroom could be heard in the parlor.

"Who would have thought that this would happen?" Steve said. As he spoke, he looked at Eddie.

Frances also watched Eddie. She was much impressed by what Steve had told her about the parallel with Stephen Daedalus and his dying mother.

"This is very different," Eddie told her.

"But it's the same, too," Steve declared.

"There's no pressure here on me to pray at Mama's bedside," Eddie reminded him.

"I know that."

"Yes, there is," Frances said.

"Yes, Eddie," Steve said.

"The atmosphere, the relationships, the characters, and the consequences of kneeling or of not kneeling and praying are all different, qualitatively."

It was evident to him that they did not agree with him.

The praying had ended. Father Fulton and the others went in the kitchen.

"Thank you, Father Fulton," Jack Ryan said.

In the parlor Eddie, Steve, and Frances missed Father Fulton's reply. But they did hear him speak to Clara.

"Now, Mrs. Boyle."

"Yes, Father, we all thank you."

"This is disgusting," Steve said.

"We do sincerely apologize. We are all very sorry about what happened on New Year's night, Mrs. Boyle."

"I'll bet they're sorry," Frances said.

"I think I understand, Father," Clara said.

"Yes, we know, we understand," Jack Boyle said.

"Thank you."

"They don't resent it," Eddie said.

"I guess not," Steve said.

"Call us any time you need a priest, Mrs. Boyle," Father Fulton said.

"We'll call you," Steve sneered.

"And may God heed our prayers for your mother, and God bless this household," Father Fulton said.

The priest was approaching the parlor. Jack Ryan and Clara were with him. He passed through the parlor.

"Good night," Father Fulton said to the three of them.

"Good night," Eddie mumbled.

Steve and Frances did not speak.

Clara Boyle and Jack Ryan let Father Fulton out at the front door.

III

"What kind of an excuse was that?" Steve demanded.

"Doesn't sound like much of a one to me," Leo smiled.

"I'd say it's a pretty sorry excuse," Steve said.

"It was," Leo nodded.

"Oh, I don't know," Jack Ryan said.

No one commented.

"What happened when you and Jack had the door closed in your face by the parish housekeeper?" Steve asked Clara.

"She slammed the door in our face," Clara said. "She thought we were trying to tell her something about an automobile accident, and about a priest being in trouble with a woman."

"I don't get it," Steve said, laughing scornfully. "How did she make that out of your trying to get a priest for Mama?"

Clara shook her head.

"I don't know."

"That's farfetched," Frances declared.

"It sure is," Steve agreed.

Molly Ryan whispered something to Jack Ryan.

"Leo," Clara said, "Cecilia Moran is going to be ready to leave soon."

"I'll drive her home."

"But Bridget isn't here yet," Steve said.

"She'll be here any minute," Clara said.

The doorbell rang.

Jack Boyle answered the ring. Dick and Jenny stood in the doorway.

IV

"I wish that Jen and I had known that you were going to have the priest here to pray for Nora," Dick said. "We would have come earlier and been here in time."

"We only decided after supper and there wasn't time to let you know so that you could get here," Clara said.

"I understand," Dick said. "I only intended to convey my regrets that Jen and I weren't here to attend and pray."

"Yes, I understand, Uncle Dick, and I'm sorry too," Clara said.

Jenny sat listening, her face a picture of unrelieved misery.

"Yes, Dick, it was only after we ate that we thought we ought to have a priest come and pray over Mama," Jack Ryan said.

"I can comprehend that," Dick said. "I intended no inferences when I expressed my regret at missing this holy occasion."

"I know you didn't, Uncle Dick," Clara said.

"Oh, Dick," Jenny exclaimed mournfully.

Dick looked at her.

"Yes, Jenny, what is it?"

"Oh, let it be, Dick."

"Yes, Jen, I have. I was only expressing our regrets."

"I'm not accusing anybody," Jenny said, still mournful.

"But, Aunt Jenny, I didn't say that you were accusing," Clara said.

"As God is my witness, I didn't accuse anybody," Jenny repeated.

"Dick, did you hear me accuse anybody?" Jenny asked, turning to her brother.

"No; why, not at all, Jen."

"Aunt Jenny, I know you didn't accuse me," Clara said, striving to hold onto her self-control.

"Dick, I swear to God that I never accused anybody." Jenny was almost in tears.

"That's true, Jenny," Dick said, trying to reassure her.

"Oh, let me alone," Jenny snapped at him.

Dick Dunne looked hurt. And then he turned accusing eyes on Clara.

"I only want to be let alone," Jenny sobbed.

"I'm not picking on her," Clara told her uncle.

"Clara," Eddie called.

Dick had jumped up, and after giving Clara a second hurt look, he bent down toward his sister and said:

"Jen, don't let anything excite your nerves."

Jenny continued to cry.

"I don't know what's the matter," Clara said.

Dick turned toward her and signaled with a nod of the head for her to leave Aunt Jenny to him.

"Oh, Dick, I'm heartsick," Jenny sobbed.

Clara turned away from them, annoyed and bewildered.

V

"She won't let up. She won't give up," Eddie said.

"What's eating her this time?" Frances asked.

"I'm not sure that I know," Clara answered.

"She hopped onto the fact that she was not called to be here when the priest came, that's the impression that I get," Eddie said.

"But we couldn't call her, there wasn't time," Clara protested.

"I know," Eddie said. "But that doesn't matter to her. She latched onto it, she had to latch onto some slight because she's got to make us feel bad for persecuting her," Eddie said.

"That's about it," Steve said.

"I don't see why she's got to go through such shenanigans," Clara said.

"But she does," Eddie said.

"She's impossible," Frances said.

"The minute you let up, she takes advantage of you," Eddie warned.

"Well, all I can say is that I wish she wasn't that way," Clara said.

"It's too late for her to be any different." Eddie shrugged.

"Yes, I guess it is," Steve said.

And it was too late for his mother to be any different from the way that she was, Eddie thought. He thought of his mother. He thought of his Aunt Jenny Dunne. The words that he had said, that it was too late for Aunt Jenny to be any different from the way that she was, were horrible. And he could do nothing about it. The thought was saddening. He had lived long enough to know that there were many horrible things in life about which nothing could be done.

"She has Uncle Dick under her thumb," Frances said.

"He depends on her," Clara said.

"I guess she's quiet now," Steve said.

"I hope she stays that way," Clara said.

"She can be made to," Eddie said. "If she causes too much trouble and disruption, she should be put out of the house."

"I'd hate to do that to the poor thing," Clara said.

"If she knows that she can't go too far," Eddie said, "you won't have to put her out."

Jack Boyle entered the kitchen, rubbing his eyes.

"Oh, hello, Jack," Steve said.

"Clara, I'd better be gettin' ready to leave." Then, turning to Steve:

"Hello, Steve."

"Yes, Jack," Clara said. "I'll fix you something to take with you."

"All right. I'll be glad when this strike is over."

"So will I," Clara said, getting to her feet. "I'll fix you some sandwiches."

VI

The family sat in the parlor. They all were getting used to the situation as it was, with his mother's condition staying unchanged.

Other interests were largely suspended. Eddie's interest was fixed here in this house and on what went on here. He lit another cigarette.

"It doesn't look like anything is likely to happen tonight," Steve said.

"She certainly is putting up a fight," Leo said.

"Yes, it seems so," Clara added.

"I'm not giving up," Jack Ryan said.

"But, Jack, there's really no hope," Steve said.

"I'm not giving up," Jack Ryan repeated stubbornly.

"There's no question here of giving up. Or of not giving up. What's happened to Mama is irreversible, it can't be undone."

"Oh, I don't know what to say," Clara broke out.

No one spoke for a few moments. There was tension in the silence.

"Does anybody want some coffee?" Clara asked.

She had to say something because she couldn't stand it any longer.

"I'll have some, please," Eddie said.

"Who else?" Clara asked.

"I'll have some," Steve said.

"Me too," Frances said.

"I got to work tomorrow, it would kill my sleep," Leo said.

Clara started toward the kitchen.

VII

Clara Boyle sat at the kitchen table. She was suddenly so tired. She had the feeling that she was going to be tired like this for all the rest of her life.

Just a few feet away from her, behind the closed bedroom door, was Mama.

Well, we all had to die sometime. But why did Mama have to die now?

How could she answer a question like that? She couldn't. Still:

—Why does Mama have to die now?

When your time came, you had to go. Everybody's time came. Her time would come someday, and then she would go too.

She didn't want to die.

She didn't want Mama to die.

Everybody had to die sometime. And nobody wanted to. She could hear voices from the front of the house. She felt like going back in there with them. She was so tired. She was not only tired; she had never been as sad as she was right now. There had never been anything like this in her life before. Of course, she had been sad when her father died. But not this sad. She had been so much younger then. Papa had died, let's see, this was January 1946, and Papa had died in November 1923. Yes, it had been November 1923. Nineteen forty-five to 1935 was ten, and 1935 to 1925 was twenty, and to 1923 was twenty-two. It would be twenty-three years ago next November that Papa had died. So it was twenty-two years ago and one month, and maybe a couple of weeks. She was too tired to figure it out to the number of days. She had been sad then. But Papa had been sick for so long. And she had been living with the Dunnes so she hadn't been right there when it happened. Besides, when you're young, you take these things better than you do when you get older. She was too sad to cry.

She ought to go to bed, but she wanted to stay up until Jack came home.

She went to the stove to heat herself a cup of coffee.

Chapter 27

I

Bridget Daugherty, the night nurse, sat by Nora's bedside, reading one of Edward A. Ryan's books.

Nora Ryan was sleeping, or at least she seemed to be asleep. She seemed to be resting comfortably, but her right eye was open wide. Its fixed look was strange.

Two oxygen tanks stood by her bedside.

Nora Ryan breathed shallowly. Now and then there was a twitch on the left side of her bed.

The house was quiet. The bedroom door was closed. The overhead light in the center of the ceiling glared.

Bridget Daugherty was reading about how the father and husband had died after a stroke. This woman, whom she had been nursing through these long nights, was the wife of the man about whose death she was reading. This was clear to Bridget Daugherty.

The book was so much like life. She knew the people in this book. She was in their home. But she would have known them even if she had not come here to take care of poor Mrs. Ryan, who was dying there beside her, may God have mercy on her soul.

She had known these people all of her fifty-three years. They were her own kind. She had never expected to read a book like this. She had never thought that books like this were written.

To think that the young man with the glasses, sleeping in the parlor of this house, had written this book. And to think that this poor woman, Nora Ryan, who was here on her deathbed, may God have mercy on her soul, was the wife of the poor man about whose death she was reading. She was filled with the wonder of God, of life and death, of this world, of heaven and hell.

Tears formed in her eyes. Bridget Daugherty stopped reading. She had just read of the death of the father of the man in the parlor, the husband of poor Nora Ryan. She brushed her tears away and said a Hail Mary to the Blessed Virgin. She closed the book and set it on the little table to her right. Then she rose, looked at Nora Ryan, and walked around the front of the bed to the left side of the bed. She gently wiped Nora Ryan's lip with a small white towel that lay on the bed beside the pillows.

Nora Ryan's left eye opened. A frightened look appeared on her face.

"How are you, darling?" the nurse asked softly.

The fear left Nora Ryan's face.

"It's only me, Bridget Daugherty."

There was perspiration on Nora Ryan's face. Bridget Daugherty wiped it with the towel.

"We'll say our morning prayers, and then I'm going to clean you up, darling."

She knelt beside the bed and blessed herself.

II

By the time that Bridget Daugherty had finished bathing Nora Ryan and changing the sheets on her bed, Steve Ryan was up and dressed. He could wake up fresh and alert even after a few hours' sleep. As an intern, he had been called out at any and all hours, to see patients. He had had to be awake and on his toes.

Steve helped the nurses feed his mother. He looked in on her. He took her temperature, listened to her heartbeat, checked her blood pressure, timed her pulse, and gave her the injections that Dr. Evans ordered. He also kept the chart on his mother.

"Good morning, Miss Daugherty," Steve said as he walked into the bedroom.

"Good morning, Doctor. She had a restful night."

"Good."

He looked down at his mother on the bed. There was a catch in his throat. This was his mother.

"Hello, Mama," he said gently.

He thought that there was recognition in her face. There must be.

"We'll see how you are this morning, Mama," he said.

He took her pulse and listened to her heart. Shaking his head, he walked to the dresser and wrote on the chart.

He did not know how she continued to live. But it was not living.

"We'll feed her now, Miss Daugherty," Steve said.

"Yes, Doctor," Bridget Daugherty said.

III

A cold dawn was about to break over a cold January day. Clara was up, rubbing sleep from her eyes, and preparing her husband's breakfast.

Steve came out of his mother's bedroom.

"Good morning," he said cheerfully.

"Good morning, Steve. How's Mama?"

"Just about the same."

Clara poured coffee for him.

"Here's a cup of coffee while I'm fixing you some breakfast."

"Thanks, Clara."

"Oh, it's nothing."

Clara put bacon and two fried eggs on a plate and set it before a vacant chair.

The toast in the electric toaster popped up. Clara took the two slices and buttered them. She placed these on a saucer beside the plate. She was pouring a cup of coffee when Jack Boyle walked in.

"Good morning," he said.

"Your breakfast is ready, Jack."

"Good morning, Jack," Steve said.

"Good morning, Steve," Jack Boyle responded.

"How would you like your eggs, Steve?" Clara asked.

"The same as Jack's."

Clara broke two eggs into a frying pan. They immediately began to sizzle.

"How's Clara's mother this morning?" Jack Boyle asked.

"Pardon me, Steve, she's your mother too," Jack Boyle quickly corrected himself.

"That's all right, Jack. She's just about the same as she was yesterday."

"Jack, will you ask Bridget Daugherty if she wants breakfast now? I'm over Steve's eggs or I would."

Before Clara finished speaking Jack Boyle had gone into Nora Ryan's bedroom.

"Miss Daugherty, would you like some breakfast now?"

"Why, yes, Mr. Boyle, I was just coming out."

"How's Mrs. Ryan?"

"She rested comfortably," Bridget Daugherty said.

Standing near the bed, he stared down at Nora Ryan. His expression was intent, and there was awe in his face. In a few seconds he followed the nurse into the kitchen.

"How would you like your eggs, Bridget?"

"Fried, please, and turned right side up, Mrs. Boyle, if you will."

"Of course I will. I'll fry them any way you like."

"Thank you, Mrs. Boyle."

Clara served Steve his breakfast and then began fixing breakfast for the nurse.

IV

Eddie, in pajamas and bathrobe, came into the kitchen just as Jack Boyle was about to leave for work. Clara handed her husband his lunch box.

"Here's some coffee, Eddie," Clara said, placing a steaming cup of coffee before Eddie.

"Thanks, Clara."

"How's Mama this morning, Steve?" Eddie asked as he put cream and sugar into his coffee.

"The same, Eddie."

Eddie stirred his coffee.

"You like scrambled eggs, don't you, Eddie?" Clara asked.

"Yes, that's all right."

Clara was already scrambling eggs.

"Did you have a good night's sleep?" Steve asked.

Eddie raised his brows at his brother.

"No."

"Oh, I'm sorry, Eddie," Steve said.

"I don't know what there is to be sorry about," Eddie said.

"I thought maybe we kept you up late talking."

"Eddie can go to bed if he wants to," Clara said. "He's the one for staying up late and talking."

"I guess that's so. Oh well, I'm sorry that you didn't sleep, Eddie. But maybe you can go back and sleep after breakfast."

"I'm not complaining."

"Here's your breakfast, Eddie."

"You do need your proper rest, Eddie."

Eddie looked up from his plate.

"I never was a big sleeper, Steve."

"Hell, I don't know why I try to control you. Nothing is ever going to."

"I'm awake now," Eddie grinned.

V

"It's a mean day."

"I don't like this weather," Frances said.

"You're not used to it any more," Steve reminded her.

"It is a cold, mean day," Clara said.

"Days like this are one of the reasons I'm glad I live in California," Frances said.

"Well, I don't like it either."

"I know you don't, Clara."

"It's nothing like the blizzard we had up at Lake George in '93," Eddie said, looking up from the letter he was writing.

"That was a big blizzard, all right," Steve said.

"A big blizzard! Why, it was the biggest blizzard of the year, the biggest ever."

"What is this?" Frances asked, laughing.

"Why, Sis, it was the biggest blizzard ever. It was the Big Blizzard of '93. That was before you was born, Sis."

"You heard tell of it, didn't you, Sis?" Steve asked.

"I did hear tell of it," Frances said. "I've heard tell of it all my live-long life."

"Yes, we sure did a heap of shoveling in '93," Steve said.

"They called us the Snow Men of '93, and that's what we was, without no exaggerating," Eddie said.

"You must have gotten awfully tired, shoveling all that snow," Clara said.

"That ain't the half of it, Sis."

"Yes, sir, I do say. I say that unless you was full in the middle of the Big Blizzard of '93 you don't know what it was like. Well, that Big Blizzard was the Biggest Blizzard of 'em all," Eddie said.

"Well, I sure hope you're right," Steve said.

Frances and Clara were laughing. But suddenly the spirit of fun was gone. Eddie fell silent. Steve tried to think of something to say.

Clara looked out the window.

"It's a raw, mean, cold morning," she said.

VI

Dr. Evans came a few minutes before nine o'clock. Clara let him in.

"Here, Doctor, let me take your coat."

He let Clara Boyle help him with his overcoat. She hung it up and then took his hat. Dr. Evans knelt to remove his boots.

"I'll see your mother now," he said, rising.

"Yes, Doctor."

Dr. Evans went through the parlor.

"Hello, Dr. Evans," Eddie said.

Dr. Evans walked by as if he hadn't heard him.

Steve came in from the kitchen.

"Good morning, Dr. Evans."

"Good morning, Dr. Ryan."

"My mother is about the same, Doctor."

"I'll have a look at her."

They entered Nora Ryan's bedroom.

"Pneumonia. I was afraid this would happen," Dr. Evans said when they came out.

"Yes, Dr. Evans."

"This makes it so much the harder but we'll try everything we can."

"How's my mother, Dr. Evans?" Clara asked.

"She's developed pneumonia, Mrs. Ryan."

Clara drew her breath in.

"That makes it worse, doesn't it?"

"Yes, it does, but we'll do all in our power and I'll be back this afternoon, Mrs. Boyle."

"Thank you, Dr. Evans."

Steve walked with Dr. Evans to the front door.

VII

"Gee, I missed something," Steve said as he sat near Eddie on the couch.

Steve had just closed the door after Dr. Evans.

"What's that, Steve?"

"Mama's got pneumonia and I missed it."

"Well, there's no real harm done."

"I know, but I don't like missing something in a patient."

"You can't do anything about it now but try to learn from the error."

"You're right."

They sat for a minute or so.

"Well, I have to get a prescription filled. I'll ask Clara what drugstore to call."

VIII

"Like to take a walk, Eddie?"

"Where to, Steve?"

"Not far, to Halsted. There's a drugstore there and Clara says it's better to go and get the prescription filled than to have it delivered."

"All right, I'll go with you, Steve."

IX

They walked briskly. It was almost too cold for conversation.

"I don't know why in hell I agreed to come with you in this weather."

"And I don't know why I was determined to go get this prescription."

Eddie kept his head bent against the raw wind. His face and ears were stinging.

"Well, Eddie, Chicago is still the Windy City."

Eddie kept his head bent against the wind. They were close to Halsted Street now.

"The weather could be worse," Steve said.

"Correct," Eddie muttered.

They reached Halsted Street and entered the drugstore. It was warm. Steve went to the prescription counter.

"I'm Dr. Ryan," Steve told the pharmacist.

"Yes, Dr. Ryan," the pharmacist said, looking at the prescription Steve gave him.

"Steve, I'm going to have a cup of coffee," Eddie called.

Eddie went to the soda fountain and sat on a stool.

"Are you going to wait for this, Dr. Ryan?" the pharmacist asked.

"Yes, I'll wait."

"It'll take ten or fifteen minutes."

"That's all right. I'll be at the soda fountain."

"All right, I'll let you know when your prescription is ready."

Steve sat next to Eddie.

"May I have coffee and a doughnut?" Steve asked the middle-aged woman behind the fountain.

"Yes, sir."

"May I have some coffee?" Eddie asked.

"Of course, dear," the woman said.

"We'll have a short wait," Steve said.

"I don't care if it's a long wait. I'm not looking forward to going back out in that."

The waitress returned with their coffee.

"Thank you," Eddie said to the waitress.

"You're welcome, dear."

"I don't understand how Mama hangs on," Steve began.

"She wants to live, Steve."

He took a sip of coffee and lit a cigarette.

"Yes, that could be. Of course, we don't know how much she knows."

"I did tell her to squeeze my hand once for 'Yes' and twice for 'No,' and asked her if she knew that I was Eddie. She squeezed once."

"That could be," Steve said.

He took a drink of coffee.

"That isn't conclusive, of course," Steve said.

"I know it isn't, Steve."

"We have no way of knowing what goes on in her mind. There are all kinds of possibilities as to how aware she might be of what's going on around her. I think she knows who we are. She knows I'm her son Steve." He took another drink of coffee.

"But I can't really be sure," he added.

Eddie finished his cup of coffee.

"You know, Eddie, I really don't know if we can say that she does know. Mama could have all sorts of impressions and fantasies about what's going on. She could be hallucinating."

The pharmacist tapped him on the shoulder.

"Dr. Ryan, I have your prescription ready."

"Thank you, I'll be right over."

Eddie picked up the check for the coffee, took a dollar bill out of his wallet, and laid it on the counter. The waitress took the bill and went to the cash register and in a moment returned with the change.

"Here you are, dear."

Eddie left a quarter on the counter.

"Thank you, dear." She smiled.

"Thank you," Steve said, awkwardly sliding off his stool.

"Oh, you're both welcome," she said.

Eddie followed Steve across the drugstore to the prescription counter to pay for the prescription. The walk back wouldn't be as bad; the wind would be at their backs.

X

Frances looked out the window. The day continued cold and dark. She had forgotten about the winter weather in Chicago. It was all the more depressing with Mama dying. Poor Mama. She didn't know what kind of weather there was. She had never felt this sad before.

"What are you doing, Franny?" Steve asked.

"Looking out the window."

"There isn't much to see."

"No, I guess not," Frances said, turning away from the window.

There was a thin little defensive smile on her lips. Steve dropped into a chair. Frances sat on the big couch. Steve let out a big yawn.

"I guess I'm kind of tired."

He stretched his arms above his head and yawned a second time.

"Why don't you go to sleep then?"

"I was thinking about it."

"You ought to. You really look tired, Steve."

"I am." Steve yawned again.

"You won't miss anything if you take a nap."

Steve looked at her, surprised.

"You're afraid that you'll miss something that's happening or being said, aren't you, Steve?"

"Well, I don't want to miss anything interesting."

Frances laughed.

"You're funny."

"Well, do you want to miss anything?"

"To be honest, no."

Steve suddenly became serious.

"Well, you know, Frances, I am in analysis."

It was Frances' turn to be surprised but she said nothing.

"And," he continued, "I don't want to miss anything that might be of importance to me in my analysis."

"Well, I don't know much about psychoanalysis," Frances began.

"It's wonderful. Everybody ought to have the benefit of it."

"Do you really believe that, Steve?"

"Yes, I do."

Then:

"No, I don't mean exactly that. What I mean is that I think everybody, or almost everybody, could get some benefit from analysis were they to go into it."

"If that's the case, shouldn't everyone be psychoanalyzed?"

"Well, yes and no."

"That's what I don't understand. How can the answer be yes and no?"

"Well, I said that I thought everyone, but I don't mean everyone, I mean almost everyone would benefit from analysis."

Frances looked at him, still puzzled.

"Let me explain what I mean, Franny."

"I certainly will let you explain."

"Everybody wouldn't go. And even if everybody wanted to, there wouldn't be enough psychoanalysts to go around."

He paused.

"Well now, to continue, a lot of people have never been to an analyst. But they manage to get along all right. They function."

"Do they need to go to a psychoanalyst?"

"No, they don't," Steve answered.

"Now you're contradicting yourself."

"No, I'm not, Franny."

"Yes, you are."

"Not at all," Steve said.

"How aren't you?"

"Well, I said that almost everybody could benefit from analysis. But it's obvious that people can get along and function without it. Now isn't that clear enough?"

"Yes, I guess so."

XI

Steve felt uneasy. He was building up anxiety. Of course, he ought to expect this. He should be able to handle his anxieties.

He laughed nervously. Then he recognized that his laugh had been compulsive. After all, Franny was the one who had pushed him off Mama's lap. And this had been traumatic for him. It had come up again and again in his analysis. Franny had been the new baby. And she was a girl. A cute little girl. She had gotten all of the attention. He could realize now, many years after the fact, that he had had an infantile regression after Franny was born. For a while he had reverted to bed-wetting. He could still remember Mama calling him "pisspot."

He was inclined to think that this must have had a traumatic effect on him.

XII

Eddie had finished correcting the last proofs on his novel, *Bernard Cleary*. It was a relief. He didn't like correcting proofs. But this was the last work to be done on the book. And now it was finished.

Steve walked in.

"Well, Eddie . . ."

"Yes?"

Steve blinked at him.

"You seem happy about something, the way you're grinning."

"I am; I've just finished correcting the last of the proofs on *Bernard Cleary*."

"Congratulations!"

"Thanks; I hate correcting proofs and I'm always glad when I've finished."

"I can see why."

For a second Steve resented the fact that Eddie had finished work on another book. He hoped to hell this wasn't Edward A. Ryan's exposé of the Ryans. Of course, he understood what Eddie was trying to do. Eddie was an artist. And even though some of the characters and situations in his books were based on members of the family and things that had happened, Eddie was not a newspaperman. He added lots of things. An artist had a right to do this. But it certainly made it hard for the rest of them when they tried to explain this. It was no wonder that there was resentment mixed in with his pride. And there might even be some sibling rivalry mixed up with it. If so, he would have to overcome it in the course of his analysis.

Should he talk it over with Eddie? Sure. Eddie might be interested. Steve opened his mouth to speak.

"Well, what are you two talking about?" Frances asked, joining them.

"Oh, we're just talking," Steve said. "Eddie has just finished correcting the proofs of his new novel, *Bernard Cleary*."

Frances looked at Eddie. He grinned at her.

He couldn't say anything about sibling envy now.

XIII

Snow flurries were being tossed about carelessly by the wind in the darkness outside.

Eddie looked out the window. How depressing the weather looked. And in this home the atmosphere was even more depressing. There was no immediate escape. He was being held here by a morbid fascination. He had thought of going out today but there wasn't any place that he really wanted to go, nothing that he really wanted to do, and no one he wanted to see.

He turned from the window and sat down on the couch. He lit a cigarette. His mother was dying. Her life was ending in hopeless death. All lives ended in hopeless death. Death was the end of consciousness. Freud had declared that no one can imagine his own death. This was true. Thinking of death, you were in fact envisioning yourself dead while you were still alive and knew it. You were aware of your own consciousness. You couldn't be dead until you were dead. And once you were dead, you wouldn't know it. If you did, you were alive, not dead.

Eddie snuffed out his cigarette, stood up, and returned to the window. Lights shone in the window across the street. A sudden gust of wind rattled the panes. He turned away and lit another cigarette.

XIV

The wind was stronger now and the thermometer had dropped.

The doorbell rang. Frances and Steve both started to get up.

"I'll get it," Clara called from the kitchen.

They heard her "Hello" as she opened the door. Then Harry Landry and his mother entered.

Michael Landry had been upstairs with his cousin Eddie Boyle. Hearing his father's voice, he rushed downstairs. Hazel Landry bent down and hugged her grandson.

"Hello, Harry, how are you?" Eddie Ryan asked.

"I'm fine, Eddie, and yourself?"

"Good."

Harry turned and said hello to the others.

"How do you do, Mrs. Landry," Eddie said to Hazel.

"Hello, Eddie."

They shook hands.

Harry and his mother sat.

"It's nasty out, isn't it, Hazel?" Clara asked.

"How is your mother, Steve?" Harry asked.

"Oh yes, it's mean and cold all right, Clara," Hazel answered.

"Well, Harry, she's no better and no worse," Steve said to Harry.

"I can tell that it's gotten meaner in the last couple of hours," Clara said.

"God, it's too bad," Harry said. "I always liked your mother very much."

"It did get worse in the last couple of hours, Clara."

"Hello, Frances," Harry said.

"Hello again, Harry."

"I know, Harry, and my mother liked you too," Steve told him.

"Yes, that's true, Harry," Frances said.

"Well, thank you both for telling me that," Harry said.

"The cold just bites into you," Hazel said, "and the wind makes it worse."

"Well, they call Chicago the Windy City." Clara smiled.

"And truly so, if you ask me." Hazel smiled back.

"I think you know how sad I feel about your mother, Steve," Harry said.

"Well, it has to get warmer sooner or later," Clara said to Hazel Landry.

"I think that we all understand, Harry," Steve said.

"I'll take it sooner rather than later," Hazel said.

Clara was laughing.

"I'll take the sooner too, Hazel, and I say the sooner the better."

"Well, Harry," Steve said, "these things happen."

"Well, I wouldn't mind being in some Florida sunshine now," Hazel Landry said.

"The real tragedy of man, I mean, no, the primary tragedy of man is his biological tragedy," Eddie said.

"That's true, Eddie," Steve nodded.

"But it's not the only tragedy," Harry Landry added.

"I didn't mean that it was, or is," Eddie said.

"Maybe I'll go to Florida a little later on in this year," Hazel said.

"You people can have Florida all you want," Frances said. "As for myself, I'll stick by California."

"Listen, I've got nothing against California," Clara said. "If you can convince Jack Boyle to go to California, I'll start singing, 'California, Here We Come' right away."

There were smiles around the parlor but they were restrained, and wan. Smiling seemed out of place at this time in this room with Nora Ryan just a few feet away dying.

"I've never been to California, but I can't conceive of myself as liking it as much as I like Florida," Hazel said.

"And it's just the opposite with me," Frances said. "I've never been to Florida, but I can't imagine myself liking it as much as I like California."

"Well, there you are," Clara said. "That's what makes horse racing."

"Yes, but it's not always what wins you money on horse races," Harry laughed.

"Well, I never bet on horse races," Steve said.

"You're better off for it, Steve," Harry said.

"Yes, Steve, with your kind of luck, you'd be in a bad way if you were a horse track gambler," Frances said.

"Don't worry, Hattie would see to it that he wouldn't become a gambler even if he was inclined that way," Clara said.

"You don't gamble much, do you, Eddie?"

"No, I don't. I once had the goofy notion that I could break a slot machine, when I knew I couldn't. I put twenty-five dollars' worth of quarters in. It was in Florida," Eddie said.

"Well, that speaks well for California," Steve laughed.

Eddie laughed.

A car door slammed. They heard Jack Boyle saying good-by to his co-workers.

"Here's Jack," Clara said.

XV

"That goddamned lunatic has killed another girl."

Jack Boyle stood in the doorway, his voice loud with indignation.

"What do you mean, Jack?" Clara asked.

"That crazy lunatic killer, he killed another girl this morning. Here it is, in the afternoon paper."

He held up a newspaper.

"Oh, I can't believe it," Clara exclaimed.

"That's four women," Jack said, anger in his voice. He held the newspaper up and then handed it to Eddie Ryan.

Eddie read:

MADMAN SLAYS FOURTH VICTIM

He held the newspaper out to Steve.

"I'd go out looking for this wild bastard," Jack Boyle was saying.

"They've got to catch him," Clara said. "My gosh, this makes four that he killed."

"And the way he does it; it makes you sick to read about it." Jack made a face.

"What was her name?" Hazel asked.

"Florence, she was called Flor, Flo—what's her last name, Steve?" Jack asked.

"What did you say?" Steve asked, looking up from the newspaper.

"What's the name of this girl that was murdered?"

Steve pushed his glasses up on his nose and looked at the newspaper.

"Florence, Flo Moscowitz."

"Poor girl," Clara said.

"This one was on the North Side," Steve told her.

"I don't want him coming to the South Side," Clara said.

"Yes, somebody should get arrested on the North Side," Frances said.

"I hope he's caught before he can kill any other women," Jack said.

"It doesn't say that all the murders were definitely committed by the same person, does it?" Harry Landry asked.

"No, it can't say that, because they ain't caught him," Jack said. "But the police seem pretty sure that it's the same guy that's committed all four."

"It must be the same guy. The murders are too much alike and there's the writing on the walls with the blood of each of his victims," Steve said.

"Are you through with the paper, Steve?" Harry asked.

"Here," Steve said, handing him the newspaper. "I'm through with it."

"Thanks." Harry reached forward to take it.

Jack unbuttoned his Mackinaw coat and went back by the front door to hang it up and to take off his rubbers.

"This is disgusting. It makes you ill," Harry said, dropping the newspaper on the floor.

"I want to see it," Clara said, picking it up.

She began to read.

Steve turned to Eddie:

"You know, some of the people walking around shouldn't be allowed to walk around, free. Watch and see, when they catch this killer, I'll bet you that he's been in a mental institution."

"Well, why are they released if they're crazy and going to kill innocent people?" Clara asked.

She put the newspaper down beside her on the couch in disgust.

"Sometimes the courts let them loose," Steve answered.

"How come?" Jack asked, sitting down.

"They get sprung on writs of habeas corpus," Steve said. "In Washington there are lawyers who make a living springing psychotics on writs of habeas corpus."

"That oughtn't be allowed," Clara protested.

"I agree with you," Steve said. "But often a judge gives short shrift to a psychiatrist testifying that some psychotic patient ought not to be let out."

"That's not right." Clara shook her head.

"I agree with you," Steve said. "But the courts wouldn't agree with me on some of the cases where I think a patient shouldn't be released. There was one case where a lawyer got a patient out on a writ of habeas corpus, and he took the patient to stay out on his farm. The patient killed the lawyer."

"He deserved it," Jack said. But then he corrected himself. "No, no man deserves to be killed. But it must go to show how lawyers who do them things are wrong."

"Oh, God, I hope the police get the man who's killed the four girls before he kills any more," Clara said.

"He'll be caught; I'm sure of that," Steve said. "But the question is —when?"

"That's it, Steve, when will he be caught?" Jack asked.

"I hope it's soon," Clara said. "Why, it's terrible to think that he's already killed four innocent girls."

"I agree," Steve said.

No one spoke for a moment. The murder of Florence Moscowitz had depressed them even more. None of them had heard of her until they read the paper that Jack brought in. But they had followed the stories. In all four instances, the girls had had their clothes torn off and had been raped. Then the victims had been hacked and sliced. Their blood had been used as ink to write messages on the walls. It shocked them to read these details. They were already shocked by their mother's stroke and her grotesque appearance. They were all living with death. The murders disgusted them.

XVI

Jack Boyle went to the basement to tend to the furnace. There was no sense in getting mad with the Ryans. None of them meant to be trouble but the truth was that none of them even thought of givin' him a hand by takin' care of the furnace. That was the trouble with them. They didn't think about things like that. But they'd think about it if there was no heat. They'd think about the furnace then, all right.

As he walked up the stairs, he was depressed. There were so many people in his home, and they had been here for so long. He couldn't throw them out, the old lady was dyin'. But he sure felt like it. After so many days and nights, he couldn't help feelin' like it.

—Goddamnit!

He felt lousy. They were all sittin' around in his parlor. He didn't feel like talkin' and he didn't feel like listenin' to their goddamned talk. He was tired.

"Clara, I'm goin' to sleep for an hour or so," he called to his wife.

He tramped upstairs to the bedroom they shared.

XVII

"Oh, Eddie, I didn't tell you about Leo," Steve said. "Last night I needed a pencil, something to write with, so I asked Leo to lend me his. Well, he handed me his Eversharp pencil. I tried to write with it and the damned thing wouldn't write."

Jack Boyle came into the room. Steve noticed him but went on talking.

"The damned pencil wouldn't write so I asked Leo what was the matter with it. Leo said, 'Oh, I forgot, there's no lead in my pencil.' "

Jack Boyle broke into a laugh.

"So Leo says he didn't have lead in his pencil?"

Steve was almost bent over laughing. They all joined him. Jack Boyle's mood had lightened.

XVIII

"Here he is," Jack Boyle said, preceding Leo and Florence into the dining room where everyone was eating supper.

"Did you two eat yet?" Clara asked.

"Oh yes, we had our supper," Leo told her.

"Yes, we ate," Florence nodded.

"Well, you can have some coffee and cake with us."

"No, I don't think I could eat any cake now," Florence said, "but thank you just the same."

"I'll have some coffee, Sis."

"Would you like some too, Florence?" Clara asked, getting up.

"All right, I'll have a cup, thank you, Clara."

Jack Boyle had sat back down to eat. He jumped up:

"Here, I'll get you chairs."

"Thanks, Jack. That's all right; I can get them myself," Leo said.

But Jack Boyle had already gone to a corner and gotten two straight-back chairs. Steve and Eddie moved their chairs down first; then Harry Landry and his mother moved theirs to make room for the two additional places.

Clara came back from the kitchen carrying two cups of hot coffee. She placed them in front of Florence and Leo. They thanked her.

"Say, Leo, what's this I hear about you?" Jack Boyle asked.

"What do you mean?" Leo smiled.

Florence looked at Jack with curiosity.

Eddie and Steve turned toward Leo.

"I been hearing things, Leo."

"Like what?"

"I heard that you were complainin' about no lead in your pencil."

Steve and Eddie burst into laughter. The front doorbell rang.

Jack, Molly Ryan, and their son Andy arrived. They could hear the laughing as they walked through the dining room and went straight into Nora Ryan's bedroom.

Nora Ryan's right eye remained open and motionless. It was disconcerting and eerie. Andy wished he could get out of the room but he was afraid to say so. His grandma was dying. He didn't know much about death but he didn't want his grandmother to die. If she was going to, though, he wished she'd hurry up and get it over with.

Jack and Molly stood with bowed heads for a minute.

They left the bedroom after saying silent prayers. Andy was glad to get out of the room. The laughter was dying down in the dining room when they entered. Andy asked Aunt Clara where Eddie Boyle was.

"In his room with Michael."

Andy ran out of the dining room up the stairs. Clara asked her brother and his wife Molly if they would like some coffee and cake. Jack Ryan said he didn't care if he did. Molly said that she would too if it was no trouble. Clara said that it was no trouble. She got up to go to the kitchen. Cecilia Moran stood up and excused herself. She went into Nora Ryan's bedroom. Molly took her place and her husband went to get another chair. The table had fallen into silence. Molly wondered if it was because of her and Jack. It must be. They had all stopped talking the minute she and Jack came to the table.

Clara came back from the kitchen with the coffee and cake.

XIX

They were still sitting around the dining-room table when Uncle Dick and Aunt Jenny arrived.

"Tom Clarkson died," Jenny announced.

"Who's he?" Steve asked.

"Won't you get chairs and sit down," Clara invited.

"He was a police sergeant and a cousin on Mother's—my grandmother's side," Eddie said.

"Oh yes, I remember," Clara said.

"I knew him," Eddie told her.

"Of course you knew him," Jenny snapped.

"I remember him too," Jack Ryan said.

"Sure you would remember. He was at the police station on State Street for years."

"I remember going to see him where there was a warrant sworn out for George Raymond," Eddie said. "George had a brutal fight with a fellow named Bill Pfeister and had beat hell out of him. A warrant was sworn out for George and I went around to see Tom Clarkson about it."

"Did he do anything, Eddie?" Jack Ryan asked.

"He said that if the person for whom the warrant had been sworn wasn't at the given address they wouldn't be able to find him."

"In other words, he told you not to worry?" Jack Boyle asked.

"That was just about it."

Jack Boyle laughed.

"And he was your cousin?" he asked.

"Yes."

"He was my mother's second cousin," Dick explained.

"That makes him our fourth cousin," Eddie added.

"Tom Clarkson was a good man," Jenny interrupted.

"Then why was he a cop?" Steve asked.

"Somebody has to be a cop, Steve," Jack Ryan said.

"That's true, Steve," Jack Boyle said.

"But I don't have to like him," Steve said.

"It's no skin off his nose now if you don't like him; he's dead," Jack Boyle said.

"Well, I say, may the Lord have mercy on his soul," Jack Ryan said.

Eddie noticed that Frances made a face. The Clarksons meant nothing to her.

"Do you want a cup of coffee, Aunt Jenny?" Clara asked.

"Let me get it myself."

"I'll get it. You sit down."

"Let me get it," Jenny insisted.

They both went to the kitchen.

XX

After doing the dishes, Clara went into her mother's bedroom. She stood looking down at her tenderly.

Poor Mama, Clara kept thinking. It made her sad. She wished this hadn't happened. She certainly hoped it would never happen to her.

She never wanted to die. But what good did it do you to wish that? Everyone had to die someday. But she didn't have to go yet. This was some consolation. One could never tell, though. You could drop dead any minute. She didn't think she would, not any time soon. Mama could die the very next minute. There was nothing that could be done to prevent it.

Clara went to the parlor and sat down. Everybody was sitting around looking sad. Mama's death was affecting all of them. Her husband Jack was affected too. It was affecting him a lot more than he would admit. He didn't say much but she knew her Jack and he was feeling it all right. But why wouldn't he? Mama had lived with them. They would be the ones who felt it the most.

"You know Mama was no trouble at all," Clara said.

"I'll second that," Jack nodded. "Most of the time we didn't even know she was in the house."

"Mama never interfered," Clara added.

"I wanted her to come to California and stay with us," Frances said.

"We tried to get her to go, Frances, but she wouldn't. Mama had never been out of Chicago and she was afraid to go that far."

"I understand, Clara."

"Yes, Ma wouldn't travel," Jack Ryan said.

"I know," Frances said.

"Well, it's only natural for Mama to be afraid to leave Chicago. She knows her way around here. Everything is familiar. And her brother and sister are here, her friends, friends she's known for years." Clara's voice trailed off.

"It's understandable," Frances said.

"I wanted her to come live with us in Washington," Steve said.

"She didn't want to move. As long as she lived here, she knew that Clara and me wouldn't ask her to do any work. She had worked hard all her life, raised her family; she didn't want any more work and she was afraid that if she went anywheres else she might have to work hard."

"I didn't invite her to Washington to put her to work at the house," Steve said; his voice was defensive.

"I didn't say you did, Steve. I was just telling you the way your mother figured it."

"Mama was a wise one," Steve laughed.

"Oh yes, she was." Clara smiled.

"She used to say, 'There's no flies on me, I'll have you know,'" Eddie reminded them.

"I heard her say that lots of times," Jack Boyle said.

The talk soothed Clara. It was making things easier for her.

"We're all going to miss her," Leo commented.

"You can say that for me too," Jack Boyle said.

"I'll miss her like I'd miss my right arm," Jenny said.

Her words came as a surprise. She had been sitting in silence as the others talked. When she spoke, it reminded them that she too had feelings and that she was sad over the approaching death of her sister. No one spoke for a moment. Then Dick said:

"Your mother was a saintly woman."

"She certainly was," Jack Ryan said.

"Yes, she was," Dick repeated.

"Mama was good," Clara nodded.

"Your mother, my sister Nora, was a walking saint all of her life," Aunt Jenny exclaimed and then broke into sobs.

XXI

The others were in the kichen. Leo joined Steve and Eddie in the parlor.

"I don't think Mama was a good mother," Leo said.

Eddie and Steve were silent.

"What made you come to that conclusion?" Steve asked.

"I was thinkin' how they was sayin' that Mama was so good and that Mama was a saint. Maybe Mama was saintly; she did a lot of prayin' and church goin' but she wasn't a good mother."

"Why wasn't she?" Steve asked.

Leo didn't answer instantly. He sat, looking off into space. Then: "Do you think she was, Steve?"

"She was an ignorant mother . . ." Steve began.

"Well, that's what I mean, I guess."

"Is that what you mean by saying she wasn't a good mother?"

"Well, she was ignorant. And that made her a bad mother."

"Is that the only reason you think she was a bad mother, Leo?"

"No, she was bad and she was ignorant. I mean I think that there are more reasons for her being a bad mother than just her ignorance."

"That's what I was trying to find out," Steve said.

"Well, did you?" Leo demanded.

"Don't take it so to heart, Leo. I didn't mean anything hostile."

"I'm not hostile."

"I want to find out for myself as much as for you."

"Well, I don't know anything about psychoanalysis."

Jack Boyle walked in and sat down. He watched Leo and Steve closely.

"I only have my own experience and common sense to go on," Leo added.

"That's plenty," Steve told him.

"Oh, I don't know, Steve. I don't know if I even meant what I said or not."

Florence and Clara walked in.

"Let's drop it, Steve."

"Well, what's going on?" Clara asked.

"Oh, we were just talking," Leo answered.

"Can we join you in just talking?"

XXII

The wind charged against the windowpanes.

"It's a cold night," Jack Ryan said.

"You picketing tonight, Jack?" Leo asked Jack Boyle.

"Yeah."

"It must be tough, huh, Jack?" Harry Landry asked.

"Oh, it ain't too bad."

"I wish the strike would end," Clara said.

"You and me and thousands of other May Motors' workers," Jack Boyle said.

"And thousands of wives of May Motors' workers," Clara added.

"It'll be settled sooner or later," Leo said.

"Yes," Jack Boyle agreed, "but there can be a lot of difference between sooner and later."

"A strike ain't no picnic," Jack Ryan said.

"You said it," Jack Boyle nodded.

"This union has to win this strike," Eddie stated.

"But the way it's dragging, nobody can win," Leo argued.

"May Motors will know if it wins," Eddie said.

"Eddie's right," Jack Boyle said. "The union has to make some kind of gain. We got to get a wage increase."

"You can't get enough of an increase to make up for what you've lost," Leo countered.

"I know that."

"Well, that's all I was saying."

"We're in for a wave of strikes," Eddie warned.

"Yes, we are, they've already begun," Jack Boyle nodded.

"If Jack's union should take a licking," Eddie explained, "there will be a crackdown against others."

"That's true," Jack Boyle said.

"Yes, I can see that," Clara said.

"Oh, we're gonna get something," Jack Boyle said.

"You're not gonna get as much as you're demanding," Leo said.

"You never do. That's why you demand more."

"That makes sense," Steve said.

"Yeah," Jack Boyle went on, "if you ask for what you want and start negotiatin', you're in a position where you can't come down. But when you ask for more than you expect, management can say that they'll give you this much, that they're willing to give you that, if you take less. That's why we ask for more so we can negotiate."

"How much do you think that you will get, Jack?" Leo asked.

"Maybe we'll get between twenty-five and thirty-five cents an hour."

"I sure would like to see Jack get about twenty dollars a week more," Clara said.

"It'll come to more than that," Jack Boyle said, "because of overtime. And we'll have lots of overtime because of the strike and the orders. Our plant's got orders that run way into 1950 and later. We got at least seven years of orders to fill."

"Ain't that good?" Steve asked.

Clara and Eddie looked toward the door. Uncle Dick and Aunt Jenny were sitting listening. They looked as though they were anxious to speak. Eddie and Clara smiled at each other. They remembered how, when they had been kids living with the Dunnes, Uncle Dick had always harped when one of them used the word "ain't."

"The way I see it, strikes are not beneficial for either the worker or the management," Uncle Dick said.

"Not unless they are decisively won or lost," Eddie said.

"If common sense were used, there wouldn't be strikes," Aunt Jenny added.

"Yeah, if common sense were used, there wouldn't be lots of things," Leo said.

"I suppose so," Jack Boyle agreed, "but I don't know. It's dog eat dog."

"Does it have to be?" Steve asked.

"I think so, I think it's human nature," Leo answered.

"I agree with that," Jack Boyle added.

"It's a tough life if you don't weaken," Jack Ryan said.

"Oh, I think people should be kind and feel gratitude," Aunt Jenny said.

She was ignored.

XXIII

"Cecilia Moran is ready to leave now, Leo," Clara announced.

He was in the parlor with the rest of the family.

"All right, Clara, I'll drive her home."

He looked over at Florence. It was almost ten o'clock. Bridget Daugherty had come to take over. Aunt Jenny was staring at him. Leo ignored the stare.

"You go, Leo, I'll wait here," Florence said.

"You don't have to worry, Florence, Leo's got no lead in his pencil," Steve teased.

"That's all you know with your psychiatry," Leo retorted.

"Well, you said so yourself."

"I'm not worried," Florence said.

"Good for you, Florence," Frances laughed.

Molly looked at both Leo and Florence with disapproval.

Cecilia Moran walked in with her coat on. She looked tired.

"Are you ready, Miss Moran?" Leo asked her.

"Yes, I am, Mr. Ryan."

"I'll get my coat and we'll go."

"Be careful of him, Cecilia," Steve said.

"Oh, Dr. Ryan, you're a card," Cecilia Moran said.

"See, Steve, it's you, not Leo, that she's got eyes for," Jack Boyle said. "It's you that's got to be watched."

"I don't know about that."

"We all know that it's Eddie who interests Cecilia," Clara said, looking at the nurse.

"Well, I do like his books."

Leo came back with his coat on and fedora hat in his hand.

"Leo's ready, Cecilia," Steve said.

"Well, I don't know if any of you men would be safe with me if you were around for long," Cecilia laughed.

"Did you hear that?" Jack Boyle asked.

"We heard it," Frances said.

"Well, good night," Cecilia Moran said.

She and Leo left the house.

XXIV

"If Cecilia Moran wants to protect herself, Eddie's the one she'd have to watch."

This fell as a surprise among them.

"Why, Frances," Clara protested.

"Well, it's true. Ask Steve if it isn't."

"That's putting me on the spot."

"Then ask Eddie himself," Frances said.

Eddie tried to look impassive but he started to grin.

"I wouldn't put it past myself," he laughed.

"Well, Eddie, I don't know that I'd put it past me, either," Jack Boyle said.

"Oh, let him talk," Clara said jokingly.

"Of course, let me talk."

"Well, I do, don't I?"

"You better."

Dick Dunne disapproved of the conversation. So did Jenny. Several times they leaned toward each other whispering.

"Eddie," Jack Boyle called.

"Yes, Jack?"

"How do you like that? Clara lets me talk."

"Well, doesn't the Constitution say that you have a right to free speech? I believe in the Constitution of my country," Clara laughed.

"Well, so do I," Jack Boyle said.

"So there's no argument."

There were more laughs.

"She'll watch you, all right, Jack," Steve called over to his brother-in-law.

"Who wouldn't? Gorgeous Jack Boyle, you're darned right, I'll watch him."

Jack Boyle grinned.

"Clara, tell me that again, I like hearing it," he said.

"Gorgeous Jack Boyle," Clara repeated.

"Hear that, everybody?" Jack Boyle asked.

Jenny Dunne started to speak but Dick shushed her.

The telephone rang.

"I'll get it," Clara said, getting up.

XXV

For a while they had been gay. The gaiety had ended. Jack Boyle was ready to leave for the May Motors picket line. He had just put his coat on when a car honked outside. Leo had returned after driving Cecilia Moran home.

"See," he said, "I timed it just right."

"Yes, you did, Jack," Clara said.

Jack Boyle said good-by and left. In a moment a car could be heard starting up. A motor was heard very briefly, and then was lost in the night.

"Is it cold out, Leo?" Eddie asked.

"Yeah, Eddie, pretty cold."

"I was just thinking about that and poor Jack having to go out and picket," Clara said.

"I can tell you, it ain't any fun picketing in cold weather. It's the same as workin'," Jack Ryan said.

"Well, at least Jack is warmly dressed," Clara said a little sadly.

"Eddie?" Aunt Jenny called.

Eddie looked at her.

"Dick and I are going to Tom Clarkson's wake tomorrow night. Are you going to go tomorrow night too?" Aunt Jenny asked. "We were thinking it would be nice if you went with us."

"No, I'm not going, Aunt Jenny," Eddie said.

Her face fell.

"Oh, Eddie, it would be a nice action to perform to pay your last respects to Tom Clarkson," Dick urged.

"I'm sorry but I'm not going, Uncle Dick."

"Mother liked Tom Clarkson," Aunt Jenny said. "She would have liked it if everybody went to his wake."

No one spoke.

"And your mother was fond of Tom Clarkson. She would have gone if she were able to."

"We know that, Aunt Jen," Clara said.

"Ma never missed a wake if she could help it," Leo said.

"She always liked to go and pray for the dear departed," Molly Ryan added.

Eddie remembered the wake for Molly's mother. That had been years ago but he still remembered the terrible sadness of that night in a West Side funeral parlor. The sadness of life was infinite, he thought.

Chapter 28

I

It was late.

"Watch your footing, Jenny."

Dick Dunne gripped her elbow.

"You too, Dick."

How would she take care of him if he fell and broke his hip?

"I am, Jenny."

They turned the corner and lowered their heads against the wind. It blew around their coats and slapped against their faces. Their eyes watered.

"Oh, it's so cold," Jenny said, almost with a sob.

"We're halfway to the next corner, Jenny."

"I hope we don't miss a streetcar."

"I don't hear one."

They reached the corner. They hadn't missed a car, thank the Lord.

"Oh, Dick, I can't stand it if one doesn't come soon."

Tears from the cold streamed down her face.

"Stand in the doorway, Jen."

They both stepped into the entrance way of the liquor store. There were no lights within the store and the area was dark. A man of medium height neared them. Dick eyed him closely. He tensed his arms. If the man tried anything with Jenny, he would give his life if necessary to protect her. The man stopped.

"You folks been waiting long?" he asked.

"No, sport, just a minute or two," Dick told him. "One ought to be coming along soon."

"I sure hope so," the man said.

Two young black men with bushy hair rounded the corner. The three of them watched with apprehension. The young blacks passed and crossed Garfield Boulevard.

"Thank heavens, here's the streetcar."

There was relief in her voice.

II

—Home, sweet home, Jenny thought.

Dick opened the door, turned on the hall light, and walked inside. Jenny followed him. He closed the door gently. It was late and he didn't want to wake up any neighbors. Jenny preceded him into the dining room and snapped on the light. Dick took off his coat, hung it in the hall closet, and put his hat on the shelf. Rubbing his hands together, he went into the dining room.

"Here, Jen, let me take your coat."

"You don't have to bother, Dick."

"It's no bother, Princess," he said, helping her slide her arms from the sleeves.

He took her coat and hung it in the front hall closet and came back.

"Do you want a cup of tea, Dick, or a glass of warm milk?"

"No, thank you, Princess."

She had had enough of this princess stuff but she was too tired to quarrel with him about it.

"I'm tired too."

"We had better turn in, Jen."

"I guess so."

He could tell that she was sad. This troubled him.

"Don't be sad, Princess."

"Oh, Dick, how can I help it?"

Dick lifted his left hand in caution.

"I didn't mean to upset you; I know how you feel."

—How can you know how I feel?

"I'm too tired to talk, Dick."

"You get some rest."

"You need your rest too. You're no longer a young man."

He wished she didn't talk about his age so often but she was concerned, he imagined. Especially now with Nora dying. And the Ryans behaving as they were. Poor Jen probably realized that he was all she had left. Just as she was all that was left for him.

III

Before getting into bed, Dick Dunne knelt to say his evening prayers. He blessed himself and said some Hail Marys for Nora. Then he said prayers for Jenny. He said a prayer for all of the dead in his family, one for himself, blessed himself, rose from his knees, and climbed into bed. He would fall asleep now thinking good thoughts.

IV

Dick was a loud snorer. Always had been. Jenny heard his snoring. He never had any trouble sleeping. The minute his head hit the bed, he fell asleep. Well, she couldn't sleep. She had slept for a little while but she was awake now. It was still dark outside, so it was still night. How long had she slept? She hoped it was for hours. She didn't want to get out of her warm bed to find out what time it was but she wished she knew. She could still hear the wind outside. Oh, she was glad to be in her warm bed. She wished she could go back to sleep. God, Dick slept like a log. No matter what happened, he could sleep. Why couldn't she sleep like that? But how could she, with him snoring all night?

V

The ash trays were filled with cigarette butts, some of them half-smoked. The apartment was cold. Wearing a sweater too big for her, Jenny was playing solitaire. She had to do something or she'd go crazy. How could she be expected to sleep with Dick snoring so loud? She couldn't close his bedroom door. After all, he wasn't a young man any more. He'd be seventy-five and he could have a heart attack or a stroke. She had to leave her bedroom door open and his too. With both doors between them closed, he could die in the darkness with no one to come to him should he call for help, no one to make him comfortable, call the doctor, maybe get an ambulance to take him to a hospital in time to save his life. She wouldn't let her brother die like a dog in the darkness in the middle of the night while she slept. What would people say?

But, my God, he made more noise snoring than a furnace. He could wake the dead.

There was no end to what she had to endure. Her poor sister Nora was dying and she wasn't even allowed to be at her bedside. She brushed the cards aside. She couldn't keep her mind on a game of solitaire. She hadn't always lived the way she had to live now. Oh, God, would she get any sleep at all? It was so cold; she was chilled to the bone. She would just have to try to sleep. She couldn't get sick now; too much depended on her. She would have to try to get some sleep. Oh, it was cold, she was shivering. Why didn't he stop snoring?

Chapter 29

I

"That was Aunt Jenny on the phone," Clara said.

"Yes? What's on her mind?" Steve asked.

They were in the kitchen.

"She and Dick can't come over until late tonight."

"Is something the matter?"

"How can you tell with her and Uncle Dick?"

"Well, I hope she's all right."

"So do I. All we need now is for her or Uncle Dick to get sick."

"That would be too much," Steve said.

"I don't know what we'd do."

"Sooner or later it's going to be a problem, Clara, you know that."

"Yes, and it worries me. I've thought about it a lot."

"If Uncle Dick dies first, what will we do about Aunt Jenny? It would be awful. Maybe, in such an eventuality, we could take her in."

"Oh, Steve, with three girls and Hattie?"

"I guess not."

"It isn't that I don't want to see something done for her, don't misunderstand me," Clara explained.

"I understand, Clara."

"I was just thinking of you and your family."

"I know, Clara."

II

"Another cold day, Eddie," Steve remarked.

"I was out earlier," Clara said, "and it isn't as cold as it was yesterday."

The telephone rang.

"I'll get it," Frances called from the dining room.

III

"Aunt Jenny's crazy," Frances said.

"But not committable," Steve said.

"Well, she's still crazy."

"She's getting even with us," Eddie said.

"Well, if that isn't crazy!" Frances exclaimed.

"It's certainly erratic behavior," Steve agreed.

"Oh, Steve, it's crazy." Frances' voice was impatient.

"She really thinks that she's getting even with us," Eddie said.

"But how's she getting even?" Frances asked.

"She's not coming over," Steve explained.

"If that's what she calls punishment, then I say let her punish us to her heart's sweet content," Frances said.

IV

"Aunt Jenny hasn't telephoned for about an hour," Steve said.

"Oh, it's been over an hour since she called last time," Clara said.

"What did she call for then?" Frances asked.

"The same reason she called the other two times, I suppose."

"Wasn't it to punish us?" Eddie asked.

"Don't leave Jack out," Clara said. "She's mad at him, too."

"Poor Jack," Frances said.

"Aunt Jenny was once a handsome woman," Eddie mused.

"She must have been, considering all I've heard about her," Steve said.

"She certainly was," Clara said, "men always seemed to fall for her."

"A couple were millionaires," Eddie said.

"I often think of how sad it is, what happened to the Dunnes," Clara said.

"It was booze that cooked Aunt Jenny's goose," Frances said.

"Yes, it was," Clara agreed.

"She could guzzle gin every day for a month," Eddie told them.

"Don't I know it!" Frances said.

"That's right," Steve said. "You lived over there for a while after Papa had his stroke."

"I wasn't thinking of that," Frances said. "I was thinking of two or three times when she had lots of money, a couple of hundred dollars, and she'd rent a room in another hotel and take me with her."

"She did that to me a number of times," Clara said.

"Where did she get the money?"

"Stole it," Eddie answered.

"She what?" Steve asked, looking at Eddie with surprise.

"Stole it. She'd take two or three hundred dollars from the cash box and go on a binge," Clara said. "She'd spend it like a drunken sailor."

"That's why she was always in debt," Eddie said; "she'd have to borrow money from the American Personal Loan Bank to cover the money she had borrowed from her cash box."

"Eddie wrote about all this in books," Frances said.

"That's right," Steve said.

V

Steve had abruptly gone into his mother's bedroom. This had affected everyone in the kitchen. They remained silent. They had been snapped back to the reason they were here.

"Gosh, I hope Mama isn't suffering," Clara said.

"She can't be," Frances said.

"I hope not."

VI

Steve Ryan came out of his mother's bedroom with an air of professional importance and a look of gravity on his face. They all stared at him, waiting.

"Mama is just about the same. There has been a slight elevation of temperature."

"What is her temperature, Steve?" Eddie asked.

"Ninety-nine point eight," Steve answered, sitting down at the table. "The elevation could be but isn't necessarily serious."

"I see," Clara said.

She wanted to cry.

VII

"We all have to die," Frances said.

"I know," Clara said, "but you keep thinking that it's a long time off."

"Yes, that's true."

"Then something like this comes along and hits you like a ton of bricks," Clara said.

Frances nodded. "It depresses me something awful. It's terrible," she said.

"We wouldn't be human if what's happened to Mama didn't depress us," Clara said.

They were sitting in the dining room.

"Our grandmother had an easy death," Clara said.

"Yes, I remember. Eddie was in Paris with Marion when she died."

"Mother died in her sleep," Clara said.

"I guess that's the best way, one of the best ways, anyway, that a person can die," Frances said.

"Poor Papa," Clara said, thinking out loud, "Papa suffered so much."

Frances nodded.

"That was a bad time too. It was so sad," Clara went on, her voice sad.

"Yes, it was, only we were so much younger then."

"Yes," Clara agreed, "but I was terribly sad when Papa died. I cried. I felt sad. But like you say, we were younger. You were just a kid; so was I. I was only in the eighth grade."

"I think I was in the fourth but I'm not sure; it could have been the third. Or the fifth."

"When you get older," Clara said, "things are different. You understand more because you've had more experience in life. Something like what's happened to our poor Mama makes you feel awful. It's different than when you're young like we were when Papa died."

"Yes," Frances agreed.

They fell into silence.

"Mama was good," Clara said.

There was a kind of comfort in talking about Mama. It didn't take away her depression; nothing could do that; but talking about Mama made it better. It helped.

"I know," Frances nodded.

"Mama would never hurt a flea."

"No, she wouldn't."

"Mama was so quiet that we hardly knew she was in the house most of the time."

Frances nodded again.

"Yes," Clara said with feeling. "She was good. And she minded her own business. Jack likes her; he didn't mind her living with us. He liked it."

"I would have liked it too if she would have come out with me," Frances said.

"She wouldn't go, not Mama. I tried to get her to go out for a visit . . ."

"I know you did, Clara," Frances interrupted.

"But you know, Franny, you couldn't get Mama to do anything she didn't want to do. No, if Mama didn't want to do something, nobody could persuade her to do it. That's the way she was."

"Yes, she was stubborn, all right."

Both sisters lapsed into their own thoughts. Moments passed in silence.

VIII

Steve and Frances sat at the table while Clara was cooking.

"When Eddie was here last June with Tommy and Phyllis, Mama would get out of the house early every morning," she told Steve, smiling.

Steve laughed.

"It must have been funny to see Mama rushing out of the house early so that she'd be gone before Phyllis started in," Frances said.

"It was in a way," Clara admitted.

Frances laughed.

"She couldn't get out fast enough," Clara said. "Every day she'd go visit one or two churches; sometimes she would visit three. And she ate every night with Uncle Dick and Aunt Jenny."

"She was doing that even before I left for California."

"I know, she did it for years. You see, the Dunnes didn't have money and Mama knew that if she ate with them and gave them money it would help them out."

"I know."

"It was so pathetic," Clara said, "what happened to Uncle Dick."

Frances nodded again. She wasn't going to let that happen to her.

"Franny, I think Mama was happy during these last years; she did what she wanted to do; she had what she needed. Mama didn't need much."

"I was always wishing that she would come out to stay for a little while with us."

"I know," Clara said sadly. "There are so many things that people want and that they never get."

"Yes."

Fran was remembering that when she was moving to California with Michael she had thought just the same thing. She had been afraid.

"Well, there's one thing, Franny, Mama's last years were more comfortable than Papa's. Of course, we were all little then so there wasn't much we could do for him; at least we were able to make Mama's last years comfortable for her."

Frances felt some sharp twinges. She could have given her mother a little time, a little bit of attention. She had neglected Mama. It was too late to let her know that she understood more now of what her mother's life must have been like. It was too late for her to thank her mother for many things that her mother had done for her and had given her. It was too late for her to tell her mother that she was sorry for the times when she must have hurt her for things she had said or done. It was too late for her to show her mother how much she loved her. Too late.

She was sad; she could not remember any sadness before that was like this. She wanted to cry.

268

Suddenly Frances went into the bedroom and flung herself across the bed, sobbing.

IX

Within a few minutes she was drying her eyes. She felt better. If she hadn't let herself go this way, she didn't know what she would have done. It had been awful, simply awful, the way she felt. She was still sad, but it wasn't the same as it was before she had let herself go.

The bedroom was dark, not really dark, dim. The air was musty. She could open the window, she supposed.

But Fran didn't move from the bed.

A lot of her life was gone, maybe more than half of it. If she lived as long as Mama, it would be just about half. What could she say for it? Too much of her life had been dribbled away. She couldn't even say how. It made her angry to think of it. But it hadn't been her fault, not entirely. She had not known any better. She had been innocent and naïve. She had not known what to do with her time, what to do with herself.

Well, she knew now. She had had to spend more than thirty years of her life finding out what she wanted to do with the rest of her life. She hadn't realized how short life was, not before this. Oh, she had known that time went by fast. After all, she knew the value of time, she lived according to a clock. She had gotten up at five o'clock in the morning, many a day, when she first got her job as a chemist in an airplane factory out in California. She had had to ride on a crowded bus for over an hour to get to work. And she had had to ride the same length of time going home at night.

It wasn't so bad now that she had her own car; she could sleep until six and be at the laboratory on time.

She had thought of time before. She remembered when she had reached thirty. She was still in Chicago and she had been going to school nights. In fact it was because she had begun to realize that time was going by that she had decided to do something about her life. She had had many sad days and many sad nights. She had thought about how so much of her life had been wasted; how her youth was gone.

She remembered why she left Chicago. She had not wanted her life to be like her mother's. She had not thought then about her mother dying. She had thought only about her own dying. But what was happening to Mama now was going to happen to all of them, and to her.

This afternoon, tonight, tomorrow, or the day after tomorrow, any day now, any minute, her mother would no longer be living here in this house or any place else, either. Her mother would be dead. Just a few feet from where she was sitting, Mama was dying. It was a wonder she didn't lose heart. Maybe she'd better knock on wood. It wasn't over yet. Everything seemed so hopeless. When you really started thinking about dying, you wondered what did matter in life. You were tempted to think that nothing did. Things might matter now but once you were dead, they wouldn't.

She guessed she was getting a little bit childish. Well, if she was, she was. She would just have to be a little bit childish, she guessed.

Oh, this was all so depressing. Nothing had ever depressed her like this. Her mother was dying. What did it all mean? What did anything mean to her mother now? All she could see was futility. In the end, that was all life amounted to. Death.

"Franny?"

"Yes?"

"Where are you?"

It was her brother Steve calling her.

"In the bedroom."

"Are you resting?" Steve asked.

"No, come on in."

"I just wanted to talk," Steve said, standing in the doorway.

Frances rose from the bed and moved toward Steve.

"Let's go back in the parlor."

Steve stepped aside to let her pass. Then he followed her.

X

"I don't know what to think," Frances said.

"What do you mean, Franny?"

"About Mama, about everything."

"Yes, I see," Steve said.

Frances waited. But whatever Steve saw, he was continuing to see without speaking of it.

"Well, Franny, she can't last much longer. You can accept it that Mama is as good as dead."

"I know, Steve, but . . ."

This was not helpful at all.

"Of course, the death of a mother is a crisis for the children," Steve said.

This was certainly true in her case, Frances thought.

"I don't know what to do."

"What can you do?" Steve asked.

"Nothing."

"There's no way to save Mama's life," Steve said. "Even if there was, Mama wouldn't be the same. She would be a vegetable. We don't know how much damage has been done to her brain but we do know that there has been damage. The probability is that the damage has been extensive, extensive enough so that, if Mama was to live, her personality, as we knew her, would be shattered."

Frances hated hearing this, but she knew that it had to be true. It just hurt. But maybe the best thing for her to do was to let it hurt. The best thing? It was the only thing that she could do. And then what? She wished she were back in California.

"You're right, Steve."

"It's just something that we've got to accept and assimilate," Steve said.

Frances nodded.

Chapter 30

I

Tom Clarkson, who had died as a retired police sergeant, was being waked at the Dennison Funeral Parlor at West Sixty-fifth Street and South Western Avenue.

It was cold, and Dick Dunne had asked for transfers when he paid the two carfares on the Sixty-third Street car. It was too cold to let

Jenny walk two blocks to the funeral parlor at Sixty-fifth Street. Besides the cold, the sidewalks were slippery and icy.

Jenny didn't want Dick to walk the two blocks. She didn't want him to slip and get hurt.

They scarcely had to wait. A streetcar was approaching as they crossed Western Avenue.

"Well, Princess, we're riding in luck tonight."

The Western Avenue car halted. Two men bumped past Dick and Jenny.

—Fatheads, Dick thought.

He helped Jenny board the car and followed her onto it. He handed his two transfers to the conductor.

"There's plenty of seats inside," the conductor told them.

"We're only going to Sixty-fifth Street, captain," Dick said.

The conductor nodded.

The streetcar passed Sixty-fourth Street and in a few more moments stopped at Sixty-fifth Street.

Getting off, Dick noticed the Dennison Funeral Parlor sign.

"Poor Tom Clarkson," Jenny said as they walked toward Dennison's.

"Yes," Dick said, supporting her elbow with his hand. "Yes, may God have mercy on his soul."

"Oh, Dick, Mother liked Tom Clarkson."

"He was a likable man."

"Yes, he was."

They were in front of the funeral home.

Jenny was almost in tears. She was thinking of her dear, darling sister Nora. Her darling sister Nora would be with them if she had not had that terrible stroke.

Dick held the front door for her. Jenny, her eyes filled with tears, stepped inside Dennison's.

II

Dick and Jenny knelt on the rail in front of the casket and blessed themselves. Dick prayed. Jenny looked as if she was praying. They knelt for about a minute or two; then they blessed themselves and rose. In awe of death, they stared at the corpse of Tom Clarkson.

Tom Clarkson had been a big heavy-set man in life. His face looked calm. The big hands were clasped together with a pair of black rosary beads in them.

"Poor Tom Clarkson," Jenny said under her breath.

They had not seen Tom Clarkson since the wake of their mother. Dick looked at the corpse for another moment.

They turned away from the casket. Helen Clarkson was sitting a few feet away. She was a heavy woman with white hair. The flesh around her neck sagged. She was wearing a black dress. She stared at her dead husband. But as Jenny and Dick approached, she turned and looked up at them.

"Jenny and I are sorry about your loss and misfortune," Dick said.

"I know you are, and thank you," Helen Clarkson said. "Tom was very fond of your mother."

"Yes, I remember, Helen, you both came to Mother's wake."

"Mother liked Tom, Helen," Jenny said. "She always talked about her cousin Tom Clarkson."

"And how is your sister Nora?" Helen Clarkson asked.

A look of suffering came upon Jenny Dunne's face. Dick became very grave.

"Oh, Helen, Nora would be here with us if she could come."

"Is Nora sick?" Helen Clarkson asked.

"Oh, Helen, she's on her deathbed," Jenny said.

Jenny was crying.

III

Jenny seemed lost. Dick sat beside her, watching. He was ready to offer solace at the first sign that she might need it. While he was on the alert, he thought of how solemn and sad death was. But death was due to the will of God. He had lived long enough to have known many who had passed on, may the Lord have mercy on all their souls.

And now he was about to lose his sister Nora. The only one he had left in the world was his sister Jen. He and Jenny were the last of the Dunne family. And this year of our Lord, Anno Domini, he would be seventy-five years old. With the will of the Lord, he and

Jenny would live many more years to enjoy the life and the years that God granted them.

But the present hours were not happy ones. Jenny, sitting beside him here in the funeral parlor, was stricken with grief. Women had tenderer hearts that could ache and break more easily than could the rougher hearts of men. And none among them possessed a heart more tender than his sister Jenny. The least little ripples of the calmer waves of life could ruffle her heart.

He let his glance travel about the big room. There was an air of unreality about the place. The faces were unfamiliar. He recognized only a few of those paying their last respects to Tom Clarkson.

A funeral home was a strange place, a place that one visited only on the solemn occasion of death. And Tom Clarkson, laid out in his casket, was strange. The majesty of death that only God understood.

"Are you all right, Jen?"

"Yes, I'm all right, don't worry about me."

Dick took a cigar, bit off the end, and spat it out. Then he lit up. A cigar always made him feel better.

"What did Tom Clarkson die of, Dick?"

"I don't know, Jenny, but I can ask and find out."

"No, I don't want to know that much; I was just wondering."

"I can inquire."

"Oh, please don't bother, Dick."

Dick didn't say anything but he would find out before they left.

Two gray-haired men sat down beside him.

"Well, Joe, Tom is gone," one of them said.

"Yes, he is, Al."

"He wasn't well when he retired," Al said.

"I heard that said, but I'd been transferred."

"He hadn't been retired for a month when he had his first heart attack."

"That so, Al?"

"Yes, Joe, less than a month."

"I beg your pardon, officer," Dick interrupted, "but did Tom Clarkson die from a heart attack?"

"Yes, he had about four before he passed away."

"You knew Tom Clarkson?" the man called Joe asked him.

"Yes, I was a cousin of his."

"Oh, you're his cousin?"

"Yes, my name is Richard Dunne, and this is my sister, Jenny Dunne," Dick said.

"I'm Sergeant Al Cruise, and this is Officer Joe Malone," Al Cruise said.

"How do you do, and how do you do, Officer Malone."

"I'm pleased to meet you," Sergeant Cruise said.

Dick and Sergeant Cruise shook hands.

"Put it there, Richard, I'm Joe Malone," Officer Malone said, reaching to shake hands.

"Glad to meet you, Joe," Dick said.

"Did you say that's your sister, Richard?" Sergeant Cruise asked.

"Yes, it is. Jenny"—Dick turned to his sister—"this is Sergeant Cruise and Officer Malone. Officer, my sister, Miss Jenny Dunne."

Dick Dunne stood up. Jenny and the two men acknowledged the introduction.

"So you're cousins of Tom Clarkson?" Sergeant Cruise asked.

"Yes, we are," Jenny said.

"A good man, Tom Clarkson was, and I'm mighty sorry to see him gone," Sergeant Cruise said. He added, "May his soul rest in peace."

"Yes," Dick Dunne said, bowing his head as Sergeant Cruise said his last few words.

"He was one of the finest men," Jenny said.

"Yes, he was, Miss Dunne," Joe Malone said. He continued, "And we both knew it because we worked with him for years."

"True enough words," Sergeant Al Cruise said.

"Oh, there's Lieutenant Duffy," Joe Malone said.

"Excuse us, please, we ought to speak to Lieutenant Duffy."

IV

Jenny had suggested that Dick talk with some of the men for a little while and she would sit and listen to some of the women.

They now stood in different parts of the big room. Dick was in the center of the room with a group of about five men, all taller than he.

A big man with gray hair announced that he felt bad about what happened to Tom but he still looked forward to his retirement next year.

A shadow crossed Dick Dunne's face. He had once thought that he would be comfortably retired.

Well, he had his health; he could thank God for that.

"Are you retired, Mr. Dunne?" one of the men asked him.

"Rats, no, I'm too young to retire."

"Maybe you are at that," the big man said, staring at him.

Dick knew that people never took him to be as old as he was. This always pleased him. He had always taken care of himself and that was one reason why he was in good health at his age. But he didn't forget that he also owed thanks to God for the state of his health.

"No, you don't look old enough to retire," the man said.

"Age, you know," Dick began, but then he paused. "Pardon me, I didn't get your name, sir."

"Oh, I'm Joe O'Mally, Mr. Dunne. I'm just a cop."

"Well, Joe, what I was about to say was that you take age . . ."

"I don't want it," another big fellow said.

"Let the man talk," Joe O'Mally said.

"Age is not only physical, it's also mental." Dick pointed to his head.

"Yes. I guess it is," the man standing next to him said. "A man is as young as he feels."

"That's what I mean," Dick nodded. "It's mental."

Joe O'Mally turned back to look down at him.

"Pardon me for the interruption, Mr. Dunne, but Rogan's pounded out his brains walkin' a beat. He didn't get what you said."

"Oh, it's nothing." Dick smiled and gave O'Mally a wink. "We'll make a mental giant out of Officer Rogan."

The men, except for Rogan, burst into laughter. Then Rogan laughed.

Dick Dunne cleared his throat.

"You're a good kidder, Mr. Dunne," Joe Malone said.

"Kidding, I'm not kidding, Officer Malone."

"Well, Joe, how will you feel when you're a mental giant?" one of the group asked.

"Ask Mr. Dunne," Joe Malone said, glancing at Dick Dunne good-naturedly.

"You officers were all friends of Tom Clarkson?" Dick asked.

"Yes, Tom and me was good friends," Joe Malone said.

"He was a good man, and a good sergeant," Sergeant Cruise said.

"You were a friend of his, Mr. Dunne?" a red-haired man asked. "I'm Sergeant Denlin, Mr. Dunne."

Dick shook hands with Sergeant Denlin.

"I'm a cousin of Tom Clarkson. I'm glad to meet you, Sergeant Denlin."

"Pleased to meet you, Mr. Dunne."

"Say, excuse me, the wife is signalin' to me," Joe Malone said, and moved off.

"The mental giant," Sergeant Al Cruise smiled.

The crowd was fairly large now. About sixty people were in the room. A man came over to talk with Sergeant Cruise. The little group broke up and Dick, who had been standing, sat down. He looked across the room at Jenny, who was talking with some woman.

V

"Tom Clarkson was my mother's second cousin, and she thought the world of him," Jenny was saying.

"My daughter went to school with his daughter," a bulky woman told Jenny. She was one of the three women with whom Jenny was talking.

"I'll bet your daughter is a lovely girl."

"She was raised right," the bulky woman said with an air of modesty.

"Is she here tonight?" Jenny asked.

"No, she isn't. She lives in Springfield. Her husband is with the State Police."

"I see," Jenny said.

"Pardon me," the bulky woman said, "I did not get your name."

"Oh, I'm Jenny Dunne. I'm here with my brother Richard, he's . . ."

The bulky woman interrupted.

"I'm Mrs. Barnes, Kitty Barnes is my name. Mr. Barnes passed away, it's two years ago this month."

"Oh, that's too bad. I'm sorry to hear that, Mrs. Barnes."

"A better man never drew breath than my late husband, Martin Barnes."

"I can believe that, Mrs. Barnes."

—She's just another ignorant Irishwoman, Jenny thought.

"I went in mourning for a year and a half," Mrs. Barnes said.

Jenny shook her head sadly.

"It makes me sad to hear this, Mrs. Barnes."

"It broke my heart."

—Do you think I believe that, you old biddy?

Jenny thought of her sister Nora. How dear, darling Nora would have liked it if she had been here tonight. She could just imagine Nora putting this biddy in her place. Her darling sister Nora might be dead this very minute.

Jenny Dunne searched in her pocketbook and drew out a crumpled handkerchief.

"What's the matter, Miss Dunne? Did you get something in your eye?" Mrs. Barnes asked.

"No, Mrs. Barnes," Jenny said, a sob in her voice. "I just thought of my sister, Nora Ryan."

"Is she ill?"

"She's at death's door."

"Oh, you poor woman!" Mrs. Barnes exclaimed.

"My darling sister Nora is dying," Jenny said, in tears.

"Oh, I'm so sorry," Mrs. Barnes said, her voice softening with sympathy.

"She might be dead at this moment," Jenny sobbed.

Several women gathered around Jenny as she sobbed. Her sobs became louder and could be heard by everyone present. Almost every eye in the room was directed at her.

Dick Dunne rushed over to her side.

VI

Clara Boyle answered the doorbell.

"Oh, Clara, I'm sorry we're so late," Jenny said.

"Come in, Aunt Jen. You too, Uncle Dick."

She and Dick stepped inside and Clara closed the front door.

"It's arctic," Dick said, reaching up to help Jenny take off her coat.

"Clara dear, forgive us for being so late," Jenny said, pulling an arm out of her coat.

"Don't think of it, Aunt Jenny."

Dick Dunne hung up Jenny's coat and his own. He followed his sister and Clara into the parlor. They all sat down.

"We were at Tom Clarkson's wake," Jenny said.

"You were?" Clara Boyle said.

"Oh, you should have seen how we were treated," Aunt Jenny said.

"They treated us correctly, fine and with good manners."

"They did?" Clara Boyle said. "Oh, that's good."

"Oh, they were so nice," Jenny said.

"Well, I'm very glad to hear that," Clara said.

"Tom Clarkson was laid out so lifelike," Jenny said.

No one showed any interest in what Jenny was saying.

"Yes, they were very friendly," Dick said.

"Oh, they were," Jenny said.

Dick nodded. Leo, ignoring the conversation, stood up and took a few steps.

"You should have heard the things they had to say about us and you should have seen them."

"That's nice, Aunt Jen," Clara said.

"It sure is," Molly said.

"It was nice," Jenny said. "Ask Dick if you don't believe me."

"We do believe you, Aunt Jenny," Clara said.

"Oh yes, it was very friendly," Dick said, looking at his sister.

Leo sat down again.

"You should have come, Brother," Jenny said, looking at Eddie.

Eddie didn't say anything.

"Eddie, I was talking to some of the cops, policemen who were friends of Tom Clarkson," Dick said. "One big cop, he wasn't smart, his name was Malone."

"I'll bet Mama could tell who he was and what his father did," Clara said.

"Of course Mama could," Steve said.

"Mama knew so many people," Clara said.

"I said to this big cop, yes, I would make a mental giant out of him, and the other policemen standing around laughed. You should have heard them."

Eddie said nothing.

"I was sorry that none of you could have gone to the wake," Jenny said.

"Yes, it was unfortunate," Dick said.

"They were all such nice people," Jenny said.

"Yes, they were, Jenny," Dick agreed.

"I don't doubt it at all," Clara said, trying to sound interested.

Uncle Dick nodded.

"And so many people asked about your mother," Jenny said. "They missed her. They certainly did."

"Mama would have been there if she could have been," Frances said.

"That's so right," Steve declared.

"So many people, and they were so sorry," Jenny said.

"I'll bet they were," Clara said.

"They really were," Jenny said. "They all said they were going to say prayers for her."

Leo rose again. He took a couple of steps backward, and then forward; he sat down again.

"Oh yes, weren't the people just grand to us, Dick?" Jenny asked him.

"Yes, they were, Jenny."

Eddie had been watching his aunt and uncle. They were clinging together, he thought, united by their gray hairs.

Chapter 31

I

Eddie Ryan thought again of his Uncle Dick and his Aunt Jenny. His mother's coming death had reminded them all of their mortality. Dick and Jenny were the oldest of the family. Their fear of death, the most terrible of all fears, was something that he would probably one day write about. Didn't Aunt Jenny and Uncle Dick realize this? They must. The thought must have crossed their minds. It must have crossed the minds of the others in the family, too. He had already written so much about them. Why would he not write about what was happening here now? He felt sure that Steve and Frances knew that he would. The others must too.

But he couldn't be sure he would be able to write about it until he tried. One morning he would wake up, sit at his desk, and start writing about it. What was happening now, this present, would be the past and would be in his memory. The experience would have crystallized in his unconscious mind.

But now he found the situation painful and the tension it generated uncomfortable. He wished that it would end. This meant wishing that his mother were dead. But that would not be the end of the ordeal for them. There would be the wake and the funeral. And suppose Torch Feeney should come to the wake? He remembered again the time when Feeney had gone to see him carrying a gun. Eddie had not shown any fear at the time but afterward he had been afraid. The idea of being afraid of Torch Feeney was humiliating.

He wished he were back in New York.

He lit a cigarette.

Clara walked in. "Jack will be coming home soon."

"We ought to be going," Molly said, turning to her husband Jack.

"I guess so," he answered.

Neither of them made a move to get up.

"It's getting late, Flo," Leo said, turning to his wife.

"Yes, we'll have to be going too."

Leo nodded and then yawned.

"I guess we're all tired," Frances said. She glanced at Eddie. "Except Eddie. Eddie, you don't ever seem to get tired."

"Oh, I get tired."

"Well, rarely," Frances said.

"Well, I'm tired," Leo said, yawning again.

"I am too," Florence said.

"We'll go, hon."

Leo rose.

"Well, folks . . ." he began.

Florence stood up.

"All right, Father," Molly said to Jack Ryan.

"We'll go too, Molly."

Molly got up.

"Well . . ." Clara said.

"Well, good night, everyone," Leo said.

II

Jack Boyle let himself in the front door.

"Hello, Jack," Clara called from the parlor.

"Hello, Clara."

"Hello, Eddie," Jack said to his brother-in-law.

"Hello, Jack. How did it go tonight?"

"Oh, all right; nothing happened. We just picketed until our turn was up and then we came back home. When we got chilled we warmed ourselves around a bonfire that was burning in a wire basket. Nothin' excitin' happened but then nobody expected anything to. The company ain't tryin' to bring in scabs yet. They're tryin' to wear us down."

"Gosh, they make enough money. They could give you men what the union's askin' for," Clara said with indignation.

"I know it, Clara, but go tell them that."

Jack gave a cynical little laugh and sat down, taking out a package of cigarettes.

"Well, I don't understand why people are never satisfied with what they've got. Why they have to have more no matter how it affects the other fellow," Clara said.

"If people thought and acted that way, we'd be livin' in heaven on earth."

"I know, Jack."

"It's a condition in society that we're never going to reach," Eddie said.

"I guess you're both right," Clara said.

Here he was, Eddie thought, almost forty-two. He didn't relish accepting this but not to accept it would amount to belief in the perfectibility of man. But it was nevertheless imperative to have faith in man, at least faith in human potentialities. Man, of course, meant men and women; and again, this meant some men and some women. But faith in man's potentialities was too general. It needed to be defined. But he was not inclined to do this now.

Steve drifted in.

"Hello, Steve," Jack said.

"Hello, Jack, how was it tonight?"

"Pretty much like it is every night."

"I see."

"It was cold but then it was last night. It's been cold almost every single night. It's been freezin' most nights."

"Well, maybe the strike will be over soon," Steve said.

"I don't know about that; I don't see any signs of it."

"Strikes are no fun," Eddie said.

"Yeah, take this one. It's hitting some of the men hard. It ain't hittin' me so hard because I've got another trade I can go back to. But I can't make as much money upholsterin' as I can in the plant, of course. We're better off than lots of the other fellas, I'll say that much," Jack Boyle said.

"That's true," Clara agreed.

"There's no chance of a settlement?" Steve asked.

"Oh, sure, there's a chance; there's always a chance."

"I mean soon?"

"Well, they're negotiatin'," Jack said, yawning.

"You're sleepy, aren't you?" Clara asked.

"Yeh, I'm gonna turn in. Like they say, tomorrow is another day."

III

"One thing about this strike, Steve," Eddie was saying, "there's been no attempt to bring in scabs."

"That's so, I guess."

"It is so. Jack goes out to picket almost every night. There's no disruption of the picket lines. There's been no violence. It was very different ten years ago."

"You mean when they had the sitdown strikes?"

"Yes."

"That's right. I hadn't thought ot it."

"The unions have grown stronger in the last ten years. They came out of the war stronger than they were when the war began. That's something I never expected."

"I don't recall that I ever thought about it one way or the other," Steve said.

"Another thing," Eddie went on. "We can expect a series of class struggles in the immediate years ahead, the immediate postwar future."

"You think so?"

Eddie nodded. He was sitting on the couch, Steve on a chair. Eddie was smoking a cigarette, Steve a pipe. The house was quiet. Everyone else was asleep, except for Bridget Daugherty.

"I guess I agree but I'd like to know why you think so."

"Because there's more to strike for."

"There is that. Take Jack and Clara. Look at how much more they've got than Mama and Papa."

"They should have more."

"I didn't say they shouldn't."

"I know, Steve, but the point I'm making is that there has been a tremendous increase in productivity since Papa was Jack's age."

"That's so."

"So, since the workers produce more, they should get more."

"I understand what you're saying, Eddie."

"Workers are better off. But relative to the increase in productivity, they're less well off than they should be," Eddie continued. "It certainly isn't difficult to perceive."

Steve grinned defensively.

"I suppose it isn't," he said, "but I haven't given much thought to problems of this kind. And when I don't give thought to something, I don't have occasion to see what's obvious."

Eddie didn't speak. He wished Steve weren't so defensive.

"But I see your point and I guess you're right," Steve added.

Eddie nodded. He was getting sleepy.

IV

A few minutes ago he had wanted to sleep. Now he didn't. But there was nothing else to do at this time of night. He could read but he didn't want to get up. He began to toss. He stopped. He lay on his back and held himself almost perfectly still. He was trying to be still. He moved his legs first, then his arms. He turned. Soon he was on his back again. His eyes were fixed on the ceiling. All of the minutes of his life had led to this one.

He turned again, this time on his left side. Then he turned onto his back. Outside, an automobile backfired. It sounded like a rifle. Maybe it was. But it wasn't.

Now it was silent. There was a world of silence with only occasional echoes of sounds. He heard nothing.

He had some seconal in his suitcase. Why hadn't he thought of it sooner? He half rolled off the couch. In the darkness he saw the black outlines of his suitcase.

Eddie was still restless when he returned to the couch but psychologically he began to prepare himself for sleep. It was soothing to know that the pill would work. Now he could wait for sleep, relaxed. The house was very quiet. He closed out all sounds. From somewhere outside, the soundless world beyond the house, he heard muted noises. But the seconal was beginning to work. A weight began to spread through his body and enter into the muscles of his arms and legs.

He was lying in a darkened room in Chicago, in the house of some member of his family. Whose home was it? It didn't matter. His gloom was as dark as the darkness of the room. Death hovered in his mind. Then he knew. It was his own death. He was dying in darkness, alone. He was helpless. He could not even call out to anyone. Everything was over. Beyond the darkness of this room where he lay dying, there was a world. He felt a pain in his left side; it was his heart. Now the pain was in his left arm. He was dying. He would die like this, alone in the darkness, and no one would know that he had been calm in his final moment. He was dying but he was not yet dead. When he was dead, he would not be dying any more. He didn't like dying. His last thought; what would his last thought be? He was thinking of what his last thought would be before he died. But he was dying now. This could be his last thought. What was it? He didn't know. He felt a twitching of muscles. He was dying, rolling off the bed and falling onto the floor, dead.

Eddie opened his eyes. He was still lying on the couch in the darkness. He had been dreaming that he had fallen off the couch and died. The house was quiet. Had his mother died? There would be a big commotion if she had. Bridget, the night nurse, would have awakened them. He was so tired but he was relieved to wake up and learn that he wasn't dead. But if he had been dead, he wouldn't have known it. What time was it? How long had he been sleeping? It couldn't have been long. He yawned, turned over on his right side, and closed his eyes. Usually when you dreamed about your own dying, it was a nightmare. There had been nothing nightmarish about his dream. It had been calm. At least, he remembered it as such. He had not had any fear. What was it all about? What about his mother? Was she still alive? His dream must have been related to her. Perhaps his dream had been a wild wish that she would die. He was wishing that she would die. They all were. Her prolonged dying was a disruption of all their lives. He was too drowsy to think. He rolled over. He was so damn tired . . .

V

Eddie could see the bluish gray of the dawn. He had slept a few hours and he was glad of that. But now a new day was beginning. Would his mother die today? If so, what then? He didn't want to think about it now. He sat up and reached for his cigarettes.

Oh, for a cup of coffee. What time was it? He wondered if Clara was up. God, he'd like some coffee. He could get up and make his own but he didn't want to. He didn't want to wake up any of the others. He didn't have to. He could make a cup of coffee without waking up the whole house if he tried. There was no need for him to make excuses.

He put out his cigarette. It had tasted harsh. It was senseless to have smoked it. His glasses, where were they? It was a little lighter now. It must be after five. He could hear activity outside. Workers going to work. That was their life. God, he wished he had a cup of coffee. He heard no stirring in the house. He closed his eyes and tried to go back to sleep. He merely tossed about more. Finally he heard footsteps upstairs.

VI

Eddie, wearing a bathrobe, sat at the kitchen table smoking. Jack walked into the kitchen, dressed and carrying the morning edition of the Chicago *Daily Representative*.

"Well, they got 'im," Jack said.

"Got who?" Steve asked, walking into the kitchen.

"That bastard who's been killing those women," Jack said, sitting down at his usual place at the table.

"I'm glad he's been caught," Steve said.

"Sit down, Steve, and I'll give you a cup of coffee and fix your breakfast," Clara said.

"I want to look at Mama first, Clara."

"How did they catch him, Jack?" Clara asked.

"I ain't read it yet, I just saw the headlines."

"Your breakfast is just about ready, Jack."

"Don't think I ain't ready for it."

"Well, here it is."

She started serving her husband. He put the paper down. The headlines read:

MURDERER CAUGHT

"I'm glad they caught that maniac," Jack repeated. "He killed a fifth girl before they got him."

"That's terrible," Clara said.

"Well, Mama's just about the same," Steve announced, walking back into the kitchen.

Jack Boyle folded up the morning paper and put it aside as he ate.

"Where did they catch him, Jack?"

"Way over on the North Side near Wilson Avenue at a hotel called the Winchester Arms. That's where he murdered the fifth girl. Someone heard her scream and called the cops. But before they got there he had stabbed her."

"Oh, that makes me sick," Clara said.

"It's awful, all right."

"That's so," Steve remarked. "It's one of those damned terrible things that happen sometimes."

"It sure is, Steve," Jack said.

Clara served Eddie a plate of bacon and eggs.

Chapter 32

I

Stanley Jablowicz had written Eddie Ryan that he was first-genera-
tion Polish and that Eddie's books about the Irish had impressed
him. His letter had touched Eddie and he had answered it. Several
letters had been exchanged and Eddie promised to look him up
when he came to Chicago. Stanley Jablowicz had sent Eddie his
telephone number.

Should he call Stanley on this trip or wait until another time?
Stanley Jablowicz was a stranger and he might feel uncomfortable
coming to the Boyle home at a time like this.

Suddenly Eddie rose from the chair and went to the telephone. It
was six-thirty.

Eddie asked for Mr. Stanley Jablowicz. The voice replied that it
was he speaking. Stanley Jablowicz spoke precisely and correctly.
Eddie told him that it was Eddie Ryan calling.

"Edward A. Ryan?"

Eddie said yes, it was. Stanley Jablowicz said that he was surprised
by the call. Eddie told him that he was in Chicago and thought that
he would telephone him. Stanley Jablowicz said that he was glad that
Eddie had and then asked what had brought him. Eddie told him
that his mother was ill. Stanley Jablowicz said that he was very sorry
to hear this and he hoped that she wasn't seriously ill and would
recover quickly. Eddie said that this was unlikely, she had suffered a
severe stroke and was not expected to recover. There was a silence at
the other end of the line. Then Stanley Jablowicz said that he was
very sorry to hear this; that he felt that he knew Eddie's mother from
Eddie's novels and it was like receiving news about someone he
knew, a friend. Eddie thanked him and asked how he was. Stanley
said that he was all right, he was well, and so was his family. Eddie
said that he was glad to hear this.

Steve was standing near the telephone. He suddenly asked Eddie to whom he was talking. Eddie ignored him. Steve interrupted again. Eddie asked Stanley to please hold on a moment; he turned to Steve and said that he was speaking to a friend. Steve told him to invite his friend over. Eddie resumed his conversation with Stanley. There was a pause before Stanley answered. He was not doing anything; he had planned to read but if Eddie really wanted him to pay a visit . . . Eddie urged him to come over. Suddenly Steve called out that their sister Frances needed a man. Stanley sounded a little bewildered but said that he would come. Eddie gave him Jack Boyle's address. Stanley said he would be there around eight-thirty.

II

They had finished eating and Clara and Frances had washed the dishes. Leo and Florence had come over; so had Jack and Molly and their son Andy. A few minutes later Dick and Jenny had arrived.

"Your friend will be here soon, won't he?" Clara asked Eddie.

She was looking forward to meeting Eddie's friend. Eddie had so many interesting friends. She almost always enjoyed meeting them.

"He should be here in about twenty minutes."

"Does he live near here?" Leo asked.

"No, he lives on the West Side."

"Oh, he's traveling a long way to see you," Clara commented.

"Whereabouts on the West Side does he live, Eddie?" Leo asked.

"Gee, Leo, I forget, I think it's somewhere in a Polish district."

"That covers a lot of room," Jack Ryan said.

"North Hermitage Avenue," Eddie said, remembering. "That's it, I think."

"What number on North Hermitage?" Leo asked.

Eddie reached over to the table in front of the sofa and took a cigarette from a pack lying there. He wrinkled up his brow, trying to remember Stanley's address.

"It's slipped my mind."

"Well, whatever his address is, if he lives on North Hermitage, he has a good long way to drive," Jack Boyle said.

"Yes, but it's not too long, particularly on a night like tonight,"

Leo said. "There won't be very much traffic because of the cold. On a night like tonight, most people want to stay home."

"It's not as cold out tonight as it was last night," Jack Ryan said.

"I don't think so either," Jack Boyle agreed.

"Maybe not," Leo said.

"Does anybody know what the temperature is?" Steve asked.

"It's thirty-five degrees," Dick Dunne said.

"That's cold enough to freeze a person," Jenny added. "When Dick and I were coming over here, on the streetcar, we both thought we'd freeze."

"Does your friend have a family, Eddie?" Clara asked.

"Yes, he's married and has a daughter Tommy's age."

"He must think a lot of you to come out on a night as cold as this."

"I've never met him but we've corresponded for a couple of years."

"What does he do?" Leo asked.

"He works for Brand & McGee; they make maps."

"Well, he ought to be here any minute now, I imagine," Clara said.

"Don't get nervous, Franny, we've got a man coming for you," Steve teased.

"For God's sake," Frances snapped.

III

During his first few minutes in the Boyle home Stanley Jablowicz was apparently disconcerted.

Here he was, actually talking with Edward A. Ryan and some of his characters. He had gone from the books to this, from fiction to life, from fiction to fact. Edward A. Ryan was a great writer and he was sitting here with him. Eddie Ryan's mother was lying on her deathbed in a bedroom. Through Eddie's books, he felt that he knew the woman. He was genuinely sorry that she was sick. He looked at Eddie's Uncle Dick and Aunt Jenny. He felt he knew them both.

He lit a cigarette and let his eyes shift from face to face. Taken all together, the Ryans were formidable. He remained silent.

After he had been there a half hour Stanley Jablowicz felt less

tense. He still didn't talk much, only answering questions about himself—where he lived, his family, his work. Several times he smiled as
he answered questions. Now the Ryans seemed less formidable, more
human; they seemed to like one another. He envied them this warm
family spirit. There was little more than politeness between him and
his brother Matthew, who owned a store on Milwaukee Avenue.
Eddie had so much that he didn't have. But envy was the least of his
feelings for Eddie Ryan.

Clara brought Stanley a cup of coffee and a slice of coconut layer
cake.

"Oh, thank you, but you didn't have to go to that trouble for me."

"It's no trouble at all, Stanley."

She turned toward her brother.

"Do you want a cup, Eddie?"

"Yes, thanks."

She turned back toward Stanley.

"Whenever Eddie's in town, I always keep the coffeepot on the
stove with a flame under it."

"He's a coffee drinker?"

"We all are but he's the biggest one in the family."

She started toward the kitchen.

"If you come around us Ryans very much, you'll get to be a big
coffee drinker too," Leo said.

"But coffee isn't addictive . . ." Stanley began.

"With the Ryans it is," Frances interrupted.

IV

For a while conversation had dropped; but now it had picked up
again.

Suddenly Steve looked over at Stanley and then at Frances. Grinning, he spoke:

"After all, Franny, you need a man."

"Do I, Steve?"

Steve turned to Leo.

"Don't you think that Franny needs a man?"

"I guess so."

"Well, Stanley's a man," Steve said, turning toward Stanley Jablo-wicz.

"But he's married," Clara protested.

"That doesn't have to make a difference."

"You better ask his wife about that," Eddie suggested.

Ignoring him, Steve turned to Franny.

"Look, Fran, we got you a man."

"Well, thank you, Steve, how kind you are!"

"You know, Steve is kind, Fran, so kind he'd give you anything so long as it belongs to someone else."

There was mild sarcasm in Leo's voice.

Steve turned to Stanley.

"Stanley, you've come in the nick of time. Our sister needs a man."

"Maybe our grandmother sent him," Clara suggested.

"I'll bet she did," Steve said.

"Mama must have told her to send a man to Frances," Clara went on.

"Yes, that must be how it happened," Steve agreed, then turning to Clara:

"Shall I explain all of this to Stanley or would you rather do it?"

"Let Clara do it, Steve," Leo said.

"You're pulling my leg or else you're pulling your sister's leg," Stanley said.

"We never pull anybody's leg, Stanley," Leo said. He turned to Eddie. "Do we, Eddie?"

"Never!"

"See, Stanley?" Leo laughed.

"I think I do see," Stanley laughed back.

"Well, Franny, you're getting a man," Steve said.

V

"I have to get ready to go now," Jack said.

—Go where? Stanley wondered. Or had he said this as a hint for him? Maybe he had overstayed his welcome.

"Jack has to go picket; he's on strike," Eddie explained to Stanley.

"For how long?"

"An hour," Eddie answered.

"Yeah, I'm on strike and I have to go out five nights a week to picket for an hour. I work for May Motors."

"That's an inconvenience, isn't it?" Stanley asked.

Jack Boyle laughed.

"An inconvenience? Well, I suppose you could call a strike an inconvenience."

"Is there any place I can drive you, Jack?" Stanley asked.

"No, thanks, but I appreciate your offer. A couple of the other fellows come by and pick me up. And they drive me back home afterward."

"Where do you go?"

"Down where I work. But after the strike is settled I'm gonna try to get transferred to the plant in Pullman. They make diesels out there at the Pullman plant. But this strike's gotta get settled first."

"How long has it been going on?"

"We're well into the third month."

"It's been longer than that, Jack," Clara interrupted.

"No, it hasn't but that's long enough."

"I should think so," Stanley said.

"Gee, it seems longer to me but you ought to know," Clara said.

Stanley rose.

"Well, I think I have to be going now."

What would his wife say when he got home?

Chapter 33

I

"We should have helped Jack get the coal in the basement, Eddie."

"I would have but for my football knee."

"Well, I should have," Steve said.

Eddie didn't comment.

"You know, he's taking an awful licking."

"Yes, I know," Eddie nodded.

"Here he is on strike. He's got to go twenty or thirty miles to picket from midnight to one five nights a week. Then, when he comes home, he comes home to a houseful of Ryans with his mother-in-law on her deathbed."

Eddie nodded.

"He finds us awake, talking away. He's got to pile into bed to get up early so he can go off to his substitute job the next morning," Steve went on.

"It would have been better for him if we had put Mama in a hospital."

"Could you have afforded that, Eddie?"

"Yes, I could have."

"As it's turning out, it would have probably been better all around."

"It looks that way, Steve."

"But Dr. Evans said that Mama shouldn't be moved."

"And it's too late now, isn't it? What do you think?"

"Oh, I think it's too late, Eddie, I don't think Dr. Evans would agree to Mama's being moved now."

"That means we're trapped."

"Oh, I know it and I'm sure that Jack understands it."

They both knew it was merely a matter of time.

"But the fact still is that Jack is taking a licking," Steve said. "And I don't think any of us would tolerate a situation like this in our own homes, do you?"

Eddie thought of Phyllis. She would have burst a blood vessel by now.

"I guess not, Steve."

"I'm pretty sure of that. I don't think Hattie would have put up with it. And Phyllis wouldn't, would she?"

"No, she wouldn't. She has very limited patience."

"She has anxieties."

Eddie nodded.

"And Leo and Florence wouldn't put up with it either," Steve said.

"I guess not."

294

II

"God, how long can this go on?" Frances exclaimed.

"I don't see how it can much longer," Steve said. "But then I didn't think Mama could last this long."

"I just don't know," Frances said, shaking her head.

"It's a rough thing when your mother dies."

Frances looked at him. How was she supposed to answer such a remark?

"Of course, the circumstances are a little bit unusual," Steve added.

"A little bit?"

"Well, maybe more than a little bit."

Frances frowned.

"Franny?"

Frances looked up, waiting for him to say something.

"Franny, try not to take it so hard."

His voice was thick.

"This is something beyond our power to prevent."

"I know that, Steve."

"But it isn't beyond our power to do something about how it affects us."

Frances said nothing.

"It's not doing Mama any good for any one of us to give ourselves up to despair."

"I know that, Steve."

Without realizing it, Frances had become defensive.

"We can't avoid facing Mama's death," Steve continued.

"Oh, Steve, I know all that, I just feel terrible," Frances blurted out.

"I know, Fran." Steve spoke gently. "We all feel terrible."

"It's the way it's happening."

"I know it's a great strain, Franny."

"You feel it too, don't you?"

"Yes."

"What do you do about it?"

"I try to understand it, to analyze it."

"Can you?" Frances said.

"Here's Eddie," Steve said, seeing Eddie enter the room before Franny spotted him.

"Hello, Steve," Eddie said abstractedly.

Fran smiled at Eddie.

"How are you, Franny?"

"Oh, I could feel worse if I tried, maybe."

Eddie nodded.

Fran looked at them, her two favorite brothers. She was glad that she had talked to Steve just now instead of to Eddie. She would have thought that it would have been the other way around, that she would have turned to Eddie instead of Steve. But Steve was a psychiatrist, that must have been why. She smiled at Eddie but she had a strong feeling of guilt in her.

III

"It's a strain, of course," Steve said again.

"I'm sure we all knew it would be," Eddie said.

He had been sharp because he was annoyed by the way Steve had spoken. That "of course" had got his goat.

"Yes, it's a strain on all of us," Steve said.

—Of course, Eddie thought.

But he didn't say it; it would hurt Steve's feelings. And why do that? The strain in this house was enough, why add to it?

IV

"What do you think of the family, Eddie?" Steve asked.

It was early afternoon. They were alone in the parlor. Clara and Fran had gone out for groceries.

"How can I answer such a question, Steve?"

"Well, I was thinking about what Fran said this morning. Remember her statement that the Ryans are an unusual family?"

"Yes."

"Do you agree with her?"

"I haven't thought about the family in that sense."

"Well, offhand, what do you think, Eddie?"

"Well, I've written a lot about them," Eddie said, smiling.

"That would go to establish that Franny is right, wouldn't it?"

"It might."

"It would at least suggest that Franny has a point," Steve said.

"Yes, but if you change the word 'unusual' to 'interesting,' Steve, you have a better hypothesis to go on."

Eddie was not interested in pursuing the subject.

"Let's consider the Ryans for a few minutes, Eddie. Let's see if they are, as Franny has said, 'an unusual family.' "

Eddie didn't say anything.

"Well now, let me see. Where do I start?" Steve said.

Eddie waited for him to continue.

"Well, to begin with, you're a Ryan. You wouldn't say that you aren't unusual?"

"What do you want me to say?"

"I don't want you to say anything, Eddie, but you know that you are unusual."

They were both silent for a few minutes.

"Would you say that Mama's life was wasted, Eddie?"

Eddie was surprised by the turn of Steve's questions.

"I don't know, I'll have to think about it."

"After all, she did produce a lot of us."

"But there was a lot of waste in her life."

"Mama's life?" Steve asked.

Eddie nodded.

"Six out of fifteen kids survived," Eddie said.

"Some of them were probably biological wastes," Steve agreed.

"Look at the time Mama spent at wakes, sitting up all night with corpses," he added.

"Would you call that waste or recreation on Mama's part?" Eddie asked, laughing.

"Both," Steve laughed back.

"She spent a lot of time praying," Eddie reminded him.

"But wait a minute, Eddie, don't you think Mama did a lot of faking about how much she prayed?"

"She was an exhibitionist."

"Her piety and holiness, her praying, were melodramatic," Eddie added.

"What are you two talking about?" Frances asked, walking in.

"Mama. We were talking about Mama's dying. Wait until Mama meets Mother in heaven," Steve said.

"Oh, they'll have a time of it," Clara said, following Frances into the parlor.

Frances smiled.

"What do you think they'll say to each other, Eddie?" Steve asked.

"Mother will probably ask Mama why she came up."

They laughed.

"And then Mother will ask how is her grandson. 'Nora, how is me grandson?' she'll ask. And then she'll ask, 'Nora, who's dead?'" Clara said.

"And before Mama answers her, she'll put her arms out and say, 'Mother, I've come home,'" Eddie laughed. "And then she'll tell Mother that Tom Clarkson died and that she heard that he had a fine wake but that she had been sick in bed and couldn't go to it."

"And Mother will tell Mama that she's seen Tom Clarkson already, that the first thing he did when he got to heaven was to go see her," Frances added.

"Mother will want all of the news, you can be sure of that," Clara smiled.

"And you can be sure that Mama will give her an earful," Frances said.

"It will be like the old days, won't it, Eddie?" Steve asked.

"It'll be just like Eddie has written in his books," Frances said.

"Well, if it is, Uncle Larry will come out and ask Mama if she hasn't got someplace else to go," Clara said.

"But will he be up there?" Steve asked.

"Of course, after all, he is the son of Grace Hogan Dunne," Eddie answered.

"That's right, Steve, Mother will see to it that all her sons and her grandsons get to heaven; but I don't know about her daughter Jenny and her granddaughters," Clara said.

"Well, don't you worry, Clara," Eddie said, "your mother's prayers will get you and Franny there."

"Won't Mama want to see God right away?" Steve asked.

"Mother will tell her that He's busy, He isn't to be bothered by any Tom, Dick, or Harry Come Lately," Eddie told him.

"But Mama will find a way to see Him in a hurry."

"But, Steve, I think Mama will want to see the Blessed Virgin Mary before she sees God," Frances said.

"You've got a point there," Steve admitted.

"She was a friend of the Mystic Rose of Jesus; Mama will want to see her too," Frances reminded them.

"Oh, Mama will have so many friends to see in heaven," Clara said.

"It'll be old home week for her," Eddie said.

They laughed.

"And she'll want to see Papa," Clara said.

"That's right, don't forget Papa," Frances laughed.

"Mama won't forget Papa; she loved him," Clara said.

No one spoke for a moment. They had felt a sudden sadness. Then Steve said:

"I don't think Mama was so dumb."

"I don't think I knew her well, Steve," Eddie commented.

"Well, one thing she was, or at least I think so, she was an individualist."

"An individualist or an eccentric?" Eddie asked.

"Let me think about that."

Eddie thought too. More than love, he felt pity for his mother.

"Can't we say that she was both? An individualist and an eccentric?" Steve asked.

"You can say it but the two words cannot be equated."

"I don't know about that, Eddie."

Eddie remembered Frances' story about Steve back in St. Michael's Grammar School. The nun had asked Steve to define a word; Steve had stood up and reeled off a definition.

"That's not what the dictionary says, Stephen Ryan," the nun had said.

"Well then, Sister, the dictionary is wrong," Steve had answered.

Eddie smiled, thinking of this story.

"An individualist does what he wants to do, doesn't he?" Steve asked.

"So does a baby," Eddie said.

"But you can't say that a baby is an individualist; his character is too unformed," Steve protested.

"Maybe eccentricity is childish," Eddie offered.

"Let me think about that."

Steve paused a minute and then went on:

"I suppose so. Yes, I suppose that many of the things that an eccentric does are infantile."

"Her behavior was often odd and eccentric, Steve, but her thoughts were stereotyped," Eddie said.

"That was certainly true of what she thought about religion," Steve agreed.

"Superstition is usually based on the most commonplace of stereotypes and she was the most superstitious of all the superstitious Ryans," Eddie said.

"More superstitious than Mother?"

"I don't know," Eddie answered.

"Of course, Mother was a Dunne, not a Ryan, but then superstition comes more from the Dunne side than from the Ryan side although Papa probably had his superstitions, too."

"Mother brought hers along with her from Ireland," Eddie said.

"Let's take her then, would you say that she was an individualist, Eddie?"

"Relative to her cultural level, I'd say yes, but we can't think of individualist in an absolute sense. It is relative."

"That's what I had in mind when I said that I thought Mama was an individualist."

"Of course, we haven't defined individualist, Steve, and unless we do in some precise sense, we can only talk around the question or issue that we have left vague."

"Well then, let's define it."

"I'm not sure I can," Eddie said.

"I can. An individualist is a person who does whatever he wants to do," Steve said.

"A lunatic does what he wants to do."

"Well then, a lunatic is an individualist."

"Then, to the eccentric, we add bizarre behavior and call it individualism?"

"Well, no, that doesn't make sense. But I still say that Mama was an individualist in her own way," Steve persisted.

"Individualism would hold that the individual is the best judge of his own wants," Eddie said.

"Doesn't that mean that an individual is someone who does what he wants to do?"

"Yes, but it is assumed that the individual is the best judge of his own wants because he is endowed with reason and can decide rationally."

"Or thinks that he is endowed with reason and that he can act rationally," Steve said.

"No, not historic individualism. It assumes that reason is a natural endowment of man."

"Aren't we quibbling, Eddie?"

"If we aren't, we will be any minute."

"I don't know about that."

"I don't think that to pose a question by making individualism a category by itself and then by loosely fitting into that category our own idea of what some person was like—I don't think that's a good question."

"Maybe not."

"We can select some aspects of behavior and prove that a given person is an individualist. If we select other aspects of the same person's behavior, we can make an opposite interpretation that is also plausible," Eddie said.

"Of course, it's the behavior that counts, not the label," Steve said.

"An individualist, definitely so when applied to Mama, is a label."

"Yes, I guess so but I still think that I would call Mama an individualist and that there is some sense in the word to what Mama was like, and what she did, or how she behaved."

"I'm more interested in the behavior than in the categorization," Eddie said.

"So am I," Steve said, rising. "But it's time for me to go in and see her."

V

"Eddie, I get so sad over Mama," Clara said, coming into the parlor where Eddie was sitting.

301

She sat down.

"I guess it had to come," she said.

"She's just worn out."

"Yes, her body couldn't take any more, I guess."

Eddie nodded. Clara probably felt their mother's fate more than she was showing.

"I'm going to miss her terribly, Eddie; she never interfered."

"Are you talking about Mama?" Frances asked, entering the room.

"Yes, I was telling Eddie how Jack and I are going to miss Mama and about how sweet she was and how she never interfered."

"I know, Clara, I feel terrible about it too."

"I guess we all do," Clara said.

"I keep wondering if she's suffering," she added.

"Oh, I don't think so, Clara," Frances said.

"I wouldn't know," Eddie said.

She must be suffering, he thought. She was conscious; she wasn't in a coma. She must be terribly frightened unless the hemorrhage had destroyed the centers through which cognizance and memory and whatever other processes were involved in being bewildered and afraid had been destroyed.

"I hope she's not suffering," Clara said.

"What did Steve say?" Frances asked.

"He said he didn't think so."

"Well then, she can't be, can she?" Frances asked.

"I wouldn't think so, not where she's paralyzed," Clara said. "If she could only talk. Just think, you have all your children around you, and you can't say a word to them, you can't tell them anything that you might want to tell them, you can't say good-by, you can't express your last wishes, you can't give them your blessing."

Clara was crying. "It's awful."

"It would have been better if the stroke had taken her quickly," Frances said.

Clara wiped her eyes, blew her nose.

"I'm sorry, I just couldn't help it."

"There's nothing to apologize for," Eddie told her.

"Oh, I know that, but I feel sorry anyway."

VI

"I've been debating with myself about something," Steve began, and then stopped.

Steve looked at Eddie and went on:

"I was wondering if I should explain the Oedipus complex to everybody."

"I don't see why."

"Well, because of Mama."

"Steve, don't you think it's hard enough for Jack and Leo? Why make it worse for them by telling them that they were jealous of Papa because they wanted to screw Mama?"

"Well, I wasn't going to be as crude as that! I was going to give them a more subtle explanation."

"If you start telling them about the Oedipus complex subtly, they won't know what you're talking about, it's too far removed from anything that they would accept. And if you're blunt about it, you'll shock them."

"I wonder."

"What would Molly and Florence say if you tell them that the character of Jack and Leo all derives from the fact that they wanted to screw their mother and couldn't?"

They were both laughing when Frances hurried into the room.

"What's going on here?"

Neither Steve nor Eddie answered.

"What is it?" Frances asked.

Steve started to answer but another fit of laughter stopped him. Then Eddie tried but he started laughing again.

"You two are making me mad!"

"We were . . ." Eddie started laughing again.

"The two of you are a pain!"

"Steve wants to explain the Oedipus complex to the Ryan family," Eddie was able to say.

"I don't see what's so funny about that!"

Eddie and Steve started to laugh again. Frances looked at them, shaking her head.

VII

"The Oedipus complex is the fundamental key to everything, Eddie."
Eddie and Steve had gone out for a walk. They had stopped at a
hamburger stand and were seated at a small table. The other tables
were empty but there were a few customers sitting at the counter.
"Yes?"
"I think it's the key to our behavior."
"That means that there's one door, one avenue to knowledge of
how our psyches are formed."
"Well, I think there is."
"One explanation is no explanation."
"I wonder about that."
Steve pressed his lips together for a second as he thought. Eddie
turned to catch the eye of the man behind the counter.
"Do you want another cup of coffee, Steve?"
"Yes, all right."
Eddie failed to catch the man's eye. He picked up the two cups
and carried them to the counter. The tall skinny counterman looked
at him.
"Two more, please," Eddie said.
The man took the cups.
He poured fresh cups. Eddie carried them back to the table, and
set them down.
"Thanks, Eddie."
They both added cream and sugar to their coffee and lit cigarettes.
"Where were we now?" Steve asked.
"I had just said that one explanation is no explanation."
"Yes, that's right. Well now, I doubt that."
"Scientifically, it's true. I am not talking of a specific and isolated
problem about relatively limited events and phenomena. I'm referring
to when you have only one explanation for a complicated mass of
phenomena or of events."
"I know what you mean."
"But let's let that ride, it's sidetracking us from the Oedipus,"
Eddie said.

"No, we can settle this question first and then take up Oedipus. Is it true that one explanation is no explanation?"

"You're merely making a question out of the proposition I stated, Steve."

"Well, a proposition is, in a sense, a question."

"A proposition is not, strictly speaking, a problem. A question is a formulation which marks out a problem."

"You know, it's not good to retire," a gray-haired customer at the counter was saying.

"Do you think it's any better to work?" the man next to him asked.

"Well, all right then, I'm making your proposition a problem," Steve said.

He squashed his cigarette in the ash tray.

A customer at the counter paid his bill and left. As he opened the door a gust of cold air came in.

"Hey, close that door," someone called. "What's it doin' open?"

"You can't go in and out of here without openin' the door, fellow," the counterman said.

"I don't care if he comes through the window, I don't like it when that cold wind whips around my ankles."

"Is one explanation no explanation?" Steve was asking.

"It explains too much. If you explain too much, you aren't explaining, you're mis-explaining," Eddie said.

"All right, I know what you mean. I'll accept it. But I don't see how that refutes Freud's theory about the Oedipus."

"Isn't it better to say Freud's hypothesis, Steve?"

"Okay, call it a hypothesis."

"I had in mind that it's part of a theory, that Freud's whole system is better taken as a theory."

"Getting back to the Oedipus," Steve said.

"It's a relationship. If a baby were raised by a wolf, it could not have Oedipus complex and relationship in its life. But babies are not raised by mother wolves, despite the tales of wolf-children. That's merely an aside, a parenthesis.

"The Oedipus relationship is that in which we see that sons love their mothers and hate their fathers. The reason is jealousy. The father is a rival for the mother's affection and love. That's the first triangle. It's the first affective experience of the infant who is to grow up to become a man. And it sets the pattern of his reactions to other women, and to men, too, during his adult life."

Steve paused and took a drink of coffee.

"Isn't that a simplification?"

"Yes, I suppose it is," Steve admitted. "But you know we have to simplify from the way that things are in life."

Eddie nodded.

"Now, let me see," Steve said, as though he were talking to himself. "What was I . . ."

Eddie interrupted him.

"We do have to simplify. We isolate. But in this case I was thinking of this—there is, I suppose, a pattern of reactions and behavior on the part of a baby and of a small child in its reactions to a parent, and to both of its parents."

"Yes, there is, of course, that's something that we can see in the Oedipus relationship," Steve said.

"There are early patterns of behavior; that is, they are acquired early."

Steve nodded.

"Well, these patterns are repeated with variations and elaborations."

"That's what happens, isn't it, Eddie, in the case of the Oedipus?"

"Yes."

Eddie lit a fresh cigarette.

"I was thinking of continuity in behavior," Eddie went on.

"Of course, there is continuity in behavior. We know that," Steve said.

"If there weren't, we couldn't say that there was anything that we would call behavior," Eddie said.

"Consistent behavior, certainly," Steve said.

"You haven't got any cats and dogs in the hamburger?" a customer was asking at the counter.

"What kind of wise-acre question is that?"

"I was only kiddin'. I want a hamburger and a cup of coffee," the customer said.

"Well, I'll make you a cat-and-dog hamburger sandwich," the counterman said.

"I believe it," another customer said.

Steve took a swallow of coffee.

"Hell, Eddie, you know what I'm getting at, what I mean," Steve said.

"I have an idea that I might know, but I don't know, in the sense of what conclusions and interpretations ought to be made, and what ones you are trying to make," Eddie said.

"We ought to discuss that," Steve said.

Eddie nodded and glanced out the window.

A train ground past on the Rock Island tracks.

"We ought to get back, don't you think, Eddie?"

"I think so."

"I'd like to continue this discussion later," Steve said.

VIII

By the time they reached the house, Steve Ryan was frowning.

"Did you two have a good walk?" Frances asked him.

"Yes," Steve snapped.

Frances was taken aback. She turned to look at Eddie. Had the two of them had a fight? They must have. But Eddie didn't seem upset. Even so, something must be wrong. Steve was practically throwing his coat on the hanger.

"Eddie?"

"Yes, Frances?"

"What happened?"

"What happened where?"

"What happened between you and Steve?"

"Nothing, why?"

"You didn't have a fight?"

"Why, no. Where did you get that notion?"

"The way he looked when you came back from your walk."

Eddie laughed.

"Maybe I was imagining things," Frances said, smiling.

"Steve didn't have much to say on the way back. I guess he started to feel a little depressed. But we didn't quarrel. There was nothing like that, Frances."

"Maybe I wasn't only imagining then."

"Eddie," Clara said, her voice agitated.

"What?" Eddie asked.

"Did something happen between you and Steve?"

"See, I wasn't imagining," Frances said.

"Nothing happened between us, Clara. There was no quarreling, nothing that would cause any hard feelings. Frances asked me the same question."

"Eddie, tell me the truth. Was there anything between you and Steve?" Clara asked.

"Absolutely nothing, Clara. We merely had a discussion."

He was annoyed that Clara didn't believe him.

"Frances asked me the same question."

"Yes, I did, Clara. I thought that they must have had a fight," Frances said.

"What did Steve say to you, Franny?" Clara asked.

"Nothing, but it was the way he talked. What did he say to you?"

"Oh, nothing, Franny, but you should have seen the look on his face and when I said hello to him, he didn't answer."

"He must be depressed about something," Eddie said.

"Well, I'm glad nothing happened between you two. It would be so awful if it ever did. You two have been such good friends all of these years."

"I don't think anything will ever come between Steve and me."

Eddie lit a cigarette.

"If Steve is depressed about something, it might be best to let him alone. If he wants to tell us he'll do it."

"You're right, Eddie," Clara said.

IX

It was a severe anxiety. He knew what was hitting him, but knowing did not relieve the anxiety. To identify and classify was one thing. He had to associate and analyze to get to the root of his anxiety. He had an idea what it was.

The Oedipus had been in his mind all day. It was his Oedipus that was involved. He had told Eddie that he had thought about explaining the Oedipus complex to the family. Was he going to tell Leo and Jack that they wanted to screw Mama? And that was why they had been jealous of Papa? Eddie had been right, of course. Leo and Jack couldn't take it.

Steve Ryan was lying in bed. The door was closed. He was more relaxed now. But there would be no relief for him until he broke through this anxiety.

Eddie was inclined to pooh-pooh the Freudian conception, or theory, of the Oedipus. Eddie should know better.

There was a sibling rivalry. The thought of Eddie pooh-poohing Freud's Oedipus theory had brought this to mind, and the phrase "sibling rivalry" had come to his mind. If Freud's theory of the Oedipus was wrong, Eddie's pooh-poohing of it ought to be right. This would be another victory for Eddie. Of course, the validity of Freud's Oedipus analysis was something separate from whether or not he was right or Eddie was right. But sibling rivalry with Eddie was now a disturbing influence in his thinking on the question. Well, there was sibling rivalry between Eddie and him. He could feel it. What about Eddie? Did he feel any sibling rivalry toward him?

Leo felt strong sibling rivalry. When he and Leo were kids they had both been full of it. And Leo still was, more so than he. Leo must have been thrown off Mama's lap for him, just as he had been thrown off for Franny. Now, where was he? Thrown off Mama's lap for the next baby to come along, Franny. And Mama's attention went to Franny. A lot of things that he had had went to Franny. He was no longer the cock of the walk at the Ryans'. When Eddie was shoved off Mama's lap for a new baby, he had gone to the Dunnes' and become the cock of the walk there. He had gotten it all. Why Eddie and not him? Why Franny and not him? Why any of them, and not him?

Eddie had told him that he couldn't explain the Oedipus to Leo and to Jack because he couldn't tell them that they had wanted to screw Mama. Of course he and Eddie both knew that this was a blunt simplification. All of his brothers, because of sibling rivalries, must have wanted to be cock of the walk with Mama. Now they never could be. Of course, he didn't want to be, and neither did they, except in the unconscious. What was it all about? It was all about what he had not been, and what the others had not been a long time ago. He was the cock of the walk with Hattie. But the frustration had been so painful. Well, that was to have been expected. That was why it had been so painful a little while ago. He hadn't been sure he could bear it.

Every male child wants to sleep with his mother. Eddie was right on one point; Leo and Jack couldn't accept their own Oedipal desires.

He had just about resolved his anxiety. Psychoanalysis was a wonderful thing, if it were rightly understood and applied.

In a minute or two he would get up and go back out there to the other rooms.

What time was it? he wondered.

Chapter 34

I

"It's going to be lonesome here without Mama," Clara said to Eddie in the kitchen.

"I imagine so."

"After all, we're used to seeing her every day," Clara said.

Eddie nodded.

"Everyone will miss her, we all loved her."

Eddie nodded again.

"But take you and Steve and Franny. None of you live in Chicago any more, and you all don't get here very often."

"I can understand, Clara."

"Jack, I mean our brother Jack, and Leo saw Mama a lot and she went to Jack and Molly's, not every day but almost every day. And Leo and Jack and Molly talked with her a lot on the telephone." Clara paused.

"But you saw her every day, every morning, and every night and were aware of her presence in the house here, Clara."

"Yes, that's what I mean. It's going to be so awfully lonesome."

"Yes, Clara, it will be."

"I hate to think of what it'll be like."

Eddie knew that his sister was suffering. He could see the sadness in her face and he could hear it in her voice.

The doorbell rang.

"I'll get it, Clara," Frances called, going to the front door.

It was Hazel Landry.

"Hello, Frances, how is your mother?" she asked.

"Oh, hello, Hazel. She's about the same. How are you?"

"I feel good enough."

Clara went to greet Hazel Landry.

"Why, hello, Hazel. It was awfully nice of you to come in all this cold."

"Not at all, Clara. I thought you might be tired, and I was sure that there would be something that I could do to help you. I had nothing to do at home."

"Harry telephoned a little while ago," Clara told her.

"Yes?"

"He said that he was downtown with Michael and that they would both be here in a little while."

"How long ago was it when he called, Clara?"

"About twenty or twenty-five minutes ago."

"Hello, Mrs. Landry," Steve said as he entered the room.

"Looks like you have a welcoming committee, Mrs. Landry," Eddie said, following Steve.

"It's nice of you to say that, Eddie, Steve."

They all stood a moment. Then Hazel Landry spoke:

"I was thinking I might clean up the house a little, Clara, if you would like me to."

"It's mighty nice of you to offer, but really, it's too much trouble for you. I'll do it myself. As a matter of fact, I was just about to start picking up a little when I heard the doorbell ring just now."

"Now, Clara, you have enough to do. It will be no trouble for me."

"Thank you so much, Hazel. We'll both do it, together."

II

"You know, Steve, I like Mrs. Landry," Eddie said.

"Oh yes, she's quite a person."

Mrs. Landry had finished helping Clara clean the house. They had worked quickly, straightening up more than really cleaning. Then she, Clara, Frances, and Cecilia Moran had sat in the kitchen to talk.

Eddie and Steve could hear them but they paid little attention to the voices.

"She's a dominating woman, though," Steve said.

Eddie didn't comment.

"She certainly dominated her husband, poor guy," Steve said.

"I know she did," Eddie said. "I was over there once when he was still alive."

"How long has he been dead? Three years?"

"I don't know. I just know he died."

"She was always overprotective about Harry. I think that was his real trouble," Steve said.

"What did her husband do for a living?" Eddie asked.

"I don't know. I did but it's gone clean out of my mind."

"Whatever it was, he seems to have left her enough for her to live in comfort," Eddie said.

"Yes, that's so. But the Landrys have been well off for as long as I've known them. Harry was always given whatever he wanted."

"That's probably his trouble," Eddie said.

"I'm pretty positive of that. He's a case of a dominating, overprotective mother."

"He doesn't seem to be hitting the bottle now."

"Come to think of it, Eddie, he seems to be drinking less since he came back from the war. And I don't think he drank so much while he was in the army, either."

"I've always thought that Harry was a nice enough fellow. But he doesn't come out that way from what Frances has to say about him."

"I don't think that he was nice to her," Steve said.

"I never knew him well but I've known him since about 1912."

"I didn't realize that you had known him so long, Eddie. In 1912, I was only two years old," Steve said.

Eddie looked off. He had been eight then, a boy in short pants.

Steve, watching him, knew that his brother was remembering other things. Well, he'd go see what Clara was doing.

III

"I was thinking about when we were kids, and lived at Twenty-fifth and La Salle, and then in the cottage at Forty-fifth and Wells," Steve said.

"Do you remember much about it all?" Clara asked.

"Some, but not as much as I wish."

"I don't remember too much about La Salle Street because that's when I was sent to Madison to live with Uncle Larry and Aunt Edna."

"How old was Mama then?" Steve asked.

"In her early thirties, I think."

Clara started to count to herself on her fingers.

"Maybe Mama was thirty-five at the time, Steve."

"Papa must have been a lot older than Mama," Steve said.

"I don't think so; he was only about six or so years older."

"Is that all?"

"I don't know for sure, Steve, but I think that's all."

"Well, I guess you know better than I do."

"Well, I've seen records and things. That's how I get the impression that I have," Clara said.

"I was only guessing," Steve said.

"Papa was young when he died," Clara said.

"I know."

"He must have died because of worry," Clara said.

"Worry could have contributed to it."

"You don't think that it would have caused his death?"

"It's not possible to say now what caused Papa's death," Steve said.

"Well, I think worry did."

"It could have been a contributing factor."

"It was a shame he died so young; it was tragic," Clara said.

Steve nodded.

"I think of Papa often," Clara said.

"What do you think about him, Clara?"

"Oh, I think of how he would have been proud of all of us if he had lived long enough to see what happened. That's one of the things I think."

"I suppose he would have been."

"Oh, I'm sure he would have been."

"Life was harder for a workingman in Papa's time, harder than it is today," Steve said.

"It certainly was. There's been progress since Papa's day."

Steve nodded.

Their talk died out.

Chapter 35

I

On the northwest corner of Garfield Boulevard and Wentworth Avenue there was a large tavern with an old-fashioned store front. Almost every time a streetcar or bus stopped, one or two men would walk in, most of them for a quick glass of beer.

Jack Boyle stopped in. He went up to the counter and asked for a beer.

"How have you been, Boyle?" the bartender asked.

"Just about the same. We're still on strike."

"I know."

"It's not as bad for me as it is for some of the fellows," Jack Boyle said. "I went back to my old trade of upholstering."

"You're lucky," the bartender said.

"I suppose I am," Jack Boyle said. "But then, it ain't all luck because I kept up my union dues and remained a member of the union in good standing. I always say even a bad union is better than no union."

"I guess you're right, Boyle," the bartender said. "It was a smart thing to do, keeping up your dues in the upholsterers'. It comes in handy now, doesn't it?"

"It sure does."

Several men carrying lunch cans entered the tavern and stepped up to the bar.

"Hello, Boyle. I ain't seen you in the last few days. Where you been keepin' yourself?" asked one of the men.

"Who, me? I've been workin'. We're still on strike but I went back to my old trade of upholsterin'."

"That May Motors strike's been goin' on for a long time now."

"You don't have to tell me," Jack Boyle said. "Every night at midnight, I'm freezin' my ass off on the picket line."

"Hey, Boyle," another man called out as he walked into the tavern.

"Oh, hello, Gorzik."

"Boyle, didn't I hear that someone was sick at your place?"

"Yeah, it's the mother-in-law."

"That's too bad, Jack. I'm mighty sorry to hear it," Gorzik said.

"Well, we all have to go someday. But to tell you the truth, I feel lousy. I liked the old lady a lot."

"This is on the house, Boyle," the bartender said, pushing a fresh glass of beer toward Jack Boyle.

"Thanks, thank you."

"Don't mention it."

"It's that serious, is it, Jack?" Gorzik asked.

"She's dying."

They were all sympathetic.

He finished his second beer. Followed by wishes of good luck and sympathy, Jack Boyle left the tavern and turned on Garfield Boulevard to walk the block to Wells Street.

II

Jack Boyle wished that he could have stayed at the tavern and had a few more. He had not felt like going home. With all that was going on now, it wasn't the same.

Depression came over him as he climbed the front stairs. He reached in his pocket for his key. What would he find inside? He let himself in. It was quiet. Was the old lady still alive? She must be or they would have telephoned him at work.

Jack Boyle hung his clothes up and turned into the parlor. No one was there. He heard voices from the kitchen.

"Is that you, Jack?" Clara called.

Well, at least it was quiet. Everyone wasn't sitting around yakking. The Ryans were all yakkers. And he was tired of coming home to it every night. He knew it couldn't be helped. No one had deliberately forced this trouble on him and Clara. No one could help it. But he couldn't help it either if he didn't like it. Hell, he didn't have to like it, even if he did have to put up with it.

He hadn't answered Clara. She called again.

"Is that you, Jack?"

"Yes, it's me."

He went to the kitchen.

"I thought you'd be here half an hour ago, Jack."

"I'm a little late tonight."

"I see you are."

"Anything new?"

"No, I wouldn't say there was anything new."

"How is your mother, Clara?"

"Just about the same."

He was feeling down in the mouth and there was nothing he could do about it. Nothing except get drunk. He liked to get drunk. But he wouldn't.

He felt tired, kind of sleepy. He wished he didn't have to picket tonight. It was so cold; he'd freeze his balls off.

"How's the weather, Jack?" Steve asked.

"Cold enough."

"I'm just about to start supper, Jack. Do you want to take a nap and I'll call you when it's ready?"

"Yes, I think I will. I stopped off at the tavern and had a couple of beers and they made me sleepy."

"I'll wake you when supper's ready."

Jack Boyle started toward the stairs.

"See you all when the grub's ready," he said.

III

"There's no use in asking the question—how much longer will this go on, Steve?" Eddie said.

"No, there really isn't, Eddie."

"I'm sure it's a question on everyone's mind here," Eddie said.

"It has to be, I guess."

"But there's nothing to do but wait, and learn whatever we can from it," Eddie said.

"That about sums it up, Eddie."

"I know it does, but it's not a pleasant summing up."

"Well, no, it isn't, but there are lots of things about which there can't be any pleasant summing up. You know that, Eddie."

"Yes, I do."

"It can't last much longer."

Eddie didn't respond. They were all wishing for her death. Eddie knew it and Steve knew it. But it was best not to admit it.

"I've never seen anything like it," Steve said.

"Oh, you must have seen cases similar to Mama's, Steve."

"Well, maybe, yes."

"There's no telling how people will die," Eddie said.

"No, there isn't."

How would he die? He couldn't think of any way except in bed. But thinking of how you might die seemed an idiotic waste of time and emotion. It was a frustrating effort, too. And decidedly depressing.

While they waited for their mother to die, they remembered things she had said and things they had said to her.

Eddie hoped that all this might be organized into a coherent sequence of events which would reveal some of the meanings of his mother's life.

There had been purpose in her life.

His mother had lived on this earth in such a way that when she died her soul would go to heaven. His mother had lived with that purpose in mind. It couldn't be said, then, that there had been no purpose in her life. She had lived for a purpose and this was it.

She must have had other purposes in her life.

"Eddie, dinner's on the table," Clara called from the kitchen.

Eddie decided to pursue these thoughts later on.

IV

While he ate, he thought about the purpose of his mother's life. His mother had had a religious purpose to her life. There were simple purposes that his mother and others lived for. There was the purpose to live for the day, for the next hour, for the next morning, or for the next meal. On Monday they lived for Tuesday, on Tuesday for Wednesday, on Wednesday for Thursday, on Thursday for Friday, on Friday for Saturday, on Saturday for Sunday, on Sunday for Monday, and again on Monday for Tuesday. Little purposes, such as these, loomed with perhaps more significance than the bigger purposes. Without these little purposes there couldn't be the bigger ones. Anyway, it was instinct to live.

"There weren't many in the tavern," Jack Boyle said.

"I'll tell you why," Clara smiled. "It's too easy to find. If a fellow doesn't get home when he's expected, the first place his wife would go to find him is that corner tavern."

"You're right, Clara," Jack Boyle laughed.

"I guess that if you want to set up a prosperous tavern, the place to locate it would be one that isn't as easy for a man's wife to find," Steve said.

"You might have something there, Steve," Jack Boyle said.

"How many times did Mama have Papa take the pledge?" Eddie asked.

"Oh, she was always dragging Papa over to the parish priest to take the pledge," Clara said.

"Mama was a smart girl in her way," Steve said.

"Oh yes, Mama wasn't dumb," Clara said.

"I kind of like that, takin' the old man to the parish priest to have him take the pledge and then him breakin' the pledge all of the time," Jack Boyle said with a laugh.

"That was a regular feature of the Ryan household," Steve said.

"Papa just liked to get drunk once in a while, that's all," Clara said.

"He did it at least once a month, didn't he?" Eddie asked.

"Not always," Clara Boyle said.

"It doesn't matter now much whether he got drunk once a month or twice a month, does it?" Jack Boyle asked.

"No, it doesn't, not now," Eddie said.

"In his day, a workingman had fewer pleasures than he has today," Jack Boyle said. "There wasn't much else for him to do but lift a few, even if it was a few too many."

"That's true," Steve said.

V

"Of course, it was different in them days," Jack Boyle said.

They were still sitting around the table talking. Leo and Florence had arrived.

"In them days, a workingman didn't have nothin' to do with himself," Jack Boyle said.

"Didn't they used to call the saloon the poor man's supper club?" Steve asked.

"Yes, that's what lots of folks called it before Prohibition days," Jack Boyle said.

"That's right," Eddie said.

"And that's what it was," Jack Boyle laughed.

"I guess so," Clara said.

"In our father's day, it was a lot different," Leo said.

"That's just what I was sayin', Leo, when you and Florence walked in here," Jack Boyle said.

"Take the life of our old man," Leo began.

"It must have been the same with my old man," Jack Boyle said.

"Today, you've got the radio, movies; you've got many things. That makes all the difference in the world."

"You said it, Leo," Jack Boyle nodded.

"And workingmen have automobiles today," Leo said.

"Not me," Jack Boyle said.

"I know, Jack, but we'll get our car someday," Clara said.

"I have no doubt about that," Jack Boyle said, "but how long is it until someday?"

"And workin' hours are much shorter today," Leo said.

"A hell of a lot shorter. In my old man's time, I don't think anybody would have dreamed of a forty-hour working week," Jack Boyle said.

"I always think of the bowling, too," Clara said.

"There was bowlin' in them days," Jack Boyle said.

"Oh, I know there was bowling, but workingmen couldn't go bowling twice a week the way you can, Jack," Clara told him.

"That's true, Clara."

"I often think of that and of Papa, when I go watch Jack bowl," Clara said.

"But Papa bowled sometimes, I think," Clara added.

"Was he good, Leo?" Jack Boyle asked.

"Gee, I don't know, Jack."

"I imagine that he was," Steve said. "I imagine Papa was good at almost anything he did."

"You've got something there, Steve," Leo said.

"My old man didn't give two hoots for bowlin'," Jack Boyle said.

"Of course, it's really only recently, and especially during the war, that bowling has become such a big sport for the workingman," Clara said.

"That's right," Jack Boyle said. "I know I didn't do much bowlin' before the war."

"I did, through the Order of Christopher bowling leagues," Leo said.

"You've been bowling longer than I have, Leo," Jack Boyle said.

"Leo's been bowling ever since I knew him," Florence said.

"Does Jack still bowl?" Steve asked.

"Jack Ryan?" Leo asked.

"Yes."

"I don't think so," Leo answered.

"He never talks about it any more," Jack Boyle said. "I guess he must have given it up."

"He used to be a good bowler," Leo commented.

"You never cared much for bowling, did you, Eddie?" Clara asked.

"Oh, I bowled but I wasn't very good at it."

"That's kind of a surprise because you were so good at sports," Clara said.

"But if I wasn't good at something I gave up on it. I only liked sports where I was good."

"That makes sense," Jack Boyle said.

"Yes," Clara said.

They had talked enough. Clara started collecting dishes. Florence and Frances helped her.

Eddie sat, thinking about what had been said. Did it mean so much?

Was it a sign of great victory for the workingman that Jack Boyle could afford to bowl twice a week and his father couldn't? What had Jack Boyle's bowling cost in suffering and sacrifice? The truth was that life was better for Jack than it had been for his own old man. Things could be a lot better. And Jack Boyle was on strike now to make things better. He would be on the picket line tonight for just this reason. His old man had been a strong union man but unions were new then and there hadn't been much help for them when the old man had his stroke and had to quit work. That simple fact had had a profound effect on his brothers and sisters. It had changed their lives. For his brother Jack and later for Leo, it had been the end of their schooling. They had gone to work.

Chapter 36

I

"Well, Eddie, I just don't know." Steve shook his head.

"Know what, Steve?"

"Whether or not Mama's aware of what's going on. I think she may be. She must have a distorted idea of what's happening."

"I would think that too," Eddie said. "And I would also think that she must be very frightened. And possibly suffering."

"Well, yes," Steve said, thoughtful.

Some moments passed.

"I wonder . . ." Steve began.

"Yes?"

"I wonder if Mama's in a euphoric state."

"I hadn't thought of that."

"She could be."

"Well, I hope she is."

"So do I, of course," Steve said.

"If she does know something of what it's all about, Steve, it must be terror for her."

"If that's so, it was probably more in the beginning when she was first stricken."

"Possibly. And possibly not."

"Human beings can get used to almost anything, Eddie."

"This is something we don't know."

"Every day at the hospital I see people living for just one more meal, one more bowel movement," Steve said.

Eddie shook his head.

They did not speak for a little bit.

"I just have an idea that Mama knows she's dying."

"Do you think she's frightened, Steve?"

"I couldn't answer that, Eddie."

There was another pause.

"One whole side of Mama is destroyed," Steve said.

"Yes."

"Well, it will be over soon."

Eddie looked questioningly at Steve.

"What do you mean by soon?"

"Oh, I mean a few days, a week. It could be more than a week, but a week is a long time."

"I see. I didn't know if you meant immediately," Eddie said.

"It could come immediately, but I don't expect it to."

"We don't really know, do we, Steve?"

"No, we don't."

II

Was Mama afraid? Eddie hoped not. It would be hideous for her, lying there helpless, waiting for death to come. He couldn't imagine a worse fate for her. Or for himself, for that matter.

What about him when his time should come? Would he be resigned or would he be angry and full of frustration? Both, probably. He felt both now. He thought of Victor Hugo's description of Balzac dying. He'd like to reread it. He thought of Dreiser. His mind had been full of death when Fran called to tell him about Mama's stroke. He had just written of Dreiser's death. Who would write of his? He wouldn't be able to; he would be locked out, unable to leave a last account.

He would die thinking of all that he had achieved. What could his dying mother think of? Did it matter? Yes, it mattered. Nora Ryan's life was a world. For Nora Ryan. These thoughts brought back his most familiar and important ideas. He must one day dignify his mother's suffering in the consciousness. This scene at Clara and Jack Boyle's was only one of millions of scenes. The outside world was full of millions of such scenes. And he was thinking of scenes other than ones in which someone was dying. But at this moment there were others dying, some in agony and some without agony.

He hoped his mother was dying without agony. Would he have reached a conclusion about this when it was time to write of the death of Nora Ryan? He didn't know.

The book about the death of Nora Ryan was for the future.

Nora Ryan was not yet dead.

III

"I keep asking myself the question over and over again," Clara said.

"Yes?"

Eddie believed he knew what Clara was going to say.

"I just keep asking myself if Mama is suffering."

"I've thought about that too."

"Yes?" Clara Boyle spoke quickly, hoping that Eddie could answer this question.

"And I just don't know."

Clara's face sagged.

"I hate to think that she is."

"She's so helpless," Eddie said, shaking his head.

"Thank heavens she's not in pain."

"I don't think she is."

"But if she knows she's going to die, that might make her suffer," Clara said.

"It seems to me, Clara, that she's been like this for so long now, Mama's aware of what's going on, she must have gotten a little used to it by now."

"Gee, I never thought of that, but maybe."

"She doesn't seem to be suffering now and she did at first."

"Oh yes, I think she did suffer at first, Eddie."

"But we can't be sure. We'll never know."

"That's right, we'll never know."

This suddenly seemed to be so horrible that she wanted to cry. But she didn't cry.

Life was hard, she thought.

IV

"There hasn't been much talk about God," Steve commented.

Eddie looked at him; the remark seemed out of place.

"Why should there be?" he asked.

"Hell, Mama's dying and she was so religious. When a Catholic is dying, God and heaven and hell and all that the Church stands for should come to mind," Steve said, talking slowly.

Eddie didn't comment. There wasn't much he could say. He wished that Steve weren't such a vulgar atheist.

"They're thinking about God, Steve, if that's what you're wondering."

"Yes, maybe they are."

"I think the ones who believe are thinking about God and praying to Him," Eddie said.

"I guess so."

"And there's not much to say about God."

"Oh, there's lots of things that they can say about God," Steve argued.

"Why should they want to?"

"Well, isn't this the time when people who believe in God speak of Him a lot? Death and hell are on their minds. If people believe in God at a time like this, they'll need Him, and think of Him, won't they?" Steve asked.

"They'll pray but they don't have to talk about God."

"I suppose you're right."

"What did I hear about God?" Frances asked, walking in.

"Not much, Frances." Eddie smiled at her.

"I was saying to Eddie that not much has been said about God around here."

"No, I haven't heard much either," Frances said.

"Of course, a strain is put on faith at a time like this," Eddie said.

"Yes, it is," Steve agreed.

"And they're afraid of losing their faith, or of having their faith damaged," Eddie went on.

"You think so?" Frances asked.

"Yes."

"Do you mean because of you and your presence here, Eddie?"
Steve asked.

"To some degree, yes," Eddie said.

"I guess that's so."

Steve looked off into space. He seemed to have lost interest in the
conversation. Suddenly he grinned.

"Well, I guess we've lost God."

"How come?" Frances asked.

"In our discussion just now. God got lost among the Ryans," Steve
laughed.

Frances smiled.

But the joke was on them, not God, Frances thought. Her mother
was dying. She could remember how sad she was when her father
died. But that was many years ago; she had been twelve years old.
Since then, she had been married and divorced; had pulled up roots
and moved to California with Michael in an effort to make a better
life for herself. It had taken her a long time to find herself. But she
had been able to get an education. She had earned the respect of the
people she worked with in California. She was a good chemist; she
did good work. She had felt that she was moving up in the world.
But now she wondered. Being with her family confused her. The
Ryan family seemed to be divided into two sets. There was her oldest
brother Jack and his wife Molly; her brother Leo and his wife
Florence; and her sister Clara and her husband Jack. They reminded
her of her past, of the days when she was a little girl living with her
mother and father.

On the other side of the fence were her brothers Steve and Eddie.
Steve was a doctor. And Eddie was a famous writer. Both of them
had made something of themselves. She had too. The three of them
weren't like the others. She felt it and she was sure Steve felt it. But
she wasn't so sure that Eddie did. He seemed to like talking to Jack
Ryan about baseball. He and Jack Ryan and Clara could talk for
hours, it seemed to her, about something that the Chicago Cubs or
the White Sox had done years ago. And Eddie liked to talk with Jack
Boyle about the union. He asked Jack questions and you could tell
from the way he listened that he respected what Jack had to say. It
was funny in a way but Eddie seemed more at home with all of them
than she and Steve did.

She loved Eddie; she loved him a lot. But when she was around him she felt unimportant.

Right now, she didn't want to continue with these thoughts. She was sad enough about what was happening without thinking about anything that would make her sadder. Maybe she'd take a walk. But it was too cold out and she wasn't used to the Chicago cold any more. She ought to be able to find a book to read. She had tried to read the newspaper but she wasn't that interested in Chicago news any more. She never got like this in California. Not as restless as she was this minute. In California she didn't have time to be. By the time she drove to work, put in a full day, and got back home, she had put in a ten-hour day. And then she had to cook for her and Michael. On weekends she had shopping and cleaning to do. And she had made friends out there. Her life was full. Here she felt closed in. Of course, there were reasons for feeling this way. It was not only that she was closed in, it was also the fact that her mother was in a room nearby breathing her last breaths on earth.

Eddie was staring out of the window at the people walking by. He turned and dropped heavily on the couch.

"How are you feeling, Franny?" he asked.

"How is anyone feeling?"

She wondered why she had answered so sharply. She loved Eddie. He hadn't hesitated about giving her money for this trip. Or the money she needed when she was getting a divorce. Or whenever she asked him to pay for anything. She loved Eddie and she had every reason to believe he loved her. It was just, well, she resented the fact that he used all of them as material for his books. She didn't want to be material for him or for anybody else. He didn't know how she felt. Nobody did. Nobody could understand how depressed she got when she thought about so many things. Nobody.

"Will you be getting to California any time soon, Eddie?" she asked.

"Possibly."

"I wish you would."

"I'll be there if I can line up some lectures out there," Eddie said.

"That would be wonderful."

She hoped he would come. He could afford to visit her. He always had told her that she was his favorite "Ryan." She'd be mad if he didn't come.

"I'll get there sooner or later," he said.

"Well, make it sooner."

"I'll come when I can, Fran. You can count on that."

"I will, Eddie," she said, smiling.

They did not say more. Frances grew pensive. She wished she were back home this minute.

Eddie noticed her mood but said nothing. Frances must be a sad girl, he thought. But she was no longer a girl; she was a woman. He looked at her.

Noticing his look, Fran smiled at him but it was a wistful smile.

Chapter 37

I

"You're going to send me some of your books, Mr. Ryan?" Cecilia Moran asked.

They were sitting at the kitchen table.

"Yes, I always keep my promise. I have your address and as soon as I get back to New York I'll attend to it."

"You'll sign them, won't you, and say something in them?"

"Yes, I shall."

"I'll certainly treasure them."

Eddie looked at her. He'd like to make her. But this was not for now.

"Well, I must get back to your mother now. I enjoyed this little talk."

"I did too, Cecilia."

II

"Cecilia Moran likes you, Eddie," Clara told him. "She's read some of your books and she was telling me how much she likes them. And you know, she's a wonderful nurse."

"She seems to be."

"Oh, she is, Eddie. Dr. Evans gets her whenever he can. He seems to think the world of her."

"He does?"

"Yes. She told me that she's taken care of many of his patients."

"If I were a doctor, I think I'd want a nurse like her for my patients," Eddie said.

"Most of her cases are old people. She was telling me that she just took care of an old man who died."

What a depressing way to make a living, Eddie thought.

"It really made me sad listening to her," Clara went on. "I'm glad I'm not a nurse. It's too hard a life."

"It must be."

"Of course, some women have to be nurses. They're needed. I don't know what the sick would do if everybody felt like me."

Eddie nodded.

"Well, we're lucky. Both of the ones we have for Mama are good."

Eddie nodded again.

"And they're both Irish Catholic. I'm glad we managed to get them for Mama."

Eddie smiled at this.

Clara smiled back at him. "Well, they both fit right in. And Cecilia Moran seems to think so much of you, Eddie."

"I'm glad to know that, Clara."

Steve joined them.

"What were you two talking about?"

"Cecilia Moran," Clara told him.

"She's an interesting subject, isn't she, Eddie?" Steve asked, smiling.

"Yes, she is."

"I was telling Eddie that Cecilia Moran thinks the world of him," Clara said.

"Oh, she does, does she?" Steve asked.

"Yes."

"I think she likes all of us."

"I'm sure she does, Steve," Clara said.

"After all, the Ryans are a likable lot," Steve laughed.

"I think they are," Clara laughed.

"You don't really care, do you, Eddie?" Steve had stopped laughing.

"I have no objection to being liked but I don't live to be liked and don't go out of my way for it."

"But you don't mind that Cecilia Moran likes you, do you?" Steve teased.

"On the contrary, I like it."

"We can tell by the way you're smiling," Clara said.

"But I've got the inside track, Eddie. I'm the doctor," Steve said.

Eddie looked at him. He had noticed before that Steve seemed attracted to Cecilia Moran. Steve's kidding had reinforced this impression. This was unusual for Steve. Steve, and all his brothers, had seemed to lose interest in all other women when they married. But there was no mistaking Steve's interest in Cecilia. God, he certainly hoped that Steve's sibling rivalry toward him wouldn't lead him to a serious infatuation with a young woman merely because he, Eddie Ryan, was interested in her. Last June, when he visited Steve in Washington, Steve had harped on the subject of sibling rivalry. It had become obvious that this was playing a big role in Steve's analysis. Hell, there was nothing so unusual about that. Steve was his younger brother.

The same thing had happened to him, Eddie, when he went to work at the Express Company. He had been told over and over again that he would never be as good as his older brother Jack. This hadn't bothered him. He didn't remember any sibling rivalry.

Well, he wasn't going to try to understand it all now. He was tired. He didn't want to think of anything more complicated than some way to make Cecilia Moran even more aware of his presence than she already was.

III

She liked working at the Boyles', liked it as much as she could any job. She didn't mind the work but she did mind the sadness that went along with it. She had to nurse so many sick and helpless people and try to make them comfortable in their last days. Well, she couldn't spend too much time thinking like this. She had to think of her patients as cases and give them the best care she could and follow doctors' orders to the letter. Nora Ryan's case was a little different. Even though Mrs. Ryan was a patient of Dr. Evans and it was Dr. Evans who had called her on the case, Mrs. Ryan's son was a doctor and Dr. Ryan sometimes acted as if he were the doctor in attendance. It made it a little hard for her. But it must be hard on Dr. Ryan too. He was young and it was his mother dying.

She wasn't complaining. No, she wouldn't complain about this job. After all, it was because of it that she had had an opportunity to meet the author, Edward A. Ryan. He was such a nice man. He didn't act at all like a celebrity. And he seemed to like her. She could tell from the way he looked at her and the things he said. He had asked her for her address so that he could send her copies of his books. He had also said that he would call her sometimes when he was on one of his trips to Chicago. She hoped he would; she liked him. She liked all the Ryans. They had so much feeling for each other. It was nice.

Oh, but she was tired. This was her second hard case in a row. Well, it wouldn't last much longer. Mrs. Ryan was putting up a hard fight but the poor woman couldn't last much longer.

Cecilia looked at her wrist watch. Time to take Mrs. Ryan's temperature. She rose from the chair.

IV

A few seconds after she had recorded Mrs. Ryan's temperature, Clara Boyle came to the door and asked her if she'd like a cup of coffee.

"Oh, thank you, Mrs. Boyle," Cecilia said as she walked into the kitchen and sat down.

It was nice of Mrs. Boyle to do this.

"If you stay around us much, Cecilia, you'll be a big coffee drinker. We all are. Especially my brother Eddie."

"I've noticed that. I hope it isn't bad for him; he's such a nice man."

"Yes, he is, and he's so kind," Clara said.

"He seems to be."

"He is. All of my brothers are. I'd be hard put to name one who's nicer than the others."

"It must be wonderful to have so many fine brothers, Mrs. Boyle."

"It is; makes me very proud."

"It ought to."

Cecilia Moran smiled. The Ryans had a wonderful family feeling.

"Do you have any brothers, Cecilia?"

"No, I don't."

"Are you an only child?"

"No; I have two sisters. They're in Wisconsin. I was born there. I came here because I wanted to be a nurse."

"Oh. I thought that you were born in Chicago. I don't know how I got that impression but I did."

"That could happen."

"And I suppose I thought you had brothers because you get along so well with mine."

"They're easy to get along with, Mrs. Boyle."

"I think so."

They both smiled.

Cecilia Moran finished her coffee and rose.

"Excuse me but I ought to be getting back to my patient."

"Yes, of course."

Cecilia Moran went back to Nora Ryan's bedroom.

V

It had been a long day. Well, it was almost over. She would be leaving soon. And when she got home she'd soak in a tub of warm water and then maybe read a mystery story until she fell asleep. She could smell something cooking. It smelled good. It was almost time for supper. She liked eating with the Ryans.

VI

Cecilia Moran was smiling. The Ryans, all but Edward, had been very talkative tonight. They were still at it.

"You know? I'm worried," Dr. Ryan said.

"What about, Steve? Hattie and the girls?" Mrs. Boyle asked.

"No, I'm worried about my baby sister."

"No need to worry about me, Steve," the young Mrs. Landry told him.

"Well, I do."

Cecilia Moran looked at Dr. Ryan. He was joking, she could tell.

"Well, I suppose I should be grateful," Mrs. Landry said.

"Frances, Steve wants to be your big brother," Edward Ryan said.

"I am her big brother," Dr. Ryan declared.

"You're one of my big brothers," Mrs. Landry corrected.

"What about me? Ain't I in this family?" Mrs. Boyle asked.

"You don't count, Clara; they don't have to worry about you. You worry about them," Jack Boyle said.

"Well, I do worry about them."

Mrs. Boyle's voice was defensive.

"But not about your baby sister," Mrs. Landry teased.

"You know I worry about you, Franny."

"Everybody worries about me and I'm the one who doesn't need it."

"That's tellin' 'em, Franny," Mrs. Boyle said.

"Listen . . ." Dr. Ryan began.

"I am listening. Don't you think I'd listen to my big brother?" Mrs. Landry asked.

"I should hope so."

"All right, Steve, out with it. Tell us why you're worried about your baby sister."

"I will if you'll all stop interrupting."

"Silence, everybody. The doctor is speaking," Jack Boyle rapped on the table.

Dr. Ryan waited a second or two.

"We haven't found a man for Franny yet."

"I've heard funnier things," Mrs. Landry said.

"I'm not trying to be funny."

"We know that. That's what makes you so funny."

"Well, I've given it a lot of thought and I'm worried."

"You're worried about Franny finding a man with her living in Beverly Hills where all those Hollywood actors are?" Mrs. Boyle asked.

"No actors for me, please," Mrs. Landry said.

"See?" Dr. Ryan said.

"Well, let me tell you something . . ." Mrs. Boyle began.

"Go ahead, Clara, you got the floor."

"Franny isn't the only one to be worried about. What about Cecilia Moran here? She's too nice a girl to be without a man."

"Oh, Mrs. Boyle," Cecilia Moran protested, her face reddening.

"Cecilia and I can take care of ourselves," Mrs. Landry said, smiling at her.

"Well, I suppose God helps those who help themselves," Dr. Ryan commented.

Cecilia Moran watched Edward Ryan. He seemed to be amused by this talk but he wasn't saying much. She was getting tired of it. And she had to be careful. She couldn't get too intimate with the Ryans. When people lost someone near and dear to them, they didn't always behave as they normally would. They could do and say things that you wouldn't expect; turn on you and make trouble. She didn't expect anything like this from the Ryans but even so she had to be on guard.

"I was just noticing the time. The others ought to be gettting here," Mrs. Boyle said.

"They'll be here," Dr. Ryan said.

Supper was finished. Cecilia Moran rose, excused herself, and went back to Nora Ryan's bedroom. As soon as she had left the room Frances turned to Clara.

"She's all right, isn't she?"

"Oh yes. She's a good nurse, so conscientious."

"Is that so, Dr. Ryan?" Leo asked, walking into the room.

He and Florence had just arrived.

"Yes, she is. She's all right but I must insist that none of you interfere with her work here."

"Did you hear that, Leo?" Jack Boyle asked, laughing.

"I heard it all right."

"Steve's gonna see to it that we don't interfere with Miss Moran's work."

"Maybe he wants to do the interferin' himself."

"I am a doctor," Steve said.

"Ain't doctors human?" Jack Boyle asked him.

"Did you hear that, Steve?" Frances asked.

"Yes, I heard it."

"Well, what have you got to say?"

"I merely consider the source," he snapped.

Jack Boyle looked at Leo and grinned.

"You guys think I'm kidding, don't you?" Steve demanded.

"Aren't you?" Eddie asked.

"I am not. I mean every word I say."

There was an edge to his voice. Jack looked at Leo, puzzled.

"I think he means it, Leo."

"You think so?"

Jack Boyle nodded. He was no longer smiling.

"Say, what's the matter? What are we talking about?" Frances asked.

"Your brother Steve," Leo said.

"I thought we were talking about Cecilia Moran," Clara said.

"Careful, Clara, she'll hear," Frances warned.

"Well, it wouldn't be a very intelligent conversation to hear," Leo said.

"I agree to that," Frances said.

"I find it kind of goofy," Leo said.

Steve suddenly got up and went into Nora Ryan's bedroom.

"I can't tell if he meant what he said," Jack Boyle said.

"Oh, I don't think so," Clara told him. "He was only kidding."

"No, he wasn't," Eddie said.

"I didn't think so either, Eddie," Jack Boyle said, shaking his head.

"He had to be," Clara argued.

Before anyone could say anything more, Steve came out of the bedroom. Looking at them sternly, he spoke:

"I don't want anybody in this kitchen unless it's necessary. I don't want any of you in Mama's room or walking around outside her door."

They all stared at him.

"What's gotten into you, Steve?" Eddie demanded.

"Nothing's gotten into me. There's too much noise out here, too much moving around, too much coming and going. I want it to stop."

"All right, Steve, we'll be quiet."

Leo's voice was low.

"Good; and stay quiet."

Leo stared at him; he didn't know what to make of Steve's tone of
voice.

"I suppose I've been put in my place," he said after a short silence.

"It's not a matter of putting you in your place."

"No?"

"No, it's a matter of Mama's condition. I want it kept quiet in
here. I don't want the kitchen used as a meeting place. You can talk
in the parlor in front of the house."

"I see."

"That's a roundabout way of saying that Steve wants to be with
Cecilia Moran without us in the way," Eddie said.

"Well, if you care to take it that way, Eddie."

Steve's voice was cold.

Eddie didn't answer.

"What d'ya say to that, Leo?" Jack Boyle asked.

"I guess it's the doctor's prerogative. Isn't that the word?"

"Yes, it is," Eddie said.

"Well, Mama is sick," Clara said, turning to him.

"I know that, Clara, but it just so happens that Steve is the loudest
person in the house."

"That's not so," Steve protested.

"Yes, it is."

Steve turned and walked out. None of them spoke. They waited
for Eddie to say something.

"He'll have to take this up with his analyst when he gets back to
Washington."

Jack Boyle laughed. In another minute they were all laughing.

VII

He heard them laughing. His stubbornness had come up in his analysis often. He thought that he had overcome it but he must have been
too confident. This was clearly a regression. It was sibling rivalry.
And Eddie was smart enough to recognize this. He had to get himself
out of this spot. He didn't want to look foolish.

He walked back to the kitchen, poured himself a cup of coffee,
and took it to the table.

"Oh, what the hell, I was only kidding."

"I knew it all along," Clara said.

"Well, it wasn't very funny," Frances said.

"Oh, Franny, it was a joke," he protested.

"Next time, make your joke funnier," Leo told him.

Steve shrugged. He could stand a little kidding. Eddie was being awfully quiet. What was he thinking?

"Well, I'd better start the dishes," Clara announced, standing up.

Steve was showing the strain, Eddie thought. It was understandable. Conditions here were bound to affect all of them sooner or later. Well, Steve had come out of it. There would be more eruptions, he was sure of that. He should be prepared for them so that they didn't get out of hand.

Leo yawned. Steve was filling his pipe.

"Let's go in the living room," Eddie suggested.

"We might as well," Steve said.

They all rose and followed Eddie. Jack Boyle looked at his watch.

"Jack and Molly ought to be getting here soon," he said, looking toward the window.

Chapter 38

I

"Why are they staying out in the kitchen?" Leo asked.

"Search me," Jack Boyle answered.

"Knowing Aunt Jenny, I suspect she's waiting to be invited in here," Eddie said, smiling.

"They don't have to be invited," Jack Boyle said. "They know they're welcome."

"You know how Aunt Jenny is, Jack," Clara said. "Right now she isn't the center of attention and that's eating her up."

"I think you're right, Clara," Frances said.

"It's all right with me if she wants to be the center of attention," Jack Boyle said.

"What's the matter with Uncle Dick?" Leo asked.

"Oh, he can't come in if she doesn't give him permission," Jack Boyle said.

"She certainly has got him bamboozled," Leo said.

"Well, he's old and she's all he's got," Clara said. "And she does take good care of him. But I do wish they'd come in here with us instead of sitting out there."

"Maybe they think we ain't good enough for them," Leo said.

"Why would they think that?" Jack Boyle asked.

"Because that's the way the Dunnes think."

"Well then, let them sit out there," Steve said.

"I just don't feel right about it," Clara said, "I'm going to ask them to come in."

She got up and started to the kitchen.

In a few minutes she came back followed by Dick and Jenny.

"Here, let me get some chairs," Jack Boyle said, getting up.

"Oh, don't bother."

Jenny's voice was almost humble.

"It's no trouble."

Eddie got up to help. Together, he and Jack Boyle brought in two more chairs. Jen and Dick thanked them.

There was an awkward silence.

"I hope we didn't interrupt you," Jenny said.

"Oh no, Aunt Jenny," Clara told her. "We weren't talking about anything in particular."

Another silence. Jenny spoke again.

"What do you hear from home, Eddie?"

"Oh, they're well."

"I'll bet they miss you."

Eddie nodded indifferently.

"Tommy is such a beautiful little boy."

"He certainly is," Clara nodded.

"Is everything well with your family?" Jenny asked, turning to Steve.

"It was the last time I heard."

"They miss you, I bet."

Steve nodded.

"Eddie . . ." Dick began.

Something was coming. Eddie knew it.

"Yes?"

"How are business conditions in New York?"

"Good, I suppose. Publishers seem prosperous."

"Then you're making a lot of money?" Jenny asked.

"I don't know; I never can tell."

"But a lot of people buy your books. I'm always hearing about them."

"It takes an awful lot of books sold to make an author rich."

"I've been thinking," Jenny said, looking at Dick, "Eddie is going to get rich and then he'll lend me the money to start a little store. I'll pay him back, of course, with interest, in no time."

"I wish I could do something like that, Aunt Jen."

"The money will be safe, Eddie, I'll make it back and pay you as fast as I make it."

"But I haven't got the money."

"It won't take that much and I'll make it back with interest in six months."

"Aunt Jenny, Eddie's telling you that he hasn't got the money," Clara spoke up.

"Doesn't Little Brother want to help his poor old aunt?"

"I would, Aunt Jen, if I had it."

"Won't you at least listen to my plans, Eddie? You'll see; you won't have to worry about getting your money back."

"Why won't you believe me when I say I don't have the money?"

"It wouldn't take a lot and it would only be for six months."

"I haven't got it, Aunt Jenny," Eddie snapped.

"You don't have to jump down my throat."

She burst into tears.

"Your Aunt Jenny was simply stating a business proposition," Dick said.

"Oh, Dick," Jenny sobbed, "he doesn't care; he's so ungrateful. Don't beg him."

Dick looked from her to Eddie and then back at Jenny. The others said nothing.

"I was only asking for what I deserve," Jenny sobbed.

Dick's look was accusing. Eddie didn't speak.

"He's no good, Dick," Jenny sobbed.

"Don't cry, Jen."

"Oh, Dick, he's no good."

"Aunt Jenny, please . . ." Clara started.

Dick stared at her, shaking his head.

"Eddie . . ." he began.

Eddie looked at him.

"Can't I talk with you for a moment, please, Eddie?"

"Don't bother with him, Dick, he's no good," Jenny said.

"About what, Uncle Dick? I told her; I haven't got the money."

"You see? I told you, Dick. He'll only insult you."

"Aunt Jenny, you'll have to stop this," Clara said.

"Eddie!"

Dick spoke urgently. Eddie rose. He started toward the dining room, his uncle behind him.

"Eddie, your Aunt Jenny is upset. I don't think that her request was unreasonable."

"But, Uncle Dick, she won't let up and I don't have the money."

"She thinks you have the money," Dick said.

Eddie shook his head in frustration.

"But I haven't. What can I do to make that clear?"

"Don't beg him for money, Dick, let him keep it," Jenny called from the living room.

"Aunt Jenny, you're going to have to stop this," Clara said.

"Yes, this is my home and I don't want any more of this fighting," Jack Boyle said.

"Don't blame me," Jenny said, "I was the one insulted."

She started to cry again. Dick rushed to her.

"Jen, don't take it so hard."

He looked at Eddie, his face hurt.

Eddie was angry. Aunt Jenny had been waiting to create a scene in which she could be the center of attention and he had let her trap him.

"We'll leave, Dick."

"Yes, I think you should, Aunt Jen," Eddie told her.

She broke into sobs.

"To think, he'd even throw me out into the street when my poor sister is lying at death's door."

Dick looked at Eddie again. He was suffering; Eddie could see this, but he was unrelenting. Aunt Jenny had been doing things like this for as long as he could remember and she wouldn't stop until she was stepped on.

Jenny's sobs subsided. She made a few low moans, sniffled a few times, and then was quiet.

She wouldn't say anything more but she would certainly think it. The way he had just treated her and Dick after all they had done for him. She had never thought that she would live to see a day when they would be so abused by their favorite nephew. And him with all that money he was making by writing lies about her. All he'd have to do was lend her enough to start a little store. That would give her and Dick something to live on, a little security. You'd think he would help them in their old age. Oh, she was heartbroken.

They had all been affected by Jenny's outburst. Clara was thinking that the way they lived was terrible, just terrible. Eddie helped them but he couldn't afford what Jenny thought he could. He was spending a lot now for the nurses and the food and Franny's plane tickets. She felt just awful. But it was her mother she felt sorriest for. Poor Mama was dying and Aunt Jenny was only making scenes. She knew that Aunt Jen felt bad about Mama. Mama had been giving them just about all of what she got from her old-age pension. It was going to be a lot harder for Aunt Jen and Uncle Dick without that money coming in. This must be worrying them.

Aunt Jen was still looking miserable. Uncle Dick sat next to her. She had him so that he believed anything she said. He always took her side in an argument. Aunt Jenny had been sulking ever since Eddie hired the nurses. This was the way she was. She always had been and there was no reason to believe she'd change.

II

A half hour had passed since Jenny's outburst and the Ryans had resumed conversation. Jenny and Dick were still sitting in the parlor.

"The Express Company is making money hand over fist," Leo was saying.

Eddie had asked him and his brother Jack about the company.

"You can say that again, Leo," Jack Ryan nodded.

"Well, we've had war prosperity," Eddie pointed out.

"We got enough orders for at least seven years. That's why I ain't afraid of any layoff," Jack Boyle said.

"Oh, there's going to be a depression," Steve predicted.

"I don't think there's going to be one, not for a while," Jack Ryan said.

"It has to come as a reaction to prosperity," Steve said.

"Oh, I don't know, Steve; I don't see a depression before '49 or '50, at least," Eddie said.

"Longer than that, I'd say," Leo added.

"Well, like I just said, we got orders that will keep us goin' until 1953 and that's without takin' into account any new orders," Jack Boyle said.

"Will your strike be settled by 1953?" Leo quipped.

"It'll have to be. But, from the look of things, I could still be picketin'."

"Jack will be bald and ready to retire by the time this strike is settled," Steve said.

"That's no jokin' matter, you know."

"The settlement of the strike or you losin' your hair?" Leo asked.

They all laughed.

"Losin' my hair doesn't bother me much. Not that I like the idea; but losin' hair ain't so much that a man can't take it. There are other things more important that a man can lose."

There was more laughing.

"What Jack's saying, Leo, is that he's got lead in his pencil," Steve said.

"I know what he's sayin'."

"Well, I'd just as soon you keep your hair, too," Clara said.

"Well, I ain't tryin' to lose it."

"He's not going to lose his hair," Dick Dunne said.

He had kept quiet for as long as he could. He had spoken even though he did not approve of the conversation. It was lowbrow and vulgar, completely ungentlemanly talk.

Jenny gave him a freezing look.

"Thank you, Dick, for the encouragement," Jack Boyle said with a laugh.

"Don't mention it."

Eddie was watching his Aunt Jenny. She looked miserable. She saw herself as a martyr and victim. This was her means for justifying what she had made of her life. He wished he had not lost his temper. But you couldn't shut her up any other way. He didn't like intimidating her but Aunt Jen would have had everybody in the house fighting unless she were stopped. Did she really believe that he had the money to give her? Probably. She always had been able to convince herself about anything she wanted to believe. Yet she looked so utterly miserable. But to make up with her would be to court another scene. This saddened him.

The others continued to talk.

III

Dick and Jenny left at around ten-thirty. They both shivered as the door closed behind them.

"It's cold, Jenny."

He held her arm firmly.

"Watch your footing, Jen."

"You too, Dick."

"I shall."

Their thoughts for one another meant much to both of them.

"It's not as cold out as the coldness in my heart, Dick."

This hit him. She had had to put up with so much tonight.

They didn't talk for some moments. They were concentrating on walking over the slippery spots of the sidewalk. They wanted to get home, get to sleep so that they would be neither cold nor sad.

They were lucky; just as they reached the corner, they could hear the streetcar coming. Well, at least one thing was happening right tonight, Jenny thought.

They sat near the center of the car.

"I hope we have the same good luck when we transfer at Sixty-third Street, Dick."

He nodded.

They were silent for a minute.

"It wouldn't have hurt Leo to offer to drive us home," Jenny said.

"I know."

"It wouldn't have taken him but ten or fifteen minutes."

Another silence. Then Dick spoke:

"Some people never think of the other fellow."

"All the Ryans are like that."

"Sixty-third Street!" the conductor called.

As the car stopped, Dick and Jenny rose.

"Watch your step, Jen."

"Don't worry; I will."

—It wouldn't matter if I didn't, she thought.

The cold struck them as they got off. They joined a small group waiting at the curb. They watched the approaching streetcar grow bigger as it drew closer. In less than a minute they were on an eastbound car.

"I'll never forget the way I was treated tonight, Dick."

He was slow in replying.

"I understand, Jen."

"I wish I did. I'll never understand why Eddie treated me as he did."

"I can't understand that either."

"What did I ever do to him?"

"Nothing, Jen."

Eddie shouldn't have talked to Jenny that way. She had always been good to him. Even if he didn't have the money to lend her, he should not have been so harsh.

"Here's South Park Avenue. White City used to be here. Remember, Dick?"

He nodded. They had lived at Fifty-eighth Street and South Park for years, the happiest years of their lives.

"There's nothing to say, Dick, no way to explain Eddie's behavior."

"It's a hard experience to digest."

"And his poor mother dying in the next room."

"But Nora is fighting, Jen."

He wanted to hope that Nora would pull through but he was afraid that only a miracle could pull her through now.

"The one thing I'm grateful for, Dick, is that Nora will never know how her children have truly turned out. That much poor Nora has been spared."

"It's hard to talk on the streetcar, Jen, let's wait until we get home."

His voice sounded tired. Dick was an old man, Jenny thought, and he had no one but her. Everything always fell on her. And she had no one.

IV

"Oh, I'm glad to be home, Dick."

"So am I."

They sat at the dining-room table.

"Dick, I don't know what to think."

"You should try not to worry."

"Try not to worry?"

He wished that what had transpired at the Boyles' had not happened.

"The way that I was talked to. Why, you wouldn't treat a dog that way."

"It was unfair."

"It was mean and disgraceful," Jenny said.

She began to cry. He felt helpless. And he ached with fatigue.

"I never did anything to them. Why should Eddie Ryan treat me as if I were dirt under his feet?"

"You're a lady, Jenny."

"I don't know what I am. I'm a brokenhearted woman."

"Jenny, don't cry, you're tired. You need sleep."

She shook her head.

"How can I sleep after the way that I was insulted?"

"You must try."

"I can't; I just can't."

She broke into sobs. Dick felt wounded. The sight of her suffering cut through him. But he was having difficulty in keeping his eyes open.

"Jen, don't let yourself be hurt."

"I can't help it."

—Damn them, why did they treat Jenny this way?

But Dick was too tired to remain angry. He felt old tonight. And an old man without money had to put up with much. He didn't like to complain. He tried to put the best face on everything that hap-

pened but sometimes it was hard. He sat with his hands on the dining-room table. He felt defeated.

"Jen, I'm so tired I can't keep my eyes open."

"Oh, Dick, I know you're tired. Go to bed."

"I have to or I'll fall asleep right here."

Through a blur of tears, Jenny looked at him. Yes, he looked old.
Old and frail. This was all she had. She didn't even have someone to
talk to in the terrible moments of her life.

Dick slowly rose from his chair.

"Good night, Jen."

"Good night."

She sat alone in the dining room.

Chapter 39

I

They were glad that Dick and Jenny had left. It was easier to talk
when they weren't around. And the scenes Aunt Jen made left them
uncomfortable. They didn't like the feeling.

"I hate to say this but I'm glad they're gone," Clara said.

"I don't miss 'em," Leo said.

"And I was ashamed of the way Jen carried on here tonight."

"It ain't your fault, Clara, you're not her keeper."

"But she's my aunt. I wish I didn't have to feel ashamed of her."

"You don't," Steve said.

"Well, I do."

"I feel sorry for her," Molly said.

"We all feel sorry for her," Clara said.

"I don't," said Leo.

"You don't mean that, Leo!"

"Oh yes, I do. Why should I? They never felt sorry for me."

"There's no reason why you should. If you don't, you don't,"
Steve said.

"Well, I don't."

"I feel sorry for Dick," Jack Boyle said.

"He had his chance," Leo said.

"He used to make good money," Clara said.

"Well, where is it now?" Leo demanded.

"He spent a lot on the Dunnes, especially Aunt Jenny."

"He was a Dutch uncle, you mean?"

"I suppose you could call him that."

"He was no Dutch uncle to the Ryans."

"Why would you expect him to be? He's only your uncle," Jack Boyle said.

"I don't expect him to be."

"Aunt Jen's drinking was the big problem for the Dunnes," Clara said.

"I think it's been over thirteen years since she's had a drink," Eddie said. "It was after Mother died. That's when she stopped."

"That's interesting," Steve commented.

"You think that it's significant that she stopped drinking after her mother died."

"Of course it is," Jack Boyle said. "Anybody who's done a lot of drinking and then quits and stays on the wagon for over thirteen years. It's got to mean something."

"It means that she gave up the bottle," Leo said, laughing.

"But it means something else, too. I would say that Aunt Jenny was jealous of Mother. And after Mother died, she must have transferred her jealousy."

"What was she trying to do, drink her mother under the table?" Jack Boyle asked.

"No, but her drinking was tied up with her mother."

"Aunt Jenny is all bound up in her family," Eddie said, "and she was ambivalent toward Mother."

"It would be hard to find a more ambivalent person," Steve agreed.

"This is all over my head," Leo said.

Jack looked at Clara.

"I have to be thinking about gettin' ready to go."

"I'll fix you a bite to take."

II

Jack Boyle had just closed the door behind him.

"I never liked living at the Dunnes'," Clara said.

"That's why you came home to live with us when you grew up," Leo said.

He paused.

"I remember once I went up there to dinner when they lived at Fifty-eighth Street and South Park. We were living in the cottage at Forty-fifth Place and Wells Street. Dick asked me why I'd come. I don't remember why I'd gone there; I think Mama sent me. But I didn't get a chance to say anything. He gave me a kick in the ass and told me to get the hell out and go on back where I belonged."

"What did you do?" Steve asked.

"I got the hell out; what d'ya think I did?"

There were laughs.

"I'll never forget it. From that day to this I ain't had any use for the Dunnes."

"You still hold it against them?" Steve asked.

"Wouldn't you?"

"I don't think so. It's not worth remembering. And Dick Dunne is an old man now. They're poor."

"He didn't have to kick me."

"I know but I wouldn't bother remembering it," Steve said.

"You weren't the one who got kicked," Frances said.

"I know, but I was talking about how I would look at it if I had been."

"Uncle Dick never liked Leo, I guess," Clara said, "even later on."

"He knew I wouldn't listen to any of his bullshit."

"But they've changed now," Clara said.

"Yes, they're old," Steve said, nodding.

"Both of 'em had plenty of chances but they threw 'em away," Leo said.

"Uncle Dick didn't throw away his chances," Eddie said. "He invested his savings in the firm he worked for and lost it all."

"Well, there are lots of things that are too bad but it ain't my fault and it ain't my fault they haven't got any money now."

"Of course it isn't, Leo," Clara said. "It's no fault of any of us Ryans."

"Who said it was?" Steve asked.

"Aunt Jenny all but said it tonight."

"Do you think that was what she was trying to say?"

"Well, she blames us and I don't like her thinking such awful things about us," Clara said.

"But nobody cares," Steve told her.

"It isn't right anyway."

"I know it isn't but it's not important."

"It's not important what any of us says or thinks except maybe Eddie," Jack Ryan said.

Eddie wished his brother hadn't said this. The remark only widened the gap between him and the rest of them.

"All I'm sayin' is that Aunt Jen shouldn't say the things she does. That's all."

"But, Clara, she's always been that way," Frances said, "so what difference does it make now?"

"I suppose you're right but I can't help not liking it."

"It's not worth talking about. That's my opinion if you want it," Leo said.

"Well, they've had a run of tough luck for a long time now. If they've ever done anything to anybody, they've sure paid for it," Jack Ryan said.

"Well, I can't help that," Leo said.

"When I'm in California, I don't have to think of any of this," Frances commented.

"But, Fran, you're so far from it and we aren't."

"Why do you think I picked California?"

"To get away from Chicago, I guess. But still, they are Mama's brother and sister. And they are my aunt and uncle."

"I know, Clara, but there are lots of things in this world you can't do anything about."

"I know but I can't just turn my back on them."

No one said anything. There was nothing more to say about the Dunnes. They were back with their own thoughts.

Papa's death had been harder, Leo thought. Papa had been hopelessly paralyzed for over a year. He had known that the days were slowly but steadily carrying him to his grave end. And he had been out of work for over a year; they had been so poor. There had been no money with which to take care of Papa. There was scarcely enough for them to keep going. Jack had gone out on the trucks at the Express Company because that paid more than working in the Payroll Department. This was where he had been working when Papa had the stroke. It still hurt remembering Papa during that time. Now it was Mama.

III

It was past midnight. Leo and Florence, Jack and Molly had all gone home. Clara, Frances, Steve, and Eddie sat waiting for Jack Boyle to come back from picketing. Even though they were tired, they didn't want to go to bed. They didn't want to leave each other.

"I can't get Papa out of my mind," Clara said, speaking softly. "The thought of him haunts me."

"I was thinking of him tonight too," Frances said.

"He was so pitiful; it was heartbreaking," Clara said.

"It was a rough thing, all right," Steve said, shaking his head.

Eddie said nothing.

"I'm going to take a look to see how Mama is," Steve said, getting up from his chair.

Eddie suddenly felt isolated. The rest of them had lived with Mama and Papa while he had lived with the Dunnes. They had not shared a childhood.

"Well, at least we can do something to make Mama comfortable," Clara was saying. "When Papa died, we were all young and couldn't do anything. Of course, Jack was wonderful to him."

"Yes, he was," Eddie said.

Steve returned to the room.

"No change; she seems to be the same."

For a moment no one spoke. Then Clara said:

"What makes me sad was that Papa was so worried about what would happen to all of us. It was terrible to see him suffering and worrying the way he did."

"Well, at least that's not true for Mama," Steve said. "She'll die knowing that we're all coming along all right."

"Yes, Steve, but Mama was worried about Jenny and Dick."

"I guess so."

Steve paused. Then added:

"Jack ought to be getting back any minute now."

"Yes, it's just about time for him," Clara said.

"Well, I'm tired, and I'm going to bed," Frances said, getting up with a yawn.

"I guess we all ought to be turning in," Steve said.

But he stayed in his chair. Frances left the room. They all said "Good night" as she walked out. A few minutes later Jack Boyle arrived.

"Hello, Jack."

"Hello, Eddie, I didn't think I'd find anyone up."

"Was it cold tonight?" Steve asked.

"Was it cold tonight? You bet it was cold tonight!"

"I'm sorry to hear it."

"No sorrier than I am to say it. We didn't do much picketing; we just stayed around the fire and drank coffee most of the time."

"Well, I'm glad you're home; I don't like to go to bed until you're here."

"Oh, there's nothin' to worry about, Clara, the company ain't gonna try to bring in scabs."

"But I worry anyway."

"You don't have to."

"I know that; I just want to wait up for you."

Jack Boyle thought this was a little foolish but he appreciated it. He guessed he ought to tell her that he liked comin' home when he knew she was waitin' up for him. But he couldn't say anything like that with Eddie and Steve here. Maybe some other time. He was damned tired now.

He got up.

"I'm turnin' in, folks. Good night."

Chapter 40

I

Nora Ryan could only see part of the room. Sometimes something looked familiar, a face, an object, something. But it didn't look the way it used to. The space of her world had changed. She could hear talking; she heard the doctor saying that her right side was paralyzed and that she could not feel anything on that side. But she had dreams of pain there. As she lay with one eye open, seeing and watching, the world stopped. On the right of her, there was nothing. It was as if there were a wall in the room blocking out everything on that side. She was helpless, as helpless as a baby. But she had no mother. She dreamed one night that she was a baby and she recognized her mother in the dreams. Was her mother dead? Her mind was too weak and tired to try to remember. An automatic acceptance was imposed upon her by her condition. She was living from one minute to another. The only thing that she knew was that she was dying. God was calling her but she could do nothing but lie here helpless until He called her for the last time.

II

Dr. Evans came early. There was something different in his manner when he came out of Nora Ryan's room. He told Steve that he would be back in the afternoon. Steve said nothing but Dr. Evans' manner upset him. He tried to hide it from the rest of them; but they sensed that there was something new in the air. They knew that it was best for Nora Ryan to die but the thought that today might be the day depressed them.

"How do you feel, Eddie?" Clara asked as she poured him another cup of coffee.

"All right, I guess."

"Maybe you shouldn't drink so much coffee, Eddie."

"Well . . ." Eddie began.

Eddie became silent. Most people didn't like to think of death. But here in the Boyle home death was staring them in the face. It might happen today. Clara and the others seemed to feel this too. He hoped that it wouldn't happen. No, he wanted it all over with. But even if Nora Ryan died today, there were many things that would still have to be done. Of course he could leave enough money with Clara to take care of things and catch a plane back to New York. But he wouldn't.

"You seem depressed, Eddie. But I guess maybe we all are."

"Well, it won't do any good for us to be down in the mouth."

"Maybe not but I don't think we can help it."

"We can't sometimes. There's nothing wrong with being depressed, Clara."

"I know. Gosh, how could a person live without being blue once in a while."

"I had a feeling that Mama was going to die today."

"I did, too, but now I'm not so sure."

"Of course, Mama can die at any moment."

"I know but I just hate to think of it."

III

Clara couldn't get the thought out of her head. Mama was going to die today. She had never felt this sad. It was like Eddie and Steve said. Mama had to die. She wanted to ask them why but she knew that there was no use asking. Mama had to die because she had had a stroke. There was no use in asking why. But she didn't want Mama to die. None of them did, she knew that. They were all sad but no matter how sad they were, no matter what they felt, they couldn't feel her sadness. Only she could feel that. And it was terrible. She wished she could cry. She wished this thing was over with. And she wished it didn't have to happen. It didn't matter what she wished. Who was she? Who was anybody in the face of the Great Leveler? And that was what death was. It wasn't only Mama who had to die.

They all did. But this was something you tried to forget. Most of the time you could until something like this came along to remind you. If it was anybody else, she wouldn't feel so bad even if it did remind her.

—Oh, Mama.

"Mama is still fighting," Frances said, entering the room.

"It seems so."

"It couldn't be anything else keeping her alive. Why, if any of us had suffered a stroke like the one she had, we've have been dead long ago."

"Maybe so."

Frances sighed.

"Oh, Clara, I don't know what to say."

"About what, Franny?"

"About Mama, I guess."

"I know what you mean. I feel that way too. I guess there isn't much we can say."

"I guess not but I've had a funny feeling all morning about her."

Clara turned pale.

"I had the same feeling this morning but I don't have it any more, do you?"

"I don't know. I don't know how I feel."

"Oh, God, I do. I feel terrible."

Clara's voice shook.

"We all do."

There was nothing more that she could say.

IV

Nora Ryan did not seem to be any worse than she had been on the day before. And yet they were all convinced that there was something going on. Death was closing in on her. And the shadow of her death was creeping in upon all of them. They might forget it for a few minutes but then the feeling would return.

That afternoon when Dr. Evans left after his second visit of the day, Clara asked Steve if there were anything about their mother's condition that Dr. Evans was holding from her. Steve said that there wasn't, not to his knowledge, honestly. Clara believed him. Frances, who was standing nearby, overheard the conversation. She didn't understand, but then she wasn't supposed to; she wasn't a doctor. She would just have to go along as she had been.

Clara kept staring at the kitchen clock. It was too soon for Jack to be home. It was still afternoon. She wished it was night. Did she? By night, Mama could be dead. No. She wouldn't be. Steve had just told her that there was no change. Well then, she wished it was night. Oh, she didn't know if she did or didn't. She didn't know anything except that she had better start thinking about fixing supper.

Chapter 41

I

After supper, Jack Boyle went out to picket. It was another cold night. Steve, Eddie, Frances, Clara, Leo, and Florence were in the parlor. Steve started talking about the paper that always seemed to be on the floor in the cottage at Forty-fifth Place and Wells Street when they had lived there.

"Do you remember, Eddie?"

"Oh yes, it was all over the place every time I came down there to visit."

"Poor Mama didn't have time to pick up with all of you kids," Clara defended.

"So Papa had to clean house on Sundays," Eddie said.

"I remember," Leo nodded.

"And so do I," said Steve, "the cottage never would have been cleaned if Pa hadn't done it whenever he could."

"I guess not," Leo said.

"But Mama never had the time," Clara protested.

No one said anything. Steve was wrapped in thought. Suddenly he spoke:

"Say, let's play we're back in the cottage and that we're kids again."

"All right, I'll be Pa," Leo said, "Flo can be Mama."

Florence stared at him, surprised.

"Let Clara be Mama," she suggested.

Eddie didn't like the idea but he said nothing.

"All right, Clara, you be Mama and I'll be Papa," Leo said.

Steve stood up and looked around.

"Have you got any old newspapers, Clara?"

"There's a stack in the kitchen; I'll go get them."

She left the room.

"When I'm Pa, I'll put the razor strap to you, Steve," Leo said.

Steve laughed.

Clara came back with a stack of papers. Steve took them. Turning to Frances, he said:

"Here, take some. We have to throw them around on the floor the way they used to be at the cottage."

Eddie watched as they spread the papers on the floor. Then Steve sat down on them. Looking up at Frances, he urged:

"Come on, Frances, sit on the floor."

"All right."

She sat. Steve started shredding the papers and rolling the strips into little balls. He threw these around the room.

"We'll be playing like this when Pa comes home from work," he said.

"All right," Frances said.

She was a little embarrassed. Clara got up and walked into the other room.

In a moment she returned and in a voice imitating her mother's said:

"Your father ought to be coming home from work any minute now."

"Ma?" Steve called.

"What do you want, you shyster?"

"Ma, what's a shyster?"

"You know what a shyster is."

"Come on and play, Steve," Frances coaxed in a little girl's voice.

"Yes, you kids go on playing," Clara ordered.

"But when are we gonna have our supper?" Steve asked.

Clara walked past them, shuffling newspapers on the floor.

"You know we don't have supper until your father gets home from work."

"Well, I'm hungry," Steve whined.

"I'm hungry too," Frances said in a petulant, girlish voice.

"I'm Pa and I'm coming home from work," Leo said, standing up.

"Come on, Franny, we'll still be playing on the floor when Pa comes home," Steve said.

"Hello, Nora, how are the kids?" Leo asked, speaking gruffly.

"Oh, Jack, I've had neuralgia pains all day."

Leo looked at the floor.

"Hello, Pa." Steve said.

"Hello, Papa," Frances said.

"Pa, I'm making a paper hat," Steve said, putting on one that he had just made.

"He won't make me one," Frances sulked.

"What the hell kind of house do I live in?" Leo asked sternly.

"Oh, Jack, I've had such neuralgia pains all day."

"I never heard of a dirty house being a cure for neuralgia."

"I want a paper boat," Frances complained.

"Well, here's a paper hat," Steve said, offering her the hat from his head.

"I don't want a paper hat."

"Will you kids shut up," Leo shouted.

"But, Papa," Frances began.

"What did I ask you to do?" Leo demanded.

He looked at the floor.

"Papa?" Frances began once more.

Ignoring her, Leo asked:

"Where's Jack?"

"He went to see his brother Eddie and Mother," Clara told him.

"So he's at the Dunnes' again, is he?"

"Oh, Jack, he's only gone to see his brother."

"And your boozin' sister and your dude brothers. I tell you, Nora, after those two sell a pair of shoes, there's not another damned thing they can do."

"Papa . . ."

Frances started laughing before she could finish her sentence.

In a moment Steve was laughing too.

"Will you kids shut up so I can hear myself think," Leo said.

Clara began to laugh too.

"I sounded like Pa, didn't I?" Leo asked.

"Well, I never knew him so I don't know," Florence said.

"Oh, he did, Florence," Clara told her.

"I think so too," Frances said.

"Let's play some more," Steve suggested.

"Oh no, let's stop," Clara said, starting to clear the floor.

II

It was after midnight.

"Mama is comatose," Steve announced, coming from her room.

"I thought she was all along," Eddie said.

"In a way she was, but she's really dying now."

"It's the end, you mean?"

Steve nodded.

"Is that noise in her throat what they call the death rattle?"

Steve nodded again.

"It's sometimes called that."

Clara came in.

"Clara?"

From the tone of Steve's voice, she knew.

"Mama's dying now," he told her.

Her face froze.

"I want to see her," she said through stiff lips.

"Go ahead."

As Clara turned to go into her mother's bedroom, Frances and Jack Boyle came into the kitchen.

"Mama's dying," Steve told them.

"Is she in any pain?" Frances asked.

"I don't know but I don't think so."

"Can I go in to see her?"

"Of course."

Frances turned and went into the bedroom.

"She's dyin', you say?" Jack Boyle asked.

"Yes."

"Do you know when it'll be?"

"No, but it'll be soon."

"I'm sorry to hear it, Steve."

"We all are, Jack, but it had to come. The big surprise is that it took so long."

"I guess so."

Clara came out of her mother's bedroom.

"Is that what they call the death rattle, Steve?"

He nodded.

"It's awful."

"I know."

III

It was almost 3 A.M. Dick and Jenny had just come back to the Boyle home. When Steve announced that the end was near, Clara thought she ought to telephone them both as well as her brothers Jack and Leo.

Jenny and Dick had arrived in less than an hour. Jack and Leo had said they both had to go to work and, unless Mama's condition was much worse, they thought they'd better get their sleep. Steve had told Clara to tell them that he would see to it that they were called in time.

Clara and Jack Boyle, Frances, Steve, Eddie, Dick, and Jenny were in the kitchen. Bridget Daugherty was in the bedroom with Nora Ryan. Jenny sat apart from her nieces and nephews. She looked sad but her expression changed and became accusing when she looked at them. Dick got up and walked to the doorway. He was quiet; his face was grave. Ever so often he would look at Jen and his face would become more grave. He tried to catch her eye but if she noticed she gave no sign. Occasionally Jenny's face would crumble as though she were about to break into sobs. But then she would straighten up in her chair and look around to see if she had been noticed.

Jenny was taking this harder than any of the others, Dick thought. He wished he could say something comforting to her but he had best refrain. With Jenny you never could tell. Sometimes her response would be wonderful but then it would be the opposite. You never could be certain about Jenny; especially when she was in such a downcast state of mind.

Everybody was ignoring her, Jenny thought. They weren't even looking at her, let alone talking to her. They had not one kind word for her. They didn't care about their poor old aunt. But what could she expect? They didn't feel anything for their own mother, who was dying in the next room. Look at them. And Nora was at death's door. Oh, God!

IV

"Three o'clock," Clara said, looking at the clock.

The door to Nora Ryan's bedroom was open.

"Oh, God, I never thought anything like this would happen," Clara said.

"Neither did I," Frances said.

"It is awesome," Eddie said.

"What's that? What's that you just said, Eddie?" Jack Boyle asked him.

"I said it's awesome."

"It sure is."

"I wonder when she'll die?" Frances asked.

"Don't talk like that," Dick snapped.

Frances frowned.

"Your mother isn't dead yet," Dick went on, "you shouldn't have thoughts of her death. You should think of her living."

"Oh, Uncle Dick."

"Where there's life there's hope," Jenny added.

"That's the spirit we all ought to have in us right now," Dick said.

Eddie looked at them. They had always been like this. Uncle Larry too. The three of them always had virtually a fetish about not thinking sad or bad thoughts. This used to enrage him but he no longer reacted to it. The truth was that he didn't care if they persisted in expressing their simple-minded ideas about thinking good thoughts and saying good things no matter what the situation.

Again, they could hear Nora Ryan's death rattle. Then the sound of a train and the mournful whistle of its engine.

Clara turned and went back into her mother's bedroom.

V

Minutes ticked away. The chill of death had settled upon the flesh of Nora Ryan. It was orchestrated by her shallow breathing, which rattled in the kitchen. They all kept getting up to go into the bedroom to look at her. Steve warned them not to speak. The last sense to go, he explained, was hearing. In her condition, Mama could misunderstand and be frightened by anything they said. None of them spoke while in her room. And when they came out they felt that there was nothing left to be said. They were numbed by the presence of death but they did not realize this. They were struggling to hold back the threatening rush of their feelings. They had accepted their mother's inevitable death. She had been too near death for too long. These days of waiting had worn away the shock. But they were tired. And the sound of her breathing filled the room. It was an ugly sound and an ugly reminder of death, their mother's death and their own deaths.

It would soon be dawn. Nora Ryan had lived into another day. They still sat, their faces grave.

Suddenly the shallow breathing stopped. No one spoke. They listened. There were no sounds.

"Doctor. Dr. Ryan," Bridget Daugherty called.

Steve rushed into the bedroom. They knew even before he came out and told them, "Mama's dead."

Chapter 42

I

Steve went to the telephone to call Dr. Evans and Jack and Leo. Eddie was tired. He decided to try to get some sleep. Clara said something about calling an undertaker but Steve said that Dr. Evans would have to pronounce Mama dead before they could call one.

II

Steve came and lay down beside Eddie. The bedroom door was open. They could hear the others talking.

"I won't go to work today," Jack Boyle was saying.

"Well, I wouldn't think so," Clara told him.

"But there won't be anything doing until tonight," Frances said.

"Mama lived a long life," Steve said, turning toward Eddie.

"How old was she?"

"Seventy-three, I think."

If he lived to be seventy-three, Eddie thought, he would have a little over thirty more years of life. He could get much more writing done. His seventeenth book would be out this year.

"Leo is going to handle the funeral arrangements," Clara was saying. "He's good at things like that."

"Oh yes, Leo will see to it that your mother has a nice funeral," Jack Boyle said.

"It won't matter to Mama," Steve told Eddie.

"But it does to them."

"I'm glad Aunt Jenny didn't make a scene," Clara said to Frances.

"Mama isn't buried yet," Eddie said to Steve.

"What do you mean?"

"Clara was just mentioning that Aunt Jenny hadn't made a scene and I was just pointing out that Mama hasn't been buried yet."

"She's made enough scenes already," Frances said in the kitchen.

"Oh, I see what you mean," Steve said.

"I'll have to call up Cecilia and tell her not to come," Clara said.

"Not yet, it's too early," said Jack Boyle.

"I don't mean right away."

"How do you feel, Eddie?" Steve asked.

"I'm tired."

"Me too."

"And I'm sorry, of course, about Mama."

"We all are but we can't say that it was unexpected."

"The expected is often unexpected when it happens."

"We'll have to go pick out a dress for Mama," Clara said.

"I was just thinking about that," Frances said.

"Remind me to call up Cecilia Moran about eight."

"I'll try to remember."

"Why don't you go to bed now, Clara, and try to get some rest?"

"I can't. I have to get little Eddie's breakfast; he'll be going to school soon."

Eddie yawned.

"I'm tired too," Steve said. "I think I'll try to get some sleep."

"So will I."

III

Eddie and Steve had been sleeping for less than two hours when they heard the doorbell ring.

"Who in the hell is that?" Eddie asked.

"Jack or Leo maybe."

They heard Jack Boyle opening the front door. In a minute Steve said:

"It's the undertaker."

"What's his name?" Eddie asked.

"I don't know. Jack Boyle's trying to find out."

"Your older brother, Mr. Jack Ryan, telephoned me and asked me to come," the undertaker was saying.

"For Christ's sake," Steve exploded.

"What's the matter?" Eddie asked.

"This is going to be a mess."

They could hear commotion and they assumed that their mother's corpse was being carried out.

"This really will be a mess," Steve said again.

"Well, why don't you do something?"

"I'm staying out of it."

Eddie turned to him, surprised.

"How old was your mother?" the undertaker was asking.

"Sixty-nine," Clara answered.

"I thought you said seventy-three," Eddie said to Steve. "Clara says sixty-nine."

"Clara's right. I forgot. Mama added a few years for the old-age-pension people."

"I see," Eddie laughed.

"Mama was seventy-three," Steve yelled into the next room.

Eddie wondered why Steve had done this. Clara ignored him and went on answering the undertaker's questions.

"What's the idea, Steve?" Eddie asked.

"I just don't like the sound of that man's voice."

"That's no reason for yelling."

"It could be."

Eddie stared at him, flabbergasted. The undertaker and Clara were still going over the arrangements. They agreed that Nora Ryan would be waked from the Funeral Parlor at Sixty-third and South Kedzie.

Finally he left.

"Good-by, Mr. Cassidy. My brother, Leo Ryan, will be in touch with you," Clara said as she closed the door.

IV

Dr. Evans arrived. Mr. Cassidy had been gone about ten minutes.

"But how could he go?" exclaimed Dr. Evans. "Those damned undertakers."

"He told me to get a death certificate from you," Clara said.

"How can I give you a death certificate when I haven't even seen your mother?"

"Oh, Doctor, I'm sorry; I didn't know."

Dr. Evans didn't say anything for a moment.

"How did he get here so quickly?" Dr. Evans asked her.

"We didn't telephone him. There must have been some misunderstanding. My older brother Jack called him," Clara tried to explain.

"Where is the doctor?" Dr. Evans asked.

"Here I am, Dr. Evans," Steve said, walking into the parlor.

"I don't understand how you could let your mother be taken away by an undertaker before I could examine her."

"I didn't talk to him; I was in the bedroom, Dr. Evans."

Dr. Evans was silent again. Then he spoke:

"We have to catch him. How long ago did he leave?"

"Only five to ten minutes," Clara said.

363

"Dr. Ryan, will you telephone Burney's Funeral Parlor and tell them they are to do nothing until I get there."

"Yes, Dr. Evans, I'll do that. Do you want me to go with you?"

"No, I won't need you. I'll go right over."

Steve went to the telephone.

V

"That was an awful mix-up," Jack Boyle said.

"I don't know why Jack had to call the undertaker so fast," Steve said.

"Cassidy wasn't going to take any chance on losing the business," Eddie commented.

"Oh, I don't think it was his fault, Eddie," Clara protested.

"I'm not saying it was, Clara, I was merely commenting on how fast he got here."

"He did get here awful fast, all right," Jack Boyle said.

"He sure did," Frances said.

"Well, I guess Cassidy had nothing to do when the call came so he came right over," Clara said. "Jack wanted Cassidy to be the undertaker. But Cassidy's place is on West Twenty-second Street. He must have an arrangement with Burney, whose place is so much closer to here."

"I guess it was my fault in a way," Steve said. "I should not have let Mama's body be taken away until Dr. Evans got here and pronounced her dead."

"That's the way it looks," Eddie said.

"Yeah, mine and Jack's," Steve said.

"Well, I wouldn't say that it was anybody's fault," Clara said.

"I should have thought faster," Steve said.

"You were so tired, Steve," Frances said.

"I should have been more on my toes," Steve insisted.

"Oh, Steve, don't worry about it, it will be all right," Clara offered.

"I hope so."

Eddie thought that his mother's death had been in keeping with her life. She had been carted out of the house fast, even before she had been pronounced dead.

"Of course Mama is dead. I listened and I couldn't pick up a heartbeat," Steve said.

"Oh, I know that," Clara said reassuringly.

Jack Boyle rose from the table.

"I'd better call my boss and tell him I won't be comin' in today."

He left the kitchen.

"I hope Dr. Evans isn't mad with us," Clara said.

"I don't think he is, Clara," Frances said.

"I hope not. He liked Mama and he was good to her. I'd feel terrible if he was mad with us."

"He didn't seem mad, Clara. He's a doctor; he surely knows that when somebody dies at home there's likely to be some confusion," Frances said.

They heard Jack Boyle speaking on the telephone.

"Yes, the mother-in-law died this mornin'," he was saying.

"We have to think about the death notice but I guess we'd better wait until Leo gets here," Clara said.

"That won't be hard," Eddie said.

"Oh, I know. I was just thinking that it was one more thing to be done."

Jack Boyle came back to the kitchen.

"Leo and Florence ought to be here soon," Steve remarked.

"Jack and Molly too," Clara added.

"We'll have to decide on when she's going to be buried," Clara said.

"I was thinking of that too," Eddie said.

"When do you think she ought to be, Clara?" Steve asked.

"I don't think she ought to be waked for more than two nights," Eddie said.

"Neither do I," Steve agreed.

"I don't either," Frances said.

"Oh, I think three nights would be better," Clara said.

"Why?" Steve asked.

"So that all of her friends have a chance to pay her their last respects."

"Can't they do it in two nights?"

"I'm not sure. People have things to do and many might not know of it in time, not to come tonight, the first night. That would leave them only one night to come."

"I think you're right, Clara," Jack Boyle said.

"Oh, I'm not sure about that," Steve said.

"I am," Jack Boyle said.

"So am I," Clara said.

"I'd rather have it for two nights," Eddie said. "But what Clara says makes sense."

"I'm still not convinced," Steve said.

"I'm sure that Jack and Leo will want it to be three," Clara added.

"But suppose the rest of us want it to be two?" Steve asked.

"It's not something to quarrel over, Steve," Eddie said.

Steve became sullen.

VI

It was a few minutes after 11:00 A.M. All six of the Ryan children were in the kitchen. Jack Boyle was there and so were Molly and Florence. Clara walked to the parlor. She sat down and sighed.

It was over. Mama was gone.

"Mama has met Mother by now," Clara said. "You can bet they were glad to see each other.'"

"Mother must have been glad to see Mama," Frances said.

"I remember once when we were living at Fifty-first and Prairie. Mama came to see Mother and dramatically announced: 'Mother, I've come home to you, I've left Jack.' Mother looked at her for a moment and then she said: 'So you've come home to roost, have you?' " Eddie said.

"Oh, I remember that; you wrote it in one of your books," Clara said.

"Yes."

"You'll have to write about all this, Eddie," Steve said.

"I don't know that I'd like that," Frances said.

Eddie said nothing.

VII

"Look at this!" Steve exclaimed.

"What?" Frances asked.

They were in Nora Ryan's bedroom.

"Call the others in, Franny."

"Clara," Frances called.

Clara walked in.

Steve was on his knees in front of an opened bureau drawer.

"Eddie?" Steve called.

Eddie came in.

"You're going through Mama's dresser?" Eddie asked.

"It has to be done, doesn't it?" Steve's voice was defensive.

"Of course it does, and we might as well do it now," Clara said.

"Let's do it systematically," Steve said, pulling out the bottom drawer.

"Steve, I don't want to take out all her clothes now."

"I'm not taking out her clothes, Clara, I'm just looking for the loot."

Steve put the drawer down on the floor. Besides the clothes, there were several envelopes and pieces of paper in the drawer. Eddie and Frances went to look.

"Here, look at these envelopes addressed to the Shrine of the Mystic Rose of Jesus Christ. There's money in them," Steve said.

"She was Mama's friend," Clara said.

"Well, they've had their reunion by now in heaven," Frances said.

"Mama hasn't been there long enough to see all her friends," Clara said.

"Here's St. Bede's," Clara said, holding up an envelope with a dollar.

She unfolded the dollar and piled it on a small stack of bills on the floor.

"And here's St. Christopher," Steve laughed, adding a quarter and a fifty-cent piece to the pile.

"And the Poor Clares," Steve said, opening another envelope and taking out four dimes.

"Oh, I've got one for the Poor Clares too," Frances said, adding three quarters.

"Here are some pennies," Eddie said.

Frances leaned forward and began stacking the coins.

"What's going on in here?" Leo asked from the doorway.

"We're gathering Mama's loot," Steve laughed.

Leo walked in and knelt down on the floor with the others.

"Say, we ought to do this more systematically," Steve said.

"All right, Steve, set up a system," Leo said.

"Well, let's see . . ."

He thought for a moment.

"I've got it! Let's empty the drawer on the floor and go through it all."

Steve stood; picked up the drawer and dumped its contents on the floor in a heap. Coins rolled around.

VIII

"Now we know the secrets of the dead," Eddie said.

"Mama didn't have any secrets; she never did anything that she had to hide," Clara said.

"But she wanted to keep some things private. A secret doesn't have to be a sin," Eddie said. "Obviously that was her purpose in keeping those envelopes in a drawer under her clothes."

"How much loot was there? I forgot the exact amount," Frances asked.

"Eighty-nine dollars and ninety-three cents," Eddie said. "That was her legacy."

Poor Mama. She had saved these pennies, nickels, dimes, quarters, half dollars, and dollars to send to convents and monasteries as offerings for prayers.

"What shall we do with the money?" Clara asked.

"Have masses said for Mama?" Leo asked.

"I don't like that idea," Steve said.

"But I think Mama would have wanted it," Leo said.

"I guess so but there ought to be something more useful we could do with it."

"What do you suggest, Steve?" Clara asked.

"We could get something for her grandchildren," Frances suggested.

"I was thinking about that," Steve said.

"Well, I'm not against it," Clara said. She turned. "Are you, Eddie?"

"No . . ."

"She's got seven grandchildren," Steve said. "Do we have enough?"

"I don't see why not," Clara said.

"I'll add whatever is needed if what you get costs more than eighty-nine dollars," Eddie said.

"You won't have to, Eddie, that ought to be enough," Steve said.

"We could get bracelets for the girls and rings for the boys," Clara said.

"That's a good suggestion, Clara," Steve said.

"What about the rest of you; do you agree?" Clara asked.

The others nodded.

IX

"No, I think that the money should go for masses," Jack Ryan said.

"But, Jack, don't you think it would be nice to give each of Mama's grandchildren a remembrance of her?"

"It's not a bad idea, Clara, but I still think Mama's money should be used for masses for her."

"Why, Jack?"

"I told you why, Steve."

"No, you didn't."

"Yes, I did."

"Oh, Steve, Jack doesn't want to go in with us and he's said so," Clara interrupted.

Jack Boyle looked annoyed but he didn't say anything.

"All I was doing was asking him why," Steve said.

"But he's told you why, Steve," Clara said.

"Why don't you drop it, Steve?" Frances said.

"Oh, all right."

X

Eddie looked out the front window at the drab street. He turned away, walked over to the couch, and plunked down. Steve drifted into the parlor.

"Well, Eddie, it's all over except for the wake and the funeral."

Eddie nodded.

"The wake," he said.

"It won't be so bad," Steve said. "Maybe you'll see some of your old friends at the wake, like Peter Moore. You like him, don't you?"

Eddie nodded.

"Yes, but I don't want to see people from the old days, people I've written about."

"But nothing will happen," Steve said.

"It will be unpleasant," Eddie's voice strained.

"But, Eddie, you ought to go to Mama's wake."

Eddie didn't answer.

"I think you should," Steve said.

Eddie lit a cigarette.

"I have a feeling that Torch will be there."

"What if he is?" Steve asked.

"I don't want to see him."

"Jack Boyle and I will throw him out if he comes and starts any trouble."

Eddie knew that they would. And he doubted that Torch Feeney would appear.

"I'll guarantee that nothing will happen if that guy shows up, Eddie. Jack Boyle and I can handle him."

Eddie didn't speak for a few moments.

His anxiety was ebbing. He felt grateful to Steve.

XI

"How do you feel now, Eddie?"

Eddie was lying down, his right arm flung over his eyes. He partially raised himself and turned to Steve.

"All right; I was merely resting."

"Maybe I ought to do the same thing."

"Maybe. There are things that I value above sleep but if you're tired, what the hell."

Eddie knew that he was making conversation. Steve sat down on the edge of the bed.

"You feel all right, then?"

"Oh yes. I just had a fit of anxiety and the only thing to do about them is go along with them."

"Your anxiety must have been connected in some way to Mama's death."

"Probably," Eddie said.

"Have you thought how Torch Feeney got into the picture, Eddie?"

"Why should I? Torch did come to shoot me once. You were there that night."

"Yes, I remember."

"After it was over, the next time I was in Chicago, I had an anxiety. And it's recurred every time I've come here since."

"The cause of your anxiety must be deeper than that."

"Perhaps."

"What do you think it's associated with?"

"I haven't thought about it in that sense."

"Why are you thinking about it this way now, Eddie?"

"I wasn't; except that you mentioned it and put it in my mind."

"Well, does that lead you to think about it?"

"No, but it has stimulated some associations."

"What associations, Eddie?"

"Oh . . . Jud Jennings for one."

"And what other associations?"

"I don't know. Peter Moore. And Jack."

Eddie paused.

"Our brother Jack?" Steve asked.

"Yes."

"Do you associate Jack with Torch Feeney?"

"I just did, more or less," Eddie answered.

"Well?"

Eddie did not say anything for a moment. Then:

"Jack used to go around with Jud sometimes after we moved into that neighborhood around Fifty-seventh and Indiana Avenue."

"Yes, Eddie?"

"I don't know; I thought I liked Jud."

There was a pause. Eddie went on:

"Sometimes I guess I admired him more than I did Jack."

"Torch Feeney or Jud?"

"Jud."

"What about Torch Feeney?" Steve asked.

"I don't think I ever thought much about him."

"Maybe Jud was a substitute brother," Steve said.

"It could be, for all I know."

"That's true; it could be. It's plausible. But do you think that it's true?"

"I don't know, Steve, I wouldn't be surprised if it were. But then again, I wouldn't be surprised either way."

"You told me once that, in writing *Jud Jennings,* he represented all that you didn't want to be or become."

"I've said that many times."

"And if Jud were a substitute older brother?"

"I associated Jack with the old man," Eddie said.

"That's what I was wondering about," Steve said.

Steve was silent, then he spoke:

"It could be true."

"What could be true, Steve?"

"It could be that the underlying theme of *Jud Jennings* is the slaying of the father."

"No, Steve, not the theme, but the motive, if that."

"Well then, the motive. That's what I meant."

Eddie didn't know what to say. This interpretation was farfetched. He neither accepted it nor rejected it. It could be true or false. The interpretation was at best a partial truth. Eddie knew that Steve accepted this interpretation. Steve was committed to Freudian psychoanalytic interpretations, and Steve was trying to apply what he had learned, or what he thought he had learned, about psychoanalysis to Eddie in order to understand himself better.

"I think there's something here, Eddie."

Eddie had been lying with his eyes closed. He opened them and looked up at Steve.

"You think so?"

"Yes, Eddie, I really do."

Steve spoke in such a way that Eddie knew that he was expecting him to agree with him.

"I don't know what to say, Steve."

"That's to be expected," Steve said.

"What's to be expected?"

"Resistance to my interpretation of why you wrote *Jud Jennings* and what it means. We have to break down our resistance before we can uncover and accept underlying meanings and motives in our psyches."

"I don't know that I'm resisting, Steve."

"Oh, you are."

Eddie stared at the ceiling. He tried to decide whether or not he was resisting Steve's interpretations. He didn't know.

"Well, what do you think, Eddie?"

"I don't know. I can't say yes or no."

"Take your time, Eddie."

Eddie looked at him in surprise. Was he serious? He had made a statement that was farfetched. He had heard Eddie say many times that it could take him as long as ten years after he wrote something to understand what was behind his writing it. And now Steve was waiting for an instant answer about *Jud Jennings* representing the slaying of the father.

"Take your time, Eddie. Give it some attention."

Steve was trying to practice on him. He thought that this was a little funny. But he would go along and let Steve question him.

"Take it easy and think, Eddie," Steve repeated.

"Suddenly, almost all thoughts go out of my mind."

"Some of them will come back."

Eddie closed his eyes. He lay, very relaxed.

He thought of Jud Jennings. He thought of him in long pants when he used to hang around Frank's poolroom at Fifty-eighth Street and the elevated station. Then he remembered Jud Jennings as a stocky kid in short pants coming around Fifty-seventh and Indiana Avenue, back in 1915 and 1916. He thought about Torch Feeney.

"Torch Feeney's mother died, sometime before I met him. His old man was a police sergeant and I think he raised them himself. There might have been a housekeeper; I don't know."

"What do you think that means?"

"I don't know that it means anything. I remember once in May or June of 1928 I met Torch one Saturday morning downtown on South Michigan Avenue. He was selling refrigerators."

"Yes?"

"I spoke to him but I didn't like him and he didn't like me. He thought that I thought that I was too good for the human race."

Eddie paused for a moment.

"He told me that I should abide by my mother. He didn't use that word. I can't remember exactly what his words were. Let's see . . ."

Steve waited for him to say more.

"I remember what it was. He told me that I should take care of my mother and stop thinking that I was too good for the human race."

"What did you say back?"

"Nothing; I simply walked on."

"What more do you make of it?"

"I've never made anything of it," Eddie said.

"But you remembered it."

"Yes. Torch didn't have a mother. I was living with Mother, not Mama. He probably resented me because of this."

"That could be," Steve said.

"Torch never seemed to like me. Not since we put on the boxing gloves. That was about 1923, in Washington Park. I had brought out my boxing gloves. He wanted to box me. I thought he'd slaughter me and I guess he had the same idea. Well, he didn't; he didn't even hit me. He kept rushing me and I jabbed him with left hooks. We were being timed for three-minute rounds but we didn't even go one. We boxed about two minutes. By then, he had a bloody nose. He held a handkerchief to it; it wasn't a pretty sight. But I remember him looking at me and saying, 'You still can't lick me.' And the incident must have remained in his mind for years. Remember that time when he came to the Healys' apartment to shoot me? He kept telling me, 'You're yellow, you're yellow, Ryan.'"

"I remember that now."

"He must have been afraid of me."

"I think so."

"That makes it idiotic that I should have notions of being afraid of him," Eddie laughed.

"It's an anxiety," Steve said.

"I know it is."

Neither spoke for a moment.

"What else, Eddie?"

Eddie thought for a moment, then:

"I liked Jud better than I did Torch."

"You did?"

"I think that generally Jud was more liked than Torch. That is my impression but I don't have much to go on."

"It could be true. But I might add that you think so because you want to think so," Steve said.

Eddie laughed. "This is amusing."

"What do you mean?"

"I mean that here we are, both of us taking pride in our ability to be objective."

"There are limits to anyone's objectivity," Steve said defensively.

"I know but I neglect facts and go on as though I were being objective."

"I think we can reasonably assume that Jud was better liked than Torch was. What I mean, Eddie, is that we think so. Of course, we both know that we can't say so absolutely."

"That's true but we want to believe it."

"We want to believe it because we think it's so. But of course we haven't finished."

"No?"

"You've opened up a process of association but you have hardly scratched the surface."

"I know. This is a question of detail that we've stopped at."

"Well?"

"It doesn't matter if Torch or Jud were the more popular," Eddie said.

"I guess not."

They both sat, silent. Eddie was annoyed with himself.

"Where were we, Eddie?"

"On Torch and Jud."

"Yes, that's right."

"But I don't know where we were going."

"Well, how do you feel now?"

"I'm all right."

"That's good, at least our talk had some good effect," Steve said.

"I suppose so."

"Steve?"

It was Clara calling him.

"I'll be right back, Eddie," He said as he rose to leave the bedroom.

XII

Eddie tried to sleep. He lay with his face toward the wall, his eyes closed. He thought of Jud Jennings. Torch Feeney. Maybe there was some underlying connection between them and his brother Jack and his father. He didn't know. It might all be in his unconscious. But even if it were, it would not change *Jud Jennings*. Jud Jennings was behind him. This wasn't the point; he himself was the point. But wasn't this a question he could leave to others? How could they know why he had written *Jud Jennings?* Was there something involved here that he didn't want to know? He wanted to know as much about himself as it was possible to know. There was much in him that he didn't know, the unconscious. There was his lost infancy. Wasn't it idiotic to be bothered about this now? He was almost forty-two years old. And he was sleepy.

Finally, he fell asleep.

Chapter 43

I

"No, Eddie, I won't," Steve said.

Eddie was surprised. Frances and Steve had come to him and announced that they would not attend their mother's funeral mass.

"We'd be hypocrites to go to a mass," Frances said.

"Are you going, Eddie?"

"Of course I'm going."

"Well, I'm not," Frances said. "I can't."

"You can," Eddie said, "What you mean is that you won't."

"All right, I won't."

"You'll hurt everyone even more than they are hurt already if you don't go," Eddie said.

"I think that you and Frances should go," Steve said.

"I don't want to," Frances told him.

"I don't either, but I'm going," Eddie said.

"Well, it was you who was responsible for Steve and me giving up our religion," Frances said.

"What's that got to do with this?"

"Maybe he's right, Fran, maybe we ought to go on account of the others," Steve interrupted.

"Do you think so?"

Steve nodded.

Frances said nothing for a few moments, then:
"All right, I'll go but I'm not going to kneel."
"Do what you want," Eddie said.

He wasn't annoyed but he did think they were being childish. He had expected that they would change their minds and attend the mass. He had gone through the motions of trying to convince them as though he had taken them seriously.

"Maybe we'll go for the sake of the others," Steve said.
"It would be cruel and idiotic not to," Eddie told him.

II

A few days earlier, on an impulse, Eddie Ryan had telephoned Arthur Bloom, a book reviewer for the Chicago *Daily Chronicle,* but had not been able to reach him. He had left his name and Jack Boyle's phone number.

Since then, all thoughts of Arthur Bloom had left him.

There was a telephone ring. Clara answered it and in a few seconds she called him. It was Arthur Bloom. Eddie knew Arthur Bloom by correspondence.

Arthur Bloom asked Eddie how he was and what had brought him to Chicago. Eddie told him that he was all right but that his mother had been ill. Arthur Bloom said that he hoped that she was better. Eddie said that no, she had died.

There was an embarrassed silence. Eddie had not meant to embarrass the man. Arthur asked him when he was going back. In a couple of days Eddie told him. Arthur Bloom then said that he would like to invite him to an affair at the Regency Room.

Steve called out and asked Eddie who it was on the phone. Eddie ignored him. Steve persisted and was now standing next to him asking who it was. Annoyed, Eddie asked Arthur Bloom to wait a moment. He put his hand over the mouthpiece and told Steve that he was talking to a man named Arthur Bloom who wrote book reviews for the Chicago *Daily Chronicle.* Steve suggested that Eddie invite him out. Eddie said that Arthur Bloom had been about to ask him to go to the Regency Room, whatever that was. Clara said that the Regency Room was the swell place to go in Chicago, that was where all the celebrities went. Steve laughed and told Eddie to tell Arthur

Bloom that sure he'd go and so would his brothers and sisters. Eddie, without thinking, told Arthur Bloom that yes, he would like to go and so would his family.

Arthur Bloom said all right, he would make arrangements to pick them up. He would call Eddie later in the day.

III

Eddie was writing letters. The others had gone to the undertaking parlor. Eddie had said he would be down in a little while.

Once alone, Eddie began to feel strange. For days they had all been crowded into Clara and Jack's home. He had scarcely been alone. Nora Ryan had, in dying, commanded their attention. And now she was dead.

He sat, pen in hand. He didn't want to write these letters. But he had to; he had to resume his normal life. And the sooner the better. But he didn't feel like starting now. He would go to the funeral parlor. He didn't want to do that either.

He lit a cigarette.

IV

It was dark when Eddie left the Boyle house. He took streetcars to Sixty-third and South Kedzie. It was a busy corner. He crossed over and went south to the funeral parlor halfway down the block. He opened the door. He took off his hat and coat. He spotted Steve.

"Hello, Eddie."

"Hello, Steve, anybody here?"

"Oh, just one or two people."

"Where do I hang my things?"

"Here, let me show you."

Eddie followed Steve to a check room.

"Wait until you see Mama."

"What do you mean?"

"You'll see."

Eddie was curious. They walked into a big room where Nora Ryan was laid out. There were chairs along the side. Eddie noticed his two sisters standing by the chairs. Jack Boyle and Leo stood near them. Also standing were a man and woman whom he didn't recognize.

Eddie went toward the coffin. He caught a whiff of the odor of flowers; there were several wreaths. As he came near, he saw his mother's face. She was wearing make-up and looked younger. But the extraordinary thing about her, and Eddie knew that this was what Steve had noticed, was that Nora Ryan looked strikingly like their sister-in-law, Molly Ryan.

He knelt in front of the coffin as though he were praying.

As Eddie turned away from the coffin, Steve came up to him.

"Well?"

Eddie was taking out a pack of cigarettes.

"Can I have one too?" Steve asked.

"Yes, here," Eddie said, offering him the pack.

"Well, what do you think?" Steve asked.

"It's eerie. She looks enough like Molly to be taken for her sister."

"I was wondering if you'd notice."

"How could I help but notice it?"

"It's the Oedipus," Steve said.

Eddie didn't comment. Frances joined them.

"Franny, Eddie thinks so too," Steve said.

"Yes, Mama does look like Molly; the resemblance is striking."

"I thought so," Frances said.

"I don't think you can miss it," Eddie said.

"I don't know if the others have noticed it," Steve said.

"I don't think they have," Frances said. "No one has mentioned it if they have."

"Jack married his mother," Steve said.

"No, he didn't," Eddie said, looking for an ash tray.

He found one, walked over to it, and put out his cigarette. Steve and Frances moved over toward him.

"What I mean, Eddie . . ."

"I know what you mean, Steve."

"It's striking proof of the Oedipus," Steve said.

"I'm willing to accept it as such but at the same time, Steve, I don't think you can say it's striking proof of the Oedipus. The question comes to mind, proof of what about the Oedipus?"

"Well . . ."

"It still could have any number of meanings," Eddie added.

"Yes, it could."

"So?"

"Well, it is unusual and striking."

"Yes, it is," Eddie agreed.

"It surprised me, all right," Frances said.

"I guess it surprised all of us," Steve said.

"So what?" Eddie asked dismissingly.

Eddie glanced around the big room.

"Those two men with Jack are expressmen. I think they're chauffeurs," Steve said.

"Oh, are they?"

"Yes, I think so."

The three of them stood looking about the big room.

V

"Yes, Mr. Ryan, we're sorry."

"Well, thank you, Tom, and thank you, Bill, for coming by," Jack Ryan said.

"Oh, we'd come, Mr. Ryan," Tom Stalansky said.

"Yes, we sure would," Bill Lesinski said.

"Well, it was still mighty nice of you both to come by like this," Jack Ryan said.

"Well, Jack, at a time like this, a man's friends ought to be counted," Tom Stalansky said.

"Well, it was sure nice of you both to come," Jack Ryan said.

"We don't get a boss like Jack Ryan every day," Tom said.

"You can say that again, Tom," Bill Lesinski said.

"Well, I sure appreciate you two fellows comin' here."

VI

Eddie had felt hungry. He, Frances, and Steve had gone to a restaurant around the corner for a quick bite. They were gone for less than thirty minutes.

"I wonder who's here," Steve said as they re-entered the big room where the casket was.

"Nobody that I know," Frances said, looking around.

"How about you, Eddie?" Steve asked.

"No."

"Well, that makes us even," Steve said.

They heard Clara saying:

"Here's my brother and sister."

Then Clara turned toward the three of them.

Jack Ryan introduced Tom Stalansky and Bill Lesinski, to Eddie, Steve, and Frances. Tom and Bill then left.

VII

It was almost eight o'clock. There was a fairly sizable crowd at the wake. The atmosphere was not mournful. From time to time people smiled and occasionally there was a laugh. There were a few small groups near the center of the room.

"It's a little like a party, don't you think, Eddie?" Steve asked.

"Irish wakes often are like parties."

"I guess you've got something there."

"What are you two talking about?" Frances asked, joining them.

"Oh, I was saying that this shindig seems like a party," Steve said.

Frances smiled.

"And Eddie said that's how Irish wakes are," Steve said.

"The McGlynns haven't come yet," Eddie said.

"Oh, they'll be here," Frances said.

"Yes, I guess so," Steve said.

"Oh, I wish it was over with," Frances said.

"I guess wakes were more colorful before people started having them in funeral parlors," Steve said.

"Funeral parlors are a blow to the Irish," Eddie quipped.

"Mama liked the old-fashioned wakes," Frances said.

"Yes, she liked to stay up all night and keep the corpses company," Steve said.

"I don't know," Eddie said, noticing a small man who had just entered.

The man walked to the casket, knelt down, and prayed.

VIII

The big parlor was noisy. There was a quality of excitement generated by Nora Ryan's children. Her death had released pent-up energy and emotion.

"Well, Mama is getting a big turnout," Steve said, coming over to Eddie.

Eddie nodded.

"Word must travel fast when somebody dies in Chicago," Steve added.

"Wakes are a big event for many people. And not only in Chicago."

"I guess so."

"The McGlynns haven't come yet," Steve added.

"I haven't seen a McGlynn for so long that I don't know if I would recognize one even if I did," Eddie said.

"Oh, I think I would."

Eddie was looking around. The room was full of strange and yet familiar or almost familiar faces. There were people here whom he must know, but he could not put together their remembered faces and their unremembered names.

"Have you seen many people you know, Eddie?"

"No."

"Neither have I."

At this moment Jack Ryan came over to Steve and Eddie, accompanied by a short man with iron-gray hair and a weathered face.

"Eddie, you remember George Egan?" Jack Ryan said.

"Oh yes, you used to be the night wagon dispatcher at Monroe and Desplaines," Eddie said, putting out his hand. "How are you?"

"Oh, I'm . . ." He did not finish his sentence.

Eddie was trying to think of something to say. George Egan had put on a lot of weight in the last twenty-five years. He looked like a beaten man. What had the years done to him?

"Are you still writing books, Ryan?"

"Yes, I am," Eddie said and, thinking that he ought to say something more, he added, "It's well enough."

"Well, I'm glad to hear it."

"Yeah, George, the kid brother did all right," Jack Ryan said.
There was another pause. Then George Egan said:
"I'll have to be getting on home."

IX

"I was glad to see George Egan," Eddie said.
"He was glad that you remembered him," Jack Ryan said.
"Was he?"
"He sure was."
"He wasn't a bad guy," Eddie said.
"No, George Egan was always okay as far as I'm concerned."
Eddie's eyes roved about to see if he could recognize any newcomers.
"George Egan doesn't run around any more, Eddie," Jack Ryan said.
"What happened?"
"His wife."
"Did she die?" Eddie asked.
"No, Eddie, she didn't die," Jack Ryan said. "She went crazy and had to be put away."
"I'm sorry to hear that."
"Yes, it was a tough thing and he's never been the same since."
Shaking his head, Eddie said:
"That's too bad."
"She tried to kill herself," Jack Ryan said.
"Yes?"
"I heard that from one of the fellows at work."
"No wonder the poor fellow looks so low."

X

The parlor was now thick with cigarette smoke. There were about fifty people there.
"Hello, Peter," Eddie said as Peter Moore came up.

"Hello, Eddie."

"I'm glad to see you."

"And I'm glad to see you, Eddie, although it is a sad occasion."

"Well, Peter, how are things?"

"Oh, I can't complain. How about you?"

"I have another novel coming out this year. I've just sent in corrected proofs on it."

"Congratulations, Eddie."

There was a distance between them. They were almost shy about speaking. Once they had been close friends. Now there was the distance of years and change between them. They were both conscious of this—and sad about it. Each of them had gone his way and each believed that it had been the only way that he could have gone.

"Well, it's good to see you, Eddie."

"And it's good to see you."

"Lots has changed since the old days," Peter said.

"Yes, I know. By the way, how is Gus Inwood?"

"He's pretty much the same. I see him fairly often."

"Give him my regards the next time you see him."

"I will."

"I like Gus," Eddie said.

He was making talk.

"Gus likes you, Eddie. He speaks of you a lot."

Clara Boyle joined them.

"Are you two having a nice talk?"

"Yes, we are, Clara," Peter said.

Eddie smiled pleasantly.

"And how are you, Clara?" Peter asked.

"Oh, I'm not bad, Peter. Of course, I don't feel happy and I can't say that I'm feeling good, considering what's happened."

"I can well understand that."

"You're looking good, Peter."

"Well, thank you, Clara, I feel good."

"And how is your family?"

"They're all well, thank you."

"I'm glad to hear it," Clara said.

They stood in the center of the big parlor, and there was a break in their conversation.

XI

Clara Boyle had a feeling of love for the people who had come here tonight to pay their last respects to Mama. Mama would be so proud. Mama had always been proud of her children. Her own feelings were the same as Mama's had been. From now on, she would kind of take the place of her mother and hold the family together. She wouldn't really take her place, nobody could do that. All she meant was that she would substitute, a little anyway, for her mother. Mama had always held them together except when they were little, and then she couldn't help it. She and Pa had been so poor that they were forced to let her and Eddie go live with the Dunnes. But Mama had been the reason why they had all become closer in these last few days. And she was going to try to keep them close. Mama would want her to.

If she thought of her mother being dead now, she would feel terrible. She did feel terrible, but she wasn't giving in to her feelings. And neither was she showing them. She would always carry a sadness for Mama, for as long as she lived. They all would.

Clara kept looking around and noticing people. And she noticed her brothers, and her sister Frances. Yes, she was proud of them.

And it was really swell that so many people had turned out. But she wasn't surprised. People had liked Mama; she didn't know of a single person who hadn't. And she knew that the turnout pleased the rest of the family.

A lot of people would miss Mama. If as many people would miss her when she died as would miss Mama, she'd be satisfied with her life.

Clara Boyle moved from one place to another and from one group to another in the big parlor. Most of the people there had spoken to her and paid their condolences. She was the oldest daughter and she guessed that this was how it should be. She didn't mean this or think of it in any way as being a rival to Frances or to her brothers; she hoped everyone would talk to them too, but most of the folks here knew she was the oldest daughter and that Mama had lived with her.

Clara suddenly turned and her eyes fell on the coffin and on her mother.

—Mama's dead.

For a second she stood stricken. Her hands started to shake. Some people moved toward her. She looked at them blankly. Then she smiled.

"Oh, I am glad you could come tonight. It's so cold. We really appreciate the way folks turned out for Mama."

XII

"Mama liked wakes with excitement," Steve said.

"She sure did," Clara agreed.

"She would have liked for her own wake to be more exciting, I believe."

"Probably."

"But, in a way, we can say that we really waked Mama at home."

"I guess you could say that, Steve."

"So I guess that Mama would say that it was a grand wake if you counted the time since her stroke."

"I think so."

Clara was interested in what Steve had been saying. She loved her brother and he was a doctor. He knew an awful lot about an awful lot of different things. And he wasn't being disrespectful when he half joked about the way Mama loved wakes. Mama wouldn't have minded it. Mama didn't mind much, anyway. She always went her own way without bothering much about what others did.

Would she ever really get used to her being dead?

"Tomorrow night will be the big night," Clara said.

"Yes, I guess so," Leo said.

The people had gone and the front door had been locked. The Ryans remained standing near Nora Ryan's coffin.

—It's almost over, Eddie thought, and it hadn't been too awful so far.

"Well, I suppose we'd better be goin'," Leo said.

"If we don't," Steve said, "we'll be put out."

"Oh, Mama wouldn't let them do that," Clara protested.

"You've got something there," Steve said.

They started toward the hall to leave.

XIII

They had all returned to the Boyle home for a snack.

"I'm satisfied with how tonight turned out," Clara said.

"Yes, everything went well enough," Leo nodded.

"Why wouldn't it?" Steve asked.

"You never can tell, Steve, how something is going to turn out," Leo said.

"I suppose not."

"The McGlynns didn't show up tonight," Clara said, "but I'm sure they will tomorrow night. They all liked Mama."

Eddie shrugged. He didn't like the McGlynns but there was no point in mentioning this.

"You don't like the McGlynns, do you, Eddie?" Leo asked.

"I don't think about them enough to like or dislike them."

"I always thought you disliked them."

"Me too," Steve said. "You don't really like them, do you?"

"No, I guess not," Eddie said.

"Oh, the McGlynns aren't bad," Clara said.

"I don't really know 'em well," Leo said.

"They liked Mama so much and were so good to her."

"Well, good for them," Steve said.

"Well, after all, Mama was likable," Frances said.

"She sure was," Clara declared.

"I'll agree with that," Jack Boyle said. "She was never any trouble for us."

"And will we miss her," Clara said.

"We all will," Leo said.

They sat silent a moment.

"The Dunnes behaved themselves," Leo commented.

"Yes, they didn't make any trouble," Steve said.

"Well, Dick never does," Clara told him.

"Oh, I don't know about that," Leo argued.

"Oh no, Leo, it's always Jenny who makes the trouble. She always was the troublemaker in the family."

"The black sheep," Leo added.

"She sure was."

Jack Boyle began to yawn. They were all getting sleepy and the conversation had fallen flat.

Chapter 44

I

Wakes tended to be more or less the same, Eddie thought. He didn't go to many but it would seem to him that they would be.

—Here today, gone tomorrow.

Inevitably, someone said this.

There was grief, but some felt a morbid pleasure at having outlived the corpse.

People didn't mind death so much as long as it wasn't their own death. What people thought at wakes was more important than what they said. This was usually true. But what people thought and what they said, as well as what they did, were all connected. But this was obvious. Well, the obvious was true.

In the morning edition of the Chicago *Daily Representative* there had been a small notice on the obituary page:

MRS. NORA RYAN

MOTHER OF EDWARD A. RYAN

The Ryans had been pleased by this. Eddie had been also.

—What will the McGlynns say? he wondered.

Maybe he ought to be ashamed of such a vanity, but why should he? The fact was that he did feel ashamed and a little guilty. But more than either shame or guilt, he was amused. The McGlynns had always been snobbish. Peter Moore had gone to the wedding of the youngest McGlynn daughter, Teresa. Afterward, when he had told Eddie about the wedding:

"Eddie, they had everyone but the janitor on the altar."

Remembering this, Eddie smiled. He looked at the clock; time to be getting over to the undertaking parlor.

II

He wished he hadn't arrived so early. He had spent so much time with his brothers and sisters. He didn't mind this but he would like to see and talk to others now.

He noticed Aunt Jenny and Uncle Dick standing near the coffin. The sight of them hurt. There was so little left for either of them. It was a shame to have to frustrate them. But Aunt Jenny's satisfaction was too often gained at other people's expense. Still, he ought to go over and talk to them. He took a step in their direction. He couldn't do it. It would be too unpleasant. He would have difficulty finding something to talk about. And Aunt Jenny was convinced that he had money. If he were to go over to talk, Aunt Jenny would swing the conversation to money. She'd start all over again about the store; he knew this.

And it wasn't much easier to talk to Uncle Dick. This had been true even when he was a boy. His antagonisms toward both of them were still unresolved.

At the same time, he felt an enormous pity for them.

Frances came up to him.

"Well?"

"Yes, Frances?"

"How are you feeling, Eddie?"

"I feel all right. What about you?"

"My mind is on California. I've outgrown Chicago, and I want to go back to my life out there."

Eddie nodded. He would like to go to California again, and visit her. She had made a new life for herself and he was pleased that she could. He was proud of Frances. It had taken courage for her to go there alone with a young son.

He looked at Aunt Jenny and Uncle Dick. No new life was possible for them.

"I was watching Uncle Dick and Aunt Jenny," he told Frances.

"They're so glum."

"I know."

"I wish I were out of Chicago," Frances said.

"I'll give you the money for your fare back."

"I was going to mention it to you, Eddie."

"Can you get a check cashed?"

"I think so. Leo could get it cashed for me."

"I'll make one out as soon as we get back to Clara's."

"Thank you, Eddie. I appreciate it."

"That's all right. I'm glad I can do it."

"You've always been good to me, Eddie."

"Why shouldn't I be?"

After a reflective pause, Frances said:

"Yes, that's right."

Eddie was thinking that he would have to send a monthly check to Uncle Dick and Aunt Jenny.

III

"The McGlynns are here," Clara told Eddie.

Eddie looked across the room. It was at least twenty years since he had last seen Billy McGlynn. He looked old and his hair was all gray. Instead of the hostility he had anticipated, Eddie felt sympathy. The man was old.

"Is he still working?" Eddie asked Clara.

"Oh yes, he's still chief plumber of the Everton Hotel."

Eddie nodded.

"Are you going to speak to them, Eddie?"

"I will in a minute," Eddie said, still watching them. They were talking with Jack and Molly Ryan.

"I ought to go over and speak to them," Clara said. "They were always nice to Mama."

"I'll talk to them later."

Clara started toward them. Steve, who had been standing nearby, turned to Eddie.

"Well, Mama's having a good turnout, I see," he said.

"Yes."

Eddie was looking around absently.

IV

"Your mother was a good woman," Billy McGlynn said.

"Yes, you can say that as many times as you got hairs on your head, and it'll still be true," Jack Ryan said.

"Oh yes," Molly Ryan said.

Billy McGlynn had spoken with feeling. He meant it, he had always liked Nora Ryan. And Jack Ryan, her husband, too. They were two fine people. And now both of them were gone. But many fine men and women were gone. In fact, he and Kitty were beginning to feel lonely. He didn't think that he had so much longer to go, himself. He was old now, and he was nowhere near the man that he once was. It wouldn't be too long before people would be coming to the same kind of a place to pay their respects to him. When the time came, he would be ready. Nora Ryan had been a good woman, just like his Kitty was a good woman.

Clara joined them and said hello. They both said how sorry they were that her mother had passed away.

"I know you are," Clara said.

V

When the two young priests entered, Billy McGlynn immediately noticed them. The saddest of all occasions was the hour of death and the sight of the Roman collar was a welcome sight at such a time.

The two young priests went up to the casket, looked momentarily at the remains of Nora Ryan, knelt down, blessed themselves, said a few prayers, rose, reblessed themselves, took another look at Nora Ryan, turned around and looked about for the members of the departed woman's family. They were here hoping to meet Edward A. Ryan. They saw Clara Boyle and walked over to join her and the McGlynns in conversation. The name of Billy McGlynn's dead brother came up. Father Deegan said that his mother and father had known Judge John McGlynn.

The talk with the McGlynns continued, but both young priests had been glancing at other faces, hoping to recognize Edward A. Ryan. They saw him on the other side of the room talking to a young man who resembled the Ryans. In a few minutes Father Arcis, with Father Deegan behind him, went over to Eddie and Steve.

"Mr. Ryan?" Father Arcis began.

"Yes?" Eddie said.

"I'm Mr. Ryan too," Steve said.

"I wanted to meet you two men. Father Deegan and I have been talking with your sister and brother, and your cousins, the McGlynns," Father Arcis said.

Father Deegan bowed and mumbled an almost inaudible "Hello."

"We're sorry about your mother, Mr. Ryan," Father Arcis went on, staring at Eddie.

Eddie waited for him to go on.

"I want both of you to know that we are sorry about what happened when your mother was stricken," Father Arcis said.

"It's not our problem, it's yours, Father," Steve said, his voice surly.

They stared at Steve, both of them taken aback.

"The servant was stupid," Father Arcis explained.

"Well, that's not our problem either," Steve said, still surly.

"We are really very sorry," Father Arcis said.

Eddie was now tense. Without thinking, he blurted:

"Father, because of the negligence, our mother almost died without the last rites of your church."

"That's true," Steve added.

"Well, I know it was very unfortunate," Father Arcis said.

"We are seeing that she is buried in your church as she wished," Eddie went on.

"No thanks to you, Father," Steve said.

"Well, we are sorry and we will pray for her," Father Deegan said.

Father Arcis was too confused to speak.

Clara had been watching the young priests talking to her two brothers and sensed that something was wrong. She was worried about what Eddie and Steve would say to them. She stepped over and quickly said:

"Father, I'd like to introduce you both to my other brother, Leo."
She led them to another part of the room. Steve smiled at Eddie.
"We told them, didn't we?"
"Yes."
"It is their problem, not ours," Steve said.
Eddie nodded. A smile crept over his face.
"You're smiling at something, Eddie."
"I was thinking of the priests."
"They're leaving now," Steve said.
"I see they are."
"I wonder what they're thinking?"
"So do I."
"I guess we gave them something to think about, all right," Steve
said, his voice smug.
"Our roles were reversed with them," Eddie said. "We told them
off rather than their telling us off."
Steve nodded.

VI

Nora Ryan's wake was almost over. Burney's Funeral Parlor
would soon be closed. The family was standing near the coffin.
Mrs. Tessie Healy, and her daughters, Marion—Eddie's former
wife—and Alice, entered. Eddie Ryan saw them; it occurred to him
that he had been expecting them.
"Look who's here!" Steve exclaimed.
Mrs. Healy and her two daughters joined the group. There were
greetings and condolences. Then Mrs. Healy, Alice, and Marion
went forward, looked at the remains of Nora Ryan, knelt as though
in prayer, rose, and returned to the group. They stood around talk-
ing.
"Eddie, you're looking good," Mrs. Healy said.
"Thank you."
"You've lost a wonderful mother," she said.
"Yes."
"She used to talk about you, Mrs. Healy," Clara said.

393

"Oh, I liked her. She used to come to see me and we got on fine together. Your mother was a saintly woman."

Clara gave Mrs. Healy a nod of agreement.

"You're looking well, Mrs. Healy," Clara said.

"Oh, thank you, Clara, I'm feeling good, too."

"I'm glad to hear that."

"Oh yes, I'm feeling as well as I ever have," Mrs. Healy said.

She turned and looked at Eddie.

"And you're looking well, Eddie," she said.

"Yes, I feel all right," Eddie said.

"You haven't changed at all. You look the same as you did when you came around our house every night," Mrs. Healy said.

Eddie smiled. He suspected that Tessie Healy was taking a dig at him. But, from her standpoint, he could understand this. He liked Tessie Healy.

"And, Marion, you're looking well," Clara said.

"Why, thank you, Clara, so are you."

"Everybody's looking well," Alice said with a laugh.

"I guess so," Steve said.

"How are you feeling, Edward?" Marion asked.

"Oh, good, and you, Marion?"

"Why, I have no complaints."

"Gee, I'm glad to see you, Eddie," Alice said.

"So am I to see you," Eddie said, looking at Alice. "All three of you."

"We are too, Edward," Mrs. Healy said. "You're always welcome at my home, you know, Edward."

"Thank you, Mrs. Healy, I appreciate that."

"We mean that, Edward," Marion said.

"We certainly do," Alice added.

"I think Eddie knows that we mean it," Mrs. Healy told her daughters.

She started shaking her head.

"I'm very sorry about your mother. She was one of the best persons I ever met," Mrs. Healy said. "Eddie, your mother was a good woman and I hope that you'll never forget her. I'll never forget the first time I met her. It was when you followed Marion to Europe and married her. Your mother was so surprised. She always came to see me even after you left and divorced Marion."

No one spoke.

"Yes, I used to love it when your mother would come to see me. She was a wise woman," Mrs. Healy said.

Alice and Steve started talking on the side.

VII

"Can't you come and see us, Edward?" Marion asked. "And bring Steve, and anyone else in your family along."

"I'd like to but I can't this time. As soon as the funeral is over, Steve and I have a reservation to fly back to New York. You know, we've been here since the day after New Year's Day."

"Oh, I'm sorry. Was your mother ill that long?" Marion asked.

"Yes, she had a stroke on New Year's Day."

"I'm so sorry. Did she suffer much?"

"I don't think so. She was in a coma until she died. Or at least I think so. Anyway, she wasn't in pain."

"Well, at least that's a little comfort, isn't it, Edward?"

Eddie nodded.

Alice joined them.

"Can't you come see us?" she asked Eddie.

"I wish I could but I can't. Right after the funeral, Steve and I have to catch a plane for New York."

"That's too bad," she said.

"If you come back to Chicago, Edward, please do visit us," Marion said.

"Don't forget, Eddie," Alice said.

"I shan't."

"Will you be coming back to Chicago, Edward?" Marion asked.

"Yes, but I don't know when."

"Well, I hope you will call and come to see us."

"I shall."

Chapter 45

I

They were back at the Boyle house. It was snowing outside.

"Ceiling zero," Jack Ryan said.

"Oh well, they can fly out tomorrow," Clara said.

"The weather might still clear up this afternoon," Eddie said.

"Well, it's all over," Leo said.

Not only was the funeral over, but Nora Ryan's life was over.

"Well, Mama lived a long life," Clara said.

"Yes, she was worn out when she died," Leo said.

"I guess you can say that," Steve said.

"Well, Mama worked hard, and she had a hard life, but she did get a lot of enjoyment out of life, too," Clara said.

"I think that's true," Steve agreed.

Eddie said nothing. His mother's life had been a poor one. Now that it was ended, it seemed to have been a pitiful one, too. But he had thought this while she was alive. Her life had been, and still was being, repeated in the lives of countless thousands of other women.

"Oh, it's a miserable day," Clara said.

"Well, we'll let Eddie and Steve get a tent and camp out in Garfield Boulevard," Jack Boyle said.

"I can just see the two of them camping," Leo laughed.

"Well, I'll join them," Frances said.

"You don't have to, Frances," Jack Boyle said.

Steve went to the window and looked out.

"It's snowing worse."

"Ceiling zero," Jack Ryan repeated.

"Say, Father Arcis gave a beautiful sermon," Clara commented.

"It was a good one," Eddie said.

"Oh yes, I liked it," Molly said.

"I thought it was a beautiful sermon," Clara said.

"What did he say to you after the funeral when he went over to you two, Eddie?" Leo asked.

"He asked me if Steve and I would have dinner with him. I told him that I was very sorry that we couldn't because we were flying back to New York this afternoon, but that I'd be glad to call him the next time I was in Chicago."

"Wasn't that nice of him!" Clara exclaimed.

"Yes," Eddie said. "And then he said, 'Well boys, by then, I hope to have my own parish.'"

Steve laughed.

"I thought that he was a nice fellow," Jack Boyle said.

"Oh, he was, Jack," Clara said to her husband.

II

It was over, Eddie thought. It had been a sad day but he was glad that he would soon be leaving Chicago. Everyone was getting edgy. There were too many people and too many emotions packed in this small house. That had been obvious this morning. Steve had gotten on their nerves. He had tried to shut him up. Finally he had snapped at him.

"Goddamn it, shut up, Steve!"

Steve had been talking, his voice pitched high, without a pause. It had been compulsive.

Steve was in a more normal mood now. Everything had gone off well at the funeral. The funeral mass had not taken too long. He had been moved by Father Arcis' sermon.

The ride to Calvary had been very sad. But it was over, he reminded himself. Almost over; he and Steve would be here another day because flights were being canceled. The damned weather. They could take a train but he preferred to fly.

So tomorrow they would be off. This whole experience would be ended.

III

"Who did you say was coming over, Eddie?" Steve asked.

"Arthur Bloom, the book reviewer of the *Chronicle*."

"Isn't he the fellow who was going to take us all to the Regency Room?"

Eddie nodded.

"He never even called, did he?" Steve asked.

"No, he didn't."

"And he's coming here now?"

"Yes, I invited him over when he phoned a little while ago."

"Did you hear that, Clara?" Steve asked.

"What, Steve?"

"The guy who was supposed to take us to the Regency Room but who didn't show up is coming over to see Eddie."

"He is?"

"Yes, he ought to be here in a half hour or so," Eddie told her.

"Good," Clara said, smiling.

"Yeah, he's somebody we want to see," Jack Boyle said, smiling back at her.

"I think we all do," Steve laughed.

"I feel sorry for the poor guy," Eddie laughed.

"Why? He might have a perfectly good reason for standing us up without even a phone call," Jack Boyle said.

"Poor guy," Eddie said, smiling.

"What do you mean, poor guy?" Steve asked. "We're not that bad."

"Well, I can hardly wait," Clara laughed.

"Jesus, Eddie, your friend doesn't know what he's walkin' into," Jack Boyle said.

"I guess not," Eddie said.

"I don't guess he's coming," Jack Boyle said.

They had been waiting for nearly thirty minutes.

"He'll be here," Eddie said.

"Yes, he will," Clara said, nodding. "Mama told me he was on his way."

"She did?" Steve asked.

"Yes, she did," Clara said. "She's already in heaven and has seen Mother. They had a good talk."

They heard footsteps on the front stairs.

"Here he is," Eddie said.

The front doorbell rang.

IV

All of them, except Eddie, stared at Arthur Bloom, a small, thin-featured man, as he limped into the Boyle parlor.

Eddie introduced them all and then asked him to have a seat.

"I thought you were going to take us to the Regency Room," Clara began.

Arthur Bloom looked embarrassed. Before he could say anything, Clara said:

"Oh, Mr. Bloom, please don't sit there. You might sit on my mother."

Arthur Bloom stared at her, bewildered.

"My mother just came back from heaven for a short visit to tell us that she is all right and all the Ryans and Dunnes in heaven are getting along," Clara explained.

He rose and turned to Eddie.

"Here, Mr. Bloom, sit there," Clara said, pointing to another chair.

Mr. Bloom sat in the chair Clara had indicated.

"Eddie tells us that you're the literary editor of the Chicago *Daily Chronicle*," Steve said.

"Yes, I am."

"But Eddie here also told us that you were going to take us all to a party at the Regency Room. We all waited for you and were disappointed when you didn't show up," Jack Boyle said.

"Why, I'm sorry, I didn't realize that . . ." Arthur Bloom was almost stammering.

"We're sorry too, Mr. Bloom," Clara told him. "I got all dressed up. So did my sister, here, and my sister-in-law over there."

"Oh, I didn't realize that you considered it a definite date," Arthur Bloom said, turning toward Eddie. "I'm really sorry that I messed up; some other time, maybe, I can make up for it."

"Oh, that's all right, Arthur," Eddie said.

"I really will try to make it up sometime," Arthur Bloom said again.

"Oh, that's all right, Mr. Bloom, don't mind; we understand, there are no hard feelings or anything. We only wanted to say that we were disappointed," Clara said.

"I'm really sorry," he said.

"Well, like I said, so are we," Jack Boyle told him.

Clara laughed.

"We'll forgive you this time," she said, smiling.

She got up and left the room. Eddie looked at Arthur Bloom. Poor guy had had enough of their horsing; he'd take him out for a cup of coffee. It would be easier to talk to him, anyway. Clara and Jack's small house was too crowded.

Clara suddenly reappeared with a sheet covering her head and face. Arthur Bloom's eyes all but popped. The rest of them acted as though there was nothing unusual about Clara walking into a room with a sheet over her head.

"I'm my mother's ghost," Clara explained.

"Welcome back home, Mama," Jack said.

"This is not my home any more," Clara said. "My home is in heaven now."

"It is, isn't it?" Steve said.

"Come on, Arthur, let's go get a cup of coffee," Eddie said.

Arthur looked at him gratefully. "Yes, I'd like that."

V

Eddie watched the snow swirling around the sidewalk. It was cold and the sidewalk was slippery.

"Be careful, the sidewalks are icy," he cautioned.

They approached the Rock Island viaduct. A freight train roared past, heading south. They walked on under the viaduct. Eddie led Arthur Bloom into a hamburger joint.

"I can see why you write books, Eddie, after meeting your family."

Eddie grinned.

"I'm very fond of them," he said.

"I see you are. They must be proud of you too."

Eddie shrugged.

"Have you another novel coming out?"

"Yes, I just finished correcting proofs on it. It's called *Bernard Cleary*," Eddie said.

They talked about Eddie's work for a while, then parted. Eddie walked back to the Boyles'.

VI

Jack Boyle staggered a little as he followed Clara into the house. He was grinning. It was after six. Jack looked around the kitchen, and a frown replaced his grin. Eddie became uneasy.

"What I want to know is how did you know where to find me so quick?" Jack asked his wife.

"I know you, Jack, and I knew where to look for you when you didn't come back when you said you would," Clara said, laughing.

"The thing I don't like about you Ryans is that you're all hypocrites," Jack Boyle suddenly accused.

Frances looked frightened. Steve was angered.

"Do you think that I'm a hypocrite, too, Jack?" Eddie asked.

"No, you're the exception, Eddie."

Steve stood up.

"I'm leaving."

He walked out of the kitchen. They all sat, surprised. Then Eddie stood.

"I'm going too."

Clara looked at him, hurt. Eddie wondered if he were doing the wrong thing. He should stand by Steve. And he would like to leave the Boyle home. Jack must want them out; he had taken a hell of a licking with all of them here for so long. It would be best if he left with Steve.

"Yes."

"Are you coming, Eddie?" Steve called back.

Eddie turned around to the others:

"I think we ought to leave."

"Take me with you," Frances said.

At this moment Steve came back into the kitchen.

"No, Franny," he said.

"We'll go downtown to the Everton Hotel and get a room," Eddie said.

Jack Boyle remained at the table, a stubborn look on his face.

"I'll pack while you call a cab," Eddie said, turning to Steve.

When the taxi came, both Steve and Eddie were packed. Eddie kissed both sisters good-by. Then he went over to Jack.

"Good-by, Jack, and thank you."

Jack stood up and shook Eddie's hand.

"Good-by, Eddie. Come see us again, any time."

"Thank you for everything, Jack."

He left the kitchen.

When he was about to enter the cab, he looked back. Frances stood in the doorway, watching them.

They rode downtown to the Loop and registered at the Everton Hotel.

Chapter 46

Jack and Clara Boyle and Frances were listening to the radio. The telephone rang. Clara jumped up and hurried to the phone.

"Hello?"

"That must be Eddie and Steve," Jack Boyle said to Frances.

"I guess so."

"Oh, we were hoping you'd call. Did you get a room all right?" Clara asked.

She listened for a moment.

"Oh, everything is all right here; we're listening to the radio."

"I guess they got a room all right," Frances said.

"Yeah," Jack said.

"Everything is fine," Clara was saying. "We're going to bed soon; we're all tired. And of course, we can't help but feel blue."

"Can I talk to them?" Frances asked, getting up.

"Yes. Here's Frances, she wants to talk to you," Clara said.

She handed the telephone to Frances.

"Hello, Steve?"

Clara walked back to the parlor. "It's Eddie and Steve," she told Jack.

"I see."

"Oh no, no trouble; everything is all right," Frances said.

"They're at the Everton," Clara went on.

"Good. You know, we were all crowded on top of each other here," Jack said.

"Oh yes, they understood."

"That's good," Jack said.

"Oh, I'm going day after tomorrow," Frances said.

"Do you want to say a word to Eddie and Steve?" Clara asked Jack.

"Sure, I'll say something; I got nothing against them."

"Frances, Jack wants to say a word to them," Clara called.

Jack Boyle stood up and walked to the telephone.

"Here's Jack," Frances said, handing the phone to her brother-in-law.

"Hello?"

"They're going back east tomorrow," Frances told Clara.

"Yeah, Eddie, we were just sittin' and listenin' to the radio," Jack Boyle said.

He listened for a moment.

"Yeah, well, have a good trip and we'll be here when you come back."

He looked at Clara.

"Here, Clara, Steve wants to say somethin' to you."

"Hello, Steve. Remember us to Hattie and the girls. Let me say good-by to Eddie."

"I'm ready to turn in," Jack Boyle said.

"So am I," Frances said.

Clara said good-by to Eddie and then hung up.

"I'm glad they called."

"So am I, Clara," Jack Boyle said.

"Gee, I'm tired," Frances said.

"We all are; it was an ordeal," Clara said.

Frances nodded.

"Clara, I'm going down in the basement to fix the furnace; then I'm turning in," Jack told her.

He went toward the basement stairs.

"I still can't believe that Mama's dead," Clara said.

"Neither can I."

They heard the winter wind rattling the windowpanes as they walked toward the bedrooms.